THE LAST TEABAG

"...help has to come from within,
then it's always there..."

Mary K Hollywood

Published by TiHi Art

Published by Tihi Art

Paperback ISBN: 978-1-0369-9175-3
Hardback ISBN: 978-1-9194263-1-0

For my late mother, Heather, who battled a few of her own personal apocalyptic events with good humour and a resilience that I can only dream of.

A Void

The bedroom ceiling is the only place in this shabby little semi-detached house not covered in small, sticky fingerprints or muddy paw prints. It's immaculate.

Seventeen very long years ago, I sat cross-legged on this bedroom floor watching Sam paint that ceiling while I drank a pint of tea and rubbed my expectant belly. Sam drew a love-heart with his finger in the undercoat above the bed. I can still just about make it out. He's probably drawing a love-heart in someone else's undercoat right now. I wish I could stop thinking about Sam, but he's still front and centre of my world, even though my world has spun off its axis.

Dark reddish hues from the sunrise are desperately trying to break through the curtains to warm up this drab space. I don't want it any warmer. This duvet is already laden with my sweat. The gently rattling ceiling fan blows a gentle and welcome breeze across my face. It's the only thing stopping me from spontaneously combusting every morning.

I don't want to lift my head off the dented pillow. I know what I'll see: piles of clean clothes, dirty clothes, clothes for charity, discarded bras, and an unworn party dress with the price tags still attached hanging on the back of the door. As usual, I distract my congested mind by imagining painting something on the ceiling as if it were a blank canvas, primed and ready for creative potential. I can almost smell the fresh acrylic paint. It's a good job I have memories of those smells. It drowns out my new body aroma.

I can't think of anything inspiring today. My mind was emptied of original and interesting thoughts as soon as my firstborn was released out of my belly like Pandora's box. I should be relieved my body is painstakingly abandoning its reproductive organs. Now that my biological clock has stopped ticking, I should be able to hear so much more. But there's not much to listen to round here, except a car door slamming shut and a revving engine outside. The menopause, like all milestones, is hysterically overrated.

The house is quiet. No one is awake. No one is asking for anything. No one is playing with their phones yet. This is my favourite part of the day. I always ruin it by looking in the pocket mirror that I stupidly keep on my bedside table. I can't resist, even though I hate watching my youthful beauty dissolve right in front of me. These saggy bags under my eyes need some haemorrhoid cream. Now that I'm nearly fifty and have birthed four humans, I have a tube on standby near every toilet and mirror.

There's another small bump on my chin. Is it a zit? Those women's magazines promised they would disappear with teenage angst or witch-hazel, but they never did. No, it isn't a zit. With one slight scratch, a stupidly long chin hair pops out. It's all creased like a newborn baby because it has been festering under my skin for weeks, waiting to burst out at some humiliating moment like the last five times. Better pluck it out now before any of my children see it and start shouting, "Art thou a witch?" like they did the last five times.

Rembrandt didn't mind staring into a mirror to see his crumbling old face. In fact, he accentuated his wrinkles and emotions with dramatic light and shadow, and received praise for it. But then, he wasn't subjected to quite the same level of derision as contemporary women. No woman gets praise for a disreputable hair on their chin. We're not allowed to show our brutal reality through the mastery of light and shadow. It probably doesn't help that I've only got fairy lights in the shape of snowmen draped across the bed frame to highlight my inner turmoil. Those should have been taken down at Christmas. It's March.

I'd need to haul this super-king body in front of the window in order for my decaying looks to be truly appreciated in a Rembrandt style. Then, I could use these early sunbeams to help create depth on my otherwise dull face in order to paint a self-portrait. I would need a dark background and dark shadows to force my cheekbones back into the light. My eyes must be looking straight back at me, ready and poised for judgement. In my imaginary world, I believe I can paint as well as he can because in here anything is possible. It is about time I asked myself some difficult questions.

On second thoughts, I don't want people to think I'm hiding something mysterious. Then they'll dig too deep. I don't want anyone to think I'm actually going mad. Am I going mad? This isn't another voice; this is my voice. This is the voice I dare not speak.

Maybe Rembrandt isn't the best style for someone who avoids confrontation. Staring into a pocket mirror is more akin to the artist Chuck Close, who painted eight-foot-high hyperrealist self-portraits. Every pore on his skin was displayed in minute detail. His paintings revealed more than a photograph could. I would be forced to paint the hair on my chin with precise detail.

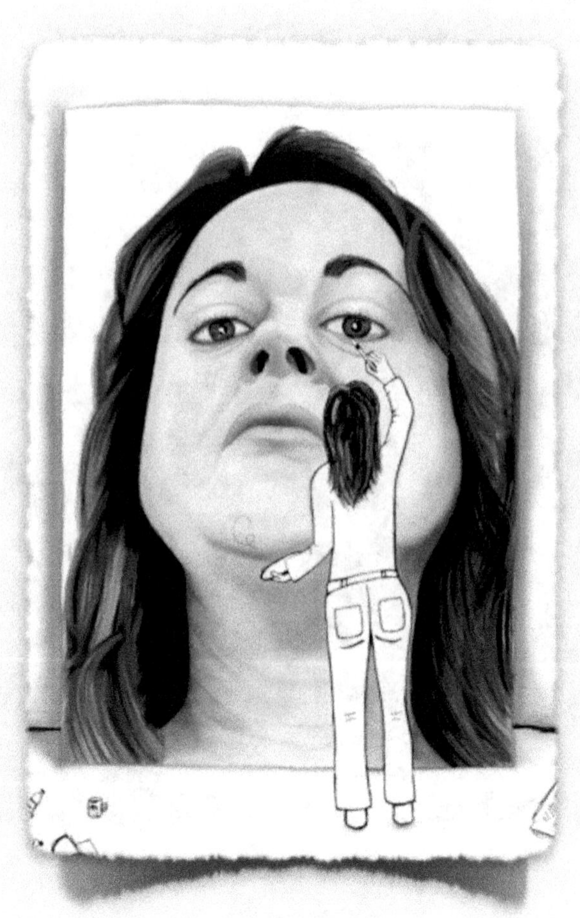

Yeah, I probably shouldn't look at myself this close up; then I won't see the flaws or feel the need to get a loyalty card at Dignitas.

Every imaginary brushstroke reveals a grim truth. That's why I don't pick an actual paintbrush up — that and it's easier to clean up an imaginary mess. That's the problem with imagination; it requires zero blood, sweat, and tears. And hoovering.

I have nowhere to go, nothing to see, no-one to ask. I should write a bucket list. It motivates most people to pretend they're adventurous. I know I won't write a bucket list; my life goals list never even got started. I was meant to be a sculptor.

My time is everyone else's time now. When will my life start? I was told I could be anything I wanted to be, but it's not true. The whole point of motherhood is to sacrifice your ego, your desires, and your whims every day so others can thrive and learn from your humility. When a certain man sacrificed a long weekend for our souls, he got an international holiday and parades for millennia; mothers get a bunch of dying flowers and a necklace made from pasta.

My heart is beating as erratically as Zoe shredding on her toy drum kit.

'Muuuuummmmmmyyyyyyyyyy.'

Speak of the devil. Those four-year-old lungs don't need to bellow – I'm just across the landing – and yet they do. It's a warning more than a request. Zoe throws open the bedroom door like a tiny SAS soldier and climbs up the side of the bed using my boobs for grip.

'Whee!! My… Boing! Boing! Boing! Is… whoa!'

Baby giraffes just fall out of their mothers and start running away from predators; why can't baby humans? I suppose we killed all the predators, so human babies need to fall out while working on Pythagoras' theorem instead. I wish I could appreciate Zoe's joy as she jumps, so carefree. It's a shame joy isn't as contagious as misery.

'What…arghh…is it…whoa…world…book…day…are… wheeeee… to school…or… ahhhh… is…it… pirates…fairies?'

Shit, it's World Book Day. Bite your lip, Nellie. This is what happens when you're used to having everything delivered to your door.

'Why didn't you tell me before the actual day, sweetie?'

'Wheeee!'

I'm a fucking artist. I can make the most amazing costumes. The kids don't ask me anymore. They don't like it when I go overboard and make little details like retracting wings or wands that sprinkle actual glitter. Ungrateful brats.

'Can I go as *Daisy Head Mayzie*, pleeeeeeeaaaase? With a real daisy growing out of my head and… and… yellow hair …and—'

'Zoe, I can't make all of that in half an hour!'

'OK, can I go as the mummy bear from *Brave?*'

'How about you go as a princess?'

'Yay!'

I think Zoe did tell me last week. She told me something about putting a hat on the cat, but I forgot because my peri-menopausal brain doesn't work like a normal brain where things are stored for later. When a woman's childbearing hips get arthritic and her knees can't carry a heavy but precious load anymore, her brain decides it would be a great idea to remove all the hormones that encouraged her to have those precious loads in the first place. Not a simple switch off the lights, or swift demolition of the working parts. No, the female body likes to wrestle with its dying organs like a honey badger on cocaine. Hormones disappear rapidly, then come back with a vengeance, then disappear again, repeatedly, every hour of every day over several years. Eventually, the ovaries get the hint and retire. As hormones diminish, they take the caring, gentle thought processes with them. What's left is a tangled web of rage and self-pity.

'Where's… boing… Daddy… boing?'

I have no idea where your beloved daddy is. The arsehole hasn't confided in me since your big sister was born. 'Still at work, sweetheart.'

I know his shift finished at midnight. I have no idea where he goes afterwards. I hope I never find out. That truth might just push me over the edge more than my wrinkly, hairy chin.

'Boing!…boing!…boing!'

I wish I could jump so high, but my ridiculously large boobs would bounce like Scraps' spaniel ears when he's chasing wasps in the long grass. These boobs replaced my child-like wonder.

I've binge-watched every genre. There's nothing left to be impressed by; even parallel universes don't raise an eyebrow anymore. I feel I have so many ropes tying me down I can barely raise my head. I could blame society for those ropes, but I tightened them. Social media makes everyone feel like an extra on The Truman Show, but we cast ourselves in that role.

'Please stop bouncing, Zoe. I feel sick.'

Women hate their bodies because of the way our bodies are perceived: a sex toy by men, competition by women, and a trampoline by young children. That's why God invented teenagers, as karma for the skipping and hopscotch days.

I must force this heavy duvet off my body and get out of—

'Whoa!'

Tom's nose is pressed so hard up against the side of the mattress it's white. He would look serious if Zoe's jumping wasn't making his head bounce.

'You didn't hear me, did you, Mummy?'

'No, no, I did not, Tom.'

'I'm super quiet, aren't I, Mummy?'

'Yes, super quiet. How long have you been there?'

'Ages. I've been watching you.'

He points at his eyes with two fingers, then points them at me as he backs out of the room. Kids are so unoriginal. But he is only six, and we can't afford to broaden his horizons with Discovery or the History Channel. Do they even exist anymore?

If I thought I looked cute in Sam's old pyjama bottoms that I cut the legs off, then I would jump out of bed and skip down the stairs singing a Pussycat Dolls song. But I know I don't, so on go the oversized cardigan and dog-bitten slippers. Saddo.

I just knocked another curled-up gold star off my reward chart on the bedroom door. Amber made that chart twelve years ago. Sam got no gold stars in his column, and only dirty shadows show how many I once had for being the "bestest mum in the world".

I can't remember the last time I could pee in private.

Zoe has banged her head on the bathroom door handle, but the bleeding doesn't stop her racing Tom downstairs to the kitchen, leaving bloody fingerprints on every single baluster. I could clone her from the DNA she has left on the stained woodchip wallpaper.

A deep breath before I kick open Peter's door. The large "Keep Out" sign does not deter me. In fact, facing up to a fourteen-year-old boy is my only chance to feel rebellious.

'What is that smell, Pete?' His room smells worse than mine.

'Fuck off, Mum!'

'Don't fucking swear at me! Remember, it's World Book Day today. You need to dress up as a character from a book, not a film or a cartoon – unless it was ripped off from a book.'

'I don't care, get the fuck outta my room!'

I am getting out of this room, and I'm going to slam the door shut to make my point, whatever that point is. No parenting handbook tells you how checking your babies are still breathing every hour turns into checking your teenagers haven't slashed their arms every hour. Instead of a baby monitor, teenagers need a hormone monitor. They could have one of those patches like diabetic patients have on their arm. When it detects blood loss, an alarm could go off on my phone, and I could raise his dopamine levels by sending him *Tom and Jerry* cartoons.

Here comes a furrier, thunderous pandemonium bounding up the stairs after being let out of the kitchen: the scruffy black rescue dog, Scraps, and the stuck-up tabby cat, Gigi, who walks like an overweight ballerina between my legs.

'Has no one fed you two, despite there being two other fully functioning humans in the kitchen? Of course not.'

Why ask them questions I know they won't answer? The same reason I ask trees, pencils, cushions, and that nail which keeps catching on my cardy: fucking Disney. I know they're only doing what the ancients did: making gods, animals, and stones look and sound like humans so they can be understood. As soon as humans learned to talk, they needed to be sure someone was listening, understanding and rewarding their every utterance; otherwise, what's the point in uttering at all?

There must be a hundred abandoned single socks on this landing, such is the strong desire to feel something, anything, through the soles of young feet. I've only got the strength to pick two up before needing a rest.

The children's bookshelf on the landing has been reorganised by tiny hands again, which means the spines of every book are facing the back so no one can see which book is which. These cheap Formica shelves look like they're trying to eat all the books in one mouthful. The tacky resin ornament of Michelangelo's *David* that Sam bought me years ago has been knocked over. *David* was supposed to represent resilience, strength, youthful beauty, and courage in the face of adversity. This *David* is fat and wearing sunglasses; I'm sure Michelangelo is eternally spinning in his grave.

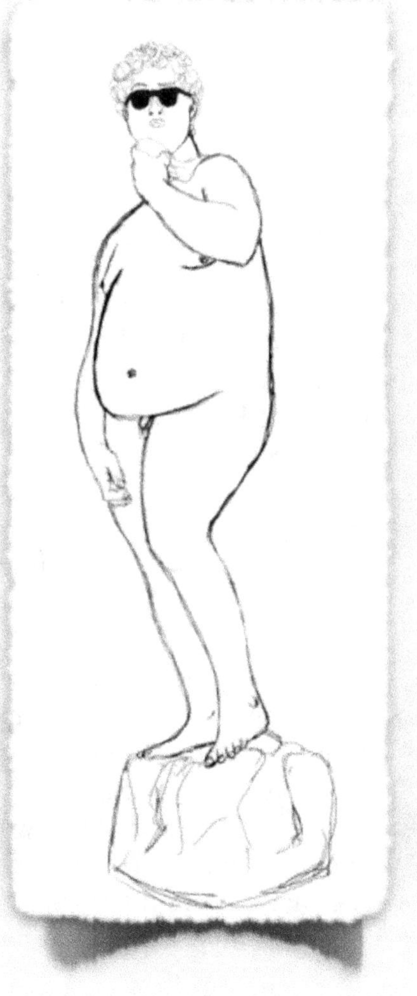

I'll transfer the dust from his head and shoulders onto my pyjama shorts, as it looks like no inanimate objects are about to burst into song to help me. No one is listening. *David* definitely isn't, nor is God. I should have realised that when he never gave me skinny calf muscles, despite years of praying. Not that it's God's fault; it's because they start selling hot cross buns on Boxing Day.

What was I doing again?

As well as socks, there's a discarded pen top, a disintegrating hair band, a sticky sweet wrapper and several clumps of cat hair. Procrastination is the only way to get me to tidy up. I'm avoiding the end of the landing and the battered door with an old pink sign that says "Amber" on it. She attempted to colour it in with a black felt pen three years ago, but the pink is slowly coming back.

I think my overwhelming need for someone to help me is what puts people and inanimate objects off helping me. Self-help is the same as masturbating; it's easy, but it's a lot more comforting coming from someone else.

Resting my head against Amber's door and holding the handle with trepidation isn't a good look for a mother of four who is supposed to be in control. My sweet sixteen-year-old daughter. I told her she could be anything she wanted to be, and she chose the classic popular bitch template. She'd sell her soul to the devil if he had lip fillers. The last time she did anything worth a gold star was the PowerPoint she created to convince us she deserved Snapchat. It was animated. I'm too easily impressed by visuals.

Now that beauty has been standardised, arseholery gets more likes. People fight over identities like the gold rush. I wanted her to be unique, so naturally she rebelled. I still hope I can save her years of achingly torturous adolescent self-doubt if she'd just listen to me. I suppose I would be denying her the value of self-discovery.

I should understand, having taught art for ten years in a secondary school full of deranged teenagers. I used to relentlessly remind them that the trials and errors in their sketchbook were worth 75% of the marks, but the final piece is only worth 25%. They rarely listened. They would leave all their efforts to the last minute, hoping they could create a masterpiece with no practice. The majority would always fuck it up. Only the obedient did it right, and their final pieces were usually boring. Which is one of the many reasons I had to leave teaching. That, and my peri-menopausal emotions making me cry when anyone dropped a pencil.

My life's sketchbook would definitely be 75% trial and error: full of doodles, anecdotes, ripped-out pages, scribbles, questions, experiments, mistakes, secrets, philosophical murmurs, unfinished creations, and frequent tea stains. I would get a reasonable grade as long as I can justify it all. What would my final piece be? I'm not ready with an answer yet.

'Amber, it's time to get up. Remember, it's World Book Day. I'm getting breakfast, don't steal my tights, or anything from my room, or from anyone else's room. I'm going downstairs, so you should get in the shower quick!'

If I walk fast, I won't hear the profanities I don't understand. Scraps and Gigi seem hell-bent on tripping me over before I feed them. They don't understand they will starve if they kill me.

The kitchen smells of a rotting tangerine that I can't find because I haven't looked for it. It's filled with the noise of barking, hissing, and two children slurping milky cereal. The expensive work surfaces that Sam and I saved up for are covered in more clean clothes, dirty clothes and abandoned clothes. There are piles of opened mail, unopened mail and junk mail that – despite being inches from the recycling bin – I cannot be arsed to throw away still. The fruit bowl is filled with hairbrushes, hair bobbles and hair-clips. I trip over chewed dog toys, decapitated cat toys, and pointless Happy Meal toys that lie scattered on the tiled floor like the remnants of soldiers after a bloody civil war. I think I put the dirty socks on the clean pile, but never mind. I don't have a proper job anymore; why can't I keep on top of this? It's hard to have a sense of achievement when all you do is wash the same clothes that were washed last week and every week before.

Tom and Zoe are scattering generous amounts of cereal and milk across the table and floor. I genuinely don't care who is going to finish first. The last time I gave out a sticker for such major events, my mother-in-law accused me of creating Peter's eating disorder. I reward no one for anything now. It saves time and glitter. In fact, it's environmentally friendly to ignore my children.

'Alexa, play Maria Callas.'

Callas' powerful lungs will drown out the competitive slurping and choking and remind me of my dear Mama, who would happily sing full soprano in her wholesome kitchen when my twin brother, Nigel, and I were young. We would pretend to hate it by covering our ears, but I would give anything to hear those high notes again. I'm pretty sure Nigel would too. I need to make a cup of tea; I'm brooding.

Zoe won. Awesome. The winner gets to wipe the soggy cereal off their face onto the floor, and then race back upstairs, inducing hiccups. Why do my children open any kind of packaging like *Edward Scissorhands*? I'll have to decant this cereal into a vase or something.

Why do I use the same mug every day? It has a thick layer of tannin on the inside. It is long overdue for a bleaching, but I was raised to believe it adds to the flavour. Frida Kahlo painted herself repeatedly because when she was bedridden, she felt like she didn't really exist. That's why I have a Kahlo mug, a Kahlo pencil case, several Kahlo pencils, a Kahlo notepad, a Kahlo scarf, a Kahlo salt and pepper set, and a Kahlo travel bag. I need to remember that I exist too.

The kettle boils furiously; it knows it's in for an overworked day. The sugary remnants of the kid's cereal are spilling down my chin like a feasting medieval king. How do I still miss my mouth? I've practised this a lot.

The burning mug of tea hurts my fingers, but I don't care. I need to know I can still feel while I stare through the kitchen window at Scraps peeing on the rickety fence. He barks at thin air.

Shit. Now I've spilled my tea all over the floor. Not again. That must be the millionth fucking time this week! FUCKING HELL. Here come the tears; they're as hard to stop as a speeding train.

Nearly every morning I spill my fucking tea in the same fucking place. I mop it up with the same fucking tea towel; the faded Van Gogh *Wheatfield with Crows* one. I bought this thirty years ago at the National Gallery gift shop. The poignancy of cleaning up with one of Van Gogh's last paintings before he killed himself is not wasted on me. I think I do it deliberately. This tea towel is a constant reminder of the fragility and loneliness of life under a brewing sky. I need to turn my pain into something beautiful.

I think this tea towel has wiped enough tea and tears for one week. Why aren't you watching over me, God? Why do you let me be so clumsy? Why do I blame God for my lack of coordination and general laziness? If there was a deity, would he have time to watch my every move? I want to believe that God is knocking my tea over rather than that I'm so useless. I don't even believe in God. My problems aren't impossible to solve; I just want someone better than me to sort them out. Divine intervention seems easier. Sometimes I need the gods to tell me what to do; otherwise, I forget.

Scraps comes bouncing in from the garden more excitedly than usual. He leaves a delightfully comical trail of muddy paw prints all the way up the stairs. That won't get cleaned today. I can't remember the last time this house was clean. I only clean if I know someone is about to visit, so I'm voluntarily antisocial. The problem with cleaning is that I make everything look nice, then everyone else makes it untidy. I can't feel anything but resentment for that. What is the point of doing anything if everyone undoes it? I shouldn't get annoyed at them just for living, but I do. In the seventies, Mama would encourage us to roll around in the mud; she thought it was hilarious. But you're not allowed to wear the same clothes twice anymore. Pointless standards rise at the same rate as inflation. Every generation wants to add to societal demands so there's a chance to reap a profit before old age.

I can hear Amber and Peter arguing, lots of doors slamming, and the dog barking. Someone is crying, and there is definitely some loud, petulant sulking going on. I really don't want to go upstairs, but I will have to. My legs feel heavier when I make them go places they don't want to go. Come on! Fear of the known can only be cured with confrontation of the inevitable.

Singularity

Zoe has emptied the box of dressing-up clothes onto the landing and scattered them everywhere. Scraps has decorated them with muddy paws, and Gigi is licking her arse right on top of Zoe's favourite fairy costume, which she is now pointing at.

'That's the dress I want, Mummy.'

Of course it is. Fucking cat! I knew she hated me. She hates me because I'm the only one who gives her medicine. Although I make her better, I'm the least favourite. How does that work, God?

Are those gravy stains, or did the cat sit there first? Urgh! How much do I actually care? My hygiene standards fell off a cliff years ago, even when hand sanitiser became a handy keyring. A wet wipe will do.

Tom doesn't fit into any of the costumes. He's sitting on his bed, thinking really hard like Rodin's sculpture in a camouflaged onesie; his soul tortured by lost things.

'Where's my other hole-in-one, Mummy? The one that makes me look like a Dalmatian?'

'I would have made you an SAS standard stab vest if you'd asked.'

I need to stop standing in the middle of the landing. I'm being used as a roundabout. I'd better get dressed too. I don't have to put any creative thought into my outfit today because I am going nowhere again. Why can't the un-employed have a dress-up day? We could meet at the park. I could just imagine myself sitting all on my own on a park bench dressed as a Viking warrior, covered in temporary tattoos and sporting a hornless helmet for historical revisionist accuracy. Do I want to be meme-worthy? Better stay inside.

I've thrown myself onto the bed face down in quite a dramatic fashion. I'm not sure for whose benefit; I'm the only one who sees this shit.

Oh God! I have no purpose, no function, no place or position. I contribute nothing; I have no worth. I have no idea of my worth because no one else does either. Not that I need constant praise for turning up day after day. The last mental disorder I need to add to this mess is narcissism. Not that the menopause is a mental disorder; it just presents like one, which is why nowadays everyone gives older women a wide berth or chocolates instead of burning them.

I have to get up. I won't open the wardrobe; I don't want to be reminded of the clothes that don't fit me anymore. My permanent belly bulge and enormous boobs make me look like I've stuffed an Easter Island statue under any slightly figure-hugging outfit.

Here comes the bra dance; in order to keep these oversized melons in a desirable arrangement, I have to coerce them into two bras so I don't get boss-eyed nipples or overspill. Now I'm exhausted and in even more pain. Have I pulled a muscle, or is it cancer? I won't do anything to find out, anyway. Just put on my joggers and an unironed T-shirt and then stare at the ceiling again; that always makes my problems go away.

I throw myself back down onto the bed, face up this time so I can stare at my phone and pretend I'm carefree. I can only drown out the cacophony of angst on the other side of my bedroom door with the self-flagellation of social media. If thirteenth-century monks had smart phones, they would've been atoning every waking hour. The daily trudge through videos of hair removal, wrinkle removal, and fat removal, competing with videos of fattening lips, fattening bottoms, and fattening breasts. If only God gave women their own sculpting tools as a gift on their first day of puberty, capitalism wouldn't need to exist.

Algorithms really perpetuate the notion that "shit sticks to shit". I don't need everybody else's inner monologue amplified; the emotional range is unmanageable. Too many inner demons have been let loose on the world. I shouldn't watch it if I don't want to compare myself to every other living being on the planet, and yet I do; such is the strong desire to find people worse off than me.

Will women ever have nothing to worry about? Only pretty, skinny women are allowed to talk on screens, so we're reduced to their mentality, which is formed by their "lived experience", which never includes struggling to find a man or sweating when looking at a doughnut.

The less I care, the more time I have to worry. I put too much value on what others think because I know how bad my opinions of them are. When you see no value in your own life, it's easy to see less in others. I think I'm grieving for my fertile body. I want my life back. I want things to be the way they used to be. It doesn't feel that long ago.

Take those rose-tinted specs off, you idiot! I was never skinny, carefree, or completely happy. I thrive on internal pain because it makes me feel more alive and gives me something to fight. It's psychological self-harm, though the scars might not be visible. Social media is like a warm swimming pool where unsettling viruses spread. It needs more chlorine.

There's a video of some government parading all its nuclear weapons in perfect straight lines. It's like watching rows of men high on Viagra walk around with their dicks out, but there's no woman to satisfy such urges. Those nuclear weapons will have to get wanked off in front of a crowd or on a test site as usual.

I scroll quickly past the videos of young people sobbing, old people laughing, and a breaking news story of a stampede of captive elephants in a zoo in Australia. There's the woman who swipes bottles off kitchen surfaces with her unshackled breasts. She's my spirit animal.

Someone is complaining about the state of the nation, again; "Britain has been asset stripped"; "Our infrastructure is in decay"; "There's wide unrest"; "We're too dependent on others"; "We're unstable". It has been a while since Britain stopped going doe-eyed at every little island it sailed past and cared for them like an evangelical Victorian workhouse matron. The Mother Nation needs to slap a large HRT patch on Norfolk and devour Cadbury World with a sinkhole to compensate for the dying throes of her Empire. I hope nobody pisses her off; otherwise, she could end up flooding our rivers with tears or bitch-slapping France.

I'll settle for a video of blackheads being squeezed. I love the idea that a backlog of dirt can be removed so easily. The easier we make life, the more we fill it full of shit.

I always scroll past talented artists. Today's artists expect a standing ovation every time they show their amazing work. No one is interested in the repetition of something that has been done before. It's like the people who post philosophy quotes. It's someone else's idea. Applause is for the original, the civilisation-rattling and the unknown. Everything else has already been discovered, presented, and applauded. That's why I gave up.

It's too quiet. How long have I been staring at my phone? There are three and a half scruffy faces staring at me through the gap in the bedroom door. Somehow, they are ready.

Amber sneers at me. 'You'll rot your brain staring at your phone all day, Mum.'

They look like the little clay figures that Anthony Gormley had made for his installation *Field for the British Isles* at the Tate Gallery back in 1994: a carpet of forty thousand miniature clay figures with naïve faces staring back at you. The expectation from their simple faces was, and still is, overwhelming.

I hurry the kids along the corridor and down the stairs towards the kitchen. Peter is a skinny, tall, pale boy; a shadow of his younger self, who would cycle up the street for several hours a day talking to any old human who dared to stop for a second. He is wearing his normal uniform without the tie and has raided the Halloween box for white face paint, cobweb spray and fake blood. I hope it's fake.

Tom is still in his onesie, but now has his combat hat on. Zoe has dropped toothpaste on her fairy dress. At least it hides the unidentified brown stains. I won't dare ask what character from a book they are each trying to represent. It would only lead to arguments or panic, and there is no time for a costume change. Amber is wearing a shrunken crop top, a ripped short skirt and laddered fishnet tights. She looks like a cabaret dancer who has been attacked in an alleyway. Has society decided whether this is empowerment or exploitation yet? I wish they'd hurry up so I can imagine myself disciplining her accordingly.

I shouldn't pretend to be so harsh; Amber has the body I've always wanted. If I looked like that, I would dress slutty too, with neon signs on my shoulders saying, "Get it here, please, I'm begging!"

I'm too scared to let anyone know what I think. I'm a silent member of society. It's not my fault. It's wrong to have an opinion. It's weak not to have an opinion. It's stupid not to agree with someone else's opinion. It's ignorant not to know every opinion since the dawn of time. It's arrogant to think I know anything. I'd be cancelled for saying what I think I know. Undermined for saying something I thought I knew. Ignored for saying something I did know. Ambushed for not realising I didn't know. Embarrassed by my obvious stupidity. Scammed because I am stupid. Hounded because I refused to accept my stupidity. Shamed for not publicising my stupidity, or threatened with harm or death because apparently I am stupid.

Is it stupid to throw ready-made snacks from the fridge to my hungry brood like they're sea-lions while they run amok searching for the right bags, coats and toast? I would argue this deserves a round of applause; it's quite a skilled operation.

'Can I have a Flitty the Floo, please?'

Zoe grabs her small yoghurt and licks it clean in seconds without a spoon. Everything that has been created to help mothers work and raise children at the same time appears to be bad for the children, the environment, and mothers. Who knew? Who cares? Despite millennia of pondering and debate, all humans have achieved is allowing the seven deadly sins to become protected human rights.

Scraps is jumping in circles in front of the door as if he doesn't want to let anyone leave. I can hear our car parking up outside. I'm tuned into its engine noise. I could pick it out at the Festival of Speed. It makes me tense. He's back. Just in the nick of time, as usual. I was hoping he'd crashed the car on his way home, then I wouldn't have to take the kids to school or face another day being ignored.

I can't open the front door to face my fate, 'Scraps! Get out of the fucking way!'

This dog is being more batshit crazy than usual. Outside, a dishevelled and even wearier Sam stares at the pavement and rummages in his pockets. Sam is very tall and still handsome, the bastard. He always appears slightly smaller than he is and can hide his double chin under a mass of grey, unkempt hair that passes for a beard. The kids fall out of the house in ascending chronological order.

'Daddy! When you go to work tomorrow, can you build me a robot horse, please, one that I can actually ride on? Tinkoo.'

I've just realised that Zoe's coat is on inside out and her shoes are on the wrong feet. Sam nods his head in blind agreement while I rearrange her.

'Morning, sir,' shouts Tom with a regimental salute. Sam put his hand out for a high five, but Tom had already marched past.

'Hmph,' grunts Peter. Sam ignores him and returns to looking at the pavement. Amber doesn't even acknowledge his presence anymore. I should do the same.

'Oh, there you are,' I say with fake enthusiasm.

Nothing! Didn't even look me in the eye, just handed me the car keys. He didn't notice the unusual dress code as the kids fought to get into the car. He just waved without looking back. I will not look at him either. I don't want him to think I'm remotely bothered by his aloofness.

The kids have battled their way into our old family hatchback. This car hasn't been cleaned since it was bought second-hand ten years ago. It has its own peculiar smell, a sort of mix of dried-up chewing gum, jelly sweets, stale coffee, mud, dog hair, and cigarette smoke, despite Sam promising for twenty years to give them up.

'Why does Daddy have to work at night-time, Mummy?'

'Because, Zoe, his factory never stops.'

'Because he's avoiding us more like,' says Amber.

Amber is too old to fall for my lies; Peter is too. How long have I got before the other two realise their parents are not the gods they think they should be? Tom isn't far off that crisis age when he realises none of his elders do trigonometry, cross-country or evaluate the calorific value of a peanut. That's when things get really interesting as a parent.

Amber grabs my phone out of my pocket and searches for music to play as we drive up our lonely street. I say lonely because it's an odd place. A former mining village with just one row of Victorian semi-detached houses on one side and fields on the other. A single red telephone box lies empty except for drunken piss at the weekend. There's only one feature that distinguishes it from most of the other villages round here, and that's the sign that says "Centre of England". There are a couple of other villages with that claim. Nobody knows for sure. Apparently, it depends on the tides and who can afford a sign.

'Your music is shit,' says Amber.

My music isn't shit; my music can sell cars, love, and anguish. Her music is all about getting high or fucked. Today's cultures colonise minds, not geography.

Amber gives up trying to explore a wider range of feelings and hands my phone to Zoe behind her. Zoe plays the first ten seconds of every song. Tom tries to drown out the intros by singing really loudly.

'Good King Wenkless last looked out, on the beast of Stephen, when the hope lay sound and out, with a lisp and demon…shone a moonie out the door…thinking it was co-oool…la la la la la la…on our way to schoo-ooool.'

'Why did Stephen have a rope called Dave?'

Being four is the best.

'BE QUIET, YOU MORONS!'

Being sixteen is the worst. Amber is lucky I don't do favourites; her fickleness is the only thing stopping me from confiscating her phone. Sure it is. The futility of the words I speak to them fall out of my mouth like a burst bin bag.

Peter snatches the phone off Zoe and switches the music off. He puts his earbuds in.

'Can I have one of those ear switches, please?' Zoe asks.

Peter hands Zoe one of his earbuds. God only knows what doom and gloom he's playing her as long as it keeps them occupied and I don't have to react.

I drive too fast on these country roads. I think it's because my first ambition was to be *Penelope Pitstop.* It was the white knee boots and a gang of unshaven men following me I desired when I was five. I'd still settle for that. Looking in my rearview mirror, I hope for an appreciative face, but Zoe is bouncing her head around, Tom is having a conversation with someone in his head as he keeps mouthing his responses, and Peter has his eyes shut. Amber has her earbuds in so she can ignore the big, wide world as well. Thank God for childlike imagination and teenage dissociation. Thank God for caffeine and a half-eaten Double Decker Sam has left in the car. I can exist in my fantasy world too.

My main fantasy is still to break down on the A444, hoping Keanu Reeves drives past and offers to help. We don't live far from Donnington Park, and he likes motorbikes. It's not completely beyond reality; I've checked. I imagine him helping me loosen the whatcha-ma-call-its on my wheel. I don't know if he likes big boobs or not. I'm not sure my dog-eared appearance and the offer of a cup of tea would be enough to make him sweep me off my feet and make my life more interesting. I doubt that's the only flaw in my plan to escape my life. I just want to create an opportunity to make him a cup of tea. I know his mother is British, and she raised him on the Two Ronnies, so he must love a cup of tea, and making tea is my biggest strength. In fact, I think it's the only reason Sam hasn't actually left me yet.

I shouldn't put my faith in celebrities. They're all one slap or tickle away from becoming a public pariah. I shouldn't need heroes at my age, but I've been hunting for one ever since Sam started tucking his T-shirt into his jeans. Celebrities replaced the priests for guidance and direction. Now we're only as clever as the celebrities we follow, some of whom can't speak without upsetting 50% of the world's population. A long time ago, the "talkies" showed the world how badly their favourite sex symbols spoke; now social media has shown the world how badly their favourite sex symbols think. Our territorial instincts don't work digitally; there are no digital lampposts to pee on, despite everyone's best efforts.

Success is so overrated; people will put up with shit as long as they look cool. I have to believe there is something better out there, even if it is unreachable, as long as it exists. Keanu is a mental screensaver; a relatively safe one, giving millions of people hope that a man can be perfect. God help the world if he ever kills a puppy.

I know I drive so fast because deep down I want to crash this car. But I can't hurt the kids; I'd have to do it on the way back. If I were to crash this car right now, it would burst open like a piñata. The road would be covered in sweet wrappers and Lego mini-figures. We're all travelling the same road but experiencing a wide range of different emotions. Amber looks like she wants to kill everyone. Peter looks disappointed, Tom looks like he's conquered the world, and Zoe grins about God knows what. My face looks ecstatic at the thought of being rescued by a movie star.

I'd better hide this smirk before the kids ask me what I'm thinking about and I have to make something up on the spot. Last time I lied so much, it got overcomplicated. I had to buy them all energy drinks so they would forget. I have enough on my plate; why crave more?

We're approaching the school; I bounce off the speed bumps as if they had been put there for someone else. The streets have swelled with superheroes, fairies, and wizards. The gates of the high school are being guarded by a short Darth Vader and a tall Oompa Loompa, "hilariously" ushering in the colourful crowd. I can't find a parking space again. The British like to design a building to house thousands with parking spaces for three. I think it's because we like a challenge. I park on the yellow zigzags. Peter hides his face. Amber shakes her head. I pretend I don't care. It's the kids who want to do stuff properly these days. We're losing eccentricity.

I have four feral children; that should be enough to make me qualify for a blue badge. Hopefully, no one will notice with so many sequins and capes on display. Amber got out of the car quickly but turned to take a photo of my clumsy parking. That will be for her digital album of my terrible parking; the only thing about me she likes to share on social media.

Zoe hands the earbud back to Peter. 'I've got song ache.'

Peter and Amber slip out of the car and melt into the bustling crowd seamlessly. Darth Vader points his shitty homemade lightsaber at Amber's incredibly short skirt, but she retorts with her standard screwed-up facial expression and totters through the school gates past the indignant Oompa Loompa. I head towards the adjacent primary school carrying overweight school bags and coats while Tom and Zoe get increasingly excited about seeing friends in different clothes. The noise, shiny fabrics and vivid colours are grating on my soul. This used to be my thing. I loved it when Amber was tiny: dressing her up like a doll, parading her in front of the less artistic parents. I used to get genuine praise for something I had created. Never won an Easter egg or book voucher though. Apparently, it wasn't fair to compare my "professional" creations to the others. Wankers.

Zoe and Tom ran off without saying goodbye. I power-walk back to the car, keeping my head down and avoiding eye contact with the equally excitable mums and dads or the lollipop man, who is pointing at my car. I need to get out of this "Lowry meets rip-off Brothers Grimm" scene as quickly as I can.

Hot Dense Point

I drive home playing louder music than the kids will let me; the car doors are vibrating hard. I need a fast-moving soundtrack to make me believe there's a more exciting scene coming next. It also helps drown out the expensive noises coming from the engine. I get carried away with that effortless feeling of putting my foot on the pedal and the car responds swiftly by dragging this lumpy body forward with more ease than I can.

This is the only part of my day, of my life, that actually raises my dopamine levels. I drive this car like I drive my body: bumping into everything in my way, filling it with crap and emergency stops every three minutes.

I need to get home. I need to speak to Sam. But I can't speak to Sam; he never responds the way I plan. It's been a long time since we had a full conversation about anything other than who is picking the kids up or dropping them off. He hasn't touched me since Zoe was conceived, not even a condescending pat on the back. He must be having an affair. I would rather think he's having an affair than face the other reality: that he now finds me unattractive.

Men look more distinguished when they get older. Women end up looking like retired wrestlers or melted mannequins. Some women are relieved to be less attractive; they don't get hassled as much. Some of us haven't been hurt so badly as to want to reject our original selves just yet. Some of us are just not getting the same attention we did when we were slimmer and younger, so need to cling on to our youthful looks with taut white knuckles.

I only have one photograph of me I like, and it was taken twenty-five years ago. I was sitting outside Ronnie Scotts in Soho at five in the morning, drinking a cup of tea in an enormous cup and saucer from the 24-hour cafe. I looked so cool; I've never been cooler since. Had I known that moment was my peak, I would have jumped into a vat of formaldehyde. Then I could've been in a Damien Hirst exhibit in the Saatchi Gallery; just as fragile and puzzling. Being cool only lasts opening night. After that, it becomes something everyone else tries to better or ridicule.

Women only have a very brief window of feeling attractive; it's why, pound for pound, makeup is worth more than gold. I suppose men only have a brief window too, except most women don't mind a dishevelled man; they look adventurous. It's a shame that just as women get adventurous, men buy sheds.

I read somewhere that collagen leaves men gradually over a longer period of time, so no one notices. For women, it's an abrupt disappearance we notice when our skin falls off our cheekbones one morning. As we get older, women have to tinker with their faces and bodies like a hobby mechanic: adding and taking bits away; waxing and polishing; frequent valeting. I'd settle for a large bow on my head like they do to unidentifiable babies.

If I was to represent myself on canvas, an old mass-produced car that someone is saving for a demolition derby would better represent my physical flaws and insecurities. I feel like an abandoned car. My twenty-five-year-old self has been held captive in that car, and the engine won't start no matter how hard I hit random buttons.

Now I know why men buy Ferraris at this age. I need to conceal myself within a shiny distraction. That's probably why older women cover themselves in sequinned tops, satin pyjamas and gold lamé leggings.

It's funny how I'm always skinny in my imaginary studio. I haven't looked like that since I was thirteen. I need to accept myself the way I am, not what I used to be. Nearly thirty-five years in this adult body and I'm still not reconciled with it. If I ran the world, I would ban mirrors, weighing scales and all fattening food. Willpower and erratic hormone levels have never played nicely together.

I'm obsessed with my body. I can't get away from it. It doesn't work properly, and I don't know how to fix it. Does everyone think this much about their body? Do skinny women have more brainpower because they're not worrying about boob sweat or chafing thighs? I want more brainpower, so I desire a more efficient body. I desperately want to think about anything other than my body.

Sam likes cars; he's a mechanical engineer. Why doesn't he want to tinker with mine? I wouldn't mind a valet; I wouldn't mind having some parts replaced. He should know better than to leave me to rust; I'll only get harder to start.

A mechanical engineer wouldn't be any different from what every doctor, gynaecologist and nurse has done to me since puberty set in: poking me with shiny, cold, metal tools, scraping, twiddling, squeezing, prodding my abdomen with their fingers, winching my legs apart, shoving one of those diagnostic tools up my vagina.

I can imagine them getting other mechanics to come in so they can suck in their cheeks and shake their heads as if the work needed will be expensive. Sparks are going to fly as I'm stitched up down below. It's not too far from the truth; the only difference is the cleanliness of the hands. I can't un-see this now.

This is why I feel detached from this body. They've taken so many bodily fluids from me they may as well build a drive-through in my crotch. And I'm only talking about "womanly" checkups here; childbirth is like having every emergency responder looking down at your expanding vagina.

Women have to accept indignity in life. For health and safety purposes, of course.

My bottom stealthily disappeared a few years ago. My body looks like Tom and Zoe created it in a game of consequences. I think Mother Earth is rearranging the fat just to stop any man from impregnating me. It's working. I feel like someone has a voodoo doll of me, and not satisfied with sticking multiple pins in all my joints, they're stuffing it with more straw.

My imagination is much more fun than reality because it's all safely under my control.

My body would be useful for a challenging life drawing class that only Jenny Saville or Lucian Freud would have the brutal honesty to contemplate. They weren't scared to paint a saggy, naked bottom draped over a stool while voluptuous breasts shrouded a hormonally induced meno-belly. At least everyone has failing eyesight after forty, so no one can see the saggy bits up close.

I'm stuck behind a very slow driver. There's no opportunity to hit a wall at full speed now.

The real problem with getting older is not having anything to look forward to. It used to be exciting not knowing what was going to happen; now the future seems boringly inevitable.

This guy is taking every corner cautiously because, unlike me, he's trying to cling onto every day he has on earth.

I'm not planning a career or family anymore, only for a house without stairs. Hope for the future is replaced with dread; free falling into the abyss while watching friends and family fall in before you. Women were told a career would set them free, but instead of being tied to a baby on their hip in a field of buttercups, we're tied to a time and a place and another socially constructed ideal. What did we win? Our own bank accounts and more taxes. Hardly worth it.

Sweat beads are forming on my head; I'm too close to this slow car. I want an accident. I want to be rescued. If I ran the world, I would ban anyone over the age of 60 from driving! Shit, that's me in eleven years! I think I've run out of time to run the world.

I thought that having two more children would keep me young. All it has shown me is how much strength and willpower I've lost. When I was young, my body could bounce back like memory foam. Now it cracks like cheap concrete. I still don't know everything, and I'm running out of time.

There's a straight bit up ahead; the only thing the Romans really left Britain was the occasional opportunity to overtake pensioners and tractors. I put my foot down.

'WHAT THE FUCK ARE YOU DOING?!!!'

A decrepit old man is hunched over the steering wheel. Shit. You bitch. Not everyone wants to go at the same pace as you. Where does this aggression come from? I used to help out at the village fete.

I'm not used to rage. I had a happy childhood. I never needed to confront my parents, so I'm not prepared to confront anyone. I went straight from breastfeeding to watching *Tenko* and *Letter to Brezhnev*. I assumed that being a strong, independent woman was preordained.

I rarely had PMT, Sam thought I was a catch. I was allowed immediate epidurals for all my children's births because of an old horse-riding accident. I've avoided pain all my life, which is why this is alien to me.

I can't maintain this speed on these windy bits of the road; my hands are shaking, and I feel dizzy. I need to pull into the lay-by.

I send gravel and dust up into the air as if I'm in a rally. This body could kill me at any moment. Sometimes, I have little control over it.

That was weird, but at least now I can breathe. I need to turn the music off and close my eyes. Here comes Mama's voice.

'Nellie! Stop overthinking again; it's time to clear the table, darling.'

Mama's forceful but ever-gentle voice always comes from deep within me. It instantly takes me back to one afternoon in 1982 when I was stressed about colouring over the line on a mermaid drawing. Mama encouraged me to clear everything from the table so I could calm down. I grumpily put everything away and then realised the table was now clear and I could start a new drawing.

'Table cleared, Mama.'

Mama always comes when I need her. She's deeply rooted in here and always will be, no matter where her body lies. Now I can open my eyes and relax.

I'm driving behind the same slow old man again. I need to resign myself to driving slowly for a bit. I must distract myself from my own hardened face. What else can I think of that won't enrage me?

Sex. Sex is the opposite of rage, or it used to be. I'm sure sex is meant to be pleasurable. I can remember that much. I wonder if Sam doesn't want sex anymore because of his body image issues. His belly is bigger than mine was when I was carrying Zoe. I don't mind a fat belly on a man. It's like the airbag has already been deployed to help with the impact of a 20-stone man landing on top of you.

It's possible he doesn't want sex with me because Tom heard us the last time and told everyone he thought he'd heard two gorillas fighting in our bedroom. Sam was genuinely offended. I didn't mind. At least gorillas are better than slapping fish or burglars, as the older two thought. It's probably because I'm more "mumsy" than "porn star" down there these days. I'm not taking up genital topiary just for his sake. I've kissed more stubble and got more hairs stuck in my teeth than he has. Kerb appeal isn't what I'm fighting for anymore. Maybe he feels the same way I do. Maybe his hormones are depleting too, leaking out with every fart. Love withers away like collagen. That's probably where it's kept.

The problem is we're stuck in a fuckless marriage, or whatever the fuck our relationship is called because we couldn't be arsed to get married. Neither of us can be bothered to carry on the mating ritual. We've run out of stories and moves because we do nothing new anymore. Sex gets added to the list of chores, and of course no one ever gets to the bottom of that list. The tension he creates from not talking to me still makes everything hurt. We're not in love; we're in situ.

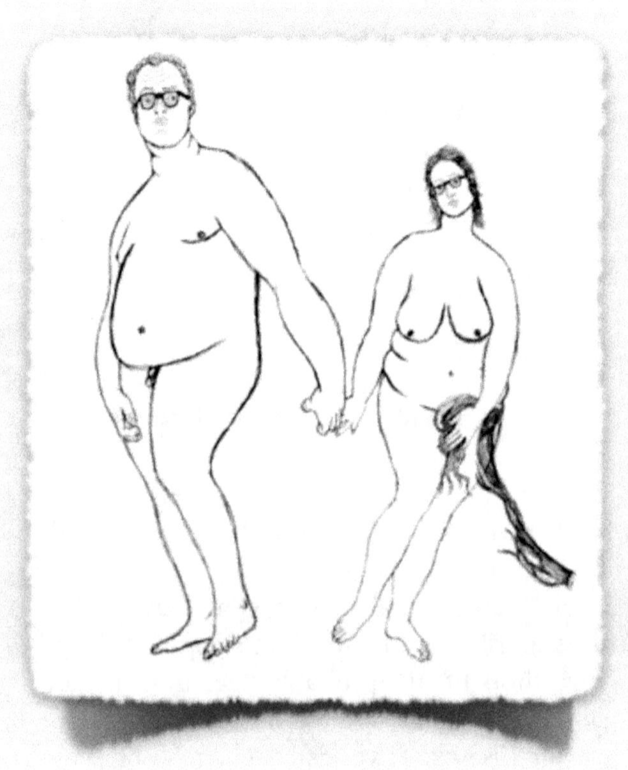

The old man driving in front has painstakingly turned into a driveway. I'm no longer forced into reflection, but I think I will continue to drive slowly. I don't want to get home now. I don't want to be reminded I'm not having fun again. If Sam did decide to touch me in an arousing way, I would need my knee support and wrist guards at the ready. Both of us would resemble Olympic shot-putters.

I'm driving so slow now I'm the one getting beeped from behind. Just one more street. My low oestrogen makes me have a low desire to do anything for anyone. Instead of berating men for starting wars, we should have been dropping evening primrose oil into their beer when they weren't looking.

I think Sam not wanting me is like when Scraps caught that pigeon. He was all excited at first but lost interest once the bird was caught because he's overfed. Sam must be getting fed elsewhere. He's definitely not excited anymore.

I have to react; I can't not react. Artists are trained to respond to every flora, fauna, table leg, vase of flowers, bare flesh, or abstract thought. To understand art is to understand everything that has ever been created. If there's no stimulus to respond to, I have to create something to fill that void and then react to it. No stone can be left unobserved. It's why I can't switch this fucking brain off.

Finally, my tiny village with my pothole-ridden road and thin strip of land I call home. My crowded sanctuary, surrounded by muddy fields and almost strangers. I slow down even more, as if I don't want to reach my destination.

I don't want to see him. I know I'm a terrible mother because the kids are crazy, a terrible wife because I don't ask him how he's doing, a terrible housekeeper because I don't bother trying to match the bedsheets with the duvet cover, a terrible provider because I won't try to sell my art for millions and a terrible friend because I don't comfort him when he's mad, but imagine throwing something at him instead.

I assume he thinks I'm shit at those things because he doesn't compliment me on any of them. Do I really need constant approval? I think I'm a good wife because I genuinely don't give a shit about toilet seat positions. He should be glad I'm not a trophy wife; trophies are another thing to dust. Boudicca and Joan of Arc set the bar too high for those who are used to labour-saving devices and mace.

I don't know if I'm good or bad at anything I do. The role of mother has been taken off the altar now that religion is derided. The Virgin Mary isn't worshipped by everyone anymore. The role of the iconic mother now has a second job, had community help removed and been given higher expectations than raising a messiah.

Rapid Inflation

I park outside Imelda's house. No-one else dares to park here. She makes everyone believe she owns the piece of road in front and the air surrounding her little terraced house. Her house emanates fear and loathing, and that's what Sam grew up with. He managed to move a whole ten yards down the road since his birth, and I thought he was adventurous.

I've parked the car with one wheel balanced on the kerb. I don't care. Imelda is twitching her curtains; I can see her in my peripheral vision. I'm not looking at her. I'm not in the mood for her passive-aggressive crap this morning. I'll take a photo of my bad parking and send it to Amber for her collection. I hope this makes her phone ping, then she'll get her phone confiscated.

I don't come from this place. This has never felt like my home. I never dreamt of being here. I'm trapped in this empty place and disbanded community where the only landmarks I know are places where the kids have thrown up or fallen down. I don't know where I belong. Armed forces kids never have a childhood home. I've always been "not from round here". I have no idea exactly where Nigel and I were born. I think he burst out on the back seat of our old Morris Minor at 85mph in the fast lane of the M40 between High Wycombe and Oxford, and I arrived shortly afterwards somewhere on the hard shoulder. Mama couldn't remember such details at the time; apparently, that was of no concern to her at that moment. I arrived on this planet in an unremarkable place, a place for flat tyres, blow jobs and speeding fines. I started life in grubby obscurity, and that's probably how I'm going to leave it. I need to free myself from the tethers of my past. The road ahead isn't a monotonous motorway with no exits; it's a choice of winding paths.

At least the empty fields opposite our houses halve the opportunities for curtain twitching. There's a lot of that round here. People are desperate for something to disapprove of. My family of six is crammed into a semi-detached house in the middle of the street in the middle part of England. Could we be anymore average and boring? Mediocre is fine; if I'm four billionth in the world, then there's still three billion nine hundred million and something worse than me.

Scraps senses my arrival and pushes his head through the cat flap. There's a recognisable noise coming through our bedroom window; Sam's snoring — it's biblical. Scraps jumps up at the door repeatedly, so I can't open it.

I squeeze past the psychotic dog to get into the house. Scraps tries to stop me from getting my wellies on. He's humped my leg, run off with a wellie and knocked over the collection of elephant sculptures on the front windowsill. I put them back; they're supposed to be for good luck. I'm never sure which way they should face. Some say face the window; some say the door. Some say east, some say west or north. That explains a lot about humanity.

'Come on, nutbar. Let's go for a walk.'

We'll cross the road to the farm fields opposite and then towards the woods on the other side. Hopefully, some newborn buds will be ready to burst out in colour and glory.

How many times do I have to throw a slobbery stick again and again for this increasingly excitable dog? This is going to be the highlight of my day. Four legs are definitely faster than two. Why did humans choose to stand up? I suppose it gives us more time to think about things other than chasing, eating, sleeping, scratching, sniffing and shagging. Although the vast majority of people are still doing one of those things right now.

I'm always so busy looking for trip hazards I don't notice the trees or the sky. I didn't notice that bloody woman with the Doberman either. She's here every day walking it on a short lead with a muzzle. Scraps launches himself onto the Doberman's leg and starts humping it. Dogs really don't do foreplay, do they?

'She doesn't like it, you know,' the woman scowls at me.

'Sorry!'

I'm not at all sorry, but I should have brought my water pistol.

'That dog should be on a lead!'

'Really sorry. He doesn't normally do this,' I lie.

I wrestle Scraps to the floor to get him away from the dog. I hold on to his back legs tightly. That dog is muzzled because of her owner's fear and lack of control. Just because she can't control her dog, why should mine be restricted as well? A dog shouldn't represent our state of mind. I hang on until she's far enough away.

Scraps tries to bound after the unwilling Doberman again. Shit. I hope no-one is filming me as I throw myself to the ground so I can hold on to his back legs again.

They've gone. I can let go. Scraps has finally forgotten and I can carry on walking with mud all up my coat. Mud on my coat is a small price to pay for a free soul. I'd rather be badly trained than muzzled.

There's a single magpie on the path in front. One for sorrow. How apt! How do magpies know to fly alone near someone having a shit day? That's why God doesn't stop wars or slim down calf muscles; he's too busy explaining everything to the magpies. I don't want to know if it's going to be a shit day; I have nothing to look forward to now. Salute it and move on.

CLAP!!

The magpies and all other birds have suddenly flown up into the air. That was a strange noise. It seemed to come from nowhere, but everywhere at the same time.

The wind blows the trees harder; it sounds like a storm is brewing. I can feel it rushing through my head. Is it going to pass without a single drop of rain or destroy my entire house? If I had *The Numskulls* in my head, they would batten down the hatches and board up my eyes and ears.

My footsteps are heavy; I'm cold. I may as well be stranded in Antarctica. A dog walk shouldn't feel like a life-changing trek. If I don't look up, I won't see the rainbow. If I don't look down, I'll fall flat on my face; such are my choices. I have to look down so I don't tread in anyone else's lazy shit.

I forgot to kill myself on the way home, idiot. How could I forget something like that?

I've stopped on the bridge above the A444. I stop here frequently to stare down at the fast-moving traffic below. So many people determined to get somewhere fast. I have nowhere important to go; that's why I don't want to get there quickly. Why do I search for meaning in everything? Even my university art tutor told me not to bother.

There are no cars on one side of the road, just a long convoy of old army trucks passing underneath the bridge towards the motorway. The pulse of each rattling chassis vibrates through every brick of the bridge and right through every one of my bones. I don't like it. I want it to stop. If I jumped off in front of a truck, I would be at peace. It would look like an accident. I wouldn't have to fuck up any more decisions. The children would get a school counsellor. Amber's always wanted one of those so she can get out of lessons. Sam could keep his mistress, who could then take responsibility for our wayward children. Zoe would love a wicked stepmother.

If my university tutor didn't want me to think about the meaning of life, then he shouldn't have taken me to see Bill Viola's *Nantes* triptych at the Royal Academy in 1992. The large-scale installation of three panels with projected video images terrified me as a student. The first panel showed the birth of a newborn baby; the last one showed Viola's dying mother; the middle one showed a man suspended in water. I'm like the man in the middle panel, in limbo, waiting to die. We start life in water; our atoms eventually return to the sea. We spend the middle bit fighting currents, riding waves, treading water and gazing at the unknown below; scared and thrilled at the same time.

Some art needs a parental advisory sticker, or at least a free cup of tea and a biscuit afterwards.

I'm not waiting to die. I can swim in any direction. I'm not a strong swimmer, though. While practising for my bronze award, I discovered I actually couldn't swim in my pyjamas without getting my hands caught in my unnecessary prolapsed pockets.

Staring over a bridge at everyone passing by isn't exercise for the mind. My mind wants to jump ship from this body because it wants something else to drive or steer. I bet one of these army tanks couldn't destroy this overladen, cumbersome body. A monster truck would have trouble toppling my industrial-strength frame. My mind has always wanted something more comfortable to travel around in. I deserve better. Bodies aren't given out as rewards, though, as far as I'm aware. I would like to move like a Ferrari, but I know deep down that I'm an indistinguishable family hatchback. I am what I drive.

I've never belonged to a religious order, no political party represents my views, not sure which social class I belong to, I'm unclassifiable. I have no manifesto; I don't know what I stand for. Why would I want to be classified? I pay no membership fees for my life. I should feel free. Instead, I feel like a needle in a fucking massive haystack: I can't be found. In fact, I'm just one of the billions of strands of hay. No one is even looking for me; there is no possibility of a glint of sunshine to show my potential. I'm not special in this world; nobody is. You're only special to those closest to you. You're only special when you die; that's when people say how special you were.

It's hard to be objective in here. When a black hole appears, I can't help but get slowly sucked in. Scraps is licking my hand. He looks up at me with his big, round, brown eyes.

'Good boy!'

My brain doesn't function properly, just like a car doesn't function properly when a tornado sweeps it up. The tornado turns the car into a deadly weapon. A new mattress once made me cry like this; it's quite random. One thought dominates all others. It should be called suppression.

Babies cry innately. I never popped one out that was laughing. Everyone has to learn to be happy, or we fall back into our factory settings; which is screaming when we don't understand.

There's no physical pain to make me stop thinking. You can't rest a brain. Thoughts are uncontested. It works like a dictatorship rather than a democracy. I can see why I'd want to send in the nukes.

'And what would happen to you, Scraps? No one's going to pick up your enormous poo.'

They'd put him in kennels before my body got cold. Dogs can sense so much. The world would be a much better place if dogs could sniff out misogyny, racism, narcissists, and vegan-pushers as well.

This is what happens when I run up against a list of questions that I can't or won't answer. Killing myself seems easier than arguing or compromising. I keep waiting to hit rock bottom so I can push myself up again, but I just keep falling. Rock bottom is too squidgy and comfy these days; I wouldn't notice hitting it. Humans like to remove the very things that make them stronger.

The convoy of army tanks carries on rumbling beneath me regardless of the life-altering trauma that nearly happened. They have no idea I just stopped their operation getting held up by a splattered body. They're welcome.

I go so close to the brink so often I now take a picnic. Yesterday I wanted to swallow bleach, but then I was distracted by the washing machine spinning out of its place. Sometimes I lose control of the wheel; I wish I had cruise control.

Thank God I didn't do it. I haven't shaved my legs, and I'm wearing these ugly flowery knickers with a hole in the seam. That crime scene image would survive longer than me if it leaked onto the internet. Shit, those flowery knickers could've become a fucking meme! If I'd had time to choose an outfit, I'd have had time to change my mind. Saved by a hungry dog and cheap knickers. I don't want to be remembered for what I complain about or all the shit stuff that has happened.

I've remembered what to do when I feel like my life has become a battle with meme-worthy moments? I need to walk home quickly. Women are pros at mood swings; we get decades of monthly practice. We know the feeling will go away, eventually. Just switch myself off and switch myself back on again. That was just a little swerve; the first time was like driving straight into a brick wall. I cried inconsolably for hours afterwards. Now I can walk away undamaged. It gets easier. That's because deep down I have stopped relying on guardian angels, gods and magpies. I have to look after myself. Not every tree falls over in a storm; some just bend with the wind. Trees get their strength from countless storms, too. Only a tree grown in a protected space or with a rotten core snaps when put under pressure. A sturdy tree has deep roots. Trees, like everything ever created, are designed to be flexible enough to go with the flow and then stand tall again. That's why paradise always looks like a garden. Hell is an empty landscape with nothing to respond to, can't think of anything worse.

I'm back in the house. Another disaster averted. I cease to exist if I throw this body away; there are no upgrades. I take my top bra off, letting more blood flow around my body. I'll leave it hanging on the coat rack so Scraps doesn't bury it in the garden again. Cup of tea, antidepressants, chewy dog toy, and get on the laptop. Gigi must have picked up on my dark mood as well, as she's forcefully brushing her fur against my leg. She's uncharacteristically needy today; I'll have to stroke her on my lap, otherwise she bites my ankles. At least I've got one hand free to throw whole Jaffa Cakes in my mouth while I wait for the laptop to remember its sole purpose.

The doctor said the peri-menopause was normal and should be like someone switching a light off. Instead, it's like someone switching the light on and off repeatedly while you're trying to change the bulb while clinging onto a super-fast ceiling fan. The doctor suggested I join a menopause support group. I imagine a menopause meeting to be like that narcoleptic meeting that went viral; except not only can no one can remember what they're talking about, two are screaming at each other, someone's crying, all the biscuits have gone, half are in the loo, some are napping and the rest are staring at each other maniacally. If Keanu was available on the NHS, that would fix all my problems.

This laptop seems even slower today. Peter must have downloaded some cartoon porn again. I'll doodle on the back of an envelope; that will help regulate my heart rate quicker than sugar.

I've been drawing the same doodle since I was twelve; when I was stuck in a maths lesson I couldn't escape. It looks like something coming to get me, like a kraken. It's always a perfect circle with curvy, wispy lines coming out from the edge of the circle. I like circles. Circles are the purest form; equally perfect from every viewpoint with no sharp edges or corners. Despite the potential for awe and wonder, this is still all I can muster. Too whimsical to make a living out of. Imagine art dealers in a prestigious auction house fighting over a piece of scrap paper with this and a teacup ring stain on it.

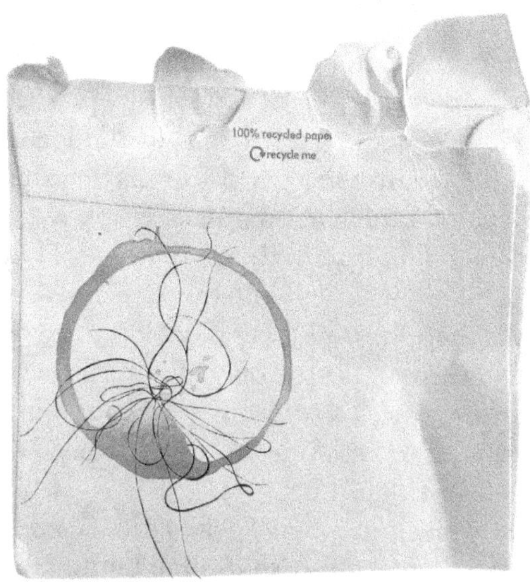

I know there's maths in art; Fibonacci, the golden section, geometry, etc. But maths was boring to me. Our maths teacher was trying to tell us that maths was order and was the language of the universe. Even back then, I knew that couldn't be completely true. The stars do not line up in an ordered pattern; daisies don't either. If maths were the language of the universe, then the countryside would look like a crocheted blanket. Some daisies are too short; some have skinny stems. Nature and any interfering gods did not create a perfectly aligned or symmetrically patterned world.

I was doodling chaos to free my mind from memorising order. Chaos makes order run free. Order stops chaos getting out of control; the maths teacher took that first doodle off my desk and threw it in the bin. I can remember quadratic equations, but I have never found a use for them. I still pine for my first drawing of chaos, though.

If I continue with this much introspection, I'm going to turn myself inside out. I need to find new buttons. Browsing the internet for buttons to add to my collection always helps me find a way out of my dark tunnels. I love the hunt, looking for a scent, scouring well-known and obscure websites for the chance to buy a button I haven't seen before. I buy mystery bundles of clothes, strip all the buttons off, sew on new cheap plastic buttons, and then put the clothes in the charity bins at the local library. It's a strange hobby. But a satisfying one. I love sorting them out. I keep them in my stack of multicoloured plastic hobby trays under the stairs. Each tray holds hundreds of buttons. They used to be organised into different styles, but the day I re-organised them into colours was the most satisfying day of my life. I get them out when I need to feel sane. It's the only chaos I have ever attempted to order. It mortifies the kids, but my problems will not be solved by changing myself to fit someone else's expectations. Cultural commitment can be exhausting.

I started the collection when I was little. Some I like just for their aesthetics, but the most important buttons connect me to points and moments in my life I want to remember. I keep those in a tin under my bed. I felt camaraderie when I studied the sculptor Louise Bourgeois, who made enormous caged "cells" filled with sentimental objects so she could wallow in her childhood issues too. She's most famous for constructing the enormous, graceful bronze spider *Maman* to represent her mother.

Her mother was clever, helpful, protective, and a weaver, like a spider. What better homage to a mother than a thirty-foot bronze statue you want to climb? Some men insist their faces are honoured; women prefer a distanced metaphor. Although that's probably because it won't show our double chin.

Bourgeois wasn't appreciated by the art world until she was very old; that stopped her being held back by conventions, manifestos or the art market. Her invisibility set her free. Can women only be free when they're invisible? My memories are hidden. Stacked and colour co-ordinated. It's more manageable than the *Venice Art Biennale.*

Those dark thoughts from earlier seem unrelatable now, but I'm still sad. At least that's an upgrade from completely fucking miserable and wanting to kill myself. I suppose I should check my website, *Bake It Happen*; maybe there will be an order for an elaborate wedding cake worth hundreds of pounds. There isn't; there's still only one order for today: fifteen cupcakes with pink fondant boobs on top, and fifteen with pink fondant penises. Another bloody hen party. It seems only the over-optimistic eat cake at the moment.

I'm bored with making cakes, but I need the money now that I've bought all those old clothes. The basic sponge cake mixture is easy, that only takes a few minutes. It's the decorations that everyone notices and pays for. I could put anchovies and pickles in the mixture, and no one would care if there was enough sugar to hide them. I stick my head in the mixing bowl and lick it clean – no one's watching.

I roll out some flesh-coloured fondant icing and start sculpting the first penis. My first sight of a real-life penis was during life-drawing classes at art college. I don't think I was the only student who hadn't really studied one before. A flaccid one, anyway. A flaccid penis is all I see these days, and that's only at the weekend, in the summer months, if Sam throws back the bedsheets in the middle of the night, and I happen to get up to need a wee, and the moon comes out on that side of the house at that particular moment. Sam is lucky I didn't build a stone circle round his genitals – it is a rare, almost sacred sight. I don't know why I care. I've been on antidepressants for so long, I don't get excited by a sugar-ring doughnut anymore.

This fondant penis is way too big; it will make the cupcake fall over. Start again.

Only the eyes ever got me aroused. That's why I fell for Sam. He was fixing a vending machine at my college. His beautiful cobalt-blue eyes met mine; I couldn't turn away. Then he smiled, and I knew I wanted to see that smile again and again for the rest of my life. No one had ever smiled at me like that before. He hasn't smiled at anyone since Zoe projectile vomited on her diarrhoea-covered mattress at 2:30 in the morning three years ago.

The non-designer jeans and the Danger Mouse T-shirt he wore that first day convinced me he would be rebellious and exciting. And he was massive. When he towered over me, I wanted to run to Bonnie Tyler to tell her I'd found a "streetwise Hercules".

His T-shirt was misleading; it's faded now. He didn't have any money, but I wasn't desperate for financial security back then. All that can be lost in one afternoon. He could fix stuff I didn't understand, build things I didn't know how to, and hit people I didn't like. It would have been easier to hire a bouncer or a handyman than to start a long-term relationship. I wanted Sam to fight my battles for me. What I didn't realise is that he would also battle me, emotionally, that is. Battles over who unloads the dishwasher shouldn't destroy a relationship, but they do; especially after the millionth time. They're tiny battles, but they wear you down eventually. I didn't know how to argue because my adoring parents never gave me the experience.

Women have strong minds rather than strong biceps, but my mind has been too busy to do a workout. He fed my weakness by being strong for me. Men think that's the right thing to do; they're hard-wired to protect us, especially from bears or other men. It's a bit like a protection racket when I think about it. Men were designed to protect, but some have turned to attack. I think they've been trying to warn us through the medium of robot sci-fi. Given enough time to evolve, everything turns on us in the end.

Now women want to feel free and free men of the obligation to look after them. We've replaced strong men with tracking apps, rape alarms, pepper spray, whistles, and drink tags. A man who can protect women from other men will not fit on a keyring. If only we could tell the good men from the bad men; unfortunately, they all look the same.

The proportions of this fondant penis are wrong. I scrunch up the icing again. There's a little satisfaction in doing that.

Jerry Hall said, "You must be a maid in the living room, a cook in the kitchen and a whore in the bedroom". Meat Loaf said, "Two out of three ain't bad". What's the equivalent for men? A couch potato in the living room, a scavenger in the kitchen, and a cadaver in the bedroom? Thoughts of leaving him enter my head every day. He doesn't make me feel good about myself anymore. Now he makes me feel worthless. My emotions seem to be tied to his; they're inextricably woven together. Sometimes, I just want my threads back, but I don't want to be the one who rips us apart. Last week I wanted to put a pillow over his big, scruffy head. But then, yesterday I was genuinely worried when he was late coming home. Thank God the antidepressants render me too apathetic to act. I don't want to find out what I've done wrong. Wishing him dead kills me. I'd be poorer without him, not just financially.

I shove a whole cooling cupcake into my mouth. I need all the sugar I can get. I might be too heavily medicated to kill him, but I worry hate always finds a way. I don't think I hate him; that's why this is so hard. If I hated him, I would act on these thoughts.

I think I'm just going through my "I hate all men phase". All women go through it periodically. I don't hate men; it's just a defence mechanism so I don't have to bother filtering out the good from the bad. It's pretty arduous. I'm glad Mama taught me how to deal with my tantrums with icing sugar.

This fondant penis is incredibly unflattering. I keep forgetting these are for decoration only. I have to eat it; it's been rolled too many times. I can't wait for the sugar rush; I may think things I later regret.

I don't really want him dead. I'm like an internet troll: when something doesn't work, I want to rip it apart or get rid of it instead of accepting it. It's easier than preparing for him leaving of his own accord. I understand the unwavering support women give awful men; a single income is hard, standing up for yourself in front of other men is hard, stopping physical abuse from other men is hard, doing everything on your own is hard. The world has never been set up for women to be on their own. It's always been set up like a Victorian workhouse that we can't leave. We need evolution to catch up and make us physically equal, but most ladies are too preoccupied with hair removal than with building upper body strength. It would be better if we could self-impregnate. Then, I would only need to look like a sea sponge. That would save a lot on depilatory cream.

The foreskin of the fondant penis needs precision, so I'll need my fine sculpting tools. When I was at university, my tutor told me that dentistry tools are the best for precision sculpting. I phoned all the local dentists, and they were more than willing to give me their old tools. I collected them, washed them, and kept them in an old Shakin' Stevens pencil case that I had held onto since primary school. Amber had a lot of questions when she found that on a shelf under the stairs next to the buttons. I can't be bothered to sterilise them in the microwave; they haven't touched clay in over twenty years.

I assumed I would be a respected artist. I could have been, but I don't know how to make money selling bits of my soul to artistically dense capitalist investors. Arse-licking wasn't part of my degree. I wanted to do an RSPCA-style home visit before selling a piece of work, just to make sure any buyer understood its meaning and how to look after it. The bank rejected that business model a long time ago. The art market works off provenance, not substance, and I don't have much of either. The perception of a successful artist is still financial gain, despite Van Gogh showing us that not to be true. Artistic success is satisfaction, moving on, being able to finish something and start another.

Everything gets turned into a business in the end; even our most basic needs have been monetised. Everything has to make your teeth whiter than ever before. We can't get our teeth any whiter. We're running out of new ideas. We're making up problems to solve. A hundred and fifty years ago, everyone had a clear idea of their position in the world. These days, you have to work it out for yourself. I'm not sure which is more stressful: being told you have to do something or being given the choice to do anything and realising you're not competent enough to do it.

If I had the time, space, and overalls for sculpting, I could sit down to observe the menopause in meticulous detail. I could try to understand the inner workings of the female body: the hormones, the reproductive system, the brain, the sweat and the swelling. I would have time to read and study a wide range of artists who have studied the female form before and cross-reference with scientific data and imagery. I could experiment with large, sagging forms and age-weary skin. After all that in-depth research, I would probably end up just representing the menopause with a model of a female body lying face down on the ground with arms and legs spread out like a fallen Leonardo da Vinci's *Vitruvian Man* making mud angels.

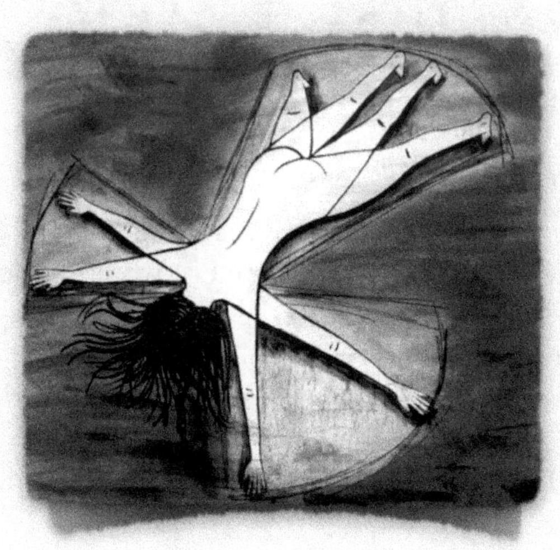

Maybe I could represent it with a video installation of a train in the distance coming towards me, and I'm standing on the tracks waiting for it. It's not the train I want to take, but I know I have to. It looks like it's moving slowly when it's far away, but as it gets closer, I realise it's going quite fast and it's not slowing down. I try to move out of its way, but I can't. The tracks move wherever I move. Then it hits me at full speed, and everything hurts.

There's a lot to unpack there. The critiques after the final pieces have been laid to rest in a gallery would hopefully give me the closure I desperately need.

I've broken the fondant penis, for fuck's sake.

Brain fog would be easy to represent: a head made entirely out of confusing and entangled wire, not connected to anything meaningful. That's probably the sugar rush, not brain fog. What everybody doesn't realise is that a woman can switch from brain fog to complete genius in the blink of a heavily mascaraed eyelash. That's why nobody understands women, not even women.

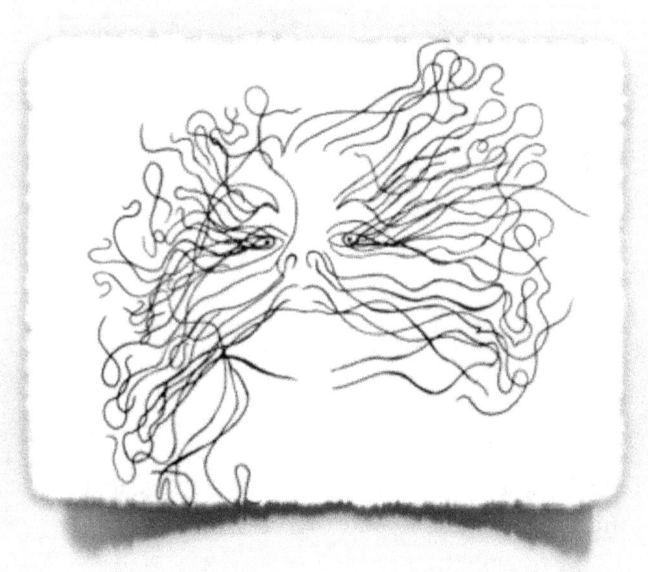

The penis now looks more like a sausage roll. For the life of me, I can't remember what the foreskin looks like up close; I always had my eyes shut at that point. Why am I bothering to paint tone and veins on the penis? I shouldn't be trying to emulate Ron Mueck's off-scale, intense, hyperreal, fibreglass sculptures of the human condition. I doubt the bridezilla wants to question the transcendence of reality when she gets her cupcake. I think she'll just want to put it in her mouth and be grateful she's not getting an STI. Pubic hair, smegma, or mottled skin might cancel the wedding. Even I'm repelled by my creation. I need to look up images of penises on my phone.

Those images repel me too. It really is a miracle anyone is born if this is the starting gun. I clear my browser history.

'Oh God, I'm so old!'

Amber has left her schoolbag hanging off a kitchen chair. I'm sure I'll find a normal picture of a penis inside this unthumbed science textbook. Now I can make anatomically perfect penises for half the cupcakes. Boobs are easy; I can do those blindfolded.

These would get a very different reaction in an art gallery. Probably a few nodding heads and elaborate adjectives expressed over a sip of expensive wine. Instead, these are going to get deep-throated by overexcited girls, and then drowned with vast amounts of Prosecco. Unfortunately, sugar pays the bills quicker than clay. I feel sick, and I hate the colour pink soooooooo much.

The Big Bang

It has taken too long to decorate these cakes. I've worked myself below minimum wage to achieve artistic perfection. There's no time to tidy up the flesh-toned chaos on the kitchen table that looks like an explosion in a fairy sex toy factory. Gigi and Scraps' white, sugary footprints are randomly scattered all over the kitchen floor. Sam's snoring still vibrates throughout the house.

I need to rearrange my boobs before I leave. I have to put my top bra back on without taking off my jumper because now I'm too cold. I've got forty minutes to get these cake boxes delivered and then get to the school gates. I'd better put Scraps in the car, then he'll think he's been somewhere.

Cars really should be powered by sugar, although the inevitable sugar low could cause a few issues at rush hour. My satnav has brought me to a pin-neat modern house with cock and balls shaped balloons adorning the front door. I have feverishly arrived at my destination. The air is bitterly cold, but my upper lip is sodden with trepidation. This street is surprisingly quiet, not even a single muffled bird song. I bet they pay extra for that on this estate. The only sound is behind the festooned front door where I'm heading; distant cackling drunk women. I've had too many drunken encounters with women; we're scary without inhibitions. I'm trying really hard not to think about the fact that I never had a hen party. Or a wedding.

The most excited and fluffiest woman answered the door. Behind her, a gaggle of wobbly women gathers quickly, screaming like football hooligans on helium. It looks more like Big Bird's coming-out parade in there. If I open the cake box quickly, I might avoid any degrading questions. The ladies all shriek in unison at the sight of fondant genitals. I do not want to go in there; I don't need a Botox party bag or a cactus-shaped dildo prize; those things aren't for carpal tunnel sufferers.

There will be a tonne of photographs taken tonight; licking sugar penises and boobs in an exaggerated manner. I bet those cakes stay uneaten; those girls won't touch a crumb of carbs. I don't care; I am neither proud nor excited about my creations. Penises and boobs are easy; representing the meaning of life on a cupcake would have been worth photobombing.

Saying I don't care is a cop-out. The only people who truly don't care are sociopaths. I'm just pissed they've got flat stomachs, gaps between their thighs and the belief they're buying into unconditional love. There is no such thing; everything is conditional. They'll find that out when their new husband walks in on them doing a poo.

Unconditional love would be too exhausting to have constantly, but every now and then would be nice. I want to feel like the woman in Klimt's *The Kiss*. It's hard to get that on your own.

I need to get out of here fast. My blood sugar is dropping.

I've parked outside the school gates with ease this time. I honestly don't remember the last fifteen minutes. I couldn't say which songs were making the car vibrate. I need to switch everything off quickly. I need peace and quiet. Scraps keeps bouncing around in the back of the car, making it rock like someone is having sex in the back. Thank God we couldn't afford tinted rear windows. The clear blue sky looks blurry for some reason.

CRACK!!

Whoa! What was that? All the birds flew out of the trees all at once, just like this morning. This was louder though, like a giant thunderclap ripped through the air. My car moved ever so slightly, or was that Scraps? He's actually quiet now, at last. A few car alarms are screaming; was every car shaken? Everyone outside ducked in unison. For fuck's sake, what holy hand grenade do I have to deal with now? I'm not sure, but it felt big. Fuck, my pelvic floor muscles are so weak. That miserable midwife did warn me.

All the congregated mums and dads are looking at the clear sky. It wasn't one of those low-flying RAF planes; I'm quite at home with the sound of a fighter jet flying so low you can see the pilot wink. It could have been a car crash with mutilated bodies strewn all over the road. Let's hope Sam's factory has blown up; it's not far from here. Shame he's not in it, if it has. I shouldn't say that. When he's not here, I want him; it's only when he's near me I want him gone. It's too complicated even for me to understand. There's nothing like a sense of foreboding to make me appreciate having a large man at hand, though.

Well, there aren't any sirens yet; everyone has returned to bitching about the school, the government or celebrity sex lives. Shame, I could do with a bit of genuine excitement, a bit of some else's drama for once. Nothing exciting happens round here. Look at them all, probably searching "loud thunderous crack" immediately. Who can find the most likely correct answer the quickest? No matter how furiously I tap away at my phone, I can't search for anything. My phone doesn't have any data. I never have any data. Fucking teenagers, fucking hotspots. I'll play a mind-numbing game on my phone so I can win at something today.

There goes the timeless high school bell, ringing faintly in the distance. I don't miss it. My brief work as a teacher had to be cut short when my bladder shrank to the size of a pea and my emotions were set to "stun". I can't tell anyone, but I'm glad I'm not a working mum anymore. Gone are the days of feeling guilty at; dropping my baby off with strangers, leaving work suddenly to care for my sick baby, other people covering my arse while I deal with my sick baby, not focussing on my job because I'm thinking about my sick baby, missing the list of milestones my baby reached while I was at work and been handed a bill bigger than the mortgage for the privilege. I was so relieved when the government decided that teaching creativity, independent thought and problem-solving skills was a waste of taxpayers' money and I was made redundant. I can't confess to anyone, because every type of feminist will throw hot coals at me from every direction.

The footpath quickly fills up with bedraggled and weary-looking Tiggers, fairies, cats, Snow Whites, wizards, hobbits and Spidermen. Most of the masks have come off, and the makeup has been contaminated with pasta sauce. Peter rushes down the path with a large white rabbit. That must be Freddy. They're constantly looking over their shoulders. At least they've slowed down to walk slowly and sensibly past a morbidly obese Cinderella; that must be Miss Hubbard. Wimps. They could outrun her. I could outrun her. Miss Hubbard gets out of breath just implying what a terrible mother I am. I told her I would not be one of those parents who changed their child so the parents of other children would stop complaining to the school.

The boys picked up their speed again. They're clearly not as frightened of the apathetic Gandalf and Indiana Jones, who are pointing at the empty sky. They pushed through a group of excited cats wearing hats and escaped down the shortcut. So he doesn't want a lift home. He could've said. I have a fucking phone. Oh shit, my phone is on silent, you idiot.

Amber clocks me looking for her in the crowd. She scowls and mouths, “Fuck off!” My taxi service is not required this afternoon. They can get the fucking bus if they want. I don’t care. I only raced over here to make sure I was available if they needed me.

Fucking helicopter parent. At least I’m not a snowplough parent, unless the snowplough was unmanned and creating a havoc-strewn, winding path of destruction in its wake. There are times I feel this body is unmanned. I’m not a stealth-bomber parent either. I can’t find the switch to drop those carefully placed, personality-destroying bombs, although I am constantly low on oxygen. I’m more of a bin lorry parent: my heavy form picks up everybody’s waste, dumps it where no one will find it and ignores the repulsive effluent that oozes from it. I even make the same noises when I start moving.

I’m actually laughing. I have to check if anyone can see me. Why can’t I laugh at my own thoughts? Fear of reprisals is driving the world crazy.

Gandalf and Indiana Jones are slowly walking back to school. The throbbing mass of jaded characters disperses almost as quickly as it emerged. I’ve got twenty minutes before Tom and Zoe are ready. That’s why Peter and Amber don’t like a lift home anymore: being stuck in a parked car with their mum asking about homework they know she doesn’t give a fuck about is probably a big enough deterrent. The other helicopter parents are descending on the primary school gates like the scene from *Apocalypse Now*, primed and ready for inane chit-chat, fake smiles and bragging rights. I hate talking to other people. Mama would talk to everyone on the school run; she was often the last mum standing. Nigel’s and my feet would be freezing. It put

me off being sociable and Nigel off being agreeable.

My phone makes a noise; it's a message from Gaba.

'Name your vagina after the last TV programme you watched; mine's *Happy Valley* 😜.'

My reply will have to be, '*Gone Fishing* 🤨'.

My message won't send. Do I need to call my vagina anything? It's always right where I left it. Unless I want to buy it a card, I think it can remain nameless.

There's an increasingly gargled symphony of ringtones and alerts going off outside; a flurried exchange of memes already. I bet someone has already linked that noise to a video of a dog farting. Everyone is shaking their heads. I'm out of the loop. This never bothered me in the eighties. The only way I'm going to find out what has happened is if I venture out towards those parents huddled in small groups; pick my clique time. Arching my back in this car seat will not make any difference. Shit, I'm going to have to move these sluggish limbs again.

I can feel the air getting colder quickly, but now I'm sweating. Everyone else is wearing scarves and hats. I've removed my jumper, revealing my short-sleeved T-shirt covered in icing sugar handprints. How am I going to spy on anyone's phones? They're all huddled around so tightly, I won't be able to casually glance. I should've put in more effort to get to know them. But once you say hello, you're whipped up into a fast-moving conveyor belt of playdates, bitch dates, coffee mornings, Prosecco nights, hot yoga, fasting and bingeing. There's Bobby's mum, the only mum who has acknowledged my existence because she organised the only party Tom has been invited to in the last two years. I don't think she likes me; she's far too nice to me. Bobby's mum crosses the road without taking her eyes off her phone — whoa! That bus had to slam on the brakes to avoid hitting her. Wish he had hit the ignorant witch, then that would be one less twat I have to deal with.

'Are you okay?' I ask.

'Yes, I'm fine, thanks, er—'

'Nellie, I'm Tom's mum from the party.'

'Oh yes, I remember, the homemaker, love that term — makes you sound all fluffy and lovely.'

Bitch witch.

'That was a bit close, wasn't it?'

'Yes, should practise what I preach, but I was too busy reading the news. Have you seen it?'

'No, my phone isn't working, battery is dead. What's going on?'

'That loud bang ten minutes ago; it was heard all the way around the world. It was massive. All they know is that it was in America. They've been hit.'

'Hit? Hit by what?'

'Don't know, but there's video of a cloud of smoke. Look!'

I have no idea what she's showing me. Her phone screen is all grey.

'Wow, that's bizarre, and we heard it over here. Must be aliens, or a meteor—'

'Don't be silly. Aliens wouldn't land in the most fortified country. They would land in Greenland or something, so they've got time to unpack and prepare.'

Daft bitch witch. No one believes in aliens any more than they believe you can make a coin appear from behind someone's ear.

'And a meteor would be seen for days, weeks before it hit us. Have you not got Discovery Plus?'

Condescending, daft bitch witch. I bet she has a performance graph of her son pinned to the fridge. I need to note that on my phone when she's not looking; my memory is too unreliable to remember grudges and that the Discovery Channel does still exist.

'We must meet up soon, Nellie.'

'Yes, we must.'

I pray she doesn't call me. I don't need my flaws ranked and filed in her memory bank. At least my children are constantly drilled and prepared for disappointment. What will happen to Bobby when he finds out not all women think he's perfect?

I need to join a different huddle, or I'll feel the need to bash her face in so she can't see my phone battery is fine. Who am I kidding? I'm more likely to sign up for Discovery Plus as soon as I get home. Thank God Bobby's mum found her pack. Time for an uncomfortable diversion. I stand near the young mums, even dafter but less inclined to condescension and bigger, flashier phones with unlimited data. Younger generations also feel the need to talk really loudly so I won't need to squint at their phones.

'I told you, Mercedes, didn't I? I told you this would happen. The government always says there's nothing to worry about, but I told you something bad was going to happen, didn't I?'

'Oh yes, you did, and look, it's happened. Will it mean they'll cancel *Desperate Housewives*?'

Finding out the truth is slow these days. A statement of fact on social media takes a dreary scroll through the comments to see if it's true, false, good, bad, expert, amateur, dangerous, helpful, sarcastic, or attention-seeking. It's like waiting to see who the winner of the 100m race is once they've tested all the urine. People have talked shite for millennia, but it floated on the wind. People who talk shite aren't the type to have the patience to commit it to stone. Now that everything is written digitally, you actually have to wade through it like a cesspit.

There's a sea of vivid colours heading this way. Let's see if I can distinguish my miniature superheroes from the rest.

'Mum! Mum! Did you hear that big noise?'

'I did, Tom.'

'What big noise? I didn't hear a noise, Mummy.'

'There was a big bang about half an hour ago, Zoe. I'm still not sure what it was.'

'Oh, we were doing a lap of horsing on the playground.'

'A lap of horsing?'

'You know, when they race each other. I came in last. I fell over a pebble.'

'Oh dear, never mind.'

'What do you think the noise was, Mum?'

'I have no idea, Tom, but it was in America apparently, so no need to worry.'

'I'm lenting for fudge, Mummy.'

'That's nice, Zoe.'

'Do you know what humples are, Mummy?'

'I have no idea, sweetie.'

'They are humps on a camel.'

'Oh, I see.'

'When I grow up, I want to be a deep-sleep diver.'

'That's nice.'

'Can we go bikeling when we get home, Mummy?'

'You can't ride a bike, Zoe.'

'Why are there no zips in our house, Mummy?'

'Get in the car.'

Primordial Darkness

If I have to listen to *Baby Shark* one more time, I am going to abandon this sinking ship once and for all. I've been listening to it for sixteen fucking years! The kids haven't shut up since I picked them up. I have no idea what they've said or what I've agreed to. I need to lie down. I need a large cup of tea.

I've dumped the car awkwardly at the end of our street. I'll take another photo. Tom races ahead with Scraps chasing him. Zoe dawdles while looking in every front garden. I carry all the school bags and the coats and the "book character eggshell art" they both created. I just dropped the Mary Poppins' paper umbrella on the ground. I try to hurry Zoe up; I'm desperate for some Wi-Fi and I need to pee.

'Look, Mummy, a curly-bodied frog!'

'It's a toy snake, Zoe.'

'Mummy, do falimgos eat pink food?'

'I don't think so… I don't know, actually.'

'Mummy, look a callerpitter, it's so hairy. Can we take it home and keep it as a pet?'

'No, sweetie. You can't keep wild creatures as pets. It's against the law. A big policeman will tell you off.'

'That's nonsenseness.'

'Those are the rules. I don't make them.'

'I'm so bored, so lovely, and so cold.'

'Ok.'

'I'm absolutely positivelylutely gabbaflasted!'

'Are you?'

'I've got cramp.'

'You don't know what cramp looks like.'

'Yes, I do; it's yellow.'

Who needs Wi-Fi? I think I'll slow down.

'Mummy, I want to rescue old people, houses, benches and paint.'

'Okay.'

'Can we go to the forest of sand later?'

'What's that?'

'The place with castles and jellyfish… where Scraps pooed in the sea.'

'Oh, the beach!'

Forest of sand, I need to write these moments of genius down.

'We couldn't be further from a beach if we tried, Zoe.'

Tom bangs on our front door. Zoe pulls her hands out of her pockets with a clump of hardened mud in each hand. She hands the mud to me, despite my hands being pretty full.

'Guess how much I love you, Mummy?'

'I don't know. How much do you love me?'

'All the houses in the world full of sugar.'

'Wow, that's a lot.'

Scraps' warm saliva or antidepressants are no match for this little one. I don't care about all the worries in the world right now, not even my blood-starved fingers.

Our front door burst open. Sam stands eagerly at the door. He's wearing his over-slept-in boxers and shrunken Millennium Falcon t-shirt. The sleeping giant awakens.

'Looks like the Millennium Falcon is about to become 3D, Dad.'

I'm not sure Sam appreciated that observation from Tom. Is Sam happy to see me or not? It's hard to tell.

'Have you heard the news, Nell? Did you hear it? That loud bang — did you hear it? Where's Amber and Peter? Are they with you?'

'I heard something. Was it aliens?'

'Don't be stupid! It's a volcano, a really big one. You have to see this.'

That is the most he has spoken to me all year. He's hugging me so tightly around my arms I might drop everything. That's new. He looks into my eyes, but I'm immune to them now. Did the Earth move? Nope. He ushers me and Zoe into the house while looking up and down the street. I'm confused. Has he forgotten that he wasn't speaking to me this morning?

Coats, bags, and shoes are all dumped in the hallway. Scraps won't stop jumping up at me. Sam steers me out of the way by holding onto my shoulders. I put the mud balls into the plant pot, which has many previously hardened clumps in it. The decorated eggs can sit with the elephants until they get a layer of dust on them. Zoe blows on the radiator.

'What are you doing, Zoe?'

'I'm woofing it because the radigator is too hot.'

Cute. The relief of removing both bras from under my jumper is immense; this is why I don't leave my house. Zoe and Tom have run into me five times as they run up and down the corridor. Am I in everyone's fucking way?

I stagger into the front room with each child sitting on one of my feet and clinging onto my legs. Sam's wide eyes are glued to the TV. He strokes his messy beard with one hand and strokes the gift shop replica of Jeff Koons' silver *Balloon Dog* with the other. I bought him that last Christmas. He has no idea that it's a famous piece of art. He just likes its smoothness. I placed my replica of the *Venus of Willendorf* next to it to add some artistic depth to the mantelpiece. Everyone thinks she's gross because she's not shiny.

Sam thought I had sculpted a self-portrait. It has a slight chip on the head where it hit the doorframe because he ducked.

I'm glad Dada is here. Sam never throws a wobbly in front of a former squadron leader. He only has the same reverence for people who are about to make him a doner kebab. Dada looks awkwardly stuck in the armchair, gripping his knees tightly. He's clenched because Imelda is sitting in her usual spot on the sofa, fiercely crocheting curse words onto a crocheted jacket for a crocheted Easter rabbit. The theme for this season's guerrilla yarn bombing scene she creates for the top of the village postbox is Reservoir Dogs. I have no idea why. The TV shows shaky footage of a funnel of smoke. It's not clear what the reporters are saying over the whooping of helicopter blades. I'm not sure if I can be arsed with another worldwide disaster. I'll clean up the various empty crisp packets that are lying everywhere instead, my usual head-in-the-sand technique. Tom and Zoe emptied their toy basket onto the floor in the noisiest way possible.

The TV footage shows satellite images of the supervolcano in Yellowstone National Park in America. It erupted on an unprecedented scale only an hour ago. A massive sonic boom ripped around the world. That's what I heard earlier… here… thousands of miles away. A mega-quake of 9 on the Richter scale has been recorded. Contact has already been lost with the states of Wyoming, Idaho, and Montana. The whole of America and Canada have both announced a state of emergency. The only footage is from hundreds of miles away; thousands are already dead. There's an immediate evacuation of everyone within a thousand miles of the volcano. The ash is spreading quickly. People as far as New York had bleeding eardrums.

'Wow! Ears bleeding, that's so cool. I want my ears to bleed,' says Tom.

'What? Are you two raising sociopaths here?' Dada asks.

'Why is there a mushroom on the weather map, Dada?'

'That is a satellite image, Zoe, showing the ash cloud forming. That ash cloud will cover most of North America and Canada in toxic ash.'

'What's a sattermite?'

'It's a big computer that orbits the Earth to watch over us.'

'What's an orbit?'

'It's the curved path of a celestial object around a planet.'

'What's a sillyteal?'

'I have no idea, Zoe.'

Dada's patience is unusually short today. I can't absorb all this information. I have to stare out of the window. A bus stops outside, releasing its own exasperated sigh. Peter and Freddy step off and go their separate ways. Freddy pulls the rabbit-eared hood back over his head, covering the top half of his face with rabbit eyes and a pink rabbit's nose. Peter closes the front door behind him as if it's made of glass. He might be tall, but he still has the face of a terrified child coming into the front room to keep company with adults, even if they are his closest relations. He's curious enough to actually come into the front room.

The TV shows footage of people smothered in ash collapsing on the streets. Peter smiles. Weird bastard. I can't believe I created that. I don't want to watch the TV screen showing people running to their cars carrying their lightest worldly possessions. Does that make me heartless? Is there an acceptable level of morbid fascination?

If Dada has to arch his neck round anymore to see from the armchair, he's going to need hospitalisation again. That's all I need. This is the first time I've seen him energised in ten years. He's been so bored since he retired. He was a fighter pilot. Pub quizzes don't release the same level of adrenaline.

'I genuinely thought it was called Jellystone Park.'

That thought probably should have stayed in my head. The adults can roll their eyes all they want; we didn't have Google in the eighties.

I've always been glad to live on a stable tectonic plate, even though this morning I wanted the earth to swallow me up. This enormous cloud of destruction won't go away with a dog lick or some Jaffa Cakes. There must have been thousands of lone magpies in America this morning. The hastily compiled graphics on the TV show the projected scale of destruction over North America.

'Flat-earthers are going to be in for a big surprise, especially in India when the ash cloud hits them from both sides,' says Sam.

There is no tragedy a typical British man won't use to illustrate a sarcastic learning point. I've never seen an apocalyptic weather map before. Zoe strokes the TV screen.

'Look, Daddy, bunting! Does that mean there're parties everywhere?'

'Those are isobars, sweetie.'

'What's an icy bar, Daddy?'

'I have absolutely no idea; ask your Dada.'

'I know where Sicily is, Dada.'

'Do you, Zoe?'

'Yes, Dada. It's on a poster on the wall in my classroom.'

Wow, everyone smiled at once! That probably registered on the Richter scale. Being cute or dumb is the only way to get a smile out of them. I can definitely do the latter still. Peter sits next to Imelda on the sofa but doesn't take his face out of his phone. He looks smug, which is never a good sign in a teenager with the internet at hand.

'Dada, there's a video on YouTube saying this is a hoax, that the footage is from a film and the noise was a nuclear bomb landing on Area 51.'

'Look, Pete, this isn't…what the…bloody hell…what the hell have you done now?'

Everyone tears their eyes away from the TV to look at Peter's costume.

'Is this a new fashion thing?' Imelda asks.

'No, Gran. It's World Book Day. It's a charity thing, I think.'

'It's an awareness thing, Pete.'

'Awareness of what, Mum?'

'Books, you idiot.'

'But I'm aware of books.'

Imelda rubs her finger in Peter's fake blood and tastes it. That's actually gross.

'Are you a goth now, Peter? That would explain a lot,' Dada asks. I think he wanted points for knowing what a goth is.

'He's a zombie, Dada. He eats dead people,' explains Tom.

'Oh right. Well, he'll be busy over the next few days then. Hope you're hungry, Pete.'

Imelda brushes the fake cobwebs off Peter's shirt.

Dada straightens his back. 'This volcano is a hundred, probably a thousand times bigger than anything a human being has ever witnessed. This could be the end of us, Pete, the end of everyone.'

'Don't deep it, Dada. They said that about Covid, but we're all still here.'

'There's no vaccine for volcanic ash,' Dada explains.

'I bet there will be,' Sam adds, as Zoe tugs on his T-shirt.

'Daddy, can you let go of the mentalpiece and get me a bisbit, pleeeeeease!'

'Sure, sweetheart. I think we could all do with a biscuit. Let's open the big selection box.'

Sam looks at me expectantly. I look back at Sam non-expectantly. Sam leaves to get the biscuits in a huff. At least I stood my ground.

I really, really could do without another worldwide drama, conspiracy theories, protests, and fundamental changes in our way of life. I'll have to do research to explain it to the kids; global catastrophes are homework for parents.

The TV is split into two screens, showing the presidential podium in America on one half and outside 10 Downing Street on the other. Another great flood has arrived, but it's not water; it's words that will drown us.

Sam returns with some Jammie Dodgers. He grabs four of them and shoves two into his mouth.

'Daddy, if you give me the Dammie Jodger, I'll smile… if you don't… stick fight!'

Sam gives the rest of the packet to Zoe. She must have magical powers.

'Tink oo Daddy.'

'What does Tink oo mean?' Sam asks.

'It's Franch for thank you, Daddy.'

Why does he look at me as if I should be able to explain that? Peter's unhealthy interest in death tolls seems to be contagious; Sam flicks between channels to find new, grim footage of dying people. This is why this family is so fucked up. They're not interested in grandiose speeches or compassion; just skip to the images of body parts. Every channel has the same pictures, except CBBC; it's showing *Octonauts.*

'Don't put on Attenborough, Dad. They always show babies dying.'

At least Tom has a line that he won't cross. Every phone in the house rings. Even Zoe's toy phone is buzzing. I don't want to answer any of them. I don't want to talk about something I can't control.

'Mummy, someone is speaking to the answer-back machine.'

'It's okay, Zoe. Better it than me.'

Sam shakes his head. 'This is going to be like Pompeii; in the future, they will dig up these Americans in their last dying throes. Maybe we'll find out which celebrities were sleeping with who after all.'

'I wouldn't want to die sitting on this sofa, surrounded by you lot,' says Imelda.

'Well, looks like you have a few days to find your perfect archaeological reveal pose, Mother.'

Sam smiles at me. I smile back. It's nice we can bond over a global disaster.

I love watching him stroke his beard. I imagine him as a Renaissance statue; carved in marble with over-accentuated curls in his beard and muscles he didn't know he had in his enormous arms. I encouraged him to grow a beard because I have Santa issues.

Michelangelo was inspired by the Ancient Greeks, who liked to add nonexistent muscles to their statues after people got bored with realistic ones. Reality has never been that inspiring, even in those inspiring times. People always want to be more than ordinary. Now we add filters, Photoshop, silicone, and hair- removal cream to make ourselves more appealing than ordinary people. We haven't progressed as a species as much as we think we have. We should never have created gods and goddesses in our own image. We're not enough. We always want more.

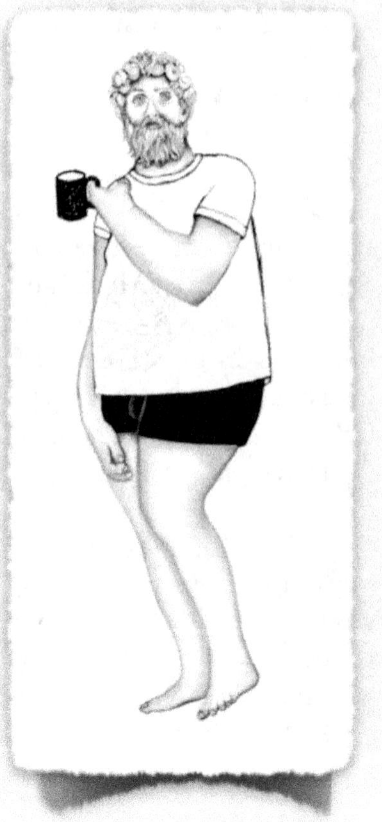

He is still handsome, not in a movie-star kind of way, but in an old warrior kind of way. I could see him with leather armour and an animal skin over his shoulder. I reckon he could still frighten away pillagers. Like our hormones override the female brain about the pain of childbirth, so they override the pain of heartache. I can't get used to this constant daisy petal pulling game of "I love him, I love him not." It's exhausting. My imagination can make anything boring or annoying look a little more exciting and therefore attractive. It keeps me going, so I don't stop myself.

This rolling news is probably going to make every fight-or-flight hormone head straight for my libido to keep me feeling safe. As long as I don't hump his leg like Scraps (there are children present). All it took was impending doom to give me a rush of hormones to the head.

Zoe is bandaging Sam's leg with tea towels and masking tape, so he's safe from my raging hormones for a while. I don't think Sam would reciprocate anyway.

Pulling his underpants out of his arse crack spoiled that whole moment. It won't be long before I wish him dead again. I'm not a murdering bitch; I just don't enjoy seeing suffering. I'm trained to accept that anything with matted hair needs an intervention.

I hope I'm still attractive enough to be put on a lifeboat should Britain sink under the weight of American and Canadian refugees being promised sanctuary here already. I'm no longer of breeding age, so my usefulness is debatable. At least my boobs would have some use. No man would throw these overboard, and even if I slipped and fell, I'd float for a good while.

In the nineties, I used to flatten my boobs in one of those bodysuit things. I was convinced I was disfigured. But then I met Sam, who couldn't help but stare at them. Mind you, if he had rested extremely large testicles on the canteen table, I probably wouldn't have been able to take my eyes off them either. He would say, "Hello boys" every time he saw me and spoke to my boobs like they were his drinking buddies. I should have been offended, but he actually made me laugh and feel more comfortable about them. I've been letting them hang freer ever since. Although I wouldn't wear one of those bodysuit things again now that they're back in fashion. Not advisable for a woman with brain fog. I've seen at least four women walking round the shops with open gussets hanging over the back of their jeans.

Why shouldn't my imperfections be on show? Nobody is perfect. Even sports cars break down. I wasted so much of my youth thinking I was ugly, when actually I was only too ugly for perfume ads; I was okay for everything else.

Sam is transfixed by the news. He should be; the American company that owns his factory has probably just disintegrated. They were already hanging by a thread and were based in Utah, which is now ground zero. His employers will be cocooned in hot ash, which will make it difficult for them to pay him. My cupcake business won't keep us afloat. It didn't last time. It didn't even cover the cost of all the phone contracts.

Chaos

Spoiler alert! Here comes the last and loudest to the orchestra of chaos: Amber storms past the front window, even the trees bend out of her way. She shuts the front door with a crash. Sam's shoulders dropped a few inches. Mine were already low; she mercifully put an app on my phone that pings when she's nearby.

'There you are!' I shouted. I still hope that one day she will reciprocate my enthusiasm for having her close.

She pokes her head round the door and sneers at everyone gawping at the TV, 'Weirdos!'

Everyone else is too busy gawping at the TV to retaliate. Her sneering was normalised some time ago.

'Have you seen the news, Amber?' I ask. I'm desperate to see her humbled by a greater power.

'Yeah. I swear if they cancel the Met Gala, I'm gonna lose my fucking shit.'

I have failed as a parent.

'Amber, don't use language like that in front of the little ones!' says Imelda.

'How can you say that while crocheting the word "Wankspangle" in gold chain stitch on the back of the Easter Bunny's jacket?' Amber replies.

'Granny, when someone swears at my school, it's like a crime scene,' says Tom.

'I'm sure it is. We need some effing crime tape in this house,' says Imelda.

Everyone stops bitching to watch the Prime Minister nervously shuffling some papers on a podium. The volcano expert they've dragged in looks really nervous too.

We might be an apex predator, but we are small fry when it comes to Mother Earth's armoury. No bullets, bombs, treaties, conventions, meetings, or quotas can stop what she unleashes. We never did stop the tide from coming in.

My senses have become so deadened that I can't feel panic anymore. I don't feel the urge to buy toilet roll or pasta; all I want to do is make another cuppa.

'Useless shitebag,' mumbles Sam.

'What's a shitebag, Daddy?'

'Um, never mind, Tom. Those people on there on the telly have a…er…. bag.'

'What's in the bag, Daddy? What is shite? Where's the bag? Is it an important bag? Can I have a shitebag, please, Daddy?'

'Er…no…I haven't got one…only politicians have them, not little boys…where's your Lego, Tom?'

'What's a polick…tish…ern, Daddy?' asks Zoe.

'Er…someone who talks rubbish…a lot…and doesn't do anything useful.'

'Is Peter a policktishern then, Daddy, coz you said he was useless and you always tell him he talks rubbish?'

'Have you got one of these shite bags, Peter? Can I have it?' Tom insists.

'No one has got a bag, Tom. That's enough,' Sam shouted. 'Bet he cocks this up as well.'

'What are cocks, Daddy?'

'For fu… never mind, Zoe. Right, I'm out of here.'

Sam attempts a dramatic exit but doesn't realise his legs had been taped together by Zoe. He falls to the floor like a demolished chimney stack. He tries to rip off the "bandages" to everyone's brief amusement.

The experts are desperately searching for something reassuring to say. Telling us that the heavier toxic ash particles will burn the throat and set like concrete inside the lungs will not calm anyone's nerves.

'That's a shit way to die. Poor bastards.' Everyone nodded in silent agreement with me.

There's no point in praying. Lava and ash are indiscriminate. Not even a god can pick and choose who to save. The prevailing winds are going to cloak America and Canada in a thick blanket of suffocating poison. Plants, animals and roofs will collapse under the weight of the ash and be uninhabitable for decades. There's no evacuation plan or food parcels for the toads or the lily pads.

'It feels like the four horsemen of the apocalypse are on their way,' Imelda says calmly. I think she's willing to let that happen.

I read somewhere that it was celebrity chefs who brought down civilisations. Every time someone sprinkles gold leaf on something innocuous, Mother Earth reaches for the reset button.

At least I have a new excuse not to take the kids to Disney World now. Tom and Zoe are playing the "floor is made of lava" game and crawling all over the sofas, chairs, and grandparents. Imelda continues crocheting without taking her eyes off the TV as Zoe crawls under her arms.

'This isn't good. You can't evacuate a few hundred million people in a few days,' says Dada. 'There are too many of them; all the planes in the world couldn't evacuate one city.'

I bet his inner voice is thinking of something useful, like how to mobilise the fleet. Shit, so many will come over here. I can't look after myself or my family, let alone displaced Americans. They eat so much.

Sam finally releases himself from his bandages, and many leg hairs by the sounds of it. He stands up, pretending none of that happened and that no one saw it. Zoe looks up at him. 'Daddy, why is everyone looking so serwious?'

'Because things might be changing for a while, sweetie. Changing quite a bit. Again. Looks like I might need to do a little bit of panic buying.'

'Can I buy some panic, Daddy? I want some panic, pleeeeeease!' she screams.

'Yes, darling, Daddy will buy you some panic. What do we need, Nell?'

'We need lots of things, but right now you need some trousers on.'

Sam runs up the stairs three steps at a time. Yesterday, he couldn't reach the remote control when it fell on the floor.

They shouldn't have said, "Don't panic buy". When will governments realise that if they treat us like children, then we'll behave like children? If I were in charge, I would give out free sweets in the parks. The supermarkets would be empty.

I peel myself away from the TV and rummage through my handbag in the hallway for any remnant of a coupon for Sam. Zoe peeks through the letterbox. Sam races back down the stairs with his trousers on.

'Sweetheart, darling, precious baby girl, could you go and get my keys and my wallet from next to the TV, would you please, sweetie? Thank you?'

'Okay, Daddy.'

Sam can't feel my eyes burning a hole in the back of his head. Maybe he can, and that's why he's avoiding eye contact. I hold the coupons out to him, but for some reason he's not acknowledging my existence. Why do I have to make a noise to get his attention? Zoe returns.

'What's this, sweetie?'

'Oh, I wasn't really listening, Daddy, so I brought you some stuff that you like: the remote control, a biscuit and some Lego.'

No amount of sweetie darlings can make her useful.

'Great, thank you, sweetheart!'

Here comes Tom with the wallet and keys; suck-up. 'Can you get me some crisps, please, Dad, and maybe an energy drink, and a meal deal and—'

Manipulative suck up.

'Do not buy him or anyone else in this house an energy drink, or I'm leaving!' I demand with what is left of my waning authority.

'Do I look stupid, Nell? I'm only going to the village shop.'

'DADDY!…remember to get stuff…and loops…and more stuff!'

'Okay, Zoe!'

Sam looks at me for clarification. He still needs a child translator. Did he intend to slam the door behind him? I'm still holding the coupons.

I really need to work on my communication skills. I'm standing here like a Giacometti statue; almost invisible to a distracted eye. Even Giacometti couldn't make me look invisible; I have too many lumps.

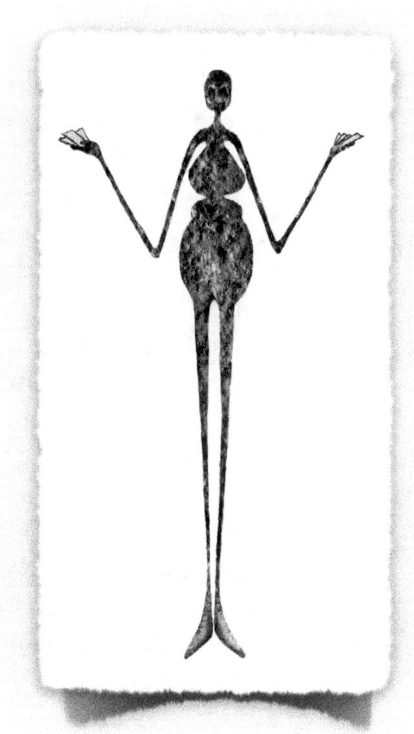

I'm going to make a round of tea. Tea makes everything bad seem far away.

I love the ritual of boiling the kettle, then choosing a specific mug for each drinker. The thickness of the ceramic, which comes from the belly of the earth, influences how the tea will taste. I don't know the exact science behind it, but the mug can't take too much heat away from the boiling water, otherwise the teabag won't brew properly. Temperature is everything. For others it's appearance; Imelda likes English bone china because it's more refined, lightweight and makes the drinker appear elegant; Sam likes a pint tankard made with a thick slab of earth covered in a blue mineral glaze that look like someone captured the sky and froze it in time; Dada likes any mug with a picture of a plane on it. I change my mug in the afternoon, while my Kahlo mug steeps in cold water. My afternoon mug is usually one of the cheap ones I see on a clearance shelf near the tills. I always feel sorry for them being left behind. That, and they're made without been over-thought or over-designed. They always make the best tea.

I drop a teabag in each mug and then pour dangerously boiling hot water over the teabag and watch the tea melt into the water in beautiful caramel brown streaks. It's hypnotic. Those brown streaks come from the belly of the earth as well. Mother Earth has quite the toolkit down there. I'm an expert at getting the right amount of milk. Everyone else gets it wrong. Each teabag has to be squeezed carefully until the desired colour is reached. Perfect.

I spill one on the floor again, just like this morning. It's fine. I can clean it up with the same Van Gogh tea towel. I'm not crying. I'm not even mad. This morning I would've happily let a lava flow take me away. It's surprising how potential annihilation cures the desire for annihilation. Is that why the brain tries to reach for the destruct button so frequently? It's a system check to make sure we can pull ourselves back from the edge. This lot won't survive without me; I've got to keep it together.

Everyone looks happier watching the news while holding a warm mug of tea. I'm a genius. I can't help thinking about Sam going to the village shop. I took Imelda there yesterday, and Imelda told all and sundry about a lump on Sam's testicles. He's had a lump there for years; I used to know their every contour. I never told him because it would make him grumpy, so I told our doctor, and he said he would check for me. Sam, or any man, never questions a doctor holding their testicles, especially when they only went in for a "routine" blood pressure check. Turns out it was nothing to worry about, so the doctor didn't tell him either.

Now that Sam has finally examined himself, or someone else has, he must have found it. The ladies in the village shop will salivate at the opportunity to share and advise Sam about his testicles in front of everyone as loudly as they can. All ladies want payback for the indignities of childbirth. All of them. There may be a brief pause in the panic buying while they anticipate his reaction. I hope the CCTV is working.

He's never tried to understand the pleasure his mother gets from his mishaps or faults. That's because he doesn't have a deep-rooted episiotomy scar. I suppose a lump on his testicle won't seem so bad now. There will be lots of Americans with lumpy bits arriving soon. We'll never get an appointment at the doctor's again. Sam has never been great with medical stuff, especially since Zoe's dramatic caesarean birth. There's nothing like a lot of unfamiliar machinery making scary noises in a room full of heavily fortified medical professionals to make a man feel useless at protecting his family. No amount of haymaking arms can deliver a baby safely. At least he wasn't referred to as a geriatric foetus container.

I have stupidly put my hand down the side of the sofa. There's a rolled-up crisp packet tied with a hairband in the middle. There's also a chewed Nerf pellet, three small Lego pieces, a penny, a child's tooth, a broken knitting needle, three chewed pencils, a chewed plastic straw, and one of my bras.

It was hard to talk to Sam after Zoe was born. Crying and peeing unexpectedly and inconsistently makes holding down a relationship or a job impossible. I couldn't work. I couldn't leave a baby at home with Imelda all day, knowing they'd be indoctrinated into a satanic crochet club. I'm quite happy making all the decisions, mopping all the bodily fluids, washing everything repeatedly, tiptoeing round my mother-in-law, being the taxi driver, the security guard, the therapist, the nurse, the cook, the cleaner, the decorator, the plumber, the window cleaner, the gardener, the secretary and the drain cleaner-upper. All he has to do is go to work and kick the car when it doesn't work.

This bra smells bad. I'll put the tooth in my pocket so it can join the other discarded baby teeth in my little souvenir box later. Everything else can go back down the side of the sofa.

What do I get from him apart from money? I get scowled at, frowned at, laughed at, left alone and left wanting. I don't get cuddled, assured, kissed, touched, included, praised, criticised, comforted, winked at, laughed with, teased, surprised, informed or loved. What do I give him? A shitload of tea and four functioning children.

We're too scared to give each other emotional support in case one of us rejects it, so we've become self-reliant and now don't need each other. Maybe he's having a midlife crisis as well. He does sweat a lot. But he doesn't have a dying uterus; he doesn't have a part of his body that is going to stop working and slowly shrivel up inside of him. The only shrivelling he can achieve is with a sudden drop in temperature. That's the only good thing about the female body — our genitals are tucked up inside, out of the way.

I'm nothing like Picasso's *Weeping Woman*; I keep my pain and anguish tucked up inside so it stains my soul, not my face, for fear of questions or retribution.

Thousands more have already been reported dead. The American news reporters look scared. Why are we here on this unstable planet? What is life all about if death is so swift and unexpected? What is the point of it all? I'm not sure there is any meaning anymore. I've been pursuing the meaning of life for so long now; I've questioned the meaning of everything. What's the point of knowing everything? The more I learn, the more I realise how stupid I was before. I had a pupil once refuse my help and say, "It's okay, Miss, I'm proud to be fick." She was happy with what she knew and loved her family. Why would she want to know anything more that would jeopardise that? I wish my brain would stop sometimes; I wish I could be happy knowing less.

I want to believe I am worth more than a nappy changer. Making babies, keeping babies alive and growing functioning adults is a worthy cause. It just doesn't feel like anyone cares anymore; mothers don't get listed in the FTSE. Now that the FTSE is crashing hard, will we be popular again? When we can't make money, making babies is our most valuable asset.

It looks like the entire world is crashing rapidly without America at the helm; every stock market graph is being put up next to the images of billowing ash. If the world goes as tits up as they're hinting at, then they won't be looking for hedge fund managers; they will need uteruses.

Well, my uterus is closing down, so what is my use now? Something new, unpredictable and exciting? My life isn't predetermined anymore. It's scary. Scary is good; scary is interesting. I really wouldn't mind mixing things up a bit. Maybe that's why Sam is probably having an affair; he's making his life a bit more interesting. I can only afford an imaginary affair. Not that it's all that imaginative, though. Imaginary sex with Keanu is exactly the same as actual sex with Sam, and because I don't want to look at myself having sex, I skip to the end anyway. My imaginary sex life is less interesting than my actual sex life, and I call myself creative.

I didn't think he would ever leave me because his dad had left when he was little. God knows what more damage his dad would have inflicted on them both if he'd stayed. Some humans like to abuse other humans so they have someone to save. Some humans create a crisis to be saved from. Humans are so fucking needy. I don't think Sam's dad wanted to save them. From the stories I've heard, he was a hit and run.

Sam is back already. He walks past the window, struggling to carry multiple carrier bags full of shopping and a large inflatable doughnut swimming ring. I don't think that's the loops Zoe was thinking of. For some well-trained reason, I rush to open the front door for him.

He looks like a man who has just discussed his testicles in public. This sturdy Victorian house creaks under the weight of his enormous, angry feet as they stomp into the kitchen. Sam sweeps all the fondant decorations on the kitchen table to one side and dumps all the bags of shopping on top. I get no eye contact again; he just turns around and heads straight out the front door.

'I'm off to work.'

He intentionally slammed the door this time. We all know the difference. I return to the front room, sit on the sofa, and wait for something else to react to.

There's new footage on the TV showing helicopter cameras trying to get close to the edge of the ash cloud. Do all the gods wait at the pearly gates like parents at a primary school waiting to pick up their children? Do those who have no god wait at the pearly gates like an abandoned child? I hope Heaven has a social services department.

Let There Be Light

Sam was definitely contemplating his testicles and not food when he panic-shopped. There are bags of sweets, popcorn, Hundreds and Thousands, cheap crisps, the cheapest biscuits, fizzy drinks, chocolate bars, chewing gum and one pint of milk. I've got hundreds of Hundreds and Thousands. I buy them in bulk. He doesn't know me at all.

'What's for dinner, Mummy?' Zoe shouts, despite being right under my feet.

'Um…soup, I think.'

'Yuck!'

'Soup with Hundreds and Thousands.'

'Ooh, yummy.'

I'll make my emergency soup; empty all the tins of soup into one saucepan no matter what the different flavours, add two tins of chopped tomatoes to hide the conflicting flavours, add heat.

Without thinking about it, I am sucking on a discarded pair of fondant boobs. I need sugar; I'm staring at another mirror. The plastic-framed mirror hanging above the microwave is surrounded by lots of postcards, photos, and kids' drawings stuffed behind it. Frida Kahlo stuck similar reminders of past connections around the mirror above her bed. She was desperate to feel a relevant part of her world too. Kahlo had her spine broken in a bus accident to be put in such a situation. I only need to be given a five-minute break from being asked for help or a cataclysmic volcano eruption to warrant such needs.

I wish I could paint as honestly as Kahlo. She painted naively, which forced people to focus on the meanings and symbolism rather than the execution. Rules always make people focus on the rules rather than the performance. Kahlo ignored the rules. Especially the one about women not being allowed to have hair in certain places.

I painfully removed my monobrow, moustache and sideburns some years ago, so would be a hypocrite to emulate her honesty if I painted like her. She thought her monobrow looked like the wings of a bird. My culture deemed mine a remnant of Cro-Magnon man or a symbol of unkemptness. Waxing was less expensive and easier than moving to Mexico and becoming a communist.

Kahlo liked to paint herself in her national dress. What is my national dress? Knickerbockers with bells on, a long Druid-like cloak, or just black leggings with a cat T-shirt? Kahlo painted her head on the body of a wounded deer once. Arrows penetrated the deer's body as it ran through a wood. Apparently, it represented fate because we are all doomed. I'm not as majestic as a young deer, nor hunted for my meat anymore. I am ready to collect dust and moths, though.

The soup is taking ages to warm up. Imaginary paintings continue to fill these brief respites. It's one way to avoid dealing with any impending difficulty and disruption to my way of life. I haven't really looked at any new art in decades, certainly not studied any. My imagination has been stuck like a scratched record since my university days. It was the last time I could afford to fully immerse myself in my art. Back then, we were given a small sectioned-off desk with three ceiling-high whiteboards in front and to the sides. We pinned actual images with actual pins to actual boards.

I was obsessed with my body even back then. Most women's bodies don't run like a well-oiled machine; they have too many complicated internal parts. They clunk about like a soapbox go-kart, using only gravity for motion. A brief kidney infection and polycystic ovaries diagnosis led to a gynaecologist informing me I wouldn't be able to conceive naturally. I panicked. I was twenty years old, believing I was saddled with a useless body. I had the boobs to attract every man I crossed paths with, but no functioning ovaries to provide a child for them. I thought I would be an outcast if I couldn't function as Mother Nature intended.

So, at university, I had the time and freedom to study a lot of female artists who had similar issues with their bodies. Kiki Smith's *Pee Body*; a sculpture of a crouching naked woman peeing out golden beads on a long thread. It repulsed and intrigued me in equal measure. It also encouraged lots of derogatory remarks from other students and reminded me why women have nothing like urinals in public spaces. It also raised the question: why do men have urinals in public spaces? They don't have them at home. One image, a thousand questions. I was more confident in handing over specimen bottles afterwards. I also studied Annette Messager's *Mes Voeux*: an installation of multiple close-up photographs of different parts of her naked body, representing the deconstruction of the idea of "woman". Nowadays, the parts needed to construct a woman can be found online and delivered to your door in a fragranced gift bag.

Rebecca Horn expressed her bodily ailments with a variety of crazy installations involving stilettos and liquid mercury. I saw her exploding piano: *Concert for Anarchy* in the Tate Gallery in 1994, but there was so much noise from crazy tourists I couldn't appreciate it. She simultaneously exhibited her work at the Serpentine Gallery, peacefully nestled in Hyde Park, there I could fully appreciate her representations of the fragility of bodily functions. Her work wasn't always pretty, but it was moving.

Then there was Sarah Lucas's *Self-Portrait with Fried Egg*; a photograph of herself with fried eggs on her boobs. It was funny, and Lucas looked badass. Most wannabe feminists stop at the image of a badass woman. That's all we're looking for.

Robert Mapplethorpe's *Portrait of Louise Bourgeois* took pride of place. It was a photo of her holding a giant bronze phallus under her arm, while grinning from ear to ear. I loved that level of confidence, and it also kept people away from bothering me while I figured out the meaning of life. An art therapist would've had a field day with such a collection of imagery. I didn't get all the answers I needed. I knew most of my answers were inside me, not what others saw when I was posing. You have to go deeper than a gynaecologist to understand each individual woman. Is that what gynaecologists are doing when they're in there.

These artists were warning us about the vulnerability and strength of the female body. Everyone pretends they will not let old age, poor health, or pervy men get to them, but they always do.

You can't go too deep when you're young. You think you can, but you're only scratching the surface of your existence because your existence hasn't fully materialised yet.

My creative response to that research was to hang up a makeshift curtain around my studio space, take my top and bra off and clumsily wrap my torso and breasts in Plaster of Paris and muslin cloth. Oblivious students passed by the curtain as I wrestled with my uncooperative boobs. I was trying to recreate, or be inspired by, Kahlo's body casts; she painted a foetus, among other grievances, on the casts as she recovered from spinal surgery.

Instead of looking like a strong female character, my boobs got burned by the chemical reaction in the plaster. I had to rip it off

my body quickly before the plaster set. It was ruined. I had to throw it in the bin. I still wonder to this day if anyone rummaged through those bins and found my boob casts with a few nipple hairs still attached.

I should make a new cast and beautifully decorate it with new grievances. I could form my boobs and meno-belly into a perfect position. Sculpt them back into an hourglass instead of an apple! It sounds drastic, but it would stop my permanently erect nipples from showing through. It would stop me from itching my nipples in public, too. It would stop them from getting tender. It would stop my chronic breast pain. It would stop them from looking droopy. I wouldn't need a bra fitting ever again. I wouldn't have these huge red ruts in my shoulders where my bra digs in. I could wear no T-shirt when it's hot, like men can. If I don't do something, my boobs will continue to grow and I'll have to start walking on all fours. I've been alive for nearly fifty years and I'm halfway through the alphabet in bras. If I reach one hundred, I will be mostly boobs.

So, the only way to make me happy with my body is to put it in a cast like a broken leg. My body only breaks when I try to squeeze it into expected rigid templates. It would be lovely to live in a world where everybody can walk down the street naked and no one bats an eyelid; it used to be like that. Religion and money ensured we covered up or stripped off, whatever the trending rules of the day might be.

People are trained to react like an obedient dog when they see a naked body. Except artists. We were trained to study naked butt cheeks and sagging breasts every Wednesday afternoon to teach us technical problem-solving skills. I became indifferent to nudity. I couldn't get aroused. That's why it was always the eyes that got me.

I needn't have worried anyway; getting pregnant is actually quite easy when you're just about to move house and you've started a new job that doesn't give maternity leave to new staff. The gynaecologist should have prescribed "bad timing" rather than mind-altering artificial hormones to cure me.

Now my body is malfunctioning again; it's nice to revisit those artistic representations. We have to be reminded that nothing is perfect, nothing runs smoothly, and nothing stays the same.

Dark Energy

The slamming of the front door just jolted me back to reality, whether I wanted to or not. Sam looks red-faced and puffed out. I'm staying in the kitchen, stirring soup at a safe distance. He runs up the stairs and looks for something loudly.

Imelda rises from her spot on the sofa and waits at the bottom of the stairs for him. She picks up one of my bras and holds it up against her flat chest, while Sam thumps back downstairs.

'I'm glad I never needed anything like this. It's a blessing I have no tits,' says Imelda.

Sam covers his ears like a toddler hearing a fire alarm for the first time, 'La la la la la la la.'

He's changed out of his work clothes and got his "I'm not telling you where I'm going because I'm having an affair" jacket on and looks like he's about to leave again.

Imelda stands in the doorway. 'Samson, where are you going?'

'There's no work tonight. The factory has stopped. Just for a few days, until they know what's happening in America. They can't guarantee paying us, so there's little point in going to work. The army has already closed the motorway.'

Shit. Shit, shit, shit, bollocking shit!

Sam walks hesitantly into the kitchen, probably hoping Imelda will get distracted by something I'm doing wrong. Imelda smugly follows him. She catches my stare. 'Looks like you'll have to go back to work, dear. Unless all those Americans decide they want cupcakes when they get here.'

'Back to work? I haven't put my feet up in seventeen fucking years unless heavily pregnant, and even then I did the dusting with a telescopic duster that Sam helpfully bought me.'

That was a firmer reply than I'm used to giving.

'The menopause didn't stop me from working, Nell. We just got on with it; we were made of tougher stuff than you lot.'

The only work I'm capable of is the Saga edition of OnlyFans. Oldest profession, my arse, when are we going to get promoted? Men have been prostituting themselves for violence as long as women have for sex.

Imelda pinches Sam's cheek as if they're in some 1950s sitcom. For all my faults, at least I'm not a mass-produced trad wife. Andy Warhol wouldn't have sold a lot of brightly coloured prints of my angry face.

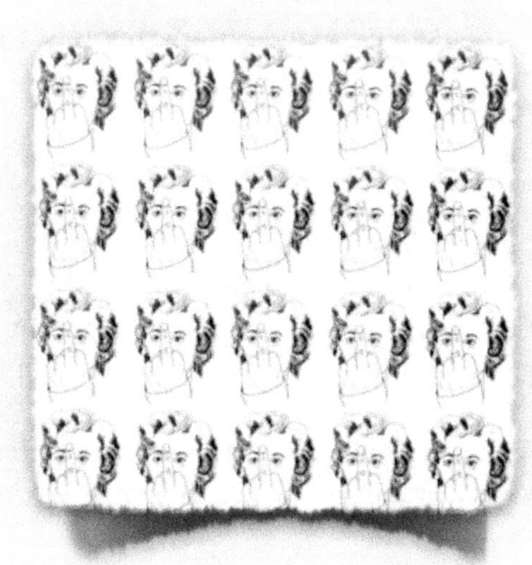

Imelda is no giant bronze spider either. My mother was. She was nurturing, caring, protective, fierce, and fragile. Imelda is a sly fox, rummaging through your detritus just to find a morsel of something that she can come back later and leave as a piling lump of shit in your way.

Sometimes I think I need a glossy, expensive coffee-table book to explain my thoughts. At least my outlet is art and crafts, not a fistfight. Sam looks like he doesn't know what to say or what to do. At least he's forgotten about leaving. I wonder who he was going to meet in that jacket.

I shouldn't ask, but, 'What are we going to do if you haven't got a job, Sam?'

'Don't worry, Nell. Money will become worthless soon.'

I'm stirring this soup so fiercely I might break the wooden spoon. I'm not used to confrontation or desperation. I like to solve problems in my head where I can control what happens and who wins.

Imelda has perfected the art of huffing and puffing; she should be reincarnated as a steam train. I'm ignoring her moaning about her garden getting ruined by the ash cloud and how this will affect the vegetable competition at the village fete. She picks up a fondant penis and lifts her reading glasses to study it. 'What on earth is this?'

'They were for a hen party. I just make what they want. I don't judge.'

'What is the world coming to!'

'The end, if you believe the news.'

'Oh, this will blow over, Nell; you'll see. A big fuss about nothing. Just need to ride it out until everyone calms down. How is your little website doing, anyway? Is the world of cupcakes on the up?'

'Actually, I've just had a new order for fifty volcano cakes with popping candy sprinkles. It's for an end of the world party.'

Tom runs into the kitchen and picks up a broken pair of fondant boobs. 'Can I eat these?'

'NO!!' All three adults shout in unison.

Tom looks genuinely disappointed. Sam grabs the rest of the imperfect genitalia and shoves them all in his mouth. Freud would break his pencil nib if he were here right now. How was I ever attracted to him? I suppose I was looking for physical attributes, not psychoanalytical profiling. I wouldn't have ripped his shirt off if he'd asked me how to stop his mother throwing dandelion seeds in other people's gardens. I bet people who have never heard of psychotherapy are the ones who don't need psychotherapy.

Imelda has never tried to understand what she did to Sam. She wasn't a professional hit-and-run enthusiast; she was more of a crash-for-cash scammer, ready to broadcast the humiliation later. She was better than what her parents did to her, and significantly better than what her grandparents did to both of them, so it is progress, albeit painfully slow. Blaming her won't solve anything; it will only add to the chips on her shoulders. I haven't forgiven my great-aunt Eloise for these enormous boobs yet. Accepting it won't make them smaller, and there's no bra supportive enough to give me closure.

I follow Imelda and Sam to the front room, where a hungry Amber has also joined us. Horrific videos of dying Americans continue to be shown on the news. I dutifully hand out the soup cocktail in mugs, with some cheese and bread. Imelda squeezes herself onto the sofa between Peter and Amber. Amber's sneering is now of Olympic standard.

'And what have you come as, Amber?'

'I'm a dancer, Gran.'

'From what book?'

'I dunno, there's got to be a dancer in some book.'

'I think you're missing the point of World Book Day; you're supposed to show your enthusia—'

'Gran, I really don't care, so don't lecture me now, OK!'

'I see manners are still evading you, my dear.'

'Mummy, will mature cheddar make me clever?' Tom asks.

'No, otherwise we'd all be geniuses.'

The hot soup is keeping everyone quiet for a while. I can't help but feel we're watching a movie, not the news. It all feels so familiar. The reactions from interviewed strangers from around the world seem to vary: some are excited, some are weeping uncontrollably, some don't care, and some just want to be on TV. Every plane that could has already left America and Canada. Every boat is on its way across the oceans to rescue whoever gets left behind. The mass evacuation of millions has started.

'This is so boring!' Amber groans.

'Do you have any respect left?' Imelda moans.

'No, Gran, I don't. No one respects me, so I don't give any.'

'Well, if you gave some in the first place, you might get some back.'

'I don't want any! I get on all right without it. Please and thank you don't get you everywhere in this life; that's a lie!'

'See, this is what happens when you don't go to church – you lose your moral compass.'

'What help is a compass? None of us are going anywhere.'

'It's not an actual compass, dear girl; it's a guide on how to live your life without upsetting others.'

'Where's yours then?'

Sam actually spat some of his soup out, not in indignation but with a wry smile. 'Don't talk to your Gran like that, Amber.'

'A bit late for that now, Samson. She's been speaking like that for so long she thinks it's normal now.'

'That's enough, ladies!' shouts Dada.

Imelda shrugs her shoulders. 'Not all of us are ladies, Bill!'

Sam's shoulders dipped. 'That's enough, Mother! Don't start.'

'Start what, Sam? Talking, giving my opinion. Freedom of speech is not allowed in this house. Oh, that's right. I forgot. Ignore it. Keep quiet and it will go away, not fester into something ugly and—'

'Mother, you weaponise your opinions. Thank God you don't understand social media, or your opinions would become weapons of mass destruction. No wonder they named hysteria after a woman's body part.'

'Yes, and when someone is talking nonsense it's called "talking bollocks" and if you're an idiot, you're a "prick" or a "dickhead". No one's ever been called a vagina when they're being stupid.'

'Yes, they have, Mother, just with an alternative word for it. Get me a notepad and pen, and I'll write down all the derogatory words for a vagina, and then you can add them to that fucking knitted diorama you're making!'

'It's CROCHET!!!'

'I WANT A PIECE OF QUIET!' shouts Tom.

The soup has nearly knocked Zoe out. I carry her upstairs, even though my arms feel heavier than my legs right now. I don't have to order the other kids out of the room. They're leaving voluntarily.

'Why is everyone so angry, Mummy? Can we go skaterolling tomorrow? Why are my legs so bendy?'

Zoe's mutterings drift off as I place her in bed; she falls asleep instantly. I could have done with more natural disasters when she was a baby. Tom lies on top of his bed with his camouflage duvet pulled up over his nose and his camouflage cap on; his eyes are the only distinguishable part of him.

'Are you okay, Tom?'

'I'm consummating.'

'Um… concentrating, I think you're concentrating. What are you thinking about?'

'What colour is hedgehog poo?'

'I think it's probably the same as all other poo.'

'Oh, okay. Night night, Mum.'

'Night night.'

What am I going to see if I peek through the gap in Peter's door?

He's lying on his bed in the dark, staring at his phone, watching live streams of the flow of death intercepted by videos of people filming themselves crying and screaming while shaving their heads and eyebrows. I think I need to put parental locks back on his phone.

The 17th-century Vanitas artists inserted "Momento Mori" onto their still-life canvases to remind their stupid, but rich,

patrons that their material wealth was pointless. We should've inserted the translation "Remember you must die" into every video game, romcom and porn magazine, then nothing would bother teenagers at all. It's healthier to face up to it rather than pretend it will never happen. Maybe his curiosity will fill the emptiness created by his growth spurt. Everything becomes a still life eventually, although today a table representing the sum total of our materialistic existence would look a little less busy.

Amber's door is firmly shut and locked. I can hear her tapping furiously at her phone, probably calling anyone who looks happy and living their best life a "bitch" or a "slut". The devil makes work for idle minds. A teenager who can't change a lightbulb shouldn't have that much power and influence. She's probably looking for a cult to join, one that celebrates nihilism but with merch.

I don't want to watch anymore news; I'll catch up with the American apocalypse tomorrow. I'm going to bed. I can't even be bothered to change my clothes. I need to lie completely still and stare at the clean, white ceiling above me. My eyes are wide open. I'm exhausted, but my mind is on some kind of rollercoaster. I don't know what is going to happen to us. No jobs, no money, no sweets, no bargaining power, no control, no peace. What do I have in my toolkit that will steer us through this? I'm going to have to create something more substantial than cupcakes. A career wouldn't be useful right now.

The American refugees won't be interested in self-portraits or a clay model; they will want something to lift their spirits and give them hope. I could do something postmodern. They like individual manifestos, the freedom to say whatever they want to say, and the freedom to be whatever they want to be. I could make a sculpture out of all the English words they can't spell or use properly. We're still clinging onto our history with grappling hooks, mainly because it makes good TV dramas.

The big and little fish are coming back across the pond. This country is going to look like a trawler net with everyone slapping about trying to breathe. We should rescue people like we rescue pets; stray people need a home too. The only problem is, a school of fish can be stunningly beautiful if they all know what they are doing, or where they're going, whereas a school of humans looks more like custard on a boombox speaker. We don't follow the laws of physics; we're naturally rebellious. Especially when put under pressure or listening to loud music.

My only fear is longer queues for everything. Immaculateness shouldn't be the expected ideal; then it becomes ordinary and boring. The inevitable collapse of the worldwide economy does bother me, but I have no answers. I might have to give teaching another go. Fuck that, I'll have to carry a weapon if I teach Americans! Scruffy, melodramatic attention seekers filled with chocolate should not teach scruffy, melodramatic attention seekers armed with guns or knives.

I can hear Dada and Imelda shuffle out of the front door and Sam mooch about downstairs. Is he going to seek solace in the arms of another woman? He's not going; he's coming upstairs. He's coming in here. Did he forget his trousers again?

He walks quietly into the bedroom. He takes his trousers off and slips under the duvet. I shuffle over to make room. We haven't been awake in bed at the same time for a very long time. I might have to play dead so I don't have to talk to him. Maybe he's only pretending to have an affair so I will fight for him. I never do, though. I don't know how to react; I feel numb. I hope he doesn't want sex. Nine months after 9/11 there was a baby boom; that's what humans do when the shit hits the fan. I'm not exactly apocalypse-body ready. If he does want sex, then I will need at least three to six months notice so I can remove unwanted skin, fat, hair, and wrinkles.

We desire so much that our present surroundings do nothing for us. We drive so fast to get away from where we are and have little desire to return to where we started. I know reality is beautiful if I would actually stop and look at it. It's only dull when I compare it to something out of my reach. Imagination can neglect reality. I've forgotten what it is.

'You all right, Nell? You seem a little focussed on the ceiling.'

What do I say? I think he's having an affair. I want to press a pillow into his face. I'm horny but hairy, and I thought about throwing myself onto a busy road this morning?

'I was just wondering. Should we take our money out of the savings? Should we try to contact your dad? What about all these Americans coming over? Have we got enough food? This is all happening so fast; I don't know what we're supposed to do.'

I despair of myself; I really do.

'Why on earth would we contact my dad? Why would you even bring that up? I haven't seen him since I was four. I don't know where he is, and I hate him. He'd upset Mum. Why would you think of that? Is impending doom not enough misery for you?'

Sam sits up, taking the duvet with him. The cold air hit my body with full force. Maybe the attempted suicide would have been a better conversation opener. He storms off.

There goes the front door slamming again. I don't think the trousers went back on. He probably doesn't need trousers where he's going. The love that we had has faded away. No-one told me it had a best-before date. I can't keep it in a box under the stairs. It's not there when I need it. What good is something you need if you can't get to it or it depends on the fragility of others? I am powerless to make him be the man I want him to be. I don't think he'd be up for learning six different martial arts and stopping speeding buses with bombs attached. I can't remember what I wanted him to be. I can't remember where I set my expectations. He assumes that because I agreed to live with him that I'm in constant alignment with him and that because his goals haven't changed in twenty years, mine shouldn't have either. Mine change hourly.

I think Mother Earth gave women the menopause to help them free themselves of the shackles of sexualisation. Someone needs to tell Joanna Lumley so she, and the rest of us panting miles behind her, can take a breather. Sam's looks have got shabbier as his body realises it definitely doesn't want to procreate more teenagers as well. Only people who trade on their looks worry about ageing. It's strength I'm more worried about losing, his as well. I want him to be strong enough to fight the bad guys, even though I never have been. I avoided those self-defence classes like a negatively charged magnet. I assumed I knew how to fight the bad guys because I only had one brother to play with as a child and we always played war games. Except I was always the German or the Native American. I was always on the losing side. That became my default setting. I accepted losing for historical accuracy, never realising I might have had a choice. By always losing, I should've discovered more about being at peace than he did by always winning. But I didn't. My only visible scars are from a C-section and a melted marshmallow. Nothing I've done has prepared me for this amount of proverbial shit. I wish I could shut this brain up.

Men are like fairgrounds. They look exciting and fun, but after a while you realise the hook a duck prizes are rubbish and you feel sick and want to go home. Breaking up with him is the only card I can play. It's the only thing I can control. But I can't leave him. I don't want to leave him. I know I have no ability to protect myself. I need him more than ever. I will continue to pay too much for a guaranteed shit prize because there's lots of flashing lights and music still playing.

I don't fear death. I've yearned for it, planned it, reorganised my calendar around it and thought about buying special underwear for it. Death frightens me less than living. Living is hard. Death is unavoidable. Life is unpredictable and out of my control.

Despite all the sandwich boards telling us the "end is nigh", we've never prepared ourselves. We assume we're going to Heaven, never caring that we're turning this place into Hell. It's easier to get someone else to rescue you from disaster instead of preparing yourself. I can't wait for someone else to rescue me anymore, because that someone else has a mind and a libido of their own.

An enormous cloud of ash-fuelled shit is about to hit an enormous metaphorical fan. I shouldn't react like the government and shut everything down. Governments are panicking because they fear death in big numbers. They've created too many graphs and league tables for mortality. We're going to go back to that grotesque fantasy fatality league again. I wonder if they give each other medals at the big summits for death tolls. That's why so many people are against the patriarchy. It feels like an endless game of football with no prize, no final whistle, and a constant supply of substitutes waiting for their turn. World leaders rant and cheer from the sidelines but take no responsibility for a piss-poor performance, which is why no one else does either.

The British used to be good in a crisis. We were fearless and so variably eccentric that we were unpredictable. Now that we're past our prime, we're panicking as much as any woman who has found a hair on her stiff upper lip. The news is already full of protests and complaining, but those only serve to distract while we figure out what to do. My Nana used to tell me that the British don't know when they've lost; they'll keep going even when the enemy assumes they've won. I need to summon up that DNA.

There won't be another lockdown. They are only threatening it to remind everyone of who is in charge. The government and the opposition are like overbearing, warring parents going through a divorce. The more they lock us in our bedrooms, the more likely we are to smoke weed and listen to *Rage Against the Machine*. Everyone feels like the children who just want to go on holiday, but all the money has been spent on lawyers. Right now, millions of people will shimmy down the drainpipe to raid the supermarkets for toilet roll. You can't stop the survival instinct once it kicks in.

Pangaea

Did I sleep? I can't remember closing my eyes or not thinking about having four children at home all day. It's been nearly a week since the schools shut. I can't remember thinking for myself amidst the new level of excitement, delirium and neurosis. And that's just the government briefings. I can't afford to waste my energy postulating on the empty ceiling this morning; I have children not to wake up for as long as possible.

The supervolcano has not stopped spewing out poisonous ash, and the stratosphere has dispersed it around nearly half the world already. Minimal sunlight is getting through the darkening skies. The influx of refugees from the American continent is filling up every municipal building. Celebrities are fighting over penthouse suites; apparently, an undisclosed influencer lost a tooth.

If I pull back these curtains, will I see more ash, acid rain or, as Peter keeps warning me; alien spawn falling from the sky? The clouds aren't fluffy anymore; they look burdened with fate. Every day is darker than the one before. The strange smell is getting stronger. The blood-red sunrise is bleeding into the blackened clouds, just as it did for Turner's famous paintings after 1815 when Mount Tambora in Indonesia erupted on the other side of the world. He didn't know it initially; catastrophic news took weeks to get around the world back then. Bliss! That eruption helped him create his beautiful range of atmospheric sky-scapes, masterfully recorded in light and colour. One supervolcano inspired a revolution in art; Turner inspired the Impressionists to add textured paint and blocks of colour. Over the next one hundred years, all the following artists focused on and dissected those blocks of colour until only one atomic level of colour could be seen — abstract art; Hilma af Klint split the atom in *Svanen* in 1915 before any scientist did, although no one noticed.

All the subset art movements appeared as a chain reaction after the fallout. The chaos theory reversed; a catastrophe eventually led to the fluttering of a million delicate wings that are only briefly noticed.

If only I were genius enough to create an opportunity to let my next career move rise from the ashes of worldwide devastation.

It's difficult when all I can summon up the energy for is dragging my apprehensive feet downstairs and putting on the kettle.

I'm still stuck in this self-loathing phase; it's harder to get out of than a comfy armchair at my age. Dada had a large print of Turner's most famous painting, *The Fighting Temeraire* hanging in our kitchen my entire childhood; a setting sun reflected in an ancient battleship being hauled back into dock by a more efficient steamboat to be broken up and retired from duty. I feel as though the sun is setting on all my heroic battles.

I wish I were so magnificent as to be worthy of such a memorial, but my battles weren't for the nation. I'm just a basic vehicle. One that makes strange noises, has unpredictable handling, an uncomfortable interior, and leaks fuel. If I knew what torque was, mine is probably shit too.

My wallowing has been made worse by the disappearance of Keanu Reeves. He, of course, gave up his seat on one of the last planes to get out of America. Everyone is hoping he's a stowaway on one of the boats. There are plenty more celebrities in the sea, literally, still paddling to get over here.

I'm fast losing all hope of anything ever getting better again. My doctor won't give me an appointment. Apparently, I'm not serious enough. I'm low on HRT and antidepressants as global supplies plummet. The government shouldn't be worried about the men rioting on our streets. When the HRT runs out, there will be an army of middle-aged women with untested and unrestrained rage ready to destroy anyone or anything in their path.

Sam has steadily filled downstairs with towering stacks of boxes over the last few days. Nobody knows what's in them, including, I think, Sam. He has promised me he paid for them and they're not from that dickhead parasite friend of his, Harvey. I don't believe him. He knows I don't believe him, but because I dared to intensify our barely talking relationship, he knows I won't ask him too many questions.

The news constantly reports on delivery trucks getting attacked and looted all over the country, and Harvey is about as trustworthy and reliable as a politician. He contemplated standing for election once; he was convinced that having a colourful past qualified him. I won't ask too many questions as long as Sam gets me teabags and milk. I don't worry about toilet rolls; I can wipe my arse with a washable flannel. I'm an armed forces daughter. But live without tea? Fuck off, world.

I poke my head into the front room. Dada and Imelda have somehow found a seat in the front room again. How do they get in? Dada is glaring at the rolling news updates: the American President has had a fistfight with the Canadian President. The Mexican president is missing. The French President has declared they will only take Canadian refugees; the Spanish President has refused to let British ex-pats fly home. Portugal has legalised all drugs. Protesters are complaining about the plastic tents being used to house refugees and keep setting them on fire. Pettiness, as always, prevails.

I shuffle along to the kitchen.

The noise of the kettle boiling seems more deafening than usual. I sneakily open one of Sam's bashed-up cardboard boxes. I can't wait any longer; my curiosity has never been tamed.

Hand towels? Why on earth would he want a box of hand towels? Is he going to open a B&B in the middle of this crisis? I suppose the refugees will need somewhere to stay if they survive the tent burning, but where?

I open another box. I'm desperately looking for more teabags as I'm going to run out soon. Fairy lights. Three boxes of fairy lights. Sam has clearly lost his mind! Is there a theme to this pop-up B&B: Santa's Grotto, *Tinkerbell*, or Valentine's Day? The next box is full of faux fur throws in garish colours. Is this what his mistress likes? I bet these are for her; I can imagine them sitting on a garish, fur-covered sofa with twinkling lights hanging from the wall and hand towels hanging on every available wall space because she saw it once on a social media post. Have I missed a trend? Hand towels must be the new toilet roll, and fairy lights, the new banana bread. I'm confused. I need to start scrolling.

The internet is very patchy; the servers in America no longer work. Most of the electrical grid in America has collapsed under the weight of ash. Refugees are bringing their TVs, looted or otherwise, with them on the planes and boats. It's a peculiar sight. Satellites aren't under control; not much is over there. Social media websites are clinging on by their fingernails. The iCloud seems to be inaccessible. Tens of thousands of family photos and videos are floating on the digital wind.

Zoe skips down the stairs with a vague attempt at parkour over the boxes in the hallway. 'Mummy, why are you cooking eggs? I hate eggs.'

'I'm not cooking; that's the volcano.'

'I thought eggs came from chickens, not volcanoes.'

'Eggs do come from chickens. The smell is of something called sulphur; it comes from volcanoes and it smells of bad eggs.'

'How do you know that?'

'I asked Siri.'

'Is Siri from space?' Zoe asks. She jumps onto my shoulders from the top of a stack of boxes in the hallway while I carry a tray of tea into the front room.

'Mummy, is the ash coming down like snow like those pictures on the TV?' she whispered straight into my ear.

'Apparently, we will only get a fine dusting.'

Somehow, I miraculously serve unspilled tea. A small child hanging off my neck isn't enough to waste a single drop. Only an existential crisis can do that. Outside just got darker than five minutes ago. Zoe looks excitedly out the window. 'Does God have one of those dimmer switchy thingies like Granny?'

'It certainly feels like he has, Zoe. All planes have been grounded out of America, even though they promised to help all those people get out.'

'Grounded? Have the planes been naughty, Mummy?'

'It's bigger than anyone imagined.'

The elders of the family sip their tea while Zoe continues her piss-poor parkour skills over the sofa and grandparents. The British government has just issued a new curfew: no one is allowed to go out on the streets after 9 pm from today until further notice. The army has been sent out to guard the supermarkets, but corner shops will have to defend themselves. Apparently, they're already empty anyway. The police are dealing with skinny, asthmatic rioters in every big city, demanding something new every day.

Schools don't prepare anyone for an apocalyptic world; kids today leave school with a proclivity for comfort-eating, sitting for long periods of time and waiting for someone to tell them what to do. Instead of schools mimicking the outside world, the outside world is mimicking schools, where the talentless suck-ups get gold stars and crying, casual bullying, gossip, wild conspiracies, perversion, and protection rackets thrive.

I bet all the gods regret making humans clever. The cleverer we get, the lazier we get. We've outsourced hunting, gathering, fighting, protection, teaching, and entertaining. We rarely achieve anything, so our core existence is never satisfied. If our ape-like ancestors had known that fishing ants out with a twig was going to lead to paying stupid amounts of money to eat live ants served with crème fraiche on a cabbage leaf in a fancy restaurant, they might not have bothered with all the intervening wars and intellectual growth. We still can't bring peace, agree on what is right and wrong, or fold fitted bedsheets.

I used to be good in a crisis. I loved solving dramas and tantrums. Now I can't predict what is going to send me over the edge until it's already pushed me off. Why would Mother Earth take a woman's strength away from her when she needs it most? Maybe that's why the Prime Minister wants to shut everything down. He's of a similar age to me. Maybe he wants to stay home and cry. Parents, teachers, police and politicians only want things banned when they can't control other's behaviour. We're all in detention, even though some of us have done nothing wrong.

Sam bursts through the front door with more boxes. I bet these are filled with Christmas crackers or potpourri.

'Bet you're all glad I went out again last night. I got a special deal,' he claims.

'I hope this isn't illegal, Samson,' says Imelda. She always puts on her posh voice when she wants to distant herself from his actions.

'I'm not doing anything illegal, Mother. I'm only doing what everyone else is doing. If we don't get it now, then we'll have nothing, because everyone else will have taken it.'

'So? Someone else won't have it because we've got it.'

'It's not my fault. Everyone else is only looking out for themselves as well.'

'You should give these boxes to the needy.'

I don't think the needy want hand towels and fairy lights. I could end this argument by revealing what Sam has got in those boxes, but I remain quiet to keep the peace and to stop our trust issues from reaching a critical level.

'We are needy, Mother! Everyone is needy. Everyone needs to eat and wipe their arse. You didn't complain when I managed to get you quilted 3-ply during lockdown.'

'I'm just saying it doesn't feel right.'

'It probably isn't right to someone, but my survival instinct hasn't been deactivated by excessive moral preaching. I'm prepared to put my body on the line if it means you lot can eat the last digestive biscuits.'

It's not irrational to panic buy; it is irrational to hoard useless shit in a crisis though. Imelda is happy to preach while eating our actual last digestive biscuit. I'm sure Sam is buying boxes of useless shit just for show. He wants everyone to think they're full of food so nobody panics.

Everybody is needy because everyone wants to be needed. The only advice I took from my mother was: "Make yourself more valuable than the money you leave in your will". I have little to leave in my will except boxes of buttons. I intentionally set the bar quite low.

Nobody plans for the end of the world. Everyone plans for plentiful riches. It's why everyone looks so disappointed all the time. End of the world? It still sounds overdramatic. The world never changes when they say that. In fact, the world continues to spin regardless of what humans do to themselves. Everyone fears for the future because they can't control it. Only gambling addicts can face such high stakes or uncertainty, and even they need a few stiff drinks to handle it.

The end of an era is always nigh. Empires, kingdoms, governments, and societies come and go frequently. They remind me of those nineteenth-century men learning to fly; every single one crashed and burned eventually. Has anyone reached the Wright brothers' phase yet? Britain has been working on, and praying for, a controlled descent for some time, but everyone forgets the turbulence.

The stock market has fully crashed on every continent. Actual printed money is already scarce, crops are already wilting, food is rationed, and it's going to get really cold. An ice age would be cool. Everyone likes snow. No one will be rioting and looting when it gets freezing.

They've just announced that schools will be shut for the foreseeable future. Fuck! Unless they're teaching GCSEs in "building a house from ash" or "how to sanitise polluted water," the kids will not need them, anyway. It's going to be a lot of cupcake baking, star jumps, and my tongue sticking out of the side of my mouth while I try to convert new maths into old-school maths on a notepad.

Zoe runs up to my face at full speed, crying, 'Muuummmyyyy!! School is shut forever… and…and…we can't do painting ever again…and…and…what's going to happen to the ladies in my school, they will be lonely…and… and—'

'Hey hey, it's OK, you can still paint. We can get the paints out here.'

'What paints? We haven't got paints.'

'Of course we have. I've got lots of paint. They're under the stairs.'

What the hell am I thinking of? I need to get better at quick and easy solutions to stop her crying that don't involve masses of cleaning up.

I'm under the stairs — an area of the house that no one else enters. My large, untouched box of acrylic paints that Sam bought me years ago is in here somewhere. This is an area of the house that I have truly given up on. I throw stuff in here as if there's a mass of conveyor belts like the baggage handling at an airport, hoping that when I need something, it will just be there waiting for me on a carousel.

Instead, there are piles of empty bags for life on the floor and several bags for life hanging from every nail or hook, filled with stuff I can't remember owning. There's the tapestry starter kit, the badge maker, the robot puppy, the daily planner, the foot massager, the self-stirring travel mug, the sumo wrestling costumes, educational toilet paper, and the dried-up remains of a Bonsai tree. Only Bond villains have the time for shit like that. I wade through these bags like a kelp forest. Bags for life are like candles; the number increases with age. I swear they're breeding in here.

Here they are — a completely untouched pack of twenty-eight tubes of acrylic paint with a pack of brand-new brushes. We haven't got any paper, so she'll have to make do with painting whatever is in the recycling bin.

Zoe is thrilled. She paints a flattened cereal box with green and purple stripes. I hope this is a good time to break some other bad news to her. 'Zoe, I'm afraid dance classes have been cancelled as well.'

'That's okay, Mummy, don't be afraid. It's only dancing. I can dance anywhere. I don't mind a few bumps and ups.'

She's right. While Zoe concentrates really hard on painting, I'm going to sit in the kitchen next to her and drink my cup of tea. I'm sticking with the only person who isn't scared shitless.

'Is there a man inside the TV, Mummy?'

'No. I hope not, anyway.'

'Then why does everyone keep shouting at it?'

'Because it doesn't shout back.'

Here comes Tom. He doesn't look as scared either.

'Mum, how much does it cost to send a parcel to America?'

'I don't think the postal service will be working over there, Tom.'

'Can I paint as well, Mum?'

'Sure, why not?'

'Where are all the helicoppers?'

'What helicopters, Tom?'

'When people need help, there are always helicoppers. Have they all gone to America to help those people?'

'Yes, I think so, probably. Well, actually, maybe not. Nothing can fly through the thick ash now, and it's already reached the east coast. Helicopters can't help them now. Every boat in the world is heading for America to pick up the ones who couldn't get a plane ticket.'

'Are we doomed?'

'Um… I hope not. Not all of us, the Disney Channel might be, but humans have survived on less than this before.'

That statement didn't go down as badly as I thought it would. They're too young to understand what doomed really means. Zoe has finished painting her flattened cereal box already. The purple and green stripes have been blended into a muddy colour and now look like a volcano. Orange and red stripes are bursting out of the top and falling ungracefully onto the ground. There are little splodges of black paint on the ground too. Those are probably people, but I'm not going to ask in case I have a breakdown. What's next on the list of keeping your children amused while the world descends into mayhem?

'I need more boxes, Mummy!'

Thank God. I couldn't think of anything. Nothing at all. When did my mind empty? Since entering my forties, my brain must have sprung a leak.

'You can't have my boxes, Zoe. I need them for something important,' says Tom.

'Mummy, I need more boxes, NOW!' shouts Zoe. She is less than a foot away from me.

'What kind of state is my kitchen in, you two?'

'Paris?' says Zoe.

'Paris isn't a state, Zoe, it's a theme park!' answers Tom.

Who do I correct first? I haven't got any more empty boxes. 'You'll have to paint the boxes Dad brought home; don't pick them up, just paint them where they are.'

'Really, Mummy?'

'Fill your boots!'

'Fill my boots with paint?' Zoe tilts her head like Scraps does when I ask him complicated existential questions.

'No, Zoe, it's a figure of speech. It means go crazy, do what you want.'

'Are you okay, Mummy?'

'I'm fine. You lot enjoy yourselves.'

'We don't have enough paint for that.'

It's hard to stand back and watch Tom and Zoe devour my tubes of paint, knowing they are unlikely to wash out of their clothes or come off the table, floor, or walls. I don't seem to mind today; such things don't seem important now.

'Mummy, when we've finished painting, can we bake a cake, pleeeeeease!'

Now she's taking the piss.

'We haven't got time, sweetie.'

'Then make time, Mummy.'

'And how do you make time, Zoe?'

'Take the clocks away, of course!'

Mary K Hollywood

The Heavens Opened

The kitchen table now reminds me of Tracey Emin's *My Bed* from 1998. She exhibited her unmade bed covered in bodily fluids, condoms, and empty vodka bottles to represent the detritus of living: excitement, arguments, serious lapses of judgement and

unexpected encounters. My kitchen table represents the detritus of childhood enthusiasm: doubt-free experimenting, questionable colour choices and unexpected outcomes. Everything that the 70s were about.

You can learn a lot about yourself from your waste; that's why animal experts always examine animal excrement. And that's why artists have got away with selling actual tins of shit as well. Not sure my children's detritus is nuanced enough to be nominated for a prize, though.

We were created from mess, from chaos. Eventually, with a bit of practice, I could probably create sophisticated organisms from this lot. If the Big Bang had just been the Big Calm, it would have been a bit boring.

It's amazing how I can use my basic knowledge of the universe to justify not cleaning up embedded paint on the walls. Artists can call up any morsel of information to justify a single unremarkable mark.

I used to keep my life clean and tidy all the time, but then the tiniest speck of dirt that came my way would make me overreact. A bit like having an allergy. I became allergic to life. Having children makes you accept the dirt, the marks made by existence, made from joy, made from doubt. I stopped overreacting and settled into barely reacting at all. There must have been a balance point that I missed along the way.

I have to accept life. Chaos and mess can feel like diving into a lake of pollen or nuts. A gin and tonic used to be my EpiPen, but I don't want to drown anymore. I have a reason to live: to keep my children alive. I can't live in fear of being fearful. Those who would regulate us are collapsing; the government, social media, councils, schools, even the crochet club is in disarray. I suppose it's to be expected when you're raised on entertainment instead of fear. All those Saturday night game shows really made the British quite docile.

When my brain has nothing to fear or panic about, it panics about small things instead. I overreact to being miserable, ignored, slighted, teased, or tripping over the bit of carpet held down with duct tape. I'm no expert, but I'm pretty sure most people don't kill themselves when they spill a cup of tea. If they did, the British would have imploded a long time ago.

I should join in the fun; I should create something of my own. I haven't made anything in years. I could use these leftover shades of the muddy brown paint Zoe has now abandoned in favour of some new muddy brown paint she's created. It's funny how everything turns to brown when you mix it together. It doesn't matter how many shades of colour you have; they all make a shade of brown in the end, just like tea, mud and the universe. I haven't drawn anything for real in ages. I probably don't know how to do it anymore. Living in a fantasy world does not sharpen those skills.

I think I'll make a collage out of all the rubbish Zoe has left behind. There's a long, woollen thread from her jumper that she unravelled from her sleeve, leaving a massive hole. There's some cardboard from an emptied box of teabags and half a cup of cold coffee that Sam left on the table earlier. All I need is a pair of scissors and glue, and I can create anything.

What shall I create? What is important to me right now? Obviously, the children, but I don't want a figurative representation of what they look like. I know what they look like. There are countless photos of them surrounding me. They are surrounding me. What needs eternally fixing in dried coffee and glue?

This spot, this place. A place we are fixed to because of ancestry, history, mortgage limitations, and now curfews. This street. I love this street, and sometimes I hate it. This house is my castle, but also my prison. I can not leave it unless I know I can return to it. It's my safe space and my torture chamber. It's where the last three children were conceived and where they all practised everything they have mastered. The walls and floors are infused with their sweat, blood, tears, and fruit juice. I've wanted to leave this house so many times, but I've also desperately wanted to return to it. This place is haunted by memories of arguments and slammed doors, but also by uncontrollable laughter and the best hugs. This is ground zero for us.

I know the lines of this street so well; I don't need a photograph to remind me. The straight, ordered lines of the man-made houses to the right contrast perfectly with the wild, natural curves of the hedges on the left. Each side forced to reconcile itself with its own form and function before reaching a vanishing point at the end of the street where they seemed to meet. Before every school run, I stare at this, reminded that there is a limit to my vision, and that depth is an illusion. The two sides never meet.

The pioneers of the Renaissance skipped for joy when they discovered how to represent such depth on a two-dimensional surface after a hundred years of trying. Then they could experiment with reality and draw the viewer's eye towards something they believed was important. It's still used in movies today, although few have any idea their eyes are being controlled.

I can paint it with cold coffee in a heartbeat thanks to repetitively teaching the same technique, every rotation on the Arts carousel, every year, to every unappreciative Year 8 student that passed through my classroom. They weren't interested in the spiritual meaning that lay on the horizon; they just wanted to hit their computer-generated target or doodle on the back of their hands.

Zoe's loose thread isn't enough to create the unkempt hedge and bare trees on the edge of the fields. I'll need to raid my emergency sewing kit that I keep next to my button boxes.

Threads are difficult to manage while swimming in PVA glue, which makes them perfect for the representation of Mother Earth's desire to battle the hedge cutters. However, the thread can be pulled into rank to represent the telephone lines that stretch across the sky, tethering the obedient houses into formation.

I can cut shapes out of cardboard rapidly. My eyes can see the shape that is needed, and I can cut it without drawing an outline. I practised hard with students who couldn't even hold a pair of scissors and who were about to impose on my break time if I didn't finish their work for them. Teaching is a noble profession, but break time is sacrosanct.

I'll use the empty Calpol box for the red telephone box so it stands out against the earthy browns. One indispensable brand to represent another.

It's not bad. It's a bit rough, but it's a start. It needs the sun. I have an orange button in my pocket that I found on the stairs earlier. There, an actual finished piece of art.

Zoe looks at my creation. Her shoulders just slumped.

'I can't do it as well as you, Mummy,' she sighs.

'You don't have to be as good as me, sweetheart. This took years of practice.'

I'll have to hide this now. I remember putting Amber off making messy art when she was about the same age. She was too young to realise that being untrained was a good thing. When do children realise they're not even close to their limitations? Adults dwell on it.

It's nice to focus on something of my own, something I've observed, something I can concentrate on that doesn't require a wet wipe or a biscuit to placate. It didn't take that long, but then it's only cutting and pasting. I'd like to draw; I'm in the mood now. I should at least try to draw something properly. Not just a quick doodle, but something well-executed. There's one clean sheet of white card from a ready meal left in the recycling. Here goes the repetitive circle motif with sweeping tentacles coming out of it, again. Every single one of these doodles ends up looking different, but they all start from the same point.

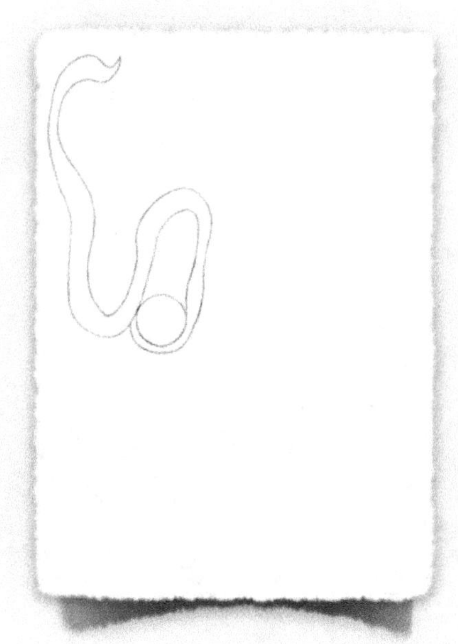

My hand hurts just holding the pencil. I am out of practice. I'm too old. I might not be able to do this anymore. I've left it too late! For fuck's sake, calm down! I'm just a bit stiff. It'll get easier. Failure isn't constant, or at least it doesn't have to be. Anyone who says, "You can do anything if you put your mind to it", didn't try scuba diving with an ear infection. There is a limit to what you can do. We are not all built the same. I couldn't be the next Queen of England without bumping off a few happily married people. It should be: "be something that brings you and others joy, and enjoy finding out what that is."

I hate the phrase "be your authentic self" as well. I don't want to be my authentic self; I can be a right arsehole sometimes. I want to be better than my authentic self. I'd rather reinvent, redesign, restore, and renovate myself. There are definitely parts that need upgrading. I've never known who I was. I didn't know what I wanted to be. I still don't. Just as I think I understand myself, I've evolved into something else. I can't keep up with my own ageing process or the catastrophic obstacles that Mother Earth keeps putting in my way.

I've forgotten how to follow my instincts. It's significantly easier to follow others. If millions of other people are all heading for the same place, it would be the same as driving straight into a traffic jam with nobody going anywhere. I need to follow my own path. It's much more of an adventure. There's no map, and I have to accept ending up at many dead ends, lost or unable to find a parking space. There have already been a few wrong turns, a few breakdowns,

some more stressful than others. They were all opportunities to fix rather than dwell.

Look at what I'm capable of when I put my mind to it. It needs a bit of colour. Shall I try to paint it? For once, I have an opportunity.

A few weeks ago, I saw the words "The only one that matters is you" hanging in a charity shop window. If charity shops are encouraging self-absorption, then the end of our era is truly nigh. I know it's not true. Any mother knows that. I don't exist on my own. I'm part of a family, a tribe, a community, a nation, and the human race. I'm at my most depressed when I think solely about myself. I need others to bring me back from the edge.

Postmodernism encourages self absorbed navel gazing. Either art predicts where civilisation is going, or civilisation, slavishly follows where the art takes them. Children bring you back from the edge, especially if they're allowed to turn the kitchen into a Jackson Pollock-esque installation in less than an hour.

Zoe has just put a gold star sticker on my T-shirt; that must have been for letting them trash the kitchen. Tom takes his empty boxes upstairs to dry on his bedroom floor. Zoe yawns and leaves a trail of muddy acrylic footprints towards the sofa. I want to finish this painting, even though my hands are aching. The creative process makes me think of endless possibilities. It's addictive. I could create an infinite number of original ideas if I had an infinite number of days to live. I'll ignore the paint on the ceiling and inside the teapot. There's no point in asking the kids to help. They'll just smear it everywhere and make it worse.

There's a lot of noise coming from upstairs. I can hear Amber screaming at Tom for using her hairdryer to dry the paint on his boxes. Now he's sneaking into my bedroom. I know the individual sound of every loose floorboard in this house. Him potentially looking in my bedside drawer is enough to stop me from painting and race up the stairs, two steps at a time. I'll have to abandon the artwork. Like my whole life so far, either hidden or unfinished.

'What are you doing in my bedroom, Tom?'

'Nothing!'

'Yes, you are. What have you got in the bag?'

'Nothing!'

'You are a terrible liar. Open the bag.'

Tom sheepishly opens the tote bag. Inside is my collection of free sachets of perfume from magazines, some loose change, a finger skateboard I confiscated off a Year 7 student twenty years ago, many types of hand cream, hair grips, and a wide variety of colourful post-it notes. Thank God that's all he found!

I follow Tom into the bathroom, where he fills empty plastic bottles with water at the sink. I've got my best stern face on, but I'm so confused I think I'm giving him mixed signals.

'What weight am I in stones and pebbles, Mum?'

'I have no idea, Tom.'

'They will need water; I heard it on the telly.'

'Who needs water, hair grips and Post-it notes?'

'The people in America, come and have a look.'

Tom is now in his bedroom, where he has sat in the middle of the floor surrounded by piles of lost and found items. I tentatively tiptoe round the junk he has amassed and sit carefully on his bed. He fills each of his painted boxes with "useful" things. He doesn't have enough sweets for all six boxes, so some boxes get more biscuits. Most boxes have at least one piece of sugary food, one sock, one hairband, three nails and two screws. He places a looped-up piece of string in each box. He adds a bottle of water and a perfume sachet to the mix.

I'm watching Tom put the lid on each box, tape it up and write "Amerika" on the top in felt pen. He draws a little picture of a stamp with the King's head on the top right corner of every box. The paint is still wet and is all over the rug he shares with Zoe. He blows on all the wet patches, but that makes him dizzy. He distracts himself by attaching some string to his model helicopter and tying the string around a hay bale from the farm set to show me how his master plan would work.

'They're too heavy for the postman's office, so I want helicoppers to drop the boxes all over America to help the people who were crying and running away.'

Now I'm crying. Tom doesn't understand why I'm crying, even though I'm trying to reassure him they are happy tears.

'You have more happy tears than sad ones, Mum.'

He's admirable, but he always leaves a trail of detritus behind him for someone else to pick up – typical fucking hero. Tom won't accept my refusal to take the boxes to the postman's office. 'I can't afford the postage!'

I refuse to give them to a courier as well. He doesn't understand they're not delivering at the moment. He sits disappointedly on the floor.

'If the postman's office won't take the boxes, then my remote-controlled flying saucer can carry them over the sea.'

Tom rummages in his toy box and finds his polystyrene flying saucer. It breaks in half as soon as he ties it to a box and tries to fly it. Plan C seems to involve a large paper aeroplane made from cardboard, but it nose-dives immediately. Plan D is small boats, so he looks for anything boat-shaped in plastic.

I can't stop the tears; my cheeks are so salty. At least I have emotions after all. I leave Tom to his delusions of competence and lie on my bed. I need to soften the noise of my despair with a suitably soundproof pillow. I don't want anyone to know what I'm feeling. I can't face the questions.

My metaphorical car has a crack in the windscreen. I've been ignoring it. My entire field of vision could be blinded by a simple bump on the road. I can't see the bumps, the loose chippings or the debris from someone else's car crash hurtling towards me. There are no advanced driver's courses for these bodies. Unless you count Buddhism, but they're not really driving, they're parked.

The bed is cold, but I am not. I stare at the ceiling, but it's blurry. What if the hole is too big for a quick squirt of resin? What if my windscreen is completely smashed? How do I get a new metaphorical windscreen? I've been driving my whole life with a massive crack in my field of vision, and I didn't realise it was a problem because that's the way it's always been. I know it's there. I can see it; it's always been there. I didn't realise it was a problem. I assumed it was normal to have a massive crack in my windscreen, especially if no one else mentioned the enormous crack. As I've got older, I've got wiser, and faster. I've realised something is not right; the dust and grit blowing into my car are annoying me, it's getting in my way, slowing me down. The hole needs filling, or the brain will automatically fill it with anxiety, fear, dread, and self-loathing. I need to fill the void. Where's that painting? I need to wipe my face dry and go back downstairs.

Instead of worrying about crashing, I should check my brakes. A car maintenance book should be the answer to the meaning of life, but there is no manual for the human brain. There's not even a little white plaque on the wall telling you what it means.

I nearly tripped on a fingerless glove going down the stairs so fast.

We are all walking this earth like tourists in the Dali Museum in Spain: bewildered, but pretending to be impressed. There are thousands of books and videos that will tell me how to be happy, how to fix my body and mind. But they don't know me, and they all say different things. I will have to write my own manual. I'm a unique make and model. I need to figure out my own needs, write them down, and refer to them when I need to. I can't wait for someone else to publish a manual specifically for me.

My art is my manual; this painting is a start. I'm going to finish it.

'Any chance of a cuppa, Nell?'

Fuck. Obviously, it is too tricky for Dada to turn on a kettle. I'm still everyone's first point of contact even when I'm trying to hide. I fucking hate being a people-pleaser.

We haven't got enough tea bags, shit. Sam is out again. Maybe I'll face the shops myself, panicky or otherwise. It's time I did something myself. I shouldn't wait for someone to save me; help has to come from within, then it's always there.

I need a coat, even though I'm boiling. Panic buying can't be that difficult; Sam always comes back with loads of stuff, nothing useful, but plenty of it. All I want are teabags; I'm not greedy. Just enough to get us through the next few days — I can't think beyond that.

'I haven't got any teabags, Dada. So, I'm just nipping out. I'll take your Land Rover, okay?'

'Okay, sweetheart.'

'Don't buy a skydiver, Mummy,' says Zoe.

'What?'

'Don't come out of the shops with a skydiver like you did last time you went shopping.'

'That was a shade sail, Zoe. I'm not going to Lidl.'

'That skydiver is still in its bag.'

'I know, I didn't realise we needed concrete to set it up.'

'Daddy said it was typical.'

'Yes, he did, didn't he?'

I get into Dada's Land Rover like a child wrestling with a climbing frame for the first time. This car is older than I am. It doesn't play music or go very fast; it forces me to drive like an elderly lion tamer. A single magpie watches me from the hedge. Are they trying to wind me up?

Adam and Eve

The supermarket car park is a mess. There's lots of beeping horns and arms waving aggressively. I park on a side street so I can slip past the mayhem and soldiers. I'm not madly keen on crowds at the best of times. I'm not madly keen on queues either, despite my British ancestry. Queues and menopausal ladies do not mix well. I peed myself unceremoniously while queuing impatiently for the self-checkout last year. The staff kindly let me use the back door to the staff room to avoid embarrassment. Apparently it's always wedged open… it's still wedged open. No soldiers in my way as I head straight through the back towards the tea aisle.

There are many people swearing and bumping trolleys inside. This is what modern anarchy really looks like. It looked cooler in the movies and pop videos. I grab an overturned trolley and browse the aisles as if I do it like this all the time.

There are discounted Valentine gifts and bright yellow fluffy Easter chicks stuffed into the end of every aisle. There's no fresh fruit or vegetables, except for grapefruit and celery. Only a cocaine fuelled chef could make a very expensive starter out of those.

The staff seem exasperated. Someone asks a disinterested soldier whether almond milk works in a chocolate mousse. I've found one pint of organic full-fat filtered milk; it's all that is left. A ripped plastic wrapper from a packet of nappies floats down the aisles like tumbleweed. There's a massive brawl in aisle six: grown men and women on the floor clutching tins of baked beans and tomato soup. A five-year-old girl kicks the shelves; her mother grabs her arm, 'Stop that, Emily! Those are real Uggs!'

Evolution used to be the survival of the fittest; now it's the survival of those who have the best shoes, who ironically aren't the fittest. There are actually people in here who have dressed up to panic-buy. I didn't think there was much point in matching my top and bottoms when all I was going to do was cling to a catering-sized packet of teabags and maybe some biscuits.

I've nearly reached the tea and coffee aisle. Anything less than fully stacked shelves of a hundred different types of tea will raise my blood pressure to DEFCON 1.

It's completely empty. Breathe. There are a few ripped teabags on the floor; they look salvageable. The only tea left is the one that declares it can "improve your mind, body and soul". I've tried them before, and they did not live up to that claim, not even close. The news didn't say they were running out of teabags. Breathe. Now I'm as mad as the lady who wanted the last tin of tomato soup. Beads of sweat are forming on my forehead.

I drift up and down the aisles looking for anything that is left on the shelves, pretending I'm not panicking at all. The sweat on my palms is making it hard to steer this trolley. I've never needed my poker face as much as I do now. The stakes are higher than in any game I've played before.

Do I need gluten-free crispbread? Toilet paper probably has an equivalent nutritional value, but crispbread definitely can't replace toilet paper. Will anyone eat chicken and ham paste? It looks like vomit. What about vegan doner kebabs? What's the point? I'll grab the last cup-a-soups and the shop-brand kitten food. I doubt

Gigi will eat those; she would rather lick the fur off long-dead roadkill than eat a rival brand. If we do end up in a barren landscape with blood-orange skies, she might just lick the jelly off. There are lots of tinned hotdogs and bags of popcorn left; thought those were essential for watching the end of the world. At least I don't have the agony of choosing between foods that make me happy and foods that make me slim. I grab a packet of Chocolate Fingers off the floor.

There's an old man clinging onto a trolley, tottering round everyone fighting. He's got a small bag of teabags next to a single roll of toilet paper. He's not very optimistic. I'll leave him be; it's not my favourite brand, anyway. There's a young man with a resting pompous face strutting through the middle, pushing his trolley like it has six gears. He's got a large box of teabags among the last of the dying potted herbs and ready meals for one. I don't need to be exposed to his shit right now.

There's a large, slightly older man with a trolley piled high with boxed wine and frozen chicken dippers. At the bottom of his trolley are two large boxes of my favourite teabags. There's enough there to keep me sane for a week or two.

My blood has just gone cold. How do I get those boxes? He's a big man, and nobody is wrestling with him for the dippers. I don't want to wrestle him either. I don't know what I am going to do. He's quite attractive; maybe I should flirt with him, maybe even run away with him — his trolley isn't loaded with faux fur throws. He's got what I want. I haven't flirted in over twenty years; I can't remember how it's done. That's bullshit. I flirted so hard with the new postman; he switched to another round. If I think about it, I won't do it.

'Excuse me, please.'

'What?!'

'I notice you've got two boxes of tea bags; would you mind—'

'Fuck off, sweetheart.'

He knows I can't do him any harm. I feel rigid, as if I've never bent over in my life. I want the teabags at the bottom of his trolley. I could outrun him, but I would have to get them first.

He's moved along a little, shoving more bottles of unscrutinised wine into his overcrowded trolley. When I'm angry and thirsty, a herd of wild horses could not drag me away from a cup of tea. My body is wobbling, which is not usually a good sign.

'I'll let you touch my boobs if you give me one of those boxes of tea.'

My boobs have their own gravitational pull, a pull that has increased with general weight gain and frenzied hormones. The man looks me up and down and checks to see who else is looking.

'OK.'

I won't look. I'll pretend this isn't my body. Breathe. The man hasn't bothered lifting my top; he's gone straight in, grabbed them and is massaging them like he's making bread dough. There is fuck-all arousal. I pretend they're like spoilers on a car; superfluous, prominent, get men excited, but don't improve the overall functionality of the whole. He's not fondling my engine, caressing my gearstick or stroking my steering wheel. It'll be over in a moment. His hands feel like old, rotting rubber.

Women can't win with their fists, so we fight with our boobs; it's more effective than mace. He can hurt my body, but he can't hurt my feelings. He keyed the car, but I didn't get thrown through the windscreen. If we're going to compete with men, we've got to behave like men. Mother Earth didn't give women big biceps, but she did give us a manipulative mindset and jiggly flesh. Got to use what's available.

The man shoves his filthy hand into the bottom of his trolley with a gratified smirk. He grabs a box of teabags and hands it over. At least he kept his side of the bargain. He walks off with a slight spring in his thuggish step. I feel sick. But I do have tea! Even the strongest man in the world has a weakness; I outsmarted him. I got what I wanted. If I had big biceps, I would've just knocked him out, then I could have taken the chicken dippers as well. I've always been okay with my weaknesses, but not my strengths.

The man turns round briefly to catch a glimpse of his prize, only for his smile to drop off his chin like fast-melting ice cream. I look behind me. The woman who berated her child for damaging her Uggs is standing in quiet fury just behind me, switching her angry eyes between me and the man. The berated child grins as if she's seen this before. She pushes past me and storms up to her husband. I don't want to be involved in this aftermath, so I rush towards the self-checkouts. In my mind, they're playing the *Rocky* theme tune on the tannoy.

I somehow reached a self-scanning station. I try to scan my few items, but I can barely hold anything properly. I feel slimy; the sweat is building up. There are screaming and crying adults in the distance; the alarms are going off, but no one cares. The soldiers are too busy getting hit with handbags and umbrellas. I need to get home as quickly as possible. I don't want to think about it; I need to think about anything except what just happened.

I'm walking so hard my knees are screaming. I'm outside, and the cold air hits me like a slap in the face. I want to collapse on the tarmac, hoping Keanu will drive past in a black limo and rescue my desperate heap off the ground. He probably wouldn't be in a limo; he'd be riding his motorbike without a helmet. Would I have the strength to hold onto his jacket as we rode off into the barely visible sunset?

The Land Rover gives me a brief respite. I'm lucky it blends in with the army vehicles as I weave away from the mayhem. I try desperately to dry my sweaty hands on my jeans before attempting to steer round abandoned trolleys on the roundabout.

I've never got used to having a physical attribute that everyone wants to look at or touch. Women walk round with what are basically two bags of sweets hanging off our shoulders. Unless they're too big, too small, droopy, lopsided, lumpy, smelly, deformed, leaking or inverted, then people point and run a mile in the other direction.

I blame the Bauhaus for trying to standardise boobs. I don't think boobs were specifically mentioned in their manifesto, but they encouraged everything and everyone to be aerodynamic, efficient, indistinct, plain, limited, and lacking quirkiness. At least their cheap designs are easier to tear down and replace without protest. I don't want to contort into a standard shape; it hurts my kidneys. A streamlined culture barely lasts one generation. There's less of it to decay, and no one misses its lack of identity.

Boobs should look like old buildings; as if they've always been there, grown like majestic old trees, filled with historical mysteries, casting the sun's light into quirky corners, like old ancestors, not temporary acquaintances. Boobs should be left to follow the golden section; the secret code found in nature. When we harness Mother Earth's secrets, we build our best architecture yet.

Old and weathered shouldn't be bad; old is wisdom, experience, growth, persistence, stamina, eccentricity, individuality, battles won, battles survived, battles lost, and laughter. We shouldn't ignore it, as we can't avoid it. Mother Earth has been through a lot more than a slight drop in hormones; her wrinkles have become the crevices men compete to conquer with oxygen tanks and prayer flags. Instead of seeing an old woman as a mountain to climb, men believe she will turn into an old hag, a witch, or a bad joke. He's foretold that we will be unbearable rather than a challenge to be revered.

I need to reclaim my middle ground. Most of the time I hide my boobs behind tight layers of polyester and Lycra, but when pushed I can let a complete stranger molest them. It's hard to find a balance between extreme behaviours. Is there any place on any spectrum where there's no shame? It would appear not.

Hopefully, the internet will completely crash soon, and the CCTV footage will have nowhere to promote my desperation. At least I have no desire to crash this car; the Land Rover would bounce off any obstacle I threw it at with classic engineered ease.

I've made it home safely, boobs intact. Sam's back. Will he be able to work out what just happened? Will he care? I will never know, because neither will he.

I struggle to open the front door with my sweaty hands. I march straight to the kitchen with my shame-filled head down. I drop my spoils of war on the floor and take both bras off. I'm not putting these bras on the stairs; these are going straight in the bin.

I shove a few wet wipes down my cleavage. Some high-strength hand sanitiser would be better, but the smell will coax a lot of questions from this lot.

I've got my best poker face on again while I make more fucking tea for everyone. I serve it with the fucking crushed Chocolate Fingers. I pray no one asks me anything about the last hour of my life. Keeping quiet is better than telling everyone everything; Nigel's revelatory therapy and the Royal Family taught me that.

Sam sits in the armchair, necking his cup of tea after stuffing a fistful of Chocolate Fingers into his mouth. He hasn't got a clue. Now he's smiling at me. I hate him so much right now. He has no idea what I've been through. He doesn't care. He doesn't ask. He just eats the receipts. Fuck off, you cheating bastard.

Pandora's Box

It's been three days since I let a grown man molest my boobs in the supermarket. The tainted teabags have nearly run out already. It's early morning. I'm sitting on my own. I can't get comfortable; it feels like the sofa is punching me however I sit. The front room is so dark I could believe a giant monster was standing outside the window, casting its shadow over me while I watch the latest news updates.

There are still thousands of boats sailing towards the American coasts: oil tankers, container ships, aircraft carriers, yachts, cruise ships, and fishing boats. They look like a massive pod of misshapen dolphins. One massive cruise ship in Florida didn't dock and sailed off into the horizon with its passengers in charge. Some experts warn that the response is too slow; some are complaining it's not enough. Some still hold out that there are hidden bunkers under Area 51 big enough to house every American so they can emerge as a super race when the land is habitable again. Some are just full of tears.

Economies are falling like a giant domino rally, with mass hysteria in China as factories shut. Rioting and looting have escalated in London and most big cities across the world as the police and army struggle to maintain order in so many places all at once. At least some people are getting to watch the grim news on a brand new, stolen, big TV. Maybe they want to inspect the details in all those apocalyptic movies to see if there are any clues on how to survive. People will always do stupid stuff if everyone else is doing stupid stuff. It's hard to do what the experts tell you to do when they can't agree on what to do.

All bank accounts have been frozen. Amber can't buy anything online; she's demonic. I treasure these early hours of the day when everyone is asleep. Movies have trained us to take the inevitable hit unless we have a big speaking part.

Presidents and prime ministers everywhere are being ignored. Calling us "Citizens of Earth" doesn't help; no one has an ID card that says that on it. Petulance, not pestilence, will destroy this world. Some of these governments need to go to the parenting classes they send us to. Apparently, there was a full-on riot in Manchester last night; no one is really talking about it, and no one cares anymore.

The UN is in disarray with not a dignitary in sight. No one knows where some of the last planes that managed to get out of America landed. Conspiracy theorists all over the world are having embolisms as the stories of mysterious disappearances roll in every five minutes. They can't make up the truth quickly enough. Someone has started a celebrity watch app where pictures of celebrities that make it to safety are awarded a green tick and those that have perished get a black stripe across them. Missing ones get a bouncing question mark. Someone else started a "Keanu Reeves Watch" app to track his whereabouts, but it crashed within hours of being created. No one knows where he is.

I want my Mama. I need someone to make me feel better about all this. I want her to tell me I'm not a slut or a whore. I want her to stroke my hair and make me feel like myself again. She would understand, probably laugh a little, but she would have made me feel better. She never taught me how to do that to myself. I shouldn't need her guidance anymore, but it's hard to let go until there's nothing to hold on to anymore.

The boob-groping teabag pimp lives rent-free in my head, even with the weight of grim foreboding on the TV trying to get in. There are too many things for me to contemplate. He will have to stay until I can replace him with the next prick to touch my boobs.

Women can't help but be preoccupied with their bodies. We are internal beings. From the moment a girl has her first period, her awareness of something inside controlling her intensifies. The fear and delight of what can come out of a female body makes a girl think a hell of a lot about what's going on in there. Men think externally; their awareness of what is vulnerable to damage and directing a stream of firepower is acute. It's not a fault; form follows function. Mother Earth knew that long before the Bauhaus got all zeitgeisty about it.

In order to warm my body, I drink the dirty tea. If only Mother Earth had given boobs echolocation or something cool instead of squeeziness.

I miss having a period. A monthly cycle connected me to the moon. I'm not sure how being connected to the moon helps a woman, but it always felt important. Why did we give up our mysteriousness?

What I need to do is draw boobs. I need to make some boobs out of clay or something. I need to visualise boobs as external; they're not a thing, not an important thing. I haven't got time to make something, because it involves planning and cleaning up – two things I'm even more fed up with doing now. I still haven't finished the painting I started on the kitchen table. I don't even know what happened to it. Like everything else, it's probably in a pile waiting to be sorted.

I have to imagine something. A sculpture. I can imagine sculpting a large-breasted woman who sits confidently with her boobs out for all to see. My muscle memory can feel the imaginary clay compliantly shifting with every scrape of my dental tool. That feeling is as embedded as any pleasure or trauma. I won't give her any facial features, no expression to misinterpret; a bit like the Venus of Willendorf. Just big, fat boobs that aren't pretty, aren't jiggly, just boobs. Boobs so big that they become ridiculous, extraneous, surplus to requirements, redundant.

I've made this one look like a circle as well. We're the ancients trying to look at themselves in the same way?

Would it work if I imagined a man in the same way? I can't exaggerate his features too much, I don't want him redundant. Not yet.

I haven't accepted that I am Mama now; I'm supposed to be the hero that I need. I'm not the same as my mother. We're not cast from the same mould; Nana was even more different. We were not like Russian dolls; each of us came out completely different from the one before. And the spawn of my wood-turning turned out two entirely idiosyncratic females again. The father makes the doll look different from the mother; it's infinitely variable what we become. I don't want to be a clone, but I wish I had her good bits. Being a mother isn't all about cleaning up the wee, poo, sick, phlegm, snot, earwax or the unidentified sticky substance on the fingertips. That's the easy bit. It's about being there for the screams of joy and screams of pain. Mothers are like gardens; you get to plant a seed, help it grow and then let it float on the wind when it's ready, not get covered in artificial grass and water features.

Sam is trying to enter the house quietly. He doesn't realise how quiet the house already is. I still don't want to know where he's been all night. He's carrying more boxes of God knows what and stacking them on top of all the others. The house looks like a warehouse.

Imelda sneaks in behind him; she's probably been twitching at her net curtains waiting for him to return. She takes up her usual position on the sofa and continues crocheting bloodstains onto a crocheted white shirt for a bunny with crosses where the eyes should be.

Zoe comes downstairs precariously, carrying all her painted recycling boxes into the hallway. She starts building a den, obstructing access to the kitchen. She's using Sam's stacks of boxes as supports and her duvet cover as a roof.

'There's enough room for one more in here. I'll let you know who I choose to save,' she yells.

I can see her thinking really hard who it will be; that's her most serious face to date. If she doesn't choose me, I will fucking disown her.

'Mummy, I love you more than all the stars in the world including the ones on computer games, and Daddy, I love you so much that I don't hate you one little bit, but I think I will save Scraps because it's funny when he farts!'

That's nice. A farting dog is worth more than the person who created you and taught you how to live. At least I was mentioned before her dad. Scraps eagerly takes his position as favourite in Zoe's den, knocking all of it over.

Dada gingerly steps over the collapsed den as he comes in from the back garden, looking like he's been rummaging in the shed. He's covered in old cobwebs, which suit his frail, elderly frame. He takes up his usual position in the armchair. I don't even get a "Hello" anymore.

Sam has made a pot of tea. He steps gingerly over the flattened den to join everyone in the front room. I know this is guilty tea, but I'll drink it anyway as we all silently watch more news.

Millions are unaccounted for; there's nobody to account for them. They keep saying, "The worst is yet to come". Some people are selling bags of ash as a health supplement; apparently, it will cure all pains. Still no mention of a teabag shortage, which can only mean our government isn't ready for complete carnage yet. Sam keeps leaning forward as if he's about to make an announcement, but then sits back down to stare at his tea.

There's a knock at the door; we all turn to see Gaba's heavily mascaraed face looking through the front room window to check she's not being ignored. Sam throws his perturbed head back and closes his eyes.

Gaba only visits when she needs something these days; she rarely leaves her house. She grew up with me, playing in the same airfield barracks, spending more time with my family than her own. We're like sisters because she won't leave me the fuck alone no matter what I say to her. We've been bursting each other's bubbles since 1976.

I love her because she knows all my secrets. I hate her because she is a constant reminder of what I could look like if I'd never had children or a husband; slightly smoother and slightly thinner. Her time is all her own time and she can do whatever she wants with it. She used to spend her time changing careers with every New Year's resolution or satisfying fetish-driven men as a dominatrix in the evenings. Some part of her must have got dislodged as a teenager, and it's been pressed up against the inside of her clitoris ever since.

One bout of antibiotic-resistant gonorrhoea put an end to that hobby; then she became a bit of a germaphobe. Now she can only satisfy her raging libido on the internet. She gets through more wet wipes than I do.

I reluctantly answer the door. Gaba doesn't look me in the eye once; she taps away on her phone and steps into the hallway.

'Hi Gab, how are you?'

'All right, I suppose. How are you? Still boring?'

'Yep, still here, twiddling my thumbs.'

Zoe runs up to Gaba while trying her best to get her princess dress over her head. She's the only one of my children who hasn't worked out that Gaba can be a drain on your emotions. Gaba loves Zoe, as she is the only one of my children she can pick up and hold like a doll. She helps Zoe with her dress, tottering in her tallest heels and tightest multi-patterned hippie dress. I can distinctly remember Gaba tottering around in her mother's high heels with a real doll when we were five years old round the back of the Captain's Mess. The heels didn't fit her back then either, and she got walloped for getting mud all over them.

'I'm going to be Princess Charming, Gaba. Would you like to play?'

'Oh yes please, I would love to be a princess; fetch me a tiara, darling!'

Zoe's legs are running before Gaba puts her back down on the floor. She runs upstairs at full speed. Gaba follows me into the kitchen.

'Have you seen the news, Gab?'

'Oh no! It's depressing. Listen, have you kicked that wanker out yet?'

'No, and for the millionth time, I'm not going to.'

'Why not? He treats you like shit. Leave him. Anyway, one of my subscribers, the one who sends me those out-of-date HRT patches, he's invited me to a massive online "end of the world" orgy tonight. You must come over; we can go split-screen. I've got an unboxed XXXL laser-guided rabbit wand to show off!'

I wish that had been a *Harry Potter* reference, and I wish penises were laser-guided.

'You do realise, Gab, that your vagina can stretch from a tampon to a baby's head. Every size fits!'

'Mine's been stretched out like pizza dough though. Anyway, will you come?'

When did gross stuff become socially acceptable? I can't roll my eyes at her; she sees that as a reward. I give her the same look I give Tom when he asks for tinned tomato soup for breakfast.

Gaba puts my junk mail into the recycling bin and tidies up my piles of abandoned clothes. I put the kettle on.

'That sounds like torture to me, Gab.'

'But it will be fun, and that's the point. Which is why you need to come with me. This might be your last chance to have any fun.'

'Your idea of fun and mine are not the same.'

'Tell me about it. I'm a professional fun-maker.'

'Really? Do you have loyalty cards? On every fifth purchase, they get a free blowjob?'

'Ugh, you know if I have to swallow another unwashed cock, I'll throw up. Nobody has real sex anymore, Nell. Get with it.'

Gaba doesn't realise she is nothing more than a contactless wanking ATM. Swipe your card and get instant gratification. As quick as making a Pot Noodle, without having to eat any of it.

Zoe runs into the kitchen, clutching three plastic tiaras. She displays them to Gaba on her arm as if she works at Tiffany & Co. Gaba chooses one and places it on her head. Zoe puts the other two awkwardly on her head and runs off. Gaba finds my feather duster, which I haven't seen in months, and starts cleaning the cobwebs off the ceiling. There's a bad one above the hob with fat and dust stuck to it. I hope she sees it.

'What's it like being a digital sex slave to the rich?' I ask.

'Rich? I wish! Supply and demand means I get peanuts, but at least I'm in control and keep all the peanuts.'

'At least! Well, those peeping Toms won't be able to use their digital binoculars soon, so you might need a new business plan.'

'You're such a killjoy, Nell.'

Gaba notices the one above the hob; I move out of the way.

I do like sex; in fact, I crave it. I just get bored listening to Gaba talk about sex. She makes sex sound as common as going to she shops; "Should I get a sliced loaf or anal beads?" The same brands are available everywhere. Instead of handcrafted, uniquely regional sex, she's been having preprogrammed, preordered universal sex for two decades now.

Sex with Sam used to be great. He was sensitive and aware. I reached the point where I didn't know where my body parts ended and his started. I miss that feeling, and I know Gaba has never felt exactly like that. Her erogenous zones have been eroded.

'So, what do you say? Are you finally going to join me for one last bash, or what?'

'I can't leave the kids and everyone else who drinks copious amounts of tea in this house. They will all shrivel up if I leave the building.'

'Stop thinking about everyone else for once. What about your needs?'

Gaba's phone rings; she turns slightly away, so it must be a dirty one. I stand in my standard, resigned position. I don't like parties. Even party-from-home ones. I'm not good with high expectations and low standards. The only way to enjoy shit like that is to be completely drunk because then everything is acceptable and funny.

I can't afford to escape my feelings with intoxicated fun anymore. Instead, I unhealthily obsess over those feelings over and over again in this never-ending inner monologue. Thinking about it, being under the influence of a warped sense of victimhood doesn't make me a safer driver either. They need to invent a breathalyser for feelings; they can make you just as volatile.

Zoe runs into the kitchen and gives Gaba a giant pink wand that makes noises when it's waved about. While whispering bizarre noises on her phone, Gaba waves the wand above Zoe's head, while she spins and giggles.

Gaba drives in the fast lane. My engine wasn't built that way; it would be the first to burst into flames if I made it go faster. But with the slightest jerk of her steering wheel, Gaba will crash. I can only watch the devastation from the hard shoulder. I always think about the aftermath; she lives only in the moment.

She used to think it was cool and that she'd get somewhere faster than everyone else. But I know she's bored. Even lots of kinky sex gets boring after the millionth time of doing it. The ancients might have added nonexistent muscles; we added fluffy pink handcuffs and banana flavoured lube to make ordinary people a bit more interesting. At least I still want sex. Gaba expected sex, got lots of sex without trying and now craves something different. She's talked about building a model railway in her spare room. There is no pot of gold at the end of any rainbow. Only a pot of antibiotics or a glass of cranberry juice.

I hand Gaba a cup of tea. Zoe runs off laughing and bumps into the doorframes.

They say you should "dance like no one's watching," but really people are "fucking as if someone is watching." We need approval for everything we do. We like watching because we like judging. Judging is a dopamine trigger; it makes people feel they know more than someone else, and it's as stupidly funny and addictive as alcohol. There's a hangover to the judgement though; if you have a conscience.

Judgement kind of worked in Victorian Britain where the gentrified judged everyone harshly, because you could call them snobby pricks and go about your day. Now, people are judged by anyone and everyone, from any class and creed, from any corner of the globe.

I would like to dance again. No one on *Strictly* ever topped themselves after a piss-poor performance. If only doctors knew that not wanting to dance is a symptom. Schools need to bring back country dancing instead of focussing on trigonometry and bleep tests. There's nothing like a do-si-do to expunge chronic social anxiety.

Gaba finishes her phone call. I successfully blocked out listening to words I've never heard in that combination before. She necks her hot cup of tea in one go. I swear her throat could withstand acid.

'Earth to Nellie! Stop fantasising and actually do something fun!'

'I don't think my needs will be satisfied at an online all-you-can-eat depravity-buffet. During the last video you blackmailed me to get involved with, I wanted to put a paper bag over my head after getting bizarre requests from those two female trainee estate agents!'

'Yeah, and after four kids everyone wanted you to put a bag over your head, and your stomach!'

'Oh, thanks, thanks, mate.'

'I'm only joking! You're beautiful, and no one really cares about stretch marks anymore. It's more about willingness. You could finally try that tea-bagging that I've had to explain to you three times already.'

'I'm a visual learner, and anyway I don't want to think about testicles every time I make a cup of tea. I'm not letting you ruin the one joy I have left.'

There are so many double entendres these days that you can't make a soufflé without getting turned on.

'If that's your only joy, why do you stay here?'

Gaba has the same confused face that Zoe has when grown-ups talk.

'Gaba, for the last time, I am not leaving my family to watch you fornicate from the sidelines.'

'Okay, but I still think you should leave the bastard. I'm here for you, babe.'

'Really, so you'll help me look after my children, will you?'

'Well, not all of them. I don't mind helping Zoe a little bit; she's still cute. I don't know why you bothered having children; they don't improve your life.'

'I had them so they can improve the world, I think.'

'That's a bit of a tall order, isn't it? They can't even keep the house tidy.'

It was my natural instinct to have babies. It was society that told me to get a job and party till dawn.

'Anyway, you say you're there for me, but not actually here, and not helping me in any way possible.'

'Oh whatever! Are you coming or not?'

'Not.'

'Fine, I'll do it on my own, as usual. You stay here and make tea.'

'Fine with me. Tea doesn't leave micro-plastics inside my vagina.'

'It doesn't make you have multiple orgasms either!'

She's never drunk my cup of tea with a chocolate-coated ginger biscuit, has she? Gaba sashays out of my house still wearing the plastic tiara. This is why I keep Gaba as a friend, because conversations like these make me glad I'm me for a change. I don't need the fuel from someone else's opinions; I'm self-propelled.

I carry the tray of tea up to the front room. Everyone stares at me. The TV, which has been on constantly for over a week, has been turned down. Everyone is looking at me as if they'd heard everything Gaba and I were just talking about. Sam has a *Mona Lisa*-kind of smile on his face; he's probably working out if he came off well in that conversation or not.

Zoe smiles at the thoughts running through her head, too. 'Mummy, I've got an idea for an end world party… but we'll have to paint the cat!'

She runs off over-enthusiastically.

'Are you leaving us to go to India, Mum?' asks Tom.

'Um…what? No! I'm not leaving you lot ever… ignore Gaba. She doesn't have a loving family like I do to turn to.'

'Where's your loving family, Nell? I thought we were just a pain in your arse!' Sam asks.

He over-confidently decided to go with, "I came out well after that conversation." I'm sure that's what Lisa del Giocondo thought too.

'I'm much happier with you lot than with a repetitive strain injury.'

Imelda continues to agitatingly crochet an off-scale bladed weapon. Zoe comes running back with a pastry brush and a tube of green acrylic paint.

'I don't hurt your bottom, do I, Mummy?'

'Not you, sweetie, not anymore,' I reply as sweetly as I can while trying to wrestle the brush and paint out of her tiny hands.

Gaia

Imelda's bottom lip is wobbling, and her crocheted weapon crumples with her ever-tightening grip. A tirade is coming; I can feel the tremors emanating through the scatter cushions. I should try to distract her with some sweets.

'I'm not sure the suffragettes threw themselves in front of racehorses so that their granddaughters could… effing play with themselves all day,' says Imelda.

'Oh, I think they did!' Dada laughs like he's watching panto, 'they threw themselves in front of horses so they could choose who or what to fuck around with, just like men have for millennia. It's a type of progress.'

Here we go. 'Imelda! Dada! Watch your language! Zoe! Tom! Go to your rooms!'

'Mum, are Granny and Dada going to break manner's rules?'

'Yes, Tom. And in a grand, pompous style, by the looks of it, off you go.'

Tom and Zoe slowly leave the room.

Imelda rests her crochet hook on her lap. 'Having it all shouldn't mean having all the bad bits too.'

Dada straightens his neck. 'Don't have a go at Gaba. Civilisation, if you want to call it that, has never allowed women the opportunity for hedonism unless they were paid, forced, or royalty. Middle-class women have never had so much opportunity for fucking things up.'

Imelda straightens her back. 'Is the level of civilisation determined by how women are treated or how women behave?'

'Well, we're fucked either way if that's the case,' Dada smiles.

I've never understood why slutty men are revered but slutty women are derided. I think it's because a man having multiple women implies he is strong and attractive, whereas a woman having multiple men implies she has repeatedly been weak and given in. Our preconceived notions follow us around like predators.

Imelda finishes sipping her tea. 'Women's behaviour is determined by the way they're treated. When women are treated like property, some behave like an antique vase that could shatter into a million pieces. When they are treated like mythological goddesses, some behave like rookie prostitutes. When they are treated like sex objects, some behave like meerkats on guard duty. It's not up to us how we're regarded. Despite years of trying, men don't know how to handle women, which is why they keep breaking them. When they find a good woman or a bad woman, they get an overwhelming obligation to tell her how good or bad she is.'

'Women do the same to men, and just as often, Imelda. Are you trying to tell me that you didn't wear a miniskirt in the sixties?'

'That was fashion, Bill.'

'That was a revolution.'

'But strangers used to come up and pinch our bottoms. Which is why the next fashion fad was long, flowing dresses again.'

'Not everyone was ready for a revolution at that point in time. Some were still scared of ankles. Most men have stopped pinching strangers' bottoms now, which is why miniskirts and letting your arse cheeks fall out of the back of your shorts have become socially acceptable again.'

Imelda sighs. 'Women never have and never will have it all, will we?'

Dada laughs. 'Men won't either. Nobody should have it all; having it all turns you into an arsehole.'

'When will we be free, Bill?'

'Freedom is bollocks. No human has been free since the first stone was thrown at another human's head. When you are born, you are dependent on your mother and father. When you reach adulthood, you are dependent on the protection of your tribe or country. If you become a parent, you are dependent on someone else for support, and you have dependents who depend on you. When you get old, you are dependent on someone younger to look after you. We have created a system to ensure you are never free, but you are safe because you can't be both.'

'I didn't get support from anyone else when I became a parent.'

'You had to work three jobs and rely on many passing strangers to look after Sam. You did not raise him in isolation or with ease. Remember who my drinking pals are, Imelda.'

'Women can't walk away from a hedonistic mistake like a man can. Not without a black eye, or a baby, or both. We can't just eat our babies like rabbits do when they're threatened.'

All eyes quickly turn to look at Sam. He hasn't raised an eyebrow; it's not the first time he's heard such a thing. I think there were moments he wished she had eaten him.

'Even Mother Earth is consuming her own at the moment, Bill.'

Dada takes a deep breath. 'Mother Earth does destroy, but only to create new. Everything is recycled into something useful in the end. She likes to clear a path for something else to prosper.'

He straightens every bone, muscle, and starched collar he has on him. I used to love these rants when I was little; lunch could take three hours on a Saturday afternoon. I used to think he should become the prime minister or at least write speeches for dignitaries, but he told me that the kind of people who are clever enough to run a country are not the kind of people who want to run a country. Made me think, what kind of people do want to run a country if it's not the clever ones? I had to stop thinking about that when I became hormonally imbalanced.

He tightens his grip on his lapels. 'Mother Earth always provides. There's always an antidote for everything bad; that's how she maintains balance. Not too much of anything, not too little either. Adapt to your surroundings, and Mother Earth will provide everything you need. She created a world where everything fits beautifully together and works in harmony. We live on a Goldilocks planet; we're just enough distance from the sun for water to exist and therefore for life to exist. Every other planet is barren.'

I remember him explaining this to me when I was little. He read Goldilocks to me every week. I would get a full debriefing after the story. I don't need to wonder how I got my overthinking brain.

He told me to be a Goldilocks mother. He told me to be strict enough to stop them from putting their fingers in electrical sockets and kind enough to make sure they can heal if they electrocute themselves. I need more Goldilocks moments; where I torture myself enough to motivate my fat arse but am compassionate enough to understand why my arse got so fat. Mother Earth does provide, albeit metaphorically and hidden in plain sight.

Imelda sips more tea. 'If Mother Earth likes balance and harmony, Bill, why did she create life-threatening childbirth for women but let men walk away?'

'One of you has to scare off predators while the other delivers a newborn. Only weak men don't come back. Imagine, Imelda, if humans had to mate by leaving semen on a passer-by and hoping they brush past a woman whose eggs are also delicately placed on her sleeve and then the fertilised ovum floated on the wind to settle on some random spot to grow.'

'That would make reality TV more interesting. Anyway, I would have been quite happy leaving my eggs near the radiator.'

'Sam wouldn't have absorbed your love of gangster movies, or your sugar cravings if you'd left him by the radiator to grow.'

'Which might have been a good thing.'

'Humans would never have evolved to question anything if they were too busy throwing their sperm over hedges or leaving their young to be hunted by apex predators.'

'We killed all the predators, Bill.'

'Only in Britain. That's why some people created porn, true crime and soap operas to satisfy our adrenaline needs.'

'I would prefer the wolves and bears to binge-watching *Bargain Hunt* repeats.'

Tom and Zoe never really left the room. They stopped halfway up the stairs, marched up and down on the middle step and returned as quietly as a couple of giddy baby elephants hiding behind Peter, who has sat down next to me. Amber appears at the door, bobbing her head about with her earbuds in.

'What are these two arguing about, Mum?'

'I think it's about who's better, men or women?'

'Simple, men are shite!'

Predictable. Amber settles herself in between Sam and Imelda, still scrolling through her phone. She wants a front-row seat if anything kicks off. Imelda sucks her lips in hard; that must be where her raw nerve is kept. She's survived many men, and she would be celebrated with rose petals at her feet if it hadn't made her such a hardened bitch.

'Granny—'

'Yes, Tom.'

'You told me God looked after us? Is it really a big woman called Earth?'

'God will look after us. He's getting rid of all the bad people. He's starting in the middle of America. It makes sense. God wants to start over. He wants carte blanche to start America again; they're too rude.'

'Gran, it's pronounced "Cate Blanchett",' says Tom.

I cry with laughter inside. Imelda looks perplexed on many fronts.

'Is God going to get rid of me, Granny?'

'No, Tom—'

'You're always saying I'm naughty. Is God unhappy with me? Will the volcano swallow me up?'

If God is looking down on us, his tongue must be worn through from all the tutting. The reason I have no spare time is that a large part of my daily life is making something shit more user-friendly. 'Tom, it doesn't work like that.'

'Are you sure, Mum?'

'God doesn't pick and choose people. It's a bit more random.'

'So it doesn't matter if we are good or bad then? God will just kill us if we're in the wrong place at the wrong time. He doesn't care about all the praying or… or—'

For fuck's sake!

Zoe stands up. 'I think God and Santa and Jesus are just playing with Earth. We are like toys; they have invisible hands.'

Even Zoe's sweet perception can't wrestle a smile out of Dada, who stares at Tom with a serious and somewhat scary face. 'Praying didn't get me where I am, Tom. Hard work and common sense are all you need. There's no big old man in the sky, deciding who should live among the clouds and who should rot beneath the earth's crust. Never made sense to me.'

'God gave you the strength and the know-how to get what you need, Bill.'

'No, he didn't, Imelda. My strength came from millennia of strong women picking strong men, helping my mother in the garden and then gruelling armed forces training. My mother would go crazy if anyone thanked a god for the food she grew, harvested, cooked, and served on the table. She'd be even more furious if you gave a god credit for raising me. Why shouldn't she get the thanks? Maybe Mother Earth wants a little bit of credit for all she's created instead of some made-up gods!'

'Made up? How dare you!' Imelda squealed like Zoe when her toys are taken away.

'Well, there are a lot of them; how do you know which ones are made up? People only believe in gods because they want to be loved by at least one person. Those who don't believe get a dog for the same reasons.'

'We are being punished for our sins. We are being punished for affairs, for stealing, for our obsession with sex, for homosex—'

'Oh, don't start, Imelda! You're not going to blame a volcanic eruption on the gay community. You've blamed everything that's gone wrong on gay people. You're worse than politicians and therapists; you can't control the future, so you blame someone else, or the past. What about the ones who fuck horses and children, the murderers, thieves, liars, terrorists, dictators, drunk drivers, human traffickers, and drug lords? Anyway, volcanoes don't erupt because people take it up the arse.'

'I'm just saying—'

'Do you think there's a homosexual thermometer in the earth's crust monitoring sexual activity? Mother Earth designed a penis to fit perfectly into many things,' Dada bellowed so loudly that Peter and Amber both removed their earbuds.

'Gran—'

'What, Peter? Are you going to give me some of your worldly wisdom too?'

'I'm just saying, Mother Earth doesn't mind gay sex; it gives women a rest.'

'Peter—'

'What, Amber?'

'Don't be so fucking stupid! Periods were designed so women could have a rest, not homosexuality.'

'Actually, Amber, you can have sex during a period; in fact, it's safer because you can't get pregnant.'

'Try having sex with a girl who's on her period, I fucking dare you!'

Peter's cheeks have flushed red. 'Mother Earth is as scary as women,' he mumbles.

Amber's eyes widen. 'Men are scary as fuck! You try putting your weak and feeble arm up to stop a hairy-arsed beast forcing his hand up your skirt!'

'You try putting your weak and feeble arm up to stop a hairy-arse beast stealing your phone and slapping your head enough it makes your hearing go strange!' says Peter.

Imelda's face is priceless; it looks like someone just sucked all the air out of her. Dada stares at Sam, who stares at Peter, who stares at the floor. Someone just realised they haven't taught Peter how to stand up for himself. Sam taught Amber to stand up for herself, but because everyone is scared of her, he left Peter alone.

Imelda looks desperate to make a valid point. 'I wasn't having a go at all men. Men build bridges, palaces, planes and cheap perfume.'

'We only create bridges to reach women, palaces to dance with women, planes to find women and knock-off perfume to bribe women. Men do everything to please women, so they can get a hug every now and then.'

'We're never pleased, though.'

'Exactly!'

Dada sounds like he's discovered a new mathematical formula that will change our understanding of the universe. 'Why are you never pleased?'

Imelda is thinking hard. 'Because men are never pleased with us. You keep trying to shape us, and nature, into something more efficient, smooth, effective, and pleasing to the eye. Something that responds to the slightest touch with instant gratification.'

'Mother Nature gave us instincts and urges. Maybe she wanted men to control her chaos; maybe she wanted bridges and perfume. Maybe she wants the occasional nip and tuck to keep all her unpleasantness to the side where no one will see it. Maybe she wanted us to emulate her creativity.'

'She created men so we wouldn't be eaten by bears; you all got a bit carried away with it.'

Dada leans forward in his chair. He looks like he needs a laser pointer at the ready. I enjoy listening to a debate without emojis, blocking and taking screenshots of memes. 'The psychology of women has been impaired for millennia because they weren't allowed to be self reliant, they were destitute without a man. They had to be married. They were made to believe they didn't need love, just protection from the elements and other men.'

'The state now provides for any woman left without a man; you can be independent, Bill.'

'Yeah, so the state can dictate how women live their lives instead of the man; that is very much dependence of a different kind. The only way a woman can be herself is to live on her own, in the woods, with minimal contact from anyone.'

'And lots of cats,' adds Sam.

I think he's been waiting to shoehorn a comment in for the last ten minutes.

'Cats don't take orders from anyone, Sam; it's why women like them so much.'

'Women are chaos, just like cats. If you can control the women, you control everything. Men worked that out a long time ago. We just haven't learned how to control them yet without making their lives a misery. Same for the cats.'

'We're not chaos.'

'Yes, you are, Mother! Men like order; women like to fuck it up. That is a well-established fact. Men like logic; women like magic.'

'Nonsense, it's men who eff everything up, it's men who start wars and don't either of you two bastards tell me anything different!'

I'm not sure whose side Imelda is on. Does she like men or not? You can't make everyone see sense when everyone can't agree on what sense is. It's all about who realises who is mad first and walks away.

'Imelda—'

'What now, Bill?'

'Wars only start to bring order to a chaotic situation. No war started because everything was okay. There's nothing to fight for when you feel safe. That's why women are still fighting for themselves because they don't feel safe. Women didn't feel heard, so they asked for the vote, women didn't feel respected so they asked for divorce, women didn't feel like an individual so they asked for their own bank account, women felt oppressed by expectations so they burned their bras, women weren't taken seriously so they started wearing trousers, women weren't respected for their intelligence so had to take artificial hormones that damaged their bodies to stop being eternally pregnant.'

'Women feel safer when there aren't any men around.'

'They also don't feel safe when there are no men around; they can't fight everyone.'

Dada leans back and tries to relax his shoulders. 'Men don't feel safe when women are in charge either. The only way for a woman to live safely is to live like a man, hide in her bedroom, or fight like a wild animal. Women shouldn't need to work for their freedom; their freedom must be protected. Men just need to treat women correctly.'

Imelda shrugs her shoulders. 'Men don't have it easy. I thought you two would appreciate that.'

'Balls! If men had to have a smear test, it would be done by a radar from the car.'

'You're a typical man, Bill. Can't take a compliment or any kind of support from a woman.'

'Female empowerment does not come from hating men, acting like men, competing with men, saying no to men, giving into men, loving men, obeying men, sleeping with men, pleasuring men, working for men, being the property of men, being able to get away from bad men, being able to defend yourself against men or being able to function without a man. It comes from being allowed to be a woman. Women sacrificed themselves at the altar of men in order to be accepted or treated fairly. They had no choice; it was the only altar left standing.'

'What a load of bollocks! Do we have to do womanly things in a womanly way?'

I reckon I could make an interesting brass rubbing of Imelda's forehead with eyebrows raised that high.

'When men try to control nature, they plant trees in rows. Women are and should be the tree that grows outside of the row or the beautiful weeds that can push up through a lump of concrete and reclaim their space. That's what I mean by womanly.

I didn't mean the delicate arse-swaying version of womanly that coaxes men off the street and into the cinema.'

Dada has always loved women. He adored Mama; I can hear her echoes through his reasoning. They survived, they learned, and they could be themselves in front of each other. That's why they were happy.

Imelda and Dada are both red in the face for different reasons. Sam returns to staring at his tea. Amber stretches her neck before the next round of verbal tennis starts.

'Imelda—'

'For God's sake, Bill, leave me alone!'

'No, men stopped protecting women because women asked them to. So some think the only alternative is to attack them, their own women. This is what happens when people interfere with millennia of social conditioning. Mother Earth took our fur away so we'd be scared of the rain and cold; she will probably take our muscles away so we become scared of wrath. They'll be no more tall and strong men around in the future because there will be double glazing and video doorbells instead. She giveth and taketh away; she's fucking slow, but she is persistent.'

Zoe stands up again. 'God hasn't taken our Daddy's muscles away, Dada.'

'That's because in this country we set our women free and now they're harder to control. This country will continue to breed large men while the women continue to run around throwing stuff at us. Control the women with endless bureaucracy, then watch the men become small and limp.'

Everyone's eyes quickly scan everyone's faces to see if that should be agreed with or scowled at.

Imelda looks Dada straight in the eye. 'Mother Earth should have given men more self-control.'

'The vast majority of men have self-control; otherwise, every woman would be raped all the time. We're taught control; it's why girls mature earlier than boys; they can slap us into line before our muscles grow. And so that boys can continue being little shits, pulling girls' pigtails so they can keep the girls in line before their emotions grow. Men evolved to be violent so we could protect. Women evolved to be emotional so they could care. The world needs both, just not from the same person at the same time. Being violent is sometimes necessary as long as it's controlled; emotions are sometimes necessary as long as they're controlled too.'

'Well, men don't have self-respect, women don't either; we definitely have equality now.'

'There I can agree with you, Imelda. It used to be women and children into the lifeboats first, but now women and children are thrown over the side like ballast. What happened to "sticking it to the man"? Wanting equality means we have to stick it to every woman and child too.'

Amber sits up from her cosy front-row seat. 'We will never be seen as equal by men while we're hunted as prey and they're carrying the guns.'

Amber squishes back into the dent in the sofa cushion. Baby steps.

'Where's your God now, Imelda? No one is looking after those innocent people; some of them are fervent believers, but no god is helping them. It's every man, woman, and child for themselves. All those prayers are blowing in the wind, unanswered, no matter which God you believe in either. They've all been abandoned.'

'There's always a reason, Bill.'

'The only people who are going to survive this are those who rely on themselves and not others, those who understand nature and can make water from their own pee. Everyone comes from the earth, eats from the earth, and returns to the earth. Everyone comes from a woman, eats from a woman and goes back to a woman in the end. Everything man-made can be destroyed in seconds, whereas Mother Earth will self-heal. There's nothing more comforting than the love of a good woman. I miss that.'

A small tear trickles down Dada's cheek. Everyone saw it. We quickly and quietly return to watch America's civilisation fall on the TV.

Mary K Hollywood

Age of Heroes

The world is unravelling before our eyes, and we're talking about the differences between men and women. Is this our way of trying to understand Mother Earth's devastation through understanding women? Or is it Mother Earth's way of trying to understand herself through listening to women's rage through the soles of our feet? She made us in her own image. That's probably why the supervolcano is enveloping the world right now; she's heard enough.

The reason I think about these things when there's an apocalypse fast approaching is the same reason I think about my BMI when my marriage is collapsing: avoidance.

Old people have a lot more stories to tell than young people. Their memories should've been banked before they disappear completely. Future archaeologists won't be able to tell our thoughts from our bones. Human knowledge is disintegrating right before our eyes. We should have engraved it into more amulets and boulders rather than secure data centres.

I wish I could read other people's minds. Sam doesn't appear too surprised by Imelda's point of view; he probably grew up with these diatribes every breakfast. Dada wants the last word; he's trained not to leave anyone behind. Amber looks like she's relishing the animosity. Tom looks hungry; Zoe looks confused. I'm fidgeting internally.

From the outside, I look as calm as a swan, but inside I am desperate to squawk. 'If we become the same as men, we lose our sacred status. We are not honorary men.'

Sam raises his head to my out of character declaration. 'Only men who can't please, enjoy or protect a woman want to control them. Women only have an upper body weakness; their minds can be the most precise ammunition in existence.'

I barely speak to him; all his rage is still focussed on his mother. I doubt I'll ever get the opportunity to really fire a laser-targeted swipe at him while she hogs all the ammunition.

'Because men know women are weaker, they think equal rights mean they have to come down to meet our level. If a woman tries to be strong, then a man will control, parade, worship, kill or punch a woman to make themselves feel stronger. Men are not allowed to appear weak, by men's and women's standards.'

Amber sits up again. 'Do men know how to treat a woman, Dad?'

'Not anymore; women have changed.' He answered more tormentedly than he deserves to.

'Women can be as strong as men!' shouts Tom.

Amber shakes her head. 'Only in superhero movies, Tom. There's no five-foot skinny bitch who could take down a team of six-foot henchmen in a unitard. I found that out the hard way.'

Sam looks puzzled. 'When did you purchase a unitard?'

'Online. I got one with a secret pocket for my phone.'

'Did you take on the boy who put his hand up your skirt?'

'I tried and I tried to look stunning and brave while I did it.'

'Superhero movies set the bar a bit too high for girls. They're meant to be a bit of escapism, not a life choice, sweetheart.'

'There are no movies about how teenage girls can stop up-skirting. Movies don't tell you anything useful.'

Sam leans back, contemplating the new information about his children's lives that he didn't know about.

'Amber—'

'Yes, Mother.'

'The strongest woman might not be as strong as the strongest man, but it's not a flaw; it's a design. Women have strength in other ways.'

'Yeah, in the jaw,' says Sam over-confidently, 'I'm just saying, women are not sacred. Being put on a pedestal is a precarious business. The higher you go, the harder the fall. Some might like the view from up there; some get vertigo; some don't know how to get down; some refuse to come down. Some get the pedestal kicked out from under them, and some pedestals are made of straw.'

'We want a pedestal, Sam, because we're so low down in the pecking order, we need one in order to look you lot in the eye. I used to stand on an actual stool just to kiss you, remember?'

Sam leans forward and looks me in the eye. I need to cross my legs as tightly as they will go. Excitement and arousal are strangers to these parts.

'Nell, when a man is put on a pedestal, he puts wheels on it to see how fast it can go downhill, and then he puts turbo boosters on the back to make it go faster than everyone else's until it crashes. I'm just saying we're different, not better. We compete to be the best among ourselves. No man wants to compete with a woman, because women compete to be the worst, especially when comparing childbirth stories.'

I haven't got any lapels, so I'm holding on to the neck of my jumper. 'If women have to be inferior for men to feel strong, then men are not as strong as they think.'

'Women don't know how to be women. Everyone keeps trying to write a new definition for women, but no one can agree on the wording. It always ends up badly written.'

'We just want to be loved and appreciated, Sam.'

'We adore women.'

'A poster of us with our boobs hanging out is not the adoration we're looking for.'

'Men fear fearless women, then we become redundant. We want fearful women because then we have something to offer them.'

'So you want to keep women fearful?' I hope my strained eyebrows are giving off the desired effect.

'No, that's not what I meant. We can't help wanting to conquer and control; it's so no one else can conquer and control us or you. Your beloved Mother Earth hard-wired us this way.'

'The whole point of civilisation is to overcome animal instincts.'

'We're getting there, Nell.'

'Some men think a "free" woman means "free for the taking".'

'But not all men. Civilising takes generations of talking and drinking beer to embed.'

'That's why it's taking you all so long. Men talking about feelings is like watching a slowly dripping tap. Women can solve all their problems before a packet of biscuits is finished.'

'Bullshit, the first answer to a problem isn't always the best answer. Anyway, we're so focussed on building all the infrastructure, we sometimes forget personal growth.'

'Stop building then; stop everything. Take a look around and enjoy it for a moment, Sam.'

'I'd love to stop. But Mother Earth designed me to build, protect, hunt, gather, and write my name on the ground with my pee. Civilisation trained me to open doors, not open doors, fight the bad guys, don't hurt the bad guys, work till you're dead and give everything you've ever earned away.'

'Boo hoo. Mother Earth designed me to sacrifice my body to whoever needs it the most and age ungracefully. Civilisation trained me to shut the fuck up for twenty thousand years, but when you do shout, make sure it really hurts! The day women won't die in order to save our children is when civilisation falls. Mothers are prepared to die to create a child.'

'Men are prepared to die to protect their children too, and you.'

Do our ungrateful brood even realise what we're saying? Do I? This is pouring out of me like a burst dam. 'Women are expected to stay at home and keep things in order when their natural instinct is to go wild.'

'You want spontaneity, Nell, but when you get it you want consistency, and when you get that you want spontaneity again, and when you get that you want it to be the kind of spontaneity that you planned in your head the previous three years, and when you get that it still wasn't what you wanted.'

'Men want to lie down and take it easy but they also want to lift heavy things until the sweat drips down their biceps, and then they want another rest with their mates and a beer and then they want to watch sweaty men chase a ball round a field and then they want to fight anyone in the wrong coloured top and then they want another rest in an A&E waiting room to show how hard they truly are.'

'What's your point, Nell?'

'I'm not sure.'

Trying to make a point is mentally exhausting if you're out of practice.

'We all do hard labour; men for forty-odd years with their hands, women for forty intense hours with their… well, you know.'

'Say it.'

'No.'

'Fucking say it, Sam. You've watched three children burst through it. It's a vagina and a uterus and a cervix and a—'

'Why do women insist on labelling every fucking detail?'

'Why do men insist on turning their heads away?'

'Because we see that detail up close. You never see it. Men are in awe of what women can do with their bodies, but also, occasionally, in disgust.'

'Ditto! Women are in awe of what men can do with theirs, and disgust is a sporting challenge for you lot. And by the way, your bits aren't so pretty close up either.'

Tom and Zoe stare at us with bemusement. Amber and Peter in surprise. Imelda and Dada would rather watch the silent devastation on the TV than engage in our battle of the sexes.

'What is a woman, Mum?' asks Tom.

'It would seem to be anything you want it to be.'

'Nell, anything is limited to what you already know.'

I'm up for this level of antagonism. I point at the gift shop replica of the *Venus of Willendorf* sitting on the mantelpiece.

'The *Venus of Willendorf* is what a woman is.'

I said that more pompously than I had intended.

'Surely we've moved on from ancient times?'

'Art can still communicate through the passage of time, Sam.'

'I'd rather communicate with that balloon dog than with that ugly, faceless woman.'

'Why?'

'It's shiny.'

'Are you a magpie?'

'It's well made.'

'It's reproduced in a factory. Even the original wasn't made by the artist; a team of craftspeople made someone else's ideas.'

'What's wrong with getting professionals to show their craft?'

'They don't get the credit or the cheque; the craftspeople are unknown.'

'So is the person who whittled that lump of stone into a fat woman a thousand years ago.'

'Twenty to thirty thousand years ago. It predates nearly all other man-made objects that we know about.'

This is one subject I am comfortable being confrontational on because I know I have more knowledge than he does. God help me if we use engine parts to analogously show the differences between men and women; I still don't know what a camshaft is.

Tom gets up and stretches to reach the replica of the *Venus of Willendorf* on the mantelpiece. He takes it down and looks at it carefully. 'So this is older than anything else in the world?'

'Yes, Tom.'

'But it says "Made in China" on the bottom.'

'Not that actual one; that's a copy.'

Sam smiles. 'Like the balloon dog. I rest my case.'

His neck will break if he arrogantly stretches it any further. Now I remember why we don't talk so often. Tom runs off, clutching the statue tightly.

'Sam, that is a replica of something significant. The other is a replica of a replica of a party gimmick. Not the same.'

'So what is the purpose of the fat, faceless woman?'

'There are a few theories; some say it's a fertility goddess. They think fat women represented the richer, wealthier and therefore healthier woman.'

'It's not the wealthy or healthy who look like that now.'

'They didn't have biscuits and multipacks of crisps back then. Anyway, others say it could be an ice age survival guide, a good luck charm, or even a dildo.'

'Hah! So it is a party gimmick as well!'

'It's the mystery of it that keeps it interesting, Sam. If it could be explained, then it would become boring. Once everyone categorises it and buys into it, then it's not punk anymore.'

'That's not punk.'

'Why not? Punk just means going against what everyone else thinks it should be.'

'Punk is the release of suppressed anger against the constraints of society. That's just a fat, faceless woman.'

I'm so tempted to shoot him with the water pistol right now.

'If it had a pretty face, would you like it more, Sam?'

'Probably.'

'Not everything needs to be aesthetically pleasing, and not all of the time. Isn't it about what you've achieved, not what you look like?'

'I don't know how it helps fertility looking like that.'

'Actually, I don't think it is about getting pregnant; I believe it's about surviving fertility. That's what women turn into when their fertility is gone. She represents reality and survival. She survived sex, she survived giving birth, she survived motherhood, she survived raping and pillaging, she survived the menopause, which means she made it to old age. I think thirty thousand years ago that was the greatest achievement of all. The history of women is like a horse race; most fell at the first hurdle: childbirth. It was rare for any to get to the wisdom age. There weren't enough finishers for the rest of us to learn from.'

'Does it have to be ugly?'

'Yeah, I don't remember seeing any pretty punks back in the day. Uglification is the ultimate punk thing to do in a society that demands perfection and beauty. She was sticking it to the man long before Siouxsie Sioux rocked up.'

'It doesn't help me; I'm a man.'

'Who interacts with women. We're not a different species. It wouldn't hurt you to read our owner's manual occasionally.'

'Show me a fucking manual, please. I would love to know how you lot work.'

Sam necks the rest of his tea. Men are supposed to be in control, but they don't understand how we work. They're towing us like an old caravan without the extra mirrors. They have no idea when our unmanageable swaying from side to side is going to tip us sideways into a ditch or off a cliff edge. It would be safer if we morphed into one campervan, then we could both sit up front.

Do men need to understand us? We barely understand ourselves; they barely understand themselves. Does anyone read those manuals? Is understanding overrated? It's no coincidence that people have lost their way as more knowledge has been gained. Art was galloping at the frontline of human achievement; now it has been reduced to belittling, ridicule and is utilised by the unwise. It's fallen to the ground whimpering. Many try to put it out of its misery.

Tom returns, still clutching the Venus statue. Sam takes it out of Tom's hands and looks at it carefully.

'That's our manual right there, Sam.'

I pray for the day he accepts me as I am and everything I believe in.

He turns the sculpture round and inspects its large bottom. 'It doesn't come with a contents page.'

'Well, the manual certainly isn't in that bit. It only works with intuition and guesswork, just like—'

'—a real woman, I see.'

Sam turns the statue round to show me the front. Tom has stuck googly eyes on her face. I pretend to scowl at Tom.

'She looks like a proper goddess now she can see, Mum.'

I want to be mad, but I cover my mouth so Tom can't see me

smiling. He takes the statue from Sam and puts it back on the mantelpiece. He places some googly eyes on the balloon dog as well. Sam also smiles a little. He likes her now she has googly eyes, of course he does.

I look straight into his googly eyes. 'Why is it that with all the knowledge we've gained from thousands of years of civilisation we still understand so little?'

'Nell, those who don't read anything believe everything they are told. Those who do read everything believe nothing they are told.'

'Do you think that if there is a God, he intentionally made us stupid so we don't get too close to the answer, just like with the Tower of Babel? Instead of forcing us to speak different languages so we couldn't reach him, he makes us stupid enough to annihilate ourselves every time we get too clever.'

Imelda turns her head away from the TV for the briefest of moments. I know Dada is chuckling inside his head.

Sam contemplates my last thought. 'Nobody knows everything about anything, Nell; whichever Supreme Being is in charge definitely wants us to need each other.'

'And wants there to be a little bit of mystery left to keep us wanting more. Women must remain a mystery.'

I've been waiting for him to understand me, but he wasn't even trying.

I stare at him intensely. 'All that's left for men to conquer and control is molten lava and the mind of a woman. You've been trying to control us, but it only made us more defiant.'

'How do we conquer you all, then?' He asks with too much genuine interest.

'You don't. We're not for taming, Sam, nor is the lava. New land wouldn't form without the lava; new people wouldn't form without the women. We need to be wild; we're incredibly boring when tamed.'

'You're incredibly scary when feral. Women are like an earthquake; everyone hides under tables when they erupt.'

'How can a big man like you be scared of a little woman like me?'

'Because, from my experience, when pressure starts building up inside a woman, a cup of tea and a biscuit isn't always enough to stop the devastation that inevitably follows.'

'Devastation is actually a new skin, somewhere for new ideas to grow. Just as forest fires clear the debris and let new trees flourish, so women have periods that clean out their uteruses to allow for new life. Clearing is important; stagnation is unhealthy.'

'Did you have to make this natural disaster sound yucky?'

How can men be turned off by women's bits when they're quite happy to stick their faces in them? I'm confused. Do they like our bits or not?

'It's only a metaphor, Sam. Periods aren't yucky after the millionth sanitary towel; they become quite mundane. If you're repulsed by your own bodily fluids, then you must be pretty uncomfortable in your own skin.'

'Oh, I am.'

We've been looking each other straight in the eye for a few minutes now. It's quite exciting. No one else is looking at us, though. Dada holds his head with both hands, Imelda continues crocheting an off-scale machine gun, Peter sits in the foetal position with his phone nestled in the middle, Amber stares into space, Tom sticks googly eyes on everything including my knees and Zoe tries to tie her doll's bonnet on to Scraps' head.

Sam leans forward again. 'So, gods come from the skies and goddesses come from the ground, and we're all stuck in the middle like a child in a custody battle. Been there, it ain't pretty.'

'Maybe we need to stop filling the voids in our lives with malleable gods and goddesses. Religion makes good people better people, but bad people worse. I've only tried to talk to God since I couldn't talk to my mother. It's comforting to believe that someone is listening and not trying to cancel you.'

'Everyone needs someone like that.'

'The void is our subconscious, Sam. We have to fill it with something, or it consumes us.'

'I'd rather fill it with biscuits than gods.'

I would rather fill it with a low-calorie doodle. The battle for women continues. I enjoyed it, although my scrunched-up forehead and serious expression might give off a different vibe. Everyone is quiet. Are they thinking about vaginas and pee streams, or are they absorbing the latest updates on the devastation? There's a new death toll graphic showing which American states have been annihilated the most.

My desire to make him want me is growing, but I almost look like the Venus of Willendorf when naked, so I definitely know now that he's repulsed by what I have become. I'm not repulsed by his ageing body shape because I still need him. Does he need me enough to let me be fat?

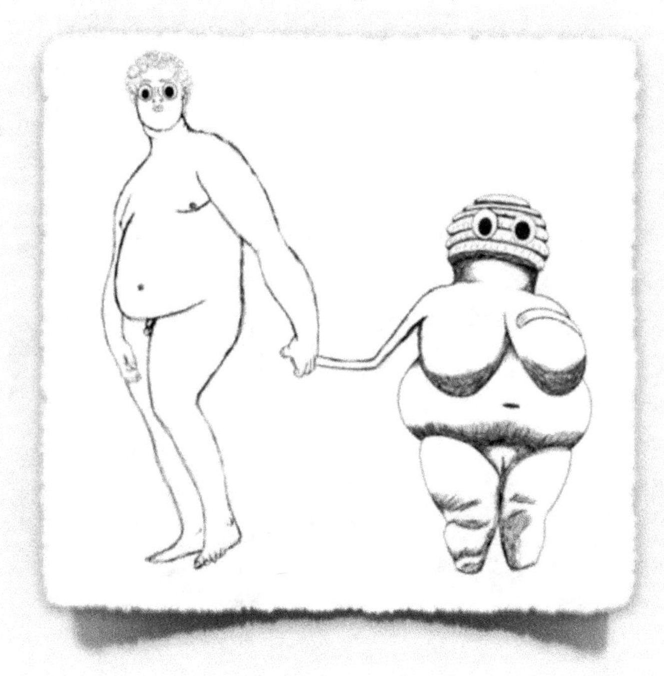

Without an actual god, I have to rely on myself, and myself is broken, which is why I still need him. He was my pendulum. If I went too high, he brought me down; if I went too low, he brought me up. Same for the left and right. But if he's not working and I'm not working, then nobody hears the time ticking away. There's nobody behind me, or him; we were supposed to have each other's backs. How do I make him want me again?

People spent millennia trying to explain the intangible, the ethereal, the abstract, the subliminal, the speculative, and the vague. Artists spent millennia trying to give form to stories and theories. The best anyone has come up with is a large, old man. Our imagination isn't as broad as we think. God isn't a large old man or a large-breasted woman; otherwise, Sam and I would worship each other rather than be ignored. God is just what we don't understand or can't control.

Michelangelo knew God was in the brain when he painted him nearly reaching Adam on the Sistine Chapel ceiling. Someone only recently noticed that on the painting, everything behind God looks exactly like a brain.

Adam didn't put in enough effort to touch and understand God; we still haven't bridged that tiny gap between the fingers.

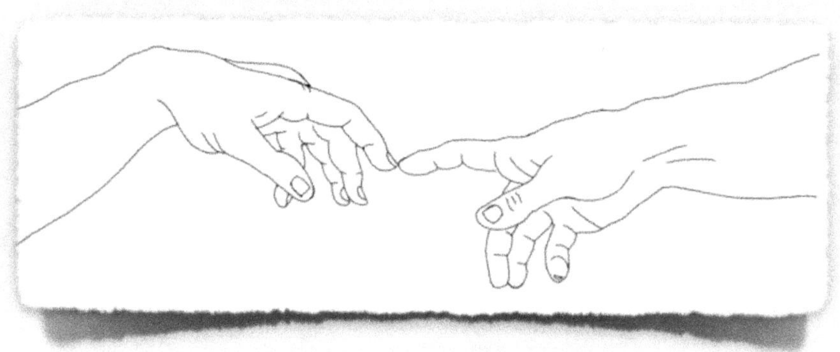

I have a strong desire to explain something that I don't understand: I'm still stuck on figuring out myself, the meaning of me and what love really feels like.

Artists don't salivate when they hear a handbell ringing; they contemplate why it's ringing, study the craftsmanship of the handbell, and absorb the beautiful sound it makes. Pavlov wouldn't have got far if he'd tested his theory on artists or menopausal women.

I wanted my god to be a very fat woman with large boobs and no facial features so she couldn't frown, look disappointed or be prettier than me.

I think it's time for another cup of tea and any biscuit crumbs I can find.

Mary K Hollywood

Primordial Soup

I've woken up on the sofa again, joylessly unaware of the time of day, or what day it is for that matter. I'm so tired my head feels like it might slip into a coma at any moment. The rolling news keeps rolling on in the corner of the room. The air feels thicker to breathe. The microscopic particles that burst out of the belly of the earth are now settling on my unread library books and filtering through my lungs into my bloodstream. The ash reached India yesterday; it's as if a large blanket has been draped over the world. Not even the rogue foot of New Zealand can poke out to escape it.

It's been two weeks since the volcano erupted. With no need to look at my calendar for swimming lessons, playdates, karate nights, and piano, I'm at a bit of a loss. Sam has been out hunting and gathering even more unidentifiable boxes. The kids are bored because the Wi-Fi is more down than it is up. The grandparents are more down than they're up because I'm using two tea bags for four cups of tea, and I've run out of proper biscuits. Nobody knows when this will end, or if it will. I can hear Imelda complaining about everything while Sam tries to make a pot of tea in the kitchen.

The ash has made the whole American continent grey; they think. Few satellites are working anymore. Millions are still waiting for boats on the coasts of America, Canada and Mexico; people are dying while queuing, or if they attempt to jump the queue. They remind me of when I visited Birmingham to see Nele Azevedo's installation of *Melting Men* sitting on the steps of Chamberlain Square back in 2014. She placed thousands of small ice figures on the steps and then photographed the little ice people melting steadily until they all disappeared. I was transfixed as their brief existence vanished right in-front of me. It made a young Amber and Peter cry so much that I never took them to an art exhibition again.

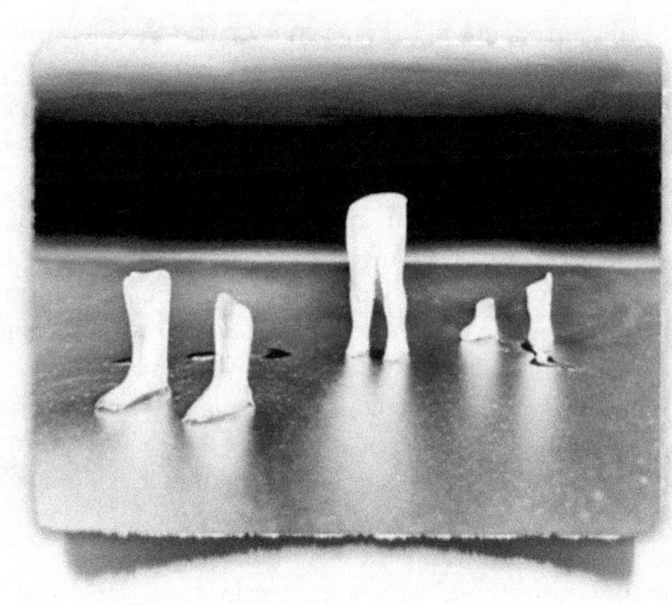

Most people put a work of art on the wall to make themselves look educated, spiritual, rich, or because it matches the carpet. I place art on my soul like a hot poultice. I don't need to buy it. I don't need to frame it. It's a memory as much of one as walking hand-in-hand with my Mama. Luckily, the art world has a big enough apothecary to accommodate every ailment since the dawn of all human thinking. I can do The Grand Tour in my mind without leaving the sofa and without the internet working.

Nobody is raising money to help anyone, as no one is allowed to access their bank accounts. Apparently, people are bargaining with bags of pasta to get toilet paper. Officially we're poor, but so is everyone else, so wealth will be measured differently now. In Britain, every shop has been closed. All current stock will be delivered in rations by the army. Apparently, I'm to wait for a box to arrive and not phone anyone to check its whereabouts. There is a 24-hour curfew for everyone, even some key workers. The last lockdown was just a dress rehearsal. It hasn't stopped Sam; he's hardly been seen except to bring even more boxes of crap into the house. During my last check, one box was empty except for polystyrene peanuts. I've stopped checking as it's too depressing.

Amber is up unusually early. She's wrapped up in her duvet, sitting on the sofa watching the grim foreboding on the TV.

'I've watched so many war movies I'm going to smash it when we live under Nazi rule,' she says.

She's probably right; she will smash something. The doorbell rings. I don't want to answer it. I can't see who it is through the undrawn curtains. Amber gets up enthusiastically to answer the door; the Wi-Fi is definitely down again. I can't find my emergency bra down the side of the sofa. I'll have to fold my arms to give off ambiguous body language instead of risking a stranger seeing my saggy boobs.

'Yeah, what do you want?' says Amber.

A small, wiry old man stands in the doorway. He's shaking so much that the old guitar on his back is making a low humming noise. He looks vaguely familiar.

'I…I…I…I…I'm…I'm…Wilfred…your…Grandad…I…I… think.'

'Whoa, this is brilliant! Are you really?'

Wow, this is the soap opera level of drama she has dreamed about since I first let her have charge of the remote control ten years ago.

'Well…um…if you are the…family of Samson Osmond Stanley…then yes…I'm his father…I…I…don't…suppose… he's…in…is…he?'

'I'll go and get him. Can't wait to see this!'

This is the level of emotional turmoil that Amber has been trained to get interested in and has been seriously lacking since school and electricity became scarce. He looks genuinely scared. I can't help but look him up and down; he's not quite the brute Imelda described him as. No one has seen a photograph of Wilfred; Sam could barely remember him. I would doubt this old man's claim if he weren't Peter's doppelgänger.

'I suppose…Imelda is here…or close by…is she?' Wilfred asks.

He nervously looks over my shoulder.

'I think she's in the kitchen; do I need a fire extinguisher handy?'

'Probably a good idea.'

Wilfred gave a knowing smile just for me. Zoe's curiosity hauls her out of her den, which is now covered with a bedsheet clipped to the bannister with clothes pegs. She fiercely relinquished a big enough gap between the towering boxes to stop everyone destroying the den with every tea break or trip to the downstairs toilet.

'Who are you?' Zoe asks. She has a boldness that took me fifty years to harness.

'Oh, I'm your granddad, sweetheart…I'm your daddy's daddy. My name is Wilfred.'

'I thought Daddy's daddy was dead; that's what Daddy said.'

'No…I'm not dead…not yet, anyway.'

Zoe smiles satisfactorily and returns to her den. Amber shoves a reluctant and pale Sam down the corridor. He walks almost on all fours to duck under the den's bedsheet. Sam looks sceptical. I don't think he recognises him either. Sam always told me he got his height from his dad, but that can't be true.

'What…what do you want?'

'Oh…just…to…you…know…um…I…just…wanted…to see you…really. How are you, son? You look…great…different… you're so much bigger than…not what I was expecting…but it's so nice to see you.'

'You're about fifty years too late for that.'

Sam towers over his father. Wilfred keeps stretching his neck muscles to look up at him. If he didn't look exactly like Peter, I bet Sam would swab the inside of his cheek with a stick instead of glare at him. I try my hardest to push a resistant Amber into the front room, but she smells of sour sweets. That's why she's wired.

'I know…but…it's been…hard…you…know…to come back…here…to this…street…I've never… been…well, not exactly…welcome…here.'

'You're still not, not here, not in this street, not anywhere.'

'Look…I wasn't expecting a fanfare or anything, I know you must hate me, but…it could be the end of the world…I just wanted to look at you…and see your family…just once…and then I'll go…I promise…I just wanted to know what you all looked like…and make sure you know…how…how sorry I am. Time has run out. I can't put it off anymore. I've wanted to come back so many times, but kept finding excuses, kept putting it off…can't do that now.'

'Well, this is what we look like. Nothing special, just ordinary folk. You've probably passed us on the street several times before.'

'No…I've been away from here. This is my first time back since…I went travelling for a bit…many places…and—'

'Well, that's nice for you…I've been stuck here all my life with a bitter mother for company, thanks to you.'

'She was born bitter, son; I didn't make her like that—'

'Don't start having a go at her! At least she was there for me.'

Amber looks like she needs a bag of popcorn perched on the edge of the sofa, arching her neck to get a better view. Sam shouts a barrage of questions at Wilfred, giving him no time to answer them. Wilfred stands firmly and silently, accepting the barrage.

'Do Daddy and our new Grandad need a fefferee?' Zoe shouts from behind her bedsheet walls.

I perch myself next to Amber on the arm of the sofa. Tom hastily joins Zoe in the den. The racket Sam and Wilfred are making is enough to entice Peter out of his room and come downstairs. He tactfully avoids touching Wilfred, Sam, and then Amber, who is now leaning against the edge of the doorframe. Peter looks like one of those metal wands avoiding the bendy wire circuit that will electrocute him if he so much as touches a hair on Amber's head.

It's nice to see a bit of aggression from Sam, but not when it's too one-sided.

'Who's Dad shouting at?' Peter asks.

'That's our other grandad. He wants to see us one last time,' Amber explains enthusiastically.

'Why last time? Is he buggering off again, or has he got a terminal disease?'

'One last time before the end of the world. It's really happening, Pete,' I explain.

'Nah, Mum, I don't believe anything they say on the telly. It's all bollocks. I've seen a video of what is really happening in America right now.'

'Oh really, and what is that?'

'This volcano is a cover-up; the footage is AI.'

'Why would anyone want to pretend this is happening?'

'To cover up some bad news; the Russians have invaded America with a drone army, and they've blown them up with nukes.'

'Pete, I don't believe any government is competent enough to pull that off; conspiracy theorists always give them too much credit. If either side had successfully blown up the other, they would be crowing from the rooftops and giving each other medals. Anyway, where has all this ash come from? Do you think they've been stockpiling it in secret underground warehouses that only a single magic key can unlock?'

Peter ignores me; I don't have enough interesting theories for him to take me on. I sneak out of the front room, tiptoe past Sam shouting at Wilfred, crawl under the den roof and head towards the kitchen. This is the holy grail of gossip I could never find. Imelda has a new facial expression: genuine fear. She has nowhere to go; there's no escape from the back garden. She is going to have to grin and bear it. She's shaking. What is she afraid of? It can't be those wiry, delicate fists of his.

'You okay, Melda? Here, sit down. Must be a bit of a shock.'

'Get that man out of here, Nell. I don't want to see his face.'

'I'll let Sam deal with him, if you don't mind. This has nothing to do with me. They need to sort it out between themselves.'

'I can't believe he's here after all this time. Get him out, please.'

'What happened, Melda? Tell me, I can help.'

It's funny how all of my insecurities dissipate rapidly when confronted with the opportunity for the tables to be turned in my favour.

'I can't talk about it…never could…it's too much…maybe some things are better left not talked about.'

'Oh, I don't know. You always say it's best these things are out in the open, not all festering inside you.'

'No…this is not the time. This is definitely not the time.'

'Has he lost weight… and height?'

'I'm begging you, Nellie, shut up!'

Shame makes people lie, and they will keep lying to keep hiding the shame.

I didn't realise the hallway had gone quiet; the shouting has stopped. Sam stares down at his dad. Wilfred shrugs his shoulders.

'I am really sorry, son.'

If Sam slams that front door any harder, it's going to come off its hinges. Do I run after him to mop his brow? Wilfred stares at the floor. I'm not sure how to clear this mess up.

'Would you like a cup of tea, Grandad?' asks Amber.

I've never seen her this committed to anything, ever. Boredom and sour sugar could start wars.

'That's very kind of you, dear, but…I…think I'll avoid upsetting anyone else…probably best I go now. Bye…everyone—'

Zoe and Tom burst out of the den, sending boxes and polystyrene peanuts flying. They are unusually deadpan. Tom presents Wilfred with a scruffy piece of paper while holding his chin up as high as it will go.

'This is a list of all the presents you've missed, including birthdays, Easters, Christmases, Halloweens, Bonfire Nights, Valentine's Days…Pancake Days…St. George's Days…It's not finished, but this is what you owe us.'

'Oh right. OK. Thank you…er—'

'I'm Tom.'

'Tom, lovely. I shall do my best…it was…lovely to meet you all.'

'Sorry it had to be like this. It must have taken a lot of courage to turn up after all this time.'

'Thank you…er—'

'Nellie, my name is Nellie.'

'Nellie, thank you. Courage is not something I'm known for. I'm the biggest coward, can't even stand up to—'

Wilfred catches Imelda's eye all the way down the corridor, through a gap in the den's sheets. He grabs the front door handle tightly.

'Please stay…just a bit longer,' I insist.

I have a cruel streak. 'Come into the front room, just for a few minutes. You are their grandad.'

'Oh, are you sure? I would love to know everything about you all.'

And I want to know what genes flow through these kids of mine. He's got Peter's slight frame. I wonder what other flaws I can blame on this old man. Zoe and Tom sit down on the floor in front of Wilfred with their arms and legs crossed as he sits tentatively on the sofa.

'My superhero name is Emmaracido,' says Zoe.

'Ignore her, Grandad, she's silly. Can you play that guitar? I don't like smooth music. I like rough music.'

'Shut up, Tom. I know all the rules: I know how to stop slapping, not to put bogeys under the table, stop running round on chairs, don't put footprints on your hair, no poo on the head.'

'That's marvellous!' says Wilfred, clapping his hands together with puzzled delight.

'Did you know that God came out of the belly of an animal?'

'No…I didn't know that, Zoe, um—'

'Can you take us to the Ferrari Park?'

'A…F…F…Ferrari park?'

'She means Safari Park, Wilfred. Can I get you a cup of tea?'

'Oh, that would be lovely, Nellie, but…oh…actually…no…I don't think so…I can't stay long.'

'Do you know Santa?'

'Oh…no, Zoe…I've not met—'

'Do you have a car?'

'Uh…no, Tom, not at—'

'Where have you been?'

'Well…that's…a—'

'Do you want to see my pencil?'

'Well, Zoe …I'm sure it's—'

'When I grow up, I'm going to be a piece of grass.'

While Zoe and Tom ask questions with impunity, Amber and Peter seem a little deflated. When they were younger, they used to discuss at great length that their missing grandfather must have been a monster of a man, all stubble, shaved head and tattoos everywhere, as that is how Imelda had sort of described him. Their hopes of a rematch between their Granny and Grandad appear to be dwindling as Wilfred's shaky hands cling onto his guitar, which is now on his lap.

'Can you play us something?'

'Um…yes…Peter, is it? I can play lots of things.'

'Cool.'

'Although I only play folk songs, I…I…doubt you've heard them.'

'Try us.'

Wilfred looks less nervous now he's playing gentle little folk songs on his guitar; the kids are amazed and delighted. I haven't seen all four of my children appreciating the same thing at the same time before.

I've heard this song; I want to join in, but I can't sing for toffee. Amber, however, can sing beautifully. How does she know this song? Who knew she could sing? I'm all caught up in this beautiful moment.

Not for long; we all stop when we hear Sam fumbling with the front door keys. He looks through the front room door. 'What the hell is he still doing here, Nell?'

I like this old man; he's harmless. 'He's their grandfather, whether you like it or not, and they're all smiling at once! Don't you dare stop this!'

'I think you should leave…Dad!'

'He's more fun than our other grandad,' says Amber.

I try to give Amber one of her own trademark side-eyes. The laughter fully stops, and Wilfred gets up, swings his guitar back over his shoulder, dips his head and heads for the front door, trying hard to dodge Sam's simmering body. He briefly turns around.

'I'll go. It was lovely to see you all. It really was…and if this is the end of the world, then I'll take this image of beautiful faces with me. Thank you.'

'You haven't earned that image!'

'Sorry, son.'

Wilfred notices Imelda's face scowling at him from the kitchen. I could see a shiver go down his back. He shuffles out of the door, trying to smile at Sam's brooding face.

Sam slams the door behind him, slides down the wall and sits on the floor in the hallway. I can hear Imelda pacing up and down in the kitchen, huffing and puffing. The children sit in the front room, grumbling that their new grandad has gone already. I put on a DVD about wizards and fairies to distract and bond as many people as possible. I can see the appeal of wands.

Binary Fission

There's another knock at the door. I take a deep breath in case there's another MIA relative behind it. It's hard to open the door while straddling a downbeat Sam to answer it.

'If it's him again, tell him to piss off back to where he came from,' Sam mumbled with frustrated rage.

'He came from this street; he was born here too. Your mum lives in his mother's house.'

How can men protect us when they have as many weak spots? I hit him with the front door.

'Darling sister, how the devil are you?'

Sam throws his head back against the wall. 'Could this day get any fucking worse?' he groans, not as quietly under his breath as he might have thought. My kick in his shin wasn't meant to be that quiet either.

'What a lovely surprise, Nigel. I wasn't expecting you. Um, um…come in. How lovely to see you both. Don't mind Sam. Just step over him. He's had a bit of a shock. In you come, I'll stick the kettle on.'

I stare daggers at Sam, but he doesn't care.

Nigel and his painfully skinny wife, Skye, awkwardly step over Sam's brooding body.

I've only met Skye twice before, so I don't know if we are at the hugging stage yet.

We're not.

There's nothing I love more than seeing my handsome, healthy twin brother and his beautiful, undamaged wife. Those fucking genes were in the womb with me, and I chose all the chubby, hairy ones! They're both pale, but that isn't unusual.

'Hi there, kids! Lovely to see you all.' Nigel shouts joyfully through the front room door without waiting for a response. Not a single head turned away from the TV.

'Who was that, Amber?' I can hear Tom asking.

'That's Uncle Nigel. He's a twat as well,' I can hear Amber helpfully reply.

I follow Nigel and Skye through the bedsheets and into the kitchen. Imelda straightens herself out and puts on her best fake smile, even pretending to enjoy the theatrical hugs and kisses. Every adult except Sam sits at the kitchen table, looking overly pleased to see each other and awaiting refreshments. The kettle boils. Nigel tells us about the state of London.

'Oh, it's awful! Everyone has gone completely mad! It's like the pandemic but without the social distancing. There's people everywhere; we're like sardines. You can't go out at night. There are police and soldiers on every corner. You can't buy a pint of milk. They're storing all the food in secret warehouses. They're talking about ration books, can you believe it? Everyone is stressed and angry. Everything is closed, even the theatres. It's like a war zone. There's nothing to do. The streets are a mess. There's rioting everywhere. I don't know what people are expecting to happen. One of Skye's yoga students got beaten to a pulp for not letting go of her backpack. Turns out it only contained her dissertation on whether elephants can paint. The thugs didn't even take it in the end. Just left the papers all over the street. The hospitals are refusing patients, even though they've got extra doctors with all the suitably qualified refugees trying to help. The Americans and Canadians are arriving in droves, but there's nowhere for them. Hyde Park looks like Glastonbury. The queue for petrol was horrendous! Do you know it took us twelve hours to get here? The traffic out of London is outrageous. Everyone is desperate to get out. Can you believe people were heckling us in the traffic jams, calling us cowards and traitors because we were leaving? It's so bad. I can't believe it got this bad so quickly. I'm sorry I didn't phone, but our landline has been damaged and my mobile connection is terrible. We had to get out. We're heading for the hills, as they say. We're going to a cottage in Wales for a bit until this all dies down. It's absolute mayhem!'

Nigel pauses to take a sip of tea. Skye stares so lovingly at her husband; it drives me mad. Should I tell her he used to pull the wings off flies and squish them with his finger to see their 'poo' come out? I shouldn't be jealous just because they're driving sports cars and I'm stuck in this dysfunctional bin lorry with sparks flying out of the back. They're designed for self-indulgence and driving off into the sunset without passengers or baggage. My extended family could look like they should be in the Wacky Races.

'Can you believe the King has let them turn Buckingham Palace into a treatment centre? He's staying at Windsor; they've got a drawbridge there. And don't get me started on those bloody neighbours of ours. Do you know what they did? Do you know? They started digging up their garden, and they've gone and dug a massive hole. They somehow got hold of a mini-digger. They've been digging since the volcano erupted. They reckon they're going to build an underground home, not waiting for planning permission, just digging a big hole. They had big plans to reinforce the sides with concrete and create a glass roof, but now they can't find supplies, let alone builders. Now we've got a massive crack in our conservatory. I'll sue them when this is all finished. All they've created is a massive muddy puddle. It's laughable. Can't wait for them to explain that when everything gets back to normal. I mean, the audacity! Who do people think they are?'

Sam staggers into the kitchen, grabs a handful of homemade cookies that Zoe made yesterday and throws them into his mouth, even though they look like bird poo. Imelda is doing a good impression of someone who has forgotten the previous drama by stuffing her face with bird poo cookies as well. Sam necks his cold cup of tea. I can't look at him when he does that; lukewarm tea is the devil's drink. He goes back up the hallway and stands in the doorway to the front room, watching his four children laugh at the TV. Hopefully, he's realising that far from being damaged by meeting their Grandad, they are all gleefully absorbed with the optimistic and brightly coloured cartoons. He hovers near the front door. He looks like he is going to leave, but this time something makes him stop. He leans against the wall, slides his back down, and sits on the floor again.

When men complain, they expect a big motherly sponge will absorb all the shit. His own motherly sponge is too busy eating her own body weight in cookies right now. The two of them must have got through a lot of sugar in the eighties.

It's funny seeing Nigel talk to everyone as if he were here last week – he hasn't been here since he announced they were eloping four years ago. He's never met Zoe. He used to visit all the time, but now he treats me like a distant relative. We shared a fucking womb for nine months and a bedroom for ten years. Fucking puberty. I miss having someone I can fight with without worrying about falling out. The only blood-boiling argument I've ever had with another human being was with him; he thought Aragorn was miscast in the *Lord of the Rings*. He only said that because he isn't a woman. I seriously lost my shit that day, but Nigel just laughed at me and never held a grudge. I like my heroes to be strong, scruffy and with a broken ankle, not lying on the welcome mat in the foetal position hugging a hedgehog door-stopper.

Nigel has changed, though; he's become someone else. Normal people strive to be different; different people strive to be normal. He needs to talk like a twat to get by in the banking community.

When we were little, he used to tell the most elaborate lies. He once told me that squash balls have a special yellow dot on them which contains poison, and if you throw the squash ball at wasps and the yellow dot touches them, they will die instantly. The sight of me throwing very bouncy squash balls at wasps was hilarious to him. Apparently, he was trying to stop me from being so gullible, but I think it was for his own entertainment.

'Nige, would you like me to phone Dada? He should be here soon, anyway.'

'Oh no, don't worry him, Sis. We won't be staying long. We just wanted to say "Hi", use your amenities, if you don't mind; the service stations are blocked up, if you know what I mean, and then we'll be out of your way. I'm sure you've got enough on your plate.'

'What about Mama? Would you—'

'No thanks. We'll be going soon; we definitely don't want to be in your way. I'm sure you're very busy, what with four children, is it now? I mean, I haven't even seen the most recent addition before; she looks adorable. But we really must get going to Wales before anymore petrol stations run out of fuel or vegan snacks. Skye, you use the toilet first, then I'll go after you. It really is lovely to see you, Sis. It's been too long. It really has.'

'Make sure it's not too long again, just in case this is the end of the world.'

I grip Nigel's arm tightly. I haven't done that since he tried to jump into a canal for laughs. For the briefest of moments, he looks me in the eye and gives me a reassuring smile. He's still in there somewhere.

'It does sound grim, Nell, but everything will be fine; it always is. Luckily, we're used to eating very little. We get by on a bottle of gin and some rice cakes. I bet your little brood needs a bit more than that, especially big Sam. What's up with him, by the way?'

'His father just turned up for the first time in over forty years. Came as a bit of a shock… to everyone.'

'Oh, I see! Wow! I bet. Couldn't have been that dear old gentleman I saw leaving your house shortly before us? He looked like he couldn't fight his way out of a paper bag.'

Imelda's shoulders suddenly stiffened. 'Don't be fooled by appearances, Nigel; anyone of any size can lay a fist on another.'

'O…kay then. Well, I'm going to nip to the loo now Skye's back. I'll let you girls have a chinwag.'

Skye stares blankly at us. We smile just as blankly back. I would love to have a proper sister. I fantasised about Nigel marrying someone amazing so I could have a friend for life. Nigel doesn't get on with Sam either. I think Sam frightens him a little bit. Our paths forked a long time ago; he's just a speck in the distance now. Nigel returns quickly, thank God.

'Right! Let's be off then. Come on, Skye! We'll catch up with you guys when things have got back to normal, hopefully in a few days, or a couple of weeks. We'll see. Lovely to see you, sis. Say hello to Dada for me! Bye, kids!'

I should be grateful I have a toilet without a queue to warrant such a visit.

Age of the Dinosaurs

It's only been a few minutes, and there's another fucking knock at the bloody front door. Amber jumps up to get it before the doorbell ring fades, probably hoping it's another new relative with a Louis Vuitton collection of emotional baggage.

'Oh, it's you, Dada.'

'Thanks, Amber. You're such a treasure! What are you doing on the floor, Sam?'

'You just missed Nigel and Skye, Bill.'

'Oh really, I'm guessing they didn't stay long then.'

'No, they just needed the loo on their way up to a cottage in Wales.'

'Sounds about right,' says an unbothered Dada. He should take up poker. Dada takes up his usual position in the front room. The kids haven't noticed him as they're still glued to the movie on TV.

'Have you heard the latest news story, Nell?'

'Which one? The one about Russians destroying America with nukes, or the one about China secretly drilling a hole through the centre of the earth, or the one about the Kardashians starting a new colony off the coast of India?'

'What news have you been watching?'

'I've stopped watching; Peter has been filling me in.'

'I would advise you to start watching again; temperatures are plummeting, and there are reports of freezing temperatures on every continent all at the same time. Everything is unprecedented. The Home Office has told people not to hoard food and bottled water, as that is making it scarce, which means they are running out, so get more. Large numbers of essential key workers are not turning up for work in many countries as they're not getting paid. Essential services are under threat; the electricity and gas are going to run out, and the water won't get treated. Satellites are struggling with the ash cloud; mobile networks are expected to have minimal usage. And with the internet servers in Europe shutting down intermittently, what's left of your beloved social media platforms won't be able to function.'

'What!' says Amber.

'No internet?' cries Peter.

'Yep! The world was once a playground of indecipherable screams of joy and pain. However, a storm has come, silencing all the screams. Everyone has left. The empty swings are now squeaking in the wind.'

I bet Dada has been working on that analogy all afternoon. Amber is frowning so hard that her eyebrows have completely changed shape.

'Don't even joke, Dada. What are we going to do without our phones?' Peter sounds genuinely scared. He, if it were possible, looks more peaky than usual. 'How are we going to talk to our friends? It will take ages to walk round to all their houses!'

'Your best mate only lives 100 yards up the road, Pete. You could shout and he'd hear you.'

'No, he wouldn't, Dada. He's always got his headset on.'

'Not for long. It'll be like the seventies — blackouts, no fuel for the car,' Dada says gleefully while rubbing his hands together, grinning.

Amber and Peter could audition for a cheap horror movie with those expressions. Wi-Fi is like magic to me; I have no idea how it works. I've prayed for a day off the internet for years, hoping to have a craft day or board games day. Now that it seems imminent, I am developing a cold sweat too. At least I have an excuse not to check my website. I can't cope with any more orders for cupcakes with the Four Horsemen of the apocalypse riding on them. Horses aren't easy to make in fondant icing; mine would give the impression that My Little Pony were coming to unleash God's judgement.

Dada isn't even trying to hide his delight. 'If the world is going to change, we will have to change with it.'

'Don't mess with us, Dada. The internet doesn't need satellites, does it? I thought it was wires. There must be some wire we could use. There must be,' says Amber.

'Some of it is satellites, but it's not that; it's the power. People operate the national grid, people press buttons, and people make sure everything works. If people aren't paid, people don't turn up. They don't work for shits and giggles. It won't be long before you won't even be able to charge any of your precious devices!'

The terrified teenagers are struggling to blink. Amber shakes her head. 'Selfish bastards, what the fuck are we going to do without fucking electricity? My ceramic curling wand, my hot-brush, my jump rope…my—'

'What about my rainbow polar bears, my mythical black rabbit skeleton and my customised fox?' says Peter.

I don't think I want to know what those things are.

'We survived for millennia without electricity,' Dada replies.

Amber has real tears welling up now. 'We haven't, Dada, not our generation. We're conditioned. We need to contact our friends immediately, not wait until later. That's barbaric! Next, we'll be cooking on an open fire and wearing fur bikinis. Animal skin is trampy. I won't be able to look for…well, for any kind of stuff… without the internet. I won't know what's out there to want so badly.'

Do I hug her or point and laugh hysterically? Deep down, I want stuff at the touch of my fingertips too. I remember the 1970s blackouts; they were cool until *Tiswas* was cancelled.

An era's worth of knowledge will be lost like the Library of Alexandria. The knowledge of how to make the internet is probably stored on the internet itself. The knowledge of what all the buttons in the car did was stored on it; I hadn't finished looking them up.

Dada shakes his head. 'You clearly don't know the meaning of the word barbaric, do you, Amber? But if things carry on the way they are, you soon will.'

He is clearly readying himself for an SAS survival week with his grandchildren. I was put through something like that when I was twelve. Nigel had a massive tantrum, and Mama had to take him home. I whittled the same piece of wood all week while Dada roasted flea-infested rabbits on an open fire. Not our best holiday.

Sam finally gets up off the floor with the same stern expression on his face he's had for a week.

'What are you smiling about, Bill?'

'Just the sound of a penny dropping, Sam. Very hard.'

'The higher the penny has to drop, the more likely it is to kill you,' says Sam.

I don't like Sam in philosophical mode. The last time he was like this, he tried to install a zip-wire from the bathroom window to the shed.

If Amber taps away any more furiously on her cracked phone, it will give her more glass splinters; her fingertips get so shiny she could buff up a diamond! There's another knock at the door, Sam shakes his head, but apprehensively answers it. I follow him out into the hallway. It's Jimmy and Carl from next door.

'Hear you've got some food stashed away, Sammy. Is it true?' Jimmy asks.

'Don't know what you're talking about, mate. I've only got as much as everyone else.'

'Ah, come on, Sammy! Everyone knows you got some boxes off Harvey. What was in them?'

'What's it to you, boys? There're not for sale.'

'Oh, we don't want to buy them. Got no money. We just thought you might want to share them, yer know, with your friendly neighbours. We could only get a few boxes of cereal — fucking muesli. Sainsbury's is boarded up.'

I bet you can get in if you show them your boobs.

'I hadn't thought of cereal. Tell you what, I'll swap a box of baked beans for 5 boxes of cereal, but not the healthy ones; I want chocolate ones.'

'OK, mate, cool.' Jimmy runs off excitedly.

I need to be more thorough. If I'd known we had baked beans, I could've made a fake chilli.

'What was all that about?' As if I couldn't hear.

Sam ignores me and delicately pulls a box from the bottom of one of the den's supporting towers. I stand at the door silently with Sam, waiting for our neighbours to return. Jimmy returns with a box of cereal boxes in acidic, colourful packaging, and Carl drags a fully popped pop-up tent behind him. Carl hands the tent awkwardly to me through the door. I fold the tent up into a neat, flat, round shape and hand it back. I'm the only one in this village who can do that. Sam hands over a box to Carl; Jimmy hands the box of cereal to Sam. Sam shuts the door hesitantly.

'Is that what's in these boxes — baked beans?' I ask with growing excitement at the thought of making a reasonably pleasant meal.

'Some of them, maybe. Problem is they'll all be after them now. We're not going to get any peace. Everyone will be on the scrounge. I'd better hide these somewhere.'

'Where are you gonna hide this amount of stuff?'

'Er, I don't know, but I'll think of something.'

'Well, while you're thinking, I need to see Mama before they ban that as well.'

'Take Bill's car and the kids. I have to get this stuff out of the way.'

Sam looks at the den towers and gestures to me to get Zoe out of sight quickly. I get the hint; she will scalp him if she witnesses him destroying the den.

'Dada, do you want to come and see Mama?'

'No thanks, darling, not today.'

'Fine. Come on, kids. Get in the car. Are you sure, Dada, last chance?'

'No thanks, off you go.'

Amber looks at me as if I'm about to ask her to draw blood. 'Do I have to go? I can't bear it.'

Peter looks up in the same way. 'And me, I just—'

'I wasn't expecting the two of you to come. I'll take Tom and Zoe. They can't remember her being any different.'

Zoe and Tom rush outside. Sam starts quietly unpicking the bedsheets, checking Zoe doesn't see him. Is he going to hide the boxes in his mistress' house? I bet she wouldn't put up with towers of cardboard ruining her decor. Mistresses are mistresses because they don't actually like having people in their real lives messing it up. Maybe she already has some boxes. I bet she has the ones filled with food.

Amber and Peter run upstairs and shut themselves in their rooms, probably contemplating their future and furiously trying to tap out their last messages. Dada falls instantly into a nap. Imelda sits on her own, quietly on the sofa. I guess no one dares to ask if she is okay.

I leave before my brain starts working overtime. We get in the car. Tom and Zoe aren't excited about visiting their grandmother. Even at their tender age, they know there's no reward, no cuddle, no secret sweets.

The roads are dead quiet. This isn't a densely populated area, so there are not a lot of army vehicles on duty. The government is allowing visits to care homes this time, so I'm not being rebellious. This is a rare opportunity to actually get out of the house and see what the world looks like.

'When I grow up, I just want to drive around,' says Tom.

'You won't be able to. The cost of petrol stops people from just driving around.'

'Then I'll get a job so I can pay for the petrol.'

'Then you won't have time to drive around.'

My stomach has filled with dread. When I'm there, I won't be happy to see her like that, and when I leave her, I will cry, but I have to put myself through it. It's been four and a half years since her stroke, just before Zoe was born. Locked-in syndrome was a harsh punishment for such a happy, sociable lady. She can only move her eyelids. It sometimes feels like she died a few years ago; the person everyone knew and loved disappeared. I wish she were still in my life. I still need a supervising adult.

The crunchy, pebbly drive to the care home seems louder than usual today. I haven't been for a few weeks; I wish she could tolerate more visits.

There seems to be less staff around than usual. I can walk straight through to the main room without being challenged. All the elderly residents are sitting in their chairs; nodding their heads, sipping tea out of brightly coloured plastic baby cups or sleeping. Mama doesn't leave her room; she lies down permanently on a bed with opera playing on a small radio most of the day. At least she looks serene lying in her bed with a white sheet draped over her body. She would look like one of those marble queens you see in cathedrals if it weren't for the breathing apparatus.

'Hello, Mama! How are you?'

I gently kiss her forehead and stare sweetly into her eyes, hoping she can read all my emotions before I blink. Mama's body is parked in a garage. It keeps ticking over thanks to the mechanics, but she's not being driven. The buttons don't connect to the right parts anymore, and her model is too old for anyone to remember how to drive it. All they can do is try to stop it from getting rustier. I wish I understood more about mechanics to make her work properly again. I'm a terrible daughter, sending her away. She never sent me away. I don't know enough about engines, but I wish we could go drag racing together again.

Mama's eyes tear up a little; she can convey a lot of emotion with her eyelids. I cry too. Zoe and Tom sit on the floor and flick through a pile of magazines on a nearby table.

A large, barrel-chested old man stumbles into the room: Alexander, Mama's favourite resident, we think. Alexander can't really sing; he roars. He used to be a percussionist in an orchestra, so he is drawn to Mama's constant music playing in her room. While roaring, he bangs his hands or any leftover cutlery on any available surface.

'Is that you, Janet, or is it Martha? I can't tell with you nurses; you keep changing.'

'No, it's me, Nellie. Remember?'

'No, sweet girl. You all look the same to me. Have you made me a cup of tea? I'm gasping. You're all trying to see me off, I'm sure of it. I've had no food today either.'

There's a plate covered with biscuits and a half-drunk cup of tea on the table next to him. He grabs a biscuit and eats it with exaggerated sound effects, much to the delight of Zoe and Tom.

'How has she been, Alexander? Is everybody okay in here?'

'We're marvellous, dear girl. Why shouldn't we be? I mean, I've not eaten for days. Who are these two delightful little people? Are they going to do a show for me?'

Alexander eats more biscuits; his long, straggly, grey and ginger beard is full of crumbs.

'They're Mama's grandchildren, Zoe and Tom, remember?'

'Dear girl, are you going to get me a biscuit, or are you planning on watching me disintegrate right here in front of you?'

I lean over the bed and stretch to reach a biscuit on the plate right next to him.

'Here's a biscuit, Alexander.'

'Oh, thank you, just what I wanted. How did you know? Now it looks like someone has left their children here. Be a doll and find out who they belong to. They don't look well-fed. Do they need some soup?'

I hover over Mama, waiting for any flicker of the eyelids. Alexander's shenanigans always make her eyes smile. He's changed the music to marching music and stomps his feet as if he were off to war. Zoe and Tom march around the room with him, much to his delight. Mama closes her eyes. I hope she can imagine what all this noise looks like.

'Do you remember, Mama, what this music means to me? When we were stationed at RAF Valley in Anglesey, Nana and Gaga came to stay with us. They wanted us to learn to ride. They bought a couple of scruffy ponies from the local sales and kept them in a tiny paddock that was on a slope. Nana painted letters on eight large ice cream containers, which she always kept for such impromptu occasions. She turned them upside down and made a tiny dressage arena. Gaga drove their old decommissioned yellow BT van up to the gate with loudspeakers attached to a tape cassette player. Nana blasted the *Radetszky March* at us while we bounced around on shell-shocked ponies on a sloping dressage arena with Gaga barking indecipherable orders at us till we fell off. No one thought to question why they had loudspeakers at hand.'

Mama opens her eyes and blinks. She remembers.

'That bloody BT van. Only Gaga could have become a farrier in his retirement, working harder than he did in his HR job. He loved shoeing horses as a hobby. He would turn up at horse shows with all his kit in the back of that van just in case a horse lost a shoe. The anvil would be tied securely in the back with baling twine. His grandchildren wouldn't be tied so securely though; we had an old tyre and a cushion to sit on, no baling twine for us. He drove around like a racing car driver, ensuring our heads hit the roof of the car when he went over a bridge. We all thought it was funny.'

Mama blinks again. Alexander has Zoe and Tom on his lap as they listen to my stories.

Alexander's eyes are like saucers. 'You know, I once took a large shit outside a pawnshop, right on the pavement!'

'Right. Thanks, Alexander. I'm going to look for a member of staff. Moaning at them shows them how much I care.'

There aren't many nurses about; one is rushing around trying to make beds, another is on the phone just nodding her head with her eyes shut. I would normally offer to help, but I would probably break some health and safety code. They all look exhausted. I go back to Mama's room.

Alexander pretends to blow a trombone while Zoe and Tom giggle at his feet.

'Mama, I'm going to take you home. I'll look after you now. I'm not leaving you here.'

'What? You can't take me home with you, dear; I don't know who you are.'

'I'm not taking you, Alexander. It's dangerous; there's not enough staff. She needs to be with me.'

'No, Martha! Janet! Andrea! Help, I'm being abducted. Help me!'

'You're not going anywhere. I'm her daughter.'

'I don't have a daughter; I only have a son, Jeremy. He's coming to get me soon. He's wonderful.'

'Alexander, your son isn't called Jeremy, he's called Robert, and he's not coming to get you. He lives in Ameri… anyway, it doesn't matter. I'll look after Mama. If I can just get her out of this bed.'

'I don't want a strange woman looking after me. I like Martha best. She gives me extra biscuits.'

'I'm not taking you, Alexander.'

'I want to stay here. I feel safe.'

Mama is restless; her eyelid flickers. Alexander grabs her other hand and gently strokes the back of it. Alexander looks me straight in the eye. His smile is forceful, yet somehow reassuring. A young nurse with forced cheerfulness pops her head round the door.

'You lot okay? You seem a bit upset, Alexander. Are you all right?'

'I'm absolutely fine, dear. Why would you think there's anything wrong with me?'

'I'll be back in a minute or two. Just got to change some more beds and put some more washing on—'

'This woman is trying to kidnap my friend.'

Alexander points earnestly at me. The nurse comes fully into the room and puts her hand on my shoulder.

'I know it looks bad, but she's happy here. You move her, she'll just get upset. And this bloody machine probably won't work if it gets moved. They like their routine.'

'But what's going to happen to them? Have you got enough food? Enough water?'

'We get supplies from the army. Don't tell anyone, though. I think it is supposed to be a secret!' she says.

'It's all very exciting, isn't it?' Alexander giggles. His deep stare ripples right through me.

'Do you understand what's going on, Alexander? Do you realise what is happening in the world? Do you know how bad it's going to get?'

'Can't be worse than the war. I was a small child back then; it was wonderful having ration books, rubble to play on. Quite an adventure.'

This doesn't feel like an adventure anyone wants. I didn't buy any tickets or book it online; I want to stay at home. I would love to have the eternal optimism of Alexander. I suppose the closer you get to death, the less you fear it. Alexander takes a deep breath in, holds his hand out like one of the Three Tenors, and starts singing.

'My Bonnie lies over the ocean, my Bonnie lies over the sea... My Bonnie lies over the ocean, oh bring back my Bonnie to me, bring back, bring back—'

Mama's face lights up; she blinks as if she's clapping her hands. The mind can override the body. It doesn't matter if the car is stuck in the mud; you can still press the buttons and make "vroom vroom" noises.

I don't want this to end. But the song is short, and the moment is already a memory.

'Where's that fucking nurse with my fucking tea?' booms Alexander.

I kiss Mama's forehead and let my tears soak into her hair. Those will leave a trace of me here. She was like Bourgeois' giant bronze spider. She can't protect me anymore because she's fallen over, but she's still there. She's too big to ignore.

'Love you, Mama, I'll see you soon.'

I'm crying all the way home. I can barely see the road; it's so blurry. The kids haven't noticed my wayward driving; they're too busy making up a ruder version of the song they have just heard. Grief is like driving your body with the cruise control switched on while negotiating a windy country lane with your eyes shut.

Continental Drift

The kids ran straight upstairs and shut their bedroom door before I could remove my bra and throw it against the wall in frustration. The front room is empty for once, so I slump onto the sofa. My face is damp and sticky with expunged tears. I need a wet wipe to remove evidence of emotional turmoil; it's as close to a chemical peel as I will ever get.

I'm not turning the TV on. The last thing I need is progressively worse news stories; they've cancelled all other TV programmes. There are no comedies, nothing to take my mind off the doom and gloom or release a shot of endorphins. I'm going to savour this peace and quiet for as long as I can.

'Fucking gods, fucking Mother Earth!!!' I scream into an empty room.

I'm angry. Why would any god or spiritual force or whoever is in fucking charge do that to a person? There's no benefit to anyone in torturing a beautiful old woman like that. My grief has been on pause for four years. Like an old VHS tape, I have a glitch where it's been paused for too long.

I know everything has to be random, but it still makes me mad. If Mother Earth had to pick out the bad guys, she'd need a jury to direct the lava flow towards them. Pain teaches me to survive. Death teaches me to live. Joy won't come to me if I pay for it, wait for it, expect it, work hard for it, or tick a lot of boxes for it. It only comes after I've felt genuine pain. I had too many epidurals; otherwise, I'd probably understand quicker.

There are many artists who painted death, rage, grief, and madness. Everyone knows what that feels like. Someone needs to paint, sculpt, or draw acceptance, but I don't think humans have collectively reached that point yet. I couldn't draw it; my feelings are too strong for the required precision. Does it need to be precise? Just create something. What can I create that will help me understand this? All the art that has ever been created from every corner of the globe since the dawn of time was created to help someone understand something. Gods are artwork.

I don't need to please a god, or sacrifice anything to a god. I don't need to believe in a god to feel worth something. I don't need to hang God on a wall while listening to someone else explain what God is to me and buy the God-shaped pencil case in the gift shop. If Mother Earth is the spiritual force driving us, then I need to understand what she is by exploring, experimenting, and creating. Then I can move on to the final piece. At least 75% of what Mother Earth has already created was just experiments; she's still looking for that last 25%: the end result. Should I look for clues in the garden? It's too cold; I'll have to look in the plant pots.

God is whatever I want it to be. Mother Earth isn't whatever I want it to be; it just is. Mother Earth isn't keeping Mama alive; the doctors and nurses are, with man-made plastic tubes. In nature, Mama would've died four years ago, and I would've grieved four years ago, and by now I would have moved on. We fear death; Mother Earth prepares for death, expects death, recycles death into life. Nothing on Mother Earth is eternal, not even herself. Eventually, she will disintegrate too. Our search for immortality must upset an entity that thrives on rebirth.

We can't accept ageing, let alone death. We fight the inevitable; we fight our demise. Without those things, we would never know we had a pinnacle. We're fighting Mother Earth, we're fighting nature, we're fighting the gods we created. We are nature. We are fighting ourselves.

We think we're better than Mother Earth because we can control her, conquer her, milk her and destroy her. We created gods to justify our own superiority, which gave us excuses to fuck about with Mother Earth. We fenced her off, contained her, pillaged her, manipulated her, sold her, experimented with her, abused her and reshaped her to fit our own needs. Imelda was right, although I'll never tell her. We treat the Earth like we treat women: shape and contort it into a compliant, fixed ideal controlled by money for easier control. Mother Earth is as pissed off as any other woman, menopausal or not.

I'm heading for my extinction-level event with fear and loathing; instead, I need to ride the lava flow on a boogie board with my greying hair blowing in the wind.

Pleasure can only be fully appreciated after pain. We happily destroy stuff just for the euphoria of something new and better. I have to accept that. I can't avoid pain.

Humans have been playing God ever since Neanderthals made their first indecipherable marks on a cave wall. They created a space inside their brains to ask: what does it all mean? That space has been expanding ever since, creating a void that not everyone knows how to fill. Now, any indecipherable marks get framed and are too expensive to see up close. Our understanding of ourselves is hidden behind bulletproof glass with a grandiose explanation next to it written in Helvetica font.

Everything man-made is art. Neanderthals were like toddlers; banging rocks together, digging in the dirt, and making marks on the walls with bodily fluids. They threw the first stone at another human's head. The gods missed an opportunity to put us on the naughty step back then; we've been out of control ever since. The Bronze Age people were like six-year-old children; throwing stuff into the fire to see if it makes a cool noise and discovering how to create shiny decorative treasure, which of course they immediately melted down into weapons to throw at the cat or their siblings. When confidence and weaponry became too destructive, the children were forced to learn how to write, speak and draw in a civilised and pious manner. The Dark Ages were those encroaching teenage years; brooding, confusing, sometimes angry, but mainly sitting waist-high in your own dirt and mess. The Renaissance was the embedded teenager who finally does some revision, learns something they already knew, believes they're a genius and doesn't need to learn anymore. The Romantic Age was when we fell in love for the first time, sometimes with ourselves, and couldn't stop staring at the wonder of beauty, and obsessively craved all the most beautiful things in the world. The Industrial Age was that moment when you've just passed your driving test and you want things to move a lot quicker and noisier. The twentieth century was the twenty-something adult whose behaviour depended on drugs, fighting, more fighting, greed, power, fractured personalities, status, casual sex, money, more money and more stuff. And then there's the millennium, the post-postmodern midult; self-righteous and indignant about everybody else around them and once all their needs are fulfilled, they go back to hunting and sex. The only problem is that adulthood moves pretty fast. We take a long time to mature, so it will seem over before we've had time to appreciate it. If the World Wars were just petty bar fights, what the hell will our mid-life crises be like? It looks like we might be cut down before our prime. We will never find out how amazing we could have been.

We've been looking for utopia or enlightenment when really it should just be the maturity to hold on to something and maybe take up a hobby. Early humans died before finding any answers, so death became something sad rather than inevitable. Our collective grief has exponentially snowballed for millennia to the point where we can't let a single person die without finding the meaning of their life. We had to create the idea of an afterlife so that we could still exist long enough to find that meaning. While we still search for meaning, we will never stop fearing death.

Not believing in a god, not fearing death, didn't make me happier. If I don't fear death or gods, then I'm the same as those that don't fear the police; I will damage myself or others until caught. People got creative at filling that void with something else: drugs and alcohol for the personal fervour, parties for communal fervour, celebrities for the iconic worship, break up songs for the hymns, quotable movies for the prayers, Pilates for the kneeling, friendship bracelets for the rosary beads, monthly subscriptions for the donations, book clubs for bible studies, AITA for confession, social media for the inquisition and CCTV for the omnipresence.

Since the camera was invented artists were free to document their own feelings, now everyone has a camera to hand or a gift voucher at Hobbycraft there's an epidemic of people copying artists and hanging their feelings on every digital or plastered wall to be critiqued, liked, shared, somewhere, anywhere.

Everyone wants to be a fucking artist now because everyone wants to be celebrated, revered, or remembered after they die. Everyone desperately wants to continue to exist. Artists are on a personal journey; a genuine artist doesn't give a shit about sipping boxed wine and nodding heads of approval. A genuine artist just keeps looking for answers to their own questions, while the answers pile up on forgotten canvases in the corner of an untidy room. Heaven was imagined for such immortality to have a home, but artists replaced that with art galleries or Halls of Fame; anywhere guaranteed to be remembered, for at least "15 minutes" of anyone's time, anyway.

Priests and curators put a lot of criteria and obstacles in the way so we are reassured heaven and galleries aren't overcrowded with people we don't like. Both are nothing more than country clubs or nightclubs: a sanctuary away from dickheads you assumed were going to hell because they weren't wearing the same shoes as you.

My desperation to get away from death and pain and the people who cause it has actually made me lazy and boring. There is no place without trouble, and there shouldn't be. Trouble keeps my heart beating.

I don't want to go to heaven; it sounds boring. I'd like to come back and give life another go. Hopefully, after everyone has rebuilt civilisation of course. If you ask most people what they want to come back as if they can be reincarnated, it's usually an animal, rarely another human. And we think we're superior. Take the guns away; we're chicken shit.

I am really in charge of my destiny. I have full control of the wheel, yet somehow I still don't know how to drive properly. The world won't be at peace until we can all drive like chauffeurs.

I'm not scared of dying, but I fear watching my children die. They have nothing to look forward to, and they haven't even finished growing. I don't care if this body goes in the ground; it's just another car going in a landfill. I don't want their bodies going into the cold, damp ground. How can I continue to care for them down there? It's so cold, it goes against every maternal instinct. I don't want to watch my kids struggle, unless it's with food packaging because that's funny. I don't want to watch them die without getting the chance to learn something useful. What if there is a heaven and they spend their eternal days discussing who their favourite influencer is, their favourite zombie, their favourite armoured vehicle, or their favourite ice cream topping? They will get bored with staying children forever. I need to stop them from dying. I have to let them live.

I'm exhausted now. But lighter. An existential crisis is a good workout for the brain. Dark thoughts burn like calories. My priorities have been reorganised.

This room is suspiciously tidy. The boxes are gone, but so are some other things: the cushions, the Lego box, even the Venus of Willendorf has gone! Shit, we've been robbed! Sam said people would be on the scrounge; someone has come in and taken the lot. Amber and Peter are upstairs, oh my god! Anything could have happened. Why take the kids' toys? And the cushions? What else have they taken?

I can feel my eyeballs strain as my eyelids open very wide. I scramble to the kitchen like Scraps when he's got the zoomies. I head straight for the tea caddy… The few remaining teabags are still there. Phew! Another crack in the earth's crust would've appeared below my feet if that caddy had been robbed. I'm not sure I can scramble up the stairs like that, so I hope the kids are fine.

The kitchen cupboards are nearly empty; most of the food has gone except for the cake-baking ingredients. The fridge only has a small pint of milk and a few vegetables left. What kind of dumbass burglar steals cushions, ancient dildos and cheese but leaves the teabags? That would be the first thing I would go for if I were robbing a place!

I can hear Sam fumbling around with his keys at the front door. How am I going to explain all this? He's going to be mad; he's going to blame me for not food-sitting. I need to get some more tears ready; he'll avoid a confrontation if I look tearful.

Sam quickly shut the front door behind him and rushed to the kitchen. I hold my breath, waiting for him; my throat hurts at the prospect of giving him bad news.

'We've been robbed.'

He looks puzzled.

'Er…no…we haven't. I've just hidden some stuff with all the boxes… just in case. Can't be too careful.'

I let out a long, furious breath. He could have fucking said, left a note or something.

'Why would anyone want to steal our cushions?' I ask, pretending it doesn't bother me at all.

'Um…anything, they'll bargain for anything…we've got to store all our stuff away.'

Sam seems odd and slightly evasive. He doesn't have anywhere to hide that much stuff except at Imelda's or his mistress's!

'Is it all at your Mum's then?'

'Don't be stupid! I don't have the energy for a guilt trip every time I want to get anything.'

I can't argue with that.

'So where is it all?'

I'm not sure I want to hear the answer.

'Never you mind.'

I fucking hate that sentence; that's worse than "at my mistress' house"! He continues to empty what's left in the cupboards; I silently watch my ingredients get taken away. If he takes the kettle, I will stab him. He takes a jar of pickled eggs and the baking chocolate. Without those, I'll have nothing left to tempt him back. He is going to leave me. This is the plan: a stealthy breakup. He's going to run away with his mistress and take all the home comforts with him and leave me with four hungry kids!

Maybe she's pregnant. When I was pregnant, I would've happily eaten pickled eggs dipped in chocolate. Sam would get me whatever weird food I wanted, whenever I wanted it. He used to bring me snacks in the middle of the night when I was breastfeeding. She must be pregnant; that's why he's taking everything. He's got someone else to prop up with cushions. Even with that lumpy testicle, he's made yet another human! Just because he can still make babies doesn't mean he has to. I can't; I'm defunct. I'm just a brain now, housed in a dilapidated vehicle. My backseat is full of junk, not potential little babies. I'm not special anymore. I'm clearly not going to be put on the lifeboats first; I'm going to be left behind to fend for myself.

I definitely don't want anymore babies, and I'm the wisest I've ever been because I don't have a baby brain making me go doe-eyed at every cute face with oversized eyes anymore. The menopause should be emancipating, but if women are only seen as baby makers, then without a baby on their hip, they are seen as not contributing anymore. They're treated as heretics, witches that should be cast out with their black cats or at least burned. No one understands intelligent women with malfunctioning bodies. They don't appear in magazines or films or anywhere to be analysed and critiqued or normalised. It's disappointing to realise that your baseline personality is "fucking pissed off" and oestrogen is what made you more approachable. It should feel like I'm shedding a skin; the old skin is falling away and a bright, fresh face is revealed. I bet snakes wouldn't look so fresh-faced if they had to grapple with tweezers and marble-effect face rollers.

Only now can I fully realise how much of my personality was dictated by hormones. It's bad enough that it was dictated by genes, breastfeeding, pollution, climate, tight jeans, tinned food, TV, pylons, daylight, not bending with your knees and scented candles.

He's filling a bag for life with the stuff from the junk drawer. None of that stuff has been useful in the last twenty years.

I don't want him to leave me. I know I wanted to leave him, but things have seismically changed. I can't bring down a mammoth, pillagers, or the banking system. I didn't fall in love with him so he could do those things, but I know I need those qualities right now. Many women don't marry for love but grow to love their husbands. Am I doing it the wrong way round? I loved him so much once; can I do it again? I didn't think love was a priority in a catastrophe, but it seems to be.

I can work as hard as any man. I've got the stamina to survive a total of one hundred and seventy-five hours of labour pains. My strength is internal; it's not in my arms. It's inside my body, wrapped in a thick skin. I want things to be brought to me so that I can care for them. I'm protective like a house. I'm sturdy, and sturdy houses are better at withstanding a storm. There's no point in telling myself; I must tell Sam before he clears the last cupboard. There'll be nothing left.

My heart is racing. I want to ask him straight out, ask him for the truth so I can stop guessing. I know I should tell him how I'm feeling, but I can't; my blood pumps too hard, and I feel sick. I feel so weak, I will fall apart. He's so casual about it, he doesn't seem remotely bothered about taking all the things we need.

'What are we going to eat, Sam?'

That is all I'm brave enough to ask. Do my head and heart even communicate anymore?

'Just the fresh stuff in the fridge and the stuff in the freezer — let's finish it all up before there are any more blackouts. If you want anything, just ask me and I'll get it.'

He's lying. He must be. This isn't right. Can't he see how distraught I am? He grabs my hand.

'Trust me, Nell.'

He is actually touching me, and not in a get out of the way kind of touch. A pulse of energy went straight from his touch, through my hand, through my heart and straight to my groin. I'm not match fit, I might faint. I have him to myself; we are alone, awake and actually looking into each other's eyes. I'm enjoying the warmth of his hand; he's actually smiling at me. I haven't felt warmth ripple through my body like that since Zoe's nappy leaked on me at the zoo.

He lets go.

He's torturing me. He's being nice, so I don't notice he's clearly running away. Now I feel frozen. I don't know what to do. I'm stuck between a massive, teetering boulder and a soft, squidgy, sticky place. Either would be suffocating. I shakily put the kettle on. Sam winds up a new clockwork radio and gathers more bags for life from under the stairs. What do I do? I'm stuck. I've never had to fight for myself before.

He shouldn't have turned the radio on. In the last twelve hours, a series of large earthquakes erupted in different parts of the world: Los Angeles, Naples and Tokyo being the worst. Every tectonic plate is jittering cumulatively. The Earth's mantle has been weakened by the supervolcano in Yellowstone as it settles down in a deep depression. I know how it feels.

'Where's your mum?' I ask, trying really hard to look relaxed.

'She went home to make jam. I think she wanted to be alone after seeing Dad again. She was a bit shaken up.'

'I bet. It must have been horrible to see that big ogre of a man again. She must have been terrified.'

'Don't start! Not even I know what went on between them back then.'

'Aren't you a bit surprised at how small he was?'

'He was huge to me when I was four, and he got bigger with every story I was told since he left. At least she stuck around.'

'Stuck like effing glue.'

'Do you have to say something horrible about her every time she's not here?'

'Sorry, but she says something horrible to me every time she is here. My whole world exists under her constant, disapproving gaze.'

'She just cares about us.'

'No! She cares about you, Sam, and only you. She wants you all to herself. She never could bear the thought of you being in the company of another woman.'

'She worries about being abandoned. She doesn't want to end up in… in a—'

'What? A care home where I abandoned my mother?'

'I'm just saying it's her biggest fear. She doesn't like being on her own. She had to do it all on her own.'

'She wouldn't be on her own if she could say something nice to everyone instead of pointing out their faults.'

'She can't help it. I thought you would understand now. Mum went through what you're going through. She was worse.'

'Worse! What the fuck does that mean?'

'I mean, she changed; she became so angry at everyone in the whole universe. I thought it was because Dad had left, but I found out later she couldn't have more children because they removed all her… you know… bits. I actually did ruin her, apparently. She was young; she's had a long time to be bitter. And they didn't have those sticky patches to help; she had to grin and bear it. So did I.'

'Oh, I'm sorry. Was a full hysterectomy hard on you too?'

'I was a child. I didn't know what was going on. My mother went from being cuddly and kind to vicious and nasty overnight. To be honest, I've only realised exactly what it was since you've been going through it too.'

'She told me the menopause was a breeze, and I'm making a fuss about nothing.'

'She doesn't remember it the same; she's probably blocked a lot of it out. It's why I still put up with her; I've forgiven her.'

'That's big of you.'

Scraps bounds in from the garden, barking. He hates raised voices, unless it's Amber; he wouldn't dare bark at her. Sam shakes his head and storms off into the front room, slamming the door behind him.

Bastard. Clever old me picked our first moment alone to pick a fight. I will always fight until we settle our differences. Both of us want to win; both of us want to be right; both of us want acknowledgment. We're both living a clipped-wing existence. We have to sit down and talk it out; otherwise, we're both going to keep throwing grenades at each other.

So, Imelda didn't go through this as breezily as she claims. She probably had no idea what she went through. If nobody talks about it, then nobody knows what is going on. Although everyone talks about it now, so everyone thinks they have the symptoms too. This is going to change me. I am going to turn into a monster like her. I've been trying to sculpt my brain into something resembling sanity; hopefully, I won't turn into a monster unless there are monster traits already there to activate. The menopause feels like a roulette wheel, not knowing which unhinged day of your menstrual cycle you're going to land on when it's finished.

The radio claims the rivers of the American continent are flowing like liquid concrete. It sounds poetic, but it really is not.

The Golden Age

Sam pretends to take a nap on the sofa. Who is he fooling? Those aren't his normal sleeping noises. It does stop anyone from asking him for stuff though. I tried a nap once, but the kids and pets wouldn't let me; they would lick my face or eat my shoes before letting me sleep.

Tom stomps through the kitchen, avoiding eye contact. He stomps out into the garden and sits in the middle of the trampoline, facing the kitchen window. He wants to be seen sulking, except his expressions keep changing as he forgets why he's sulking and looks at the flies instead. I've forgotten if sulking is good or bad for children? I'm not sure if any two parenting experts agree on anything. I should check on Zoe, though; she's probably taped raisins to his bed again.

Zoe has turned her side of the bedroom into a hospital. She is treating every single toy she owns. Her large monkey has a plastic funnel over its mouth; her doll is bandaged head to toe in toilet paper, and Tom's transformer has a bendy straw coming out of its backside. Zoe has used all of Tom's t-shirts as blankets, making the bedroom look like a colourful army hospital. I think I know why Tom is sulking now. Zoe pulls the t-shirt blanket over Barbie's eyes.

'She didn't make it, Mummy.'

Looks like Zoe is the only one actually preparing herself for a global apocalypse. I slowly walk to my bedroom. I'm going to sulk and stare at my white ceiling again. Gigi has already claimed the bed for herself, but she will have to share as I curl up around her furry body. Are we all going to go the same way as Barbie? Existing requires so much effort. I bet the world would be better if humans purred like cats.

Zoe dramatically opens the bedroom door, carrying her enormous teddy bear. She throws it on top of me and Gigi. 'Can you look after Willow? She's poorly. She's got chicken spots. She needs one of your special cuddles. I'll be back for her when she's better.'

Willow is covered in small, round red dots that smell of lipstick. I only have one lipstick that Gaba bought me years ago. Looks like I don't have any now. Zoe shoves Willow around my back and wraps the teddy's arms around me. This is the best cuddle I've had in ages.

Amber walks into the bedroom like an overpaid supermodel. She checks if she has reached the accepted level of inappropriate clothing in my large mirror. I suppose I have been of little help in those areas, so she outsourced those skills to others, hoping eyeliner or a lacy thong will rescue her from disaster or boredom. Everybody wants to be the pale blue dot in a sea of beige.

Her skirt is so short I can see the gusset of her knickers. Her top is so tight I can see every seam and hook and eye fastener on her bra. She's driving as if she's got the roof down, probably so she can feel the fresh air rush over every pore of her skin. It's a shame so many men think they can jump in her car without being invited. It is glorious to feel the air reach every part of your body; why do we make it so difficult for girls to feel free? I shouldn't get all prudish now; I used to pull my skirt up and my top down, desperate for anyone to take a look and hope that I was fuckable.

Losing your virginity is like getting a new car; it's exciting. You want the best model; you think you're going to look cool; everyone tells you that you are going to look cool, and you can't wait to get started. The reality is everyone now thinks you're a show-off; it smells strange; you can't drive very fast for a while; and you're scared to touch any buttons.

'I'm going out; I dunno when I'll be back.'

'Where are you going, Amber?' I ask, not really wanting to know the details in case I have to disapprove of them.

'There's an end of the world party, an all-nighter; I won't be back till… well, whenever.'

'Well, I don't want you going to a party right now. It's dangerous out there. You're only—'

'I don't really care what you think. You can't stop me. I'm sixteen now; I can think for myself. You lot are miserable and boring. I need some fun. There's fun to be had at this party. I'm going. Just try to stop me.'

'At least tell me where it is.'

'I don't know yet.'

Amber storms off. She wants autonomy. She wants anarchy. She wants freedom. It's the first instinct of an adult brain. I should be proud. Our education system is supposed to squash those instincts; it's meant to make them diligent and hardworking. It's also meant to make them polite and smartly dressed. Amber's outfit is proof that Amber's needs are not being met. Our education system did not prepare anyone for anarchy.

The world we have created is not safe for girls; it never has been. She's cooped up. I'm not surprised she wants to escape. I do too.

For extra dramatisation, Amber slams the front door behind her on her way out. I dare not move in case I catch Willow's chicken spots or get my eyes gouged out by Gigi. A car speeds off outside with my morally experimental daughter inside. The slamming clearly didn't disturb Sam's pretend sleep downstairs. She left unchallenged. Zoe comes back into the bedroom.

'Is Amber going to be okay?'

'Yes, Zoe. She's technically a grown-up now.'

'I can't wait to be drone-up.'

'Really?'

'Yes, when I'm a drone up, I'm going to teach people how to draw cucumbers.'

Zoe has drawn two slices of cucumber on two pieces of badly cut-out paper. She tapes them over my eyes.

'There you go. You relax, Mummy. I'll put myself to bed.'

Tom stomped back upstairs because no one was watching him in the garden. He pokes his sullen face round the bedroom door.

'The rain makes the jumpoline sizzle.'

I lift one of my paper cucumber slices. Should I tell him it makes his hair frizz as well? I blow him a kiss; he smiles and goes to his room.

I didn't know it was raining. It should never have become acceptable to never leave your house.

Mary K Hollywood

Mass Extinction

It's early, early. The fine ash particles in the air are hurting my lungs. At least I've got hot flushes, a cat, a dog, and an oversized teddy bear to keep me warm. I don't care about their howling protestations; I need to pee.

The curtains are hiding a yellowy frost on the windowpane. The cold air is desperately trying to penetrate from outside, as if it too wanted to escape the slowly encroaching darkness. The newly formed spring buds didn't get a chance to open this year. At least no one has to worry about global warming anymore.

My brain needs a rest. I can't put it in a splint. I can't take the weight off it. My brain is limping; it will heal out of shape and make out of shape thoughts. I can't think straight with a limp. No one goes through life without a physical injury, so no one should expect to get through life without a mental injury now and then. My leg isn't broken, but it feels numb. Scraps must have cut off the blood supply all night. I'm walking like a drunk; I hope I make it to the toilet before I pee myself.

I'm scared to peel the paper cucumber slices off my eyes in case the tape takes a few eyebrow hairs with it. I can see in the bathroom mirror they did nothing for my dark, baggy eyes.

Amber's door is ajar. I hope she returned home alive… I can tell by the two feet of giant hairy legs sticking out from under the Korean boy band duvet set that Sam eventually found a place to sleep last night. I smile for a moment and then stagger down the stairs.

Amber is barely alive, sitting at the kitchen table with her catatonic head stuck to the tabletop with what looks like vomit. Her arms are drooping towards the floor. Gigi hides under her chair, licking the vomit. The smell of cold sick is vile and an unwelcome reminder of the hint of sulphur as the two noxious fumes mingle together.

There's a despondent knock at the front door. I answer it as slowly as I can. I'm less enthusiastic about visitors than I ever have been before.

It's Gaba. She looks as if she has had no sleep. Her eyes have dark rings around them too; her cheeks are puffy.

'What the hell happened to you?'

'I've got no internet. My landlord has switched off the heating. I don't know where to go. Any chance I could have a shower?'

'Sure, you know where it is, but don't touch my anti-ageing shampoo!'

Gaba slowly walks up the stairs, clutching the bannister rail as if she's on a ship in a storm. Scraps runs after her, barking furiously. Amber somehow disappeared, leaving a perfect cast of her screwed-up face in the dry vomit. I suppose it's my responsibility to clean this up. If it didn't smell so much, I would frame it.

Nothing appears to be working. The internet, the heating, the electricity, even the water pressure is low. I hope Gaba doesn't mind a cold, dribbly shower; it might actually help her. I can boil a saucepan of water with the camping stove Sam left here. I might even use a whole teabag for myself while no one's looking. The silence provides time to think; there's a lot to think about.

I could see this as another opportunity to lose weight, but I will probably waste it making stupid amounts of cake and cookies. I doubt there's much salad in an apocalyptic world, and I'll need cake energy to help fight the pillagers. I don't want to contemplate not being able to have cake without a cup of tea.

My phone isn't working, so I have no idea how far away the apocalypse is now. The clockwork radio informs me, though. Why did I wind it up?

Yellowstone is just billowing smoke now, like it's puffing on a large cigarette after two weeks of tantric sex. The first flotilla of boats with more American and Canadian refugees is due in British ports any day now. There were reports of people being thrown overboard and many mutinies as soon as the food ran out. No one has any idea how many will get here. The UK is gripped by food shortages. The warehouses can't be restocked because of the no-fly zones and all the cargo ships being used to transport refugees. Apocalypse preppers are being hunted down like a Pokémon challenge. This is worse than lockdown. This time we can leave our homes but go nowhere, buy nothing and not even ridicule a celebrity-laden song; it's all been so fast.

Mama would have loved a situation like this; she would have seen it as an opportunity to do something new and exciting. She would have had the kids performing a show on the sofa: a re-enactment of the Tambora volcano eruption in a Victorian workhouse scenario with full costumes made from tea towels and old coats.

Sam comes down the stairs, rubbing his head. I would've liked to have seen how Amber turfed him out of her bed.

'Turn the radio up, Nell.'

'Do we have to?'

I like him scruffy; he looks more like a warrior. I might make him some pretend armour out of cardboard, like I did for Peter when he was little.

Campi Flegrei, the supervolcano in Italy, has erupted. That's not far from here. A couple of other supervolcanoes have erupted in the last fourteen hours. That's why the air is so thick; I thought it tasted different. Massive earthquakes have been recorded in many locations along the Pacific rim, causing tsunamis, with one heading straight for the earthquake-hit Tokyo. The world has cracked like an overboiled egg. My body aches just thinking about it. Billions dead. That's a lot. This is an extinction-level event. Shit. The emergency services are buried under the same rubble. Zoe appears in the doorway in her Highland cow onesie.

'Mummy, why is Gaba sleeping on your bed?'

'She was very tired last night, sweetie. Let her sleep.'

'Oh, she was awake when I woke her up!'

There are reports of ballistic missiles causing explosions over disputed territories all over the world; every grudge match is being played out while so many are distracted. There aren't enough correspondents in the world to communicate all the bad news. Sam stands completely still next to me in the kitchen; neither of us has rehearsed the next move.

Dada bursts through the front door, carrying a big bundle wrapped in a thick blanket. He carefully places the bundle on the kitchen table and unwraps the blanket to reveal a pile of shotguns and pistols.

He lines them up in order. 'I thought you'd like this one, Sam; got a bit of weight behind it. It's a bit old-school, but I've cleaned it up. It won't injure the shooter anymore. You do know how to use a gun, don't you, Sam?'

'I don't know. It didn't come up in my City and Guilds training,' says Sam.

Sam gingerly takes the old rifle without taking his eyes off Dada.

'This one is perfect for you, sweetheart, small and light. You remember how to shoot, don't you? You remember what you've been taught, don't you?'

Dada hands me a small pistol with sectionable fervour. I was thirteen the last time I held a gun. It was an open day at the barracks. I only remember the gorgeous soldier standing over my shoulder with his hands on mine.

'I don't remember how to use a gun, Dada.'

'Right, I'll show you again. It's very easy. Come here.'

Dada grabs my arm hard. He stands behind me, puts the pistol in my hand and holds it tight. I'd forgotten how strong he is. I can feel the cold sweat on his hand. He helps me aim towards the back door. Sam is still standing, holding his rifle incorrectly. He puts his gun down on the table.

'I don't need a weapon; I am a weapon,' says Sam.

Yep, I'm making him some armour. I think a Viking-esque leather skirt, or whatever that's called. I don't have the internet to find out, but I can improvise.

'Yes, you're big, we know, Sam. But you're still made of flesh, and bullets coming from a tiny man will still kill you, and then your bigness just makes it harder for us to bury you,' Dada replies.

'What happens when you run out of bullets, Bill? Everything that is man made isn't being made by men right now, in case you haven't noticed.'

'I've got plenty of bullets, Sam, don't worry.'

'That's a question for another day. Right now, we need core strength.'

'Not sure there's a lot of that in that enormous body of yours either. What we need is a plan, a strategy, a line of defence, anything! Civilisation is on the brink.'

'Guns emasculated men. I'm not scared, Bill. Are you?'

'Not scared, prepared.'

'Prepared for what? Armed robbery? A shootout at the O.K. Corral? This is Britain, the only people with guns are farmers, drug dealers and, obviously, former fighter pilots. Unless you're going to hijack a cow, snort a shedload of cocaine or attend one of your reunion lunches, you won't need guns.'

Dada flew Sea Harriers in the Falklands War, and he has inherited trauma from Grandpa, who fought in both World Wars. That pent-up energy has to be released somehow. Dada turns to look up at Sam, leaving me to practice my aim.

'What will I need then, Big Sam? I can't grow another six inches before the anarchists start walking down the street.'

'Anarchists?! They're too busy dyeing their hair and getting their platform boots on; you've got time to do cartwheels to get away from them.'

Zoe comes running into the kitchen and stops dead in her tracks.

'Who's Mummy shooting at, Dada?'

'It's okay, Zoe, Mummy isn't shooting at anyone yet; she's just practising.'

'Is Mummy going to be a baddie? I don't want my mummy to be a baddie.'

'Mummy's not a baddie, but she needs to stop baddies coming into the house.'

'What baddies? Why are they coming here? Daddy, you said there are only baddies on TV. I need a gun. Can I have a gun?'

'Wouldn't hurt, Sam.'

'What! Bill, she's four! She's not having a gun!'

'I want one! I don't want to be killed by baddies. Give me a gun, pleeeeeeease Daddy!'

'No way, no guns. She nearly castrated me with a tin opener once; she's not having a gun!'

'But, Daddy, please!'

I drop my aiming arm and place the gun on the table. I rummage through the bags for life on the table and bring out Tom's Nerf gun.

'Here, Zoe, you can use this.'

I look at Zoe calmly, then switch quickly to stare at Dada incredulously.

'But this is Tom's, Mummy. I'm not allowed to touch his stuff.'

'He's got another. This is yours now. See if you can find all the pellets.'

Zoe's eyes widen as she holds the Nerf gun with both hands.

I stare Zoe straight in the eye. 'Right, some ground rules.'

'Show me the writing, Mummy! Show me where the rules are written!'

'You can't read yet, Zoe. When you can read, I'll show you the rulebook.'

She'll never remember. Zoe runs off looking for pellets. Now I look Dada straight in the eyes to make sure he's looking at me.

'Dada, no guns for the kids. Put these away for now. The anarchists haven't arrived yet.'

'You two can't bury your heads in the sand this time. You both have to face up to reality soon. This is the start of a new world.'

'What have you got left to protect yourself with, Bill?'

'Oh, don't worry about me, Sam. I've got loads more at home.'

Sam looks a little surprised. I do not. Dada wraps the guns and knives back up and rummages through the bags for life on the kitchen table.

'What is all this stuff, Nell?'

'Let's see: snorkels, buckets, spades, wellies, sun hats, woolly hats, waterproof ponchos, towelling ponchos, inflatable animals, inflatable armbands, a pop up chair, a pop up tent, an inflatable boogie board, fishing nets, a frisbee, kites, umbrellas, poo bags, plastic cups, plastic plates, a miniature plastic salt and pepper set and a plastic bag filled with other plastic bags. I've only been prepping for rainy afternoons in the garden, Dada, not the destruction of the civilised world.'

I hand Dada a huge – I mean often used as a laundry bag huge – empty bag for life.

'I never thought I'd be storing weapons in these unless it was cardboard swords or water pistols.'

Dada puts the weaponry and ammunition into the bag and carefully places them under the stairs.

Sam looks perplexed. 'Out of all of us, I didn't know you feared death the most, Bill.'

'I don't fear death, Sam! I only fear the method of death. I'm not dying because some arrogant world leader made a calculated poor decision or because some addict couldn't get a sugar fix! I will defend myself and my family against every dick for brains that heads this way. Will you?'

'Well, yeah, but not with a rusty old gun. I don't want to kill anyone, or I'll become the same as them. I'll defend. I'll protect, just in my way.'

'That's your problem, Sam. You do everything your own way, a way that no one knows or understands. This is war now. This isn't just food shortages or blackouts; this is death and destruction on a global scale. It's started. It's bloody started!'

Dada looks feverish now. The electricity comes back on. Sam and Dada rush to the front room and turn the TV on.

'Muuuuuuuuuuuuuummmmmmmmmmmm!'

Tom runs like a demented ferret downstairs. I get to the bottom quickly enough to pick him up mid-fall off the last three steps. I carry him into the front room.

'Wh…wh…wh…where's…where's…my…superhero deluxe figurine set? Someone has stolen it, and…my…box of string?'

I look at Sam, who won't look me in the eye.

'I've just hidden a few things, safekeeping, you know.'

'No, I don't know. I haven't got a clue. Why are you taking all our stuff? Tell me!'

'You wouldn't understand!'

He's selling it, he's hiding it, he's giving it to his mistress's children because they're better behaved. A superhero figurine has no bargaining power in a food crisis. It must be for her.

All I can do is stare at the back of his head. I know he can feel it. It usually works. Luckily for him, Tom is distracted by Zoe playing with his confiscated Nerf gun. Why does he have to be in control of my emotions? Why can't I fully hate him? I need to calm myself down before I say anything that will make things worse.

Garden of Eden

I've watched too much disaster porn on TV. I don't want to turn away in case I miss something, but I don't want these images in my memory bank either. Gaba descends downstairs wearing my only going-out outfit and covered in thick makeup. It needs to be thick enough to compete with the filters she uses on her phone. She won't let anyone see her without her "face" on. She's trying to smooth out her wrinkles and dents to show her essence; like a Brancusi sculpture rather than her grim reality, which is more like a Halloween mask. Twentieth-century artists were very good at getting people to "look over here" while performing a magic trick beyond most people's comprehension with their other hand.

I put on my best poker face every hour; it's the same thing. There are multiple ways to hide our insecurities and the dents. The car loses value once it has a mark. Although there's not enough foundation in the world to stop her walking into doorframes and falling over her own feet when she moves her head too quickly. Gaba is more interesting to know than the facade is to look at. Our best times were pyjama nights with every dent and wrinkle on show. She is fun to drive when no one else is looking.

'Didn't think you'd mind if I borrowed your dress, Nell, seeing as you're never going to wear it. Seems a shame to waste these sequins. Thanks for letting me rest. I feel great. Got any food. I'm starving?'

Gaba sprays herself with an excessive amount of perfume all over her body and under her dress; desperate to make herself appear better than she already is. I don't use my looks to get anything because what I need doesn't need an infantilised man to get it for me. The prospect of losing her looks generates more fear in Gaba than in me. I only fear one man not finding me attractive. She fears them all.

Imelda has brought round her newly made jam, made from all the frozen fruit she stores over winter that has been forced to defrost. She has also brought round all the cupcakes I have ever given her in the past, which are now defrosting on the coffee table. I get soggy garlic bread, melted ice cream and peas to add to the impromptu feast. I don't need another mouth to feed, but it looks like I've got one. Sam watches Gaba eat the last cheese string with increasing incredulity. I watch everyone else pull a disgusted face when they try Imelda's jam.

Peter and a cleaner Amber succumb to the smell of food and sit on the sofa. We're all sitting in the room together. Everyone's combined body heat warms the room up a little. Their dragon breath looks yellowy to match the frost on the inside of the windows. The heating has come back on, but in the time it will take to heat the house, the power will probably go off again. Dada has his old military coat on with his floor-length scarf that Mama knitted him twenty years ago. Imelda has her mittens and winter hat on – the mittens make it very awkward to eat cupcakes covered with jam. Gaba seems agitated and keeps scratching at the frost on the window like a crack addict waiting for their dealer.

Sam turns up the volume on the TV. There's shaky footage of a group of people in blue overalls inside a minibus being escorted by the army through an angry mob who are hurling abuse and stones at them. They're outside the Eden Project gift shop in Cornwall. A reporter shouts at the camera, trying to explain what is going on, but it makes little sense.

Tom looks confused. 'Where are those people going?'

'I think they are going to climb trees or go jungling,' says Zoe.

She's not far off; apparently, they're going to live inside the biomes to see if they can survive this encroaching apocalypse.

'Can we go, Mum? I liked the Eden Project.'

'I didn't, Tom. It was too hot; I thought I was going through the whole menopause in one afternoon.'

'Is the menopause exotic, Mum?'

'Not even close. The menopause is like a slow-motion, low-budget, amateur dramatic death scene.'

There are more soldiers protecting the volunteers' passage through the protesters than there were at the supermarket. The government just stated that it hopes things will calm down soon and that this experiment won't be necessary. We've left it until now to experiment with human survivability? It's probably a good job my anti-depressants are going to run out soon, then I can react to this appropriately. It looks like a select few have been sent to paradise, but everyone else has been condemned to hell. I'm not sure if I'm bothered about not being invited. I wouldn't want a long demise with strangers; I think I'd rather have a quick exit. When the going gets tough, the tough step over the self-destructive.

Apparently, ten couples of childbearing age volunteered to test the possibility of riding out apocalyptic events. While everyone else struggles with freezing temperatures and food shortages, they will learn how to grow crops and food under UV lighting. The government is trying to deny a cover-up. The real pearly gates better equip St Peter with riot gear and tear gas. They're young; they will have to be if they're going to re-populate the next generation. Their heads are down, and they don't seem happy at being saved. I suppose they had to say goodbye to many family and friends.

Amber looks pissed. 'Who chose them? What makes them so special? It's not fair. They're not the prettiest, are they? That one's a right minger! If they're gonna create the next generation of humans, they could've at least picked some pretty ones.'

'A bunch of supermodels wouldn't survive five minutes in there, Amber,' Sam grumbled.

'What do they win, Dad?'

'The chance to recreate civilisation.'

Other governments had secret plans in similar biomes. Apparently, the governments wanted to keep this entire operation secret and their identities anonymous to protect them. They claim the volunteers were picked randomly by an AI computer and given twenty-four hours' notice. Some pairs of animals were selected to enter the biomes as well, but only small animals can be catered for: there's no room for goats or cows. Roast rabbit and duck will be on the menu, but no witchetty grubs. Not exactly a hardship.

Without the internet, Peter can only create his own conspiracy theories; he believes there are extensive tunnels underneath the biomes, built in secret in case of an apocalyptic event. He reckons they are stocked with enough food for ten years. In this age of misinformation, liars and the imaginative thrive.

'We haven't got enough food for the weekend, let alone two years,' I say while bingeing on a catering-size packet of raisins.

'People react to something stupid with more gusto than something clever,' says Sam. He's desperately trying to open a single packet of ketchup, which bursts open over his hands, making him lick his hands clean.

They selected key skilled people; a doctor, a nurse, a midwife, a soldier, a gardener, a farmer, a chemist, a biologist, a physicist, an engineer, a comedian, a maths teacher, a carpenter, a cook, a plumber, a dentist, an optician, a team builder, a yoga instructor and a therapist. AI found ten couples where both the husband and wife had one of these skills. There was no place for politicians, criminals, spiritual leaders, athletes, or pop stars. The king refused a ticket; he prefers to go down with the ship. Although everyone knows his heirs have been sent to a secret location. The list of offended subgroups is growing by the minute. Anyone who wants to be different can't be different in such a small sample of humanity; they have to be obedient, not overdramatic, and without previous physical injuries in order to survive each other.

'If only they needed a cupcake baker, then you could have gone, Nellie! Twenty years ago, a teacher and an engineer might have had a chance,' says Imelda.

Imelda can be such a bitch sometimes. I taught a cover physics lesson once; the kids had to explain the lesson plan to me. I would not want to be responsible for saving civilisation.

Dada shakes his head. 'I can see why they didn't knock on our door. We've got a guerrilla yarn bomber, a fighter pilot with no plane, an ageing tart, a couple of teenage delinquents and a… what is it you do again, Sam?'

Nobody is really sure exactly what Sam does for a living. He works in a factory, but what he does in that big metal box is anyone's guess. He never talks about work, and nobody asks him how his day was. He could be the cleaner, a forklift truck driver, a security guard, or he might just hold up the girders. He's not answering.

'Told you AI would take over the world, didn't I, Mum?'

'Pete, unless AI can design a vacuum cleaner that does the stairs, cobwebs, and the toaster, then it shouldn't decide who could survive eating tins of cold beans.'

'I'm glad I'm not in there then; I hate baked beans,' he replied.

Sam shakes his head even more. Is he realising that the rations that he purportedly found won't satisfy this bunch of fussy eaters? There are only three meals that they all enjoy. Is it too late to tell him what they are?

'You lot will have to eat your vegetables once we've run out of beige food,' says Dada.

'I don't eat beige. I eat cucumbers!' Tom replies.

'That's great, but we might be running out of cucumbers as well; they don't keep so well.'

'Tell me you're joking?' says Tom. Finally, a little bit of trepidation is creeping in.

'I'm not joking. You need skills to survive, just like the reporter said. What skills have you lot got?'

Tom raises his hand. 'I can start a fire, Dada. We did it at forest school.'

'Good lad! Well, that's something.'

'What the fuck is forest school?' Amber asks, 'We never had that. I'd have got excluded for starting a fire when I was at primary school!'

'I can make a bow and arrow, Dada.'

'Really, Zoe? That might actually be helpful. How do you make them?'

'You buy them from the toy shop.'

'What are we going to shoot an arrow at anyway? There are no wild bears round here,' Amber moans.

'If you looked up from your phone just now and then, you'd see rabbits, pheasants, deer. There's plenty for now,' Dada explains.

I'm not shooting, skinning or gutting a fucking deer! Dada made me do a rabbit once, and I was violently ill and nearly made me vegetarian. I like my meat sealed in clingfilm.

That group won't save humanity without a creative mind, someone who can think outside the box, someone who can problem-solve, multitask, and create something from nothing. Someone who can bottle up decades' worth of rage without suffocating. They're all the same age; there is no one older to teach them how to drink tea through a hosepipe. It's crazy to think that Gen X could have been peak civilisation; we were the last age group to deal with boredom. We squandered our training experimenting with couscous.

Imelda looks over-concerned. 'I think they should have picked a few more gardeners to look after that place; it'll get overgrown; they'll get greenfly.'

Amber looks pissed off. 'I think they should've picked celebrities, put some cameras in there so we could watch them survive for real.'

'God help humanity if it was descended from celebrities,' I laugh.

'You like celebrities, Mum. You've got that picture of Keanu Reeves in your bedside drawer. Don't pretend you're not interested in their lives as well,' says Amber.

I'm not taking this on my own. 'Imelda has a picture of Alan Titchmarsh in her potting shed, Sam has a picture of Rachel Riley in his wallet, and Dada has a picture of a Spitfire in his. Everyone has a fantasy.'

I'm not apologising for mine. Happy thoughts keep you healthy; I have to get them from somewhere. If I can't get joy in reality, then my imagination is where it will thrive. It's cheaper than pills.

'Anyway, Keanu Reeves is a universal donor to celebrity fantasies; he's like O-negative blood, everyone likes him.' I think I'm over-explaining my predicament.

Sam takes out his wallet and places a pound coin on the coffee table. 'It's time for our annual family sweepstake; who out of that lot is going to die first? My money is on the maths teacher.'

'I'm in!' Gaba says. She over-excitedly rummages around in my clutch bag and pulls out a pair of surgical gloves wrapped in a tight ball. She places them on the table. 'Who needs an optician? They're going to want to be blurry-eyed after a couple of years looking at each other!'

Imelda checks her pockets and retrieves a tiny rolled-up ball of discarded wool, which she places on the pile. 'The comedian will be first. I've seen him on telly; he's rubbish.'

Dada gets out his wallet and puts down ten ten-pence pieces in a neat pile. 'I know the soldier will be the last one standing.'

Amber puts her hand down the side of the sofa cushions and finds a twenty-pence piece. 'The blonde one is gonna leave first, in a black bag.'

Peter rummages in his pockets and brings out a half-used packet of chewing gum. 'The guy with the designer beard, he likes comfort too much.'

Tom places a piece of string from his pocket on the table. 'I hope they all survive and live happily ever after.'

Zoe places a Nerf pellet on the table. 'I think Santa lives on the moon.'

Everyone looks at me. I rummage around in my night bra and pull out a single teabag, which I place on the pile. 'I think we should clear out Dada's greenhouse.'

Everyone stops smiling and starts contemplating. Everyone knows the greenhouse is not big enough for all of us.

Tom looks at me seriously. 'Mum, are we going to die? Are we going to be eaten by crocodiles?'

'We don't have crocodiles in this country, sweetie.'

'Are we going to be eaten by cats and dogs then?'

'No… cats and dogs wouldn't eat us.'

'They would if we ran out of their food. Have you got enough cat and dog food, Mum?'

I don't know how to answer that. Enough for how long?

'Yes, I've got plenty, Tom. Don't worry. This is a lot of fuss about nothing; you'll see. This will all blow over in a couple of weeks, and that lot will walk out all sheepishly with nothing but a place on Strictly.'

It's all going a bit *Chicken Licken* in here. This is my strength; appearing fearless when inside I'm bricking it. It might actually be useful now.

The electricity goes off again; the TV dies.

Amber sucks all the air out of her face. 'I'm not sticking around here with you lot of saddos. If it is the end of the world, then I'm going to drink, dance and party the night away. I don't want to end it stuck in here watching a broken telly!'

Amber stomps up the stairs, hitting every step as hard as she can to emphasise how sad she thinks everyone is. Everyone's apparent lack of excitement could damage those loose floorboards.

She doesn't want to miss out on what everyone else is doing. She doesn't want to get trolled or cancelled just because she didn't turn up, nod her head in agreement and make everyone else feel supported in their ritualistic pursuit of social acceptance by arbitrary rules. I wonder if she'd let me come.

Gaba presses her face up against the frosty window, looking eagerly outside for excitement too. 'I would rather die than survive this.'

'Why wouldn't you want to survive, Gaba?' Sam asks. There was a hint of "Let me help you with that," about him.

'I don't want to live in a post-apocalyptic world, Sam. Everyone is miserable and scrounging around for food. Doesn't sound like fun to me.'

'But death? That really is the end… there's no hope…there's no chance to enjoy anything anymore if you're dead…at least if you survive there's a chance of another party at some point.'

'My needs are met. I make sure of that every day.'

'Your needs are selfish and easy; of course you met them.'

'Could've been hit by a bus on any of the last eighteen thousand days, Sam. At least I'll die with a smile on my face.'

'Don't try to fool us into thinking you've been having the time of your life. You're lonely, hungry and scared, otherwise you wouldn't be here.'

'I don't have to explain myself to you, Sam.'

'I don't need your explanation; I can work it out for myself.'

Amber comes back downstairs with two coats on.

Sam shakes his head. 'And where are you going?'

'Don't pretend you care, Dad!'

Amber storms out of the door with Gaba eagerly scuttling after her. 'I'll go after her. I'll be the responsible adult, don't worry. Wait for me, Amber!'

Someone's rechargeable vibrators aren't working. Gaba has left her surgical gloves on the table. I can imagine the panic attack when she's confronted with a room of disillusioned heterosexual teenage boys whose highlight of the evening is brushing their fingers past her crotch. She hasn't touched a real human man since she was twenty-two. At university, I contemplated embroidering a tent with all the people Gaba had slept with up until that point, just like Tracey Emin did, but I realised I would have needed an industrial-sized marquee, even back then.

She used to call a one-night stand "flamboyant wanking". There is no Alka-Seltzer for the sexual hangover, only a long shower and more alcohol to blot it out of her memory. If the internet hadn't been invented at about the same time as the gonorrhoea incident, I think she would be in a nunnery or an asylum by now.

I should intervene, but my energy levels aren't responding.

I'm less worried about Amber. I know she has the strength to crush any teenage boy's fingers. Amber won't let herself be demeaned.

'Should we go after them, Sam?'

He's looking at me coldly, 'Not unless you're looking for debauchery as well.'

I'm convinced nobody my age has sex anymore unless they're a newspaper columnist.

Tom looks confused. 'Mum, does anarchy mean we can do whatever we want?'

'Sort of. What do you want, Tom?'

'Food and my own rules.'

'Okay, any food you hunt down yourself, you can control how much of it you want to eat.'

'Okay, and I want to go to bed when I want.'

'Okay, there's no school anymore, but you have to be really quiet all night because you know how angry adults get if we don't get our sleep.'

'Okay.'

'And if you're going to be in control, then make sure you tidy up after yourselves because I'll be doing nothing as well.'

'Well, there's no need for—'

'And while we're at it, your sworn enemy can take all your toys because he's bigger than you.'

'That's not fair!'

'Anarchy isn't fair; it's about being the biggest and most aggressive.'

'But James Parker wouldn't take my toys.'

'How do you know?'

'Anyway, our daddy is bigger than everyone on the planet, so we can keep our toys.'

'But you're in control now, so Daddy doesn't have to come to your rescue. Anarchy has no rules and weird costumes.'

'I don't like anarchy anymore.'

The electricity comes back on again, so does the TV. The angry mob has broken into the Eden Project. The maths teacher lies motionless on the floor. Sam sweeps his useless hoard into his hand and smiles to himself. He threw the teabag back at me. It hit me in the face. I'm fuming and aroused. When will my body and mind ever line up?

Sam smiles at Tom. 'You see, Tom, with anarchy you can't protect against pricks with guns or bigger muscles; that's why endangered animals have to be put in pens and artificially inseminated to keep their species alive.'

'I hope that lot packed some test tubes then, Sam.'

'Or long rubber gloves!' He laughs.

We're both laughing. At the same time. At the same thing. The planets have just aligned. I need to blow on these glowing embers.

Evolution

The ceiling looks different this morning; there's a faint hint of a cola-spray stain. I'm tempted to stick something on it with a broom handle — a picture of Keanu, a picture of Sam laughing, a picture of the kids?

The skies are getting darker and colder more quickly now that the debris from the other supervolcanoes is mingling in the stratosphere. It feels like twilight before a snowstorm in midwinter all the time. The clouds look like they're all going in different directions, trying to get somewhere else fast. The clockwork radio claimed yesterday that other volcanoes in Indonesia keep erupting – they've stopped counting how many. Numbers don't seem to register anymore.

I worry about Amber and her anarchic aspirations, Sam's lumpy testicles, Peter's paranoia, Imelda's awful jam, Gaba's immune system, Dada weaponising the kids, Nigel's distance, Mama's deterioration, Wilfred's catch up Christmas list, Tom's missing toys and Zoe's obliviousness to the impending doom that will arrive at our door sooner or later.

Maybe the doctors were wrong about Sam's testicle. They didn't diagnose my perimenopause until I'd been tested for rheumatoid arthritis, fibromyalgia, multiple sclerosis, dementia, endometriosis, anxiety, heart disease, and liver failure. He could be dying. Shit.

I'm not sleeping much; I can't rest. I have too many thoughts in this head; I can't process them properly when I'm awake. I've got pre-traumatic stress disorder. It's not a vicious circle; it's a merciless spiral trying to pull me in. Do I panic? I don't feel panicky. This is what lots of suicidal thoughts train you for: the real life or death moments. It's like I've been training for a crisis my whole life. I can resist the temptation to fall into the abyss now. I can walk past, have a little look, and head straight for the gift shop.

Tom and Peter came into the room to turn the TV on. I've just realised I fell asleep on the sofa again. The electricity must have come on briefly. The boys sat on the floor as close to the TV as they could get, flicking through all the channels trying to find more gory details.

'I didn't give birth to you lot just so you could sit and watch TV!'

'But you knew it was coming, didn't you, Mum?'

Tom is practising at being a smart arse. I think they're suffering from omnipresent withdrawal syndrome. It will take more than a bit of ash and worldwide starvation to humble our God complex.

The Pacific Ring is literally on fire; the emergency news broadcasts have lost count of all the earthquakes and tsunamis. We're into hundreds of millions more dead; hundreds of millions more are missing. There are billions starving and without clean water. I have no idea how my despair fits into this. Am I lucky to have a few bottles of mineral water hidden under the stairs among the windbreaks and guns? I actually am; their value has rocketed; pound for pound more expensive than gold. I don't really want to see the news, but I need to know when I need to really panic. There's no one to take your cues from anymore. No gods are responding to anyone's prayers; governments are scattered. Even the council won't return a single call. Dada wants to arm everyone for a shootout; Mama doesn't even know this is happening. I wish I could be like Zoe: happily playing on the floor with a couple of empty crisp packets and a handful of rusty clothes pegs. She attached the clothes pegs to the crisp packets, turning them into horses.

Sam steps through the front door quietly, hoping no one notices he has been out all night again. I'm not going to question him; I don't know if I care anymore. I can't even look authoritative in front of a four-year-old. I've lost my power. Zoe will never know what I was capable of.

There are massive protests in Parliament Square demanding action, food, and a promise to protect the British people. But there's still no statement from the Prime Minister – nobody seems to know where he is.

Zoe writes her name on her arm. 'Why don't they make everyone share everything like you make me and Tom do, Mummy?'

'Because, like you and Tom, most people won't share even when told to. Even if it's the most obvious and sensible thing to do. Anyway, why are you writing your name on your arm?'

'To check I'm the right person.'

It would seem the only people enjoying this global disaster are a company called PopUpEden. They somehow created a pop-up biosphere complete with plants and insects to help support a family of four throughout this difficult period. The company only asks for payment in water.

Sam pokes his head round the door. 'Harvey got one of those. It's only a tent, a packet of seeds and some mealworms; someone's always got time to con someone else.'

The TV dies again, and all the lights do too. There's an eerie silence throughout the entire street. I used to love being reminded of life before fridges, but this time I can't really enjoy it. Every time this happens, it could be the start of it.

I manage to get Sam's attention. 'It's so cold now; we need more jumpers and blankets. Where is all our stuff? We need the cushions! I can't make this place look homely without scatter cushions!'

'It's safe, that's all you need to know,' says Sam, more firmly than I would like.

'I need to know; I have to know; not knowing is killing me.'

'Not now, Nell. One crisis at a time, please.'

'When then? We've got little food, little comfort, no Amber, no plan, what are we going to do?'

'Please trust me; when the time's right, I'll tell you everything. I need to go out again. I'll see you later.'

Sam leaves again. How did I get to this stage in my life, having no one reliable to turn to? They have me. They rely on me to cook, clean, wash, buy, sort, tidy, find, get, remember, organise, play, fight, decide, order, pick up, create, throw out, bargain, plead, beg and deny everything they do in their own lives. I'm the one they rely on, and I haven't got a clue.

Scraps bounds into the room and puts his slobbery face on my lap. I can't stop the apocalypse, I can't stop the army, I can't stop the anarchists, I can't stop my immediate family. Why don't I sort my buttons out? That always helps me calm down.

I can't find my button boxes. They, and most of the bags for life, are not under the stairs anymore. Where are they? I only leave them in one place. Nobody else touches my buttons. What the fuck has he done with my buttons? If he's swapped them for a bunch of bananas, I will finally kill him. He knows I'll go fucking crazy if I don't have my buttons. He knows how much they mean to me. Why would he hurt me so much? He's punishing me. He actually hates me. He wants me to be in pain. I would rather he hit me, then I would have a bruise to show everyone, but the bruises are all on the inside. They still hurt. I don't understand what's going on. I'm going to go crazy if I can't find my buttons, but they're not anywhere. My blood is boiling, my heart is racing, and my head is hurting. I need to sit down before I fall over.

I've forgotten what a woman is supposed to do in this situation. Time to lift some mental weights again; get my sketchpad. If my mind is strong, then it can carry the weight of opinion, the forces of negativity, and the burden of responsibility. How do I lift mental weights? It sounds clever, but it means nothing. I am trained to lift mental weights; it's all I've ever done.

Start by doodling on a page, start with my circle. See where I take it this time. I'm in the perfect frame of mind for great art: we've got mystery, revelation, risk, and emotional danger. My brain is like a Petri dish, most hospitable to the germ of an idea.

There was a time when I couldn't draw a circle; it was always bent out of shape. I've had so much time to perfect the circle now. Why can I never remember that I can make progress with practice? There's a weight right there.

I could use this doodle as a mind map; that's how all good art projects start. I'll write "apocalypse" in a curly font in the middle and see what else comes to mind. Food, obviously, bottled water, heating — what else are we missing? I suppose toilet paper has to go on there. Thank God Zoe is out of nappies now, but wet wipes; I will need a tonne of those, and tissues, and nappy bags for the inevitable accidents. I'll need sweets to shut them up when I'm tired. I'm going to need a lot of sweets. I don't want to stock up on UHT milk; that stuff is disgusting in tea. It makes me feel as if I were in a cheap hotel. I might not have a choice, though. There's no point in getting bread, only the ingredients for bread. I know how to bake. Ingredients last much longer than the final product, as I discovered during lockdown – the kids won't binge eat flour or yeast on its own. My bread might not be as squidgy as Hovis, but it was almost edible. I won't be able to take butter, but margarine will last longer than me. I'm going to have to learn how to make chicken dippers in the shape of dinosaurs, without chicken. This mind map looks pretty; I can breathe normally again. The pencil is mightier than the sword, unless I wield the pencil like a five-year-old. Finger tapping on a keyboard was even mightier than the pen before the power cuts. But tapping is too quick; handwriting makes you think carefully before putting down the next word.

I haven't dared tell the kids we've run out of spaghetti; I'm too scared. I'll add a pasta machine to the list. Mad Max never thought of that, did he?

The mind map is getting big now. It's the most aesthetically pleasing mind map I've ever created. It deserves a place on the fridge next to Tom's painting of a tank, Zoe's handprint and Peter's counsellor's business card.

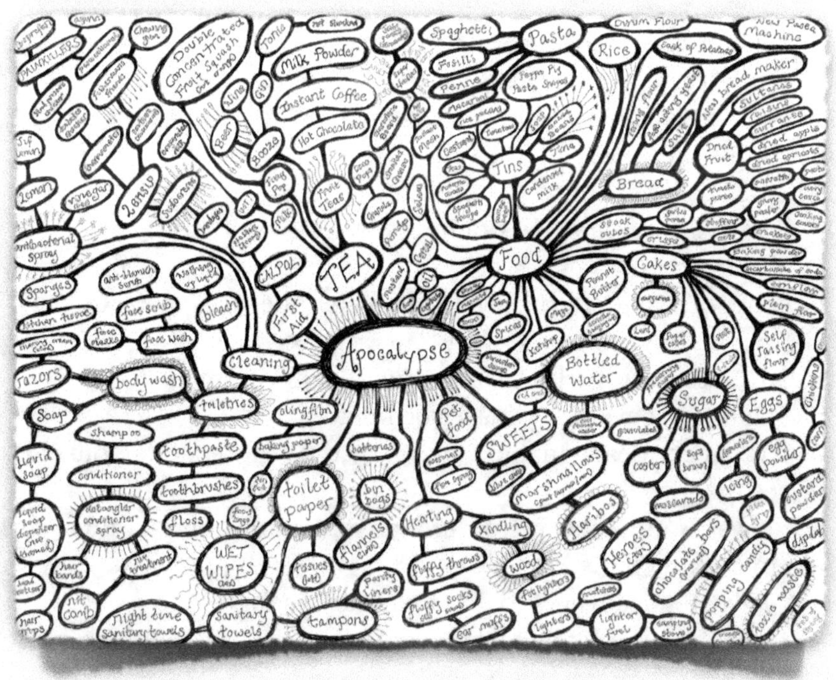

I like mind maps. Like the start of any art project, I feel everything and anything is possible. Is there any fun to be had during an apocalypse?

I wish I had chosen a simpler font, though. These curls are cramping up my carpal tunnel. Sam is home again. That bloody mistress of his can't be far away.

'Where are my buttons, Sam? I can't find them anywhere; have you swapped them?'

'Are you mad? I'm not that stupid. I've put them somewhere safe in case we get robbed.'

'Thanks, but you could have said. I was about to take the crowbar to every house on the street!'

Sam rummages through empty drawers, while I continue to add unnecessary patterns to my apocalyptic shopping list. This list isn't far from a normal weekly shop; mothers are always apocalypse-ready.

'What are you looking for, Sam?'

'Batteries; do we have any?'

'Not many, but there's a couple in the drawer by the microwave. I have no idea if they're used or not; they just appeared there one day.'

'Thanks. What are you doing?'

'Writing a list.'

'A list of what? A bucket list of celebrities you want to sleep with before the end of the world?'

'No, actually it's a list of ingredients, so I can make food. If we have flour, we have many loaves of bread.'

'Not a bad idea actually, I knew you'd work something out. Let me see the list.'

He was waiting for me to think of something? I was waiting for him to do something.

'I have no idea where to get it all from, though.'

'Leave that to me; you were always better at the thinking stuff; I'm better at the getting-it bit.'

'Really? Okay, I suppose. Do you want me to do anything else? It helps me to do something?'

'Um…yeah, pack the kids' clothes and stuff without them seeing.'

'What? How do I do that?'

'And a bag for us, imagine we're going on holiday but to somewhere really cold and unpleasant.'

'Okay, that's normal for us. Are you going to give me a hint as to why?'

'Can you keep a secret?'

'Of course.'

'Then how did Mike and Phil know I once wore your silk nightie to bed when I had that skin rash?'

'That was not me. I don't speak to them. Oh…she didn't, did she? I'm sorry.'

'They're subscribers. Gaba sells our secrets as well as her own. It's okay; my mother tells more people more intimate stuff than that, but that is why I'm not telling you where I'm going; you have to trust me.'

My temporary confidence is giving me that little bit of strength to ask the question I am dying to ask so I can trust him.

'But…but… just answer me this…are you having an affair? Is there another woman? Are you leaving me? Are you going to run off like… like—'

Shit, he looks mad.

'Like who? My Dad? I don't believe it. Is that what you think? Is that what you think of me?'

I think I just let Schrödinger's angry cat out of the box.

Sam stares at me, unable to speak. Love has changed. It's gone from butterflies in the stomach to a pain similar to trapped wind because I'm too fearful to let out my thoughts for fear of being demoralised. Those butterflies have climbed back into their chrysalises. The chrysalises have calcified like stone babies without realising. The stones sit there as a constant reminder of all that wasted potential. Am I wrong to ask, to doubt? With no answers or information, I have to fill in the blanks myself.

Peter stumbles into the kitchen. 'Any food, Mum? I'm actually hungry for once.'

Zoe and Tom scramble down the stairs looking for food, too. As soon as they see Sam, they each grab one of his legs and climb up his body.

Imelda comes through the front door. 'Only me. I've brought more jam.'

Dada is right behind her, carrying a large sack. 'Got some knives. Been sharpening them all day. Where shall I put them, Sam?'

'Under the stairs, Bill, if you please, out of the way of the kids.'

Tom has reached Sam's shoulders. Zoe keeps sliding down his t-shirt. Tom touches the top of Sam's head and cheers as if he'd planted a flag on top. They both jump off and run towards the fridge.

Sam hasn't taken his eyes off me this whole time. 'Give me that list.'

He looks at the list while puffing his cheeks out a lot. He'd better not crumple that up; it's art.

'I don't think Harvey deals in fast-acting yeast.'

'That's not what I've heard. Give it back; you'll have to take a photo of the list.'

'My battery is dead, just give me the list; I'll return it when I'm done. Why do we need icing sugar? Were you thinking of *Bake Off* instead of *I'm a Celebrity*?'

'Sugar paste preserves cakes. I'm not an idiot.'

'Fine, I'll be back later.'

Sam grabs the microwave and storms out of the front door, slamming so hard this time that the pictures on the walls rattle. He didn't deny having an affair; he just ignored my questions as usual. The trouble with living inside my head is I'm mad at him for things he only did in my head. Have I made things a lot worse? I didn't think it could get worse, but it just did. I'm sure I should have at least half of everything, but he's taking the lot. As long as I get to keep the kettle, he can keep the fucking microwave.

He'd better not lose that mind map; I'm already missing it.

According to the radio, the gas has been cut off permanently. The power stations are understaffed as key workers decided they don't need money when there's nothing to buy and nothing to live for. The shipping forecast is moderate to poor, though.

I wish I could send Scraps round to lick their hands and make them feel better. They need to sort out their buttons as well.

Everyone else has gathered round the kitchen table. It's painfully quiet; nobody is talking, scrolling, or watching anything. The only sound is the crunching of the last thawed-out pizza. My handheld culinary blowtorch made the crusts extra crusty. Nobody has complained about the strange taste. The rest of the food from the freezer has thawed, although the ambient temperature in here seems to be lower than the fridge, anyway. It looks like breakfast tomorrow will be blow-torched lasagne and blow-torched hash browns.

It's so dark I reckon I can convince Tom and Zoe it's bedtime. I have no idea what time it is exactly; no timepiece works anymore, and my circadian rhythm is way off kilter. Amber sways back into the house. She has partied hard. I'm jealous.

'Where have you been?'

'Do you really want me to tell you in front of this lot, Mum?'

'Where's Gaba? Was she with you?'

'I don't know where Gaba went. She got scared and ran off.'

'You can't keep disappearing like this Amber, we need to know where you are.'

'Why? You're not going anywhere. I'm not sitting around waiting for shit to happen. I don't need you lot.'

'Then why are you here now?'

'All I need is a shower and some new clothes, then I'll be off again.'

'Well, the shower isn't working because we have no gas.'

'You lot are fucking useless!'

'It's not my fault that the power stations aren't working; I'm not in charge of that!'

'Yeah, but it's your generation who are fucking it up for everybody else, isn't it?'

'I'm sorry, was my generation laying down the red carpet for your generation to tiptoe across too much for you all?'

'There's no red carpet in this shithole!'

'Yes, there is; it's just metaphorical.'

'What fucking use is a metaphorical one? I want a real red carpet. I deserve it!'

'What have you done to deserve anything?'

'It's my human right, Mum.'

'Human rights were made up by humans; they don't actually exist. And I'm pretty sure it's not written down anywhere that you should have a red-carpet existence. An easy life is actually fucking hard to get.'

The power comes back on, as does the TV. Is the national grid powered by Amber's fury? If so, there's definitely enough for everyone.

'I'm having a shower right fucking now, nobody better get in my way!'

She didn't hear me about the gas, did she? She has no idea how anything works. Surprisingly, Imelda has finished stuffing her face and stood up. 'Well, I'm not sure I need to witness any more carnage. I've had enough for one day. I'd better go home.'

'I'll walk you home; it's about time I head off as well.'

'Thanks, Bill.'

I hope she's referring to the carnage on the TV.

The Stone Age

Sam is back. Again. He's probably watching the house from behind a hedge, waiting for the grandparents to leave. I hate the fact that he can just leave and no one asks why. If I had left the house without warning, I would have been reported to social services.

He lies down on the sofa. Should I ask him anything this time? He's actually smiling; don't spoil it. He's holding a small wooden box. Maybe the cat died; I haven't seen her today.

'I thought they'd never go. Look what I managed to get, Nell!'

He pulls out a large spliff.

'You're kidding. Where did you get that? I thought you were getting food.'

'These are easier to get than cornflakes at the moment.'

I'm not sure I like his smile. It's not his loving smile; it's an uncaring smile. That smile doesn't make my heart go pitter-patter.

'Come on, you know you want one.'

'I thought we agreed to give that up for the sake of the kids?'

'Why did we agree to give up feeling happy?'

I can feel my eyes welling up. Sam has just confirmed that he isn't happy. I have to leave him; it's the right thing to do. Why don't I want to do it then? Because he's the only one who knows where the biscuits are hidden. Did he swap the microwave for a spliff?

Peter walks into the front room; he doesn't look impressed by his dad lying back on the sofa giggling.

'Do you want one, son? I don't mind, seeing as it is the end of the world.'

'No thanks, Dad, smoking pot only makes the demons sleepy, not dead.'

'You're petulant with a capital arse, Pete.'

I think I would have preferred him asking for a drag too. Disapproval seems harder to accept. I shouldn't have taught my children right and wrong; there will be nothing left for them to discover for themselves.

Sam grins from ear to ear while holding in a long breath full of smoke. He's wrapped in two puffer jackets with the hoods up. He looks relaxed. It's funny; getting high is how finding gods got started. It looks like civilisation is going to be bookended by smoke and mirrors.

Peter stares at Sam, trying to pretend his inane grinning isn't bothering him. Sam giggles, Peter turns away to watch the news intensely while simultaneously playing with his tethered phone, hoping to play one last game before the electricity goes out again. Do I need Sam to be switched to reality? Instead of always driving behind him, I should try to overtake and take the lead before we both veer off the road.

Sam's grinning is exhausting even to me now. Amber trots down the stairs in what must be the last fresh clothes she owns. She still looks dishevelled. She smells the air and looks at her dad, grinning on the sofa.

'Nice, and you're having a go at me for having a bit of fun.'

'This isn't fun, Amber. This is escapism.'

Sam makes smoke rings; he's got better at them.

'What have you got to escape from, Dad? Us?'

Amber looks down at Sam with another disapproving gaze. Is there anything teenagers won't disapprove of? I make myself comfortable on the other sofa, anticipating and hoping for an honest tirade to flow out of Sam's mouth. Sam sucks in a deep drag.

'No, darling. I'm not escaping you lot.'

Sam closes his eyes and carries on smiling. Amber turns on her wobbly heels and leaves the house. Was that it? Hardly worth waiting for.

Peter lifts his head from his barely working phone. 'I can't get in touch with Freddy anymore, Mum. What shall I do?'

'Use your legs to go a hundred yards up the road and check on him!'

'Will you come with me? You know what his mum can be like.'

'Sure, I haven't seen an unrelated adult in ages, and Scraps' frozen pee isn't helping the garden.'

I search for my bra among the shoes in the hallway. It's hard to put it on under layers of jumpers. Scraps doesn't want to go outside, so I drag him out.

Peter puts his earbuds in to walk the short distance. We haven't been alone together for over seven years, and he doesn't want to interact with me, just keep me as backup. He's transitioning from complete dependence to complete independence; it doesn't happen overnight. He has to not need me at some point, otherwise he'll hate adulthood.

The ground outside has a furriness to it; it feels slightly otherworldly. Scraps seems scared, even though there's no one about. Freddy is the son of Sam's line manager at the factory. That's why they can afford to live at the top end of the street, in one of the detached properties. That doesn't irritate Sam that much at all; he hardly ever mentions it. Freddy's mum isn't the most popular line manager or villager. Sam calls her Moses because a sea of people can be seen to move away from her when she walks the factory floor. She likes to remind me of how gifted Freddy is. Little does she know, his only talent is setting up fake profiles on social media to troll his classmates.

Peter knocks pathetically on the door because deep down he's probably hoping nobody is in.

I can feel my legs stiffening in the freezing cold despite wearing jeggings underneath my jeans. Freddy eventually opens the door still wearing the rabbit onesie he wore on World Book Day a couple of weeks ago; it's covered in stains and spills. He probably smells awful, but the cloud of cannabis smoke lingering around him is overpowering it.

Peter looks his friend up and down. 'You alright, mate? You look rank. I can't get my phone to work, can you?'

'Mine works a bit.'

Wow! That was enthralling. Freddy staggers back into his front room. Peter seems to have taken that as an invitation, so am I. Freddy's mum is comatose on the sofa; the floor is covered in rubbish, empty wine bottles and mouldy potatoes with electrodes coming out of them. Freddy slumps back into the large indent on the sofa and unpauses his game. Peter clears a space next to him and sits down. Despite being asked to come with him for support, apparently I don't warrant a fucking seat. I'm not clearing a space next to Freddy's mum; I don't want to be the one who disturbs her. Scraps won't even come inside; it's too repugnant for a dog.

'Not watching the news then, Fred?'

'Nah, it's too depressing, mate.'

'Haven't you heard? The Americans aren't dead; they're hiding in underground bunkers in Area 52. The government is keeping them hidden until everyone else is dead, and then they can rise up again.'

'You still buying into all that shit? You can't hide a few hundred million people underground in a couple of days. It would take them weeks just to set up the queue barriers.'

'Nah, they're not saving everyone. Just Silicon Valley residents and a few Oscar winners.'

'It doesn't really matter, does it? We're all going to die.'

'Is this how you want to go? Stoned and fighting zombies?'

'Is there a better way?'

Dying as you lived. Piss-poor imagination these kids have today; the only skill they have in abundance is avoidance techniques.

'Where's your dad, Fred?'

'Don't know. Don't care.'

'What do you mean?'

'Apparently, he has another family he'd rather be with. Mum knew he was having an affair, going on for years. He paid for her kids to go to university, wouldn't even buy me a new games console. As soon as the shit hit the fan, he buggered off to be with her, didn't even say goodbye.'

Every mother's worst fear. More than bears or rivers of volcanic ash. Peter looks way out of his depth. I'm not sure if I can doggy paddle my way out with worldly advice.

Freddy looks up at Peter. 'It's alright though, mate, managed to swap his golf clubs for this bit of weed. Don't reckon his collection of railway signs will be of much use to anyone though, but you don't know what they want until they knock on your door.'

'What use are golf clubs at a time like this, Fred?'

'They really hurt when they hit you. I should know.'

'Do you need anything? Food? Water?' says Peter, like we have a surplus!

'Nah, not really hungry, mate. Dad's wine collection is keeping us healthy, safer than the water Mum said.'

'Look, I'd better go. If you need anything, make sure you come and see me. I'm not far away, alright?'

'Yeah, sure.'

If only every antagonist or warmonger that has ever existed knew that all you have to do to keep people passive is make them push digital fruit or diamonds into rows. We see ourselves out of the house. Peter's head is lower than usual as we walk back down the street.

'You okay, Pete?'

'I think so, Mum.'

Seeing adults stoned is one thing; they're suppressing a life of strain, sacrifice, and anticlimax. It's sad to see teenagers stoned, though; they're suppressing low expectations or emptiness.

I try to distract his thoughts. 'I thought computers were created to improve our lives. They seem, like most creations, to encourage vicarious living instead of brutal reality. Passive creativity has its place, but when it dominates, it renders people unable to create for themselves.'

'What the fuck does that mean, Mum?'

'Unless this supervolcano throws up a flaming labyrinth with rivers of acid, an unnecessary timer, useless rewards and hungry dragons, computers haven't prepared you lot for anything.'

Peter laughs a little.

I see an opportunity to let a thought squirm out of my head. 'We've recklessly designed stuff to erase human endeavour and creativity. We're not built for lazy leisure, we're designed to panic, run, think, postulate, create, wield, fight, lose, overthink, sing at the top of our voices, have a tea break, take a deep breath, rethink, get back on the horse, charge, clean up and celebrate till dawn.'

'You're right, Mum. But would any of those things help us survive what's coming now? We haven't got many teabags left, let alone any horses.'

'We can't match Mother Earth's force, but she made us clever.'

'Not all of us. All the intelligence humans have is dependent on an on/off switch working.'

'We used to be fuelled by scraps found on the floor, or berries hanging from bushes. Just because we now need sophisticated buildings and networks, it doesn't mean we can't survive, Pete.'

'Everyone is too complicated and needy.'

'We are stupid and reckless with our intelligence. We don't know how to use it. The human body is too limited for our expanding ideas. We want more than it can offer.'

'I don't feel like I have any scrap of intelligence rattling around in this new, lanky body.'

'Intelligence doesn't grow with your bones, Pete. Teenage-hood is like when you run out of iCloud storage; you're forced to buy a terabyte, and then your photo collection goes from looking overflowing to insignificant. Your brain still has the same amount of knowledge; it's just that there's room for a bit more now you've upgraded to an adult body. For some, it can seem overwhelming to fill that vast extra space, but it's nice to know it's there if you need it.'

'But I'm not smart, Mum. The last thing I got congratulated on was doing my first poo in the potty. It's all been downhill since then.'

'Sorry, but I'm not apologising for that. It was a momentous occasion for me. I nearly hired a brass band when Zoe did hers. I didn't realise you were clinging on to your first achievement like you clung onto your childhood teddy bear. There's plenty of time to achieve something new; you haven't had the opportunity yet.'

'Do you think I'm stupid, Mum?'

'No. We call people stupid when we don't understand what they're doing.'

'Am I too complicated and needy?'

'Complicated? No, not that I've noticed. Everyone is needy. You'll fill up that hard drive soon enough. Just don't fill it with screenshots of computer game league tables. Try the occasional sunset or dive into the sea.'

'I didn't think I would need to be clever. I thought the robots were going to do everything for us.'

'The robots probably won't get built now. Which is probably a good thing; they would probably chew through their own charging cables, jump off mezzanine floors, digest liquids, or inhale fumes to deactivate their safety features – anything to suppress their own self-loathing. We shouldn't create computers in man's own image.'

Peter laughs a little again. 'So not even AI can save us from this disaster.'

'Not without a functioning plug and socket, Pete. AI only sped up what humans programmed it to do; it was limited to our knowledge.'

'So what are we going to do without the power to think faster?'

'We'll think of something, I promise. We're British; we might take a while to get going but once we get going, we're difficult to stop.'

Peter smiles and gives one of his earbuds to me. I put it in my ear as we walked back home. I think I need to lie down. I can't save the world from itself, but I can start with one inert teenager at a time.

The Human Bottleneck

The electricity hasn't come back on since yesterday. That's the longest period without power so far. The blowtorch has run out of gas. I can't pretend to cook anything, I can't pretend to watch anything, but more importantly, the kids can't charge their devices to play even the basic games. The water makes funny noises when it comes out of the tap, and it doesn't look clean. This is the beginning of the end. I really, really, really do not want to get out of bed. It's my birthday today. I didn't remind anyone, so no one remembered. I can hear Zoe running up and down the hallway, laughing. The lack of power isn't bothering her because her happiness is not fully dependent on it yet; she's powered by Hundreds and Thousands and giddy hope. When they run out, I'm hiding.

I need to find out what's making her laugh so much, see if it needs thwarting, and then come back to bed. The view from my bedroom window is bleak. The ground is solid with frost; the few spring leaves that have fallen from the trees are in different shades of yellow. There is no blue. This is a very limited palette; I would only need burnt umber and some thinner. It looks like autumn already; the Earth is in full menopause now. Nothing will get a chance to grow unless summer gets a chance again.

Sam is fast asleep, curled up on the floor in the front room, covered in the dog's fleece and surrounded by empty baked beans tins. Where did he get those? Zoe giggles while staring down at him, waiting for him to wake. His eyes opened with a start.

'Daddy, did you know that birds don't kiss, they smudge!'

'Any breakfast left, Sam? Or did you eat all our supplies?'

'Leave me alone, Nell. I was hungry.'

'We're all hungry!'

This is why a woman's body stocks up on fat, in case of moody men in times of crisis.

Zoe tries to turn the telly on. 'What's wrong with the telly? I want to watch *Gromice and Wallet.*'

Zoe drops the remote control on Sam's head while she looks for something else to do. 'I'm jumping over cats today.'

Gigi hisses in the hallway. Maybe I should jump over cats as well while I stagger towards the kitchen.

After my little exchange with Peter the other day, I've realised I do have some knowledge at my disposal. Why don't I use it? Because I know there's an easier option in the biscuit barrel or under the sink. That's where my secret bottle of gin is hidden. I would love to drink the lot, knock myself out. Then I won't have to face a day of uncertainty or trying to placate teenagers suffering from electricity withdrawal.

Peter comes downstairs, probably to tell everyone that aliens are holding the Americans hostage in vast underground cities left by the dinosaurs. When will he realise I don't care? If the dinosaurs want to rule the world again, that is fine with me. If aliens want to be our masters, that is also fine with me. As long as we are enslaved to make teabags, I'm totally okay with anyone getting a grip of this cataclysmic situation.

I'm holding on to the kitchen worktop too tightly; my knuckles are pale white. I really want that gin now, but all I'm getting is pain. Peter watches me. I don't want the taste, only the aftereffects. I want to block everything out too.

'Does Dad feel better now, Mum? All his troubles gone?'

'Shut up. No one likes a smartarse. This is hard to deal with — the hardest thing ever. I don't know what we're supposed to do. I'm sure your dad just wanted to forget about some things for a moment.'

'Getting stoned can't be the answer.'

'No-one gets stoned to answer a problem; they get stoned to avoid answering a problem.'

I rummage in the cupboard under the sink. I'm not thinking about it; my hands just search for it. I've found it; the half-empty bottle of gin looks so clean and clear; it looks clearer than the water. I want to feel it gurgling down my throat, knowing it will put my mind at ease.

Peter grabs the bottle from my hands; he wrestles it away from me. Not all teenagers want their parents to be indifferent. I honestly didn't think he was this strong.

'This won't help, Mum.'

Peter grabs the bottle and pours the gin down the sink, with his other arm outstretched to keep me back.

'No, Peter, don't – please. I beg you, don't!'

'You've got to be strong. We can get through this if we try. You've got to try, but you need to be fully conscious to try! I need you, we need you, Dad needs you even though he won't admit it. It's not the end of the world. You said we were your world, and we are all still here.'

The gin spirals down the sink. There's a loud gurgling sound as if a small but rabid monster living in the u-bend just sucked it all up. I put my head in my hands. Peter relaxes his arm and holds me tight as I weep. Sam staggers into the kitchen with the dog fleece wrapped round his shoulders. He walked straight past us as if this were a normal sight. He opened the empty cupboards, looking for something. I straighten myself up and wipe the tears away with my sleeve. He's right; I can't give up yet; if I do, I may as well throw my children off a bridge in front of moving traffic.

'Thanks, Pete.'

Peter smiles at me. Sam finds what he was looking for: a large bag of mini marshmallows he had hidden on the top shelf that only he can see into the back of. He opens them and shoves huge handfuls into his mouth as he staggers back to the front room.

'Are you strong enough to hold him back from the marshmallows?'

'Not yet, Mum.'

I wind up the clockwork radio. I don't know why. I don't want to know how much worse it is. Someone has declared tap water unsafe for human consumption unless boiled. That gin would have been the safest thing to drink. Sam comes back from the front room looking slightly refreshed.

'Right, I'm going out one last time.'

He grabs his jacket and tries to put it on over the fleece. He leaves. What does "One last time" mean? He's not coming back? He's not going to die with us? He can't bear to watch us suffer? He needs the comfort of another woman to get him through this? He needs more beans? He needs more marshmallows? The front door slammed one last time.

The news sounds like playground noise in the background; there's so many people talking over each other. London is struggling with smog, as the smoke from the refugee street fires fills the already crowded air. The prime minister is officially missing.

Dada hovers in the hallway. Nobody noticed him arrive. 'What bloody use are politicians when you need them – run away as soon as it gets a bit tough. Anyway, where's Sam when you want him, or has he buggered off as well?'

'He's not buggered off; he's doing something; he just won't tell me what. He'll be back later, hopefully. Then you can interrogate him yourself.'

'Just want to make sure he's looking after you, Nell, and not someone else, that's all, sweetheart.'

'I don't know what he's doing.'

'As long as you're okay with it.'

'I don't really have any choice.'

'Everyone has a choice, darling.'

Peter tries to get one teabag to make three cups of tea using an old teapot and a camping stove. Yesterday, I taped one emergency teabag to the top of an empty cupboard, and I will not surrender it until I know I have reached my final hour on this planet.

I've been trying to make my HRT patches last longer as well. At first, I left them on for a few days more, but now I've cut them into quarters. I hope there's a hormone rehab centre in this bleak future I'm facing.

'I can't believe so many people are dead, Dada; it's awful.'

'Everyone's got to go someday.'

'But I don't want to be melted by lava, suffocated by ash, squashed by falling masonry, starved, dehydrated, frozen to death, murdered—'

'When you're dead, you're dead. I don't think it matters how.'

'I'd like to go peacefully, Dada, at my choice, satisfied, fulfilled, loved.'

'Then you'll need to feel like that twenty-four seven, in case a lump of masonry does fall on your head. No one feels like that all the time.'

'Well, as long as I could have a little bit of that, I'd be fine.'

Peter gives me a cup of weak black tea. It's disgusting, but I drink it all in one go. Tom runs into the front room wearing his woollen hat and gloves, looking for a better place to hide from Zoe in another epic game of hide and seek. There's a knock at the door. Dada offers to get it as I stare down the hallway with bated breath. Sam left a crowbar leaning against the wall in case we have any unwanted guests.

It's Nigel and Skye. I can see the tops of a few stranger's heads behind them.

'Dada, what a pleasant surprise! How the devil are you? Hope you don't mind us dropping in again, Nell. Where is she?'

Who the fuck has Nigel brought with him? There's one, two, three, four, five, six fucking strangers coming into my home. I'm not that accommodating to strangers at the best of times, least of all when I'm rationing teabags. I suppose I've got to greet them properly.

'Darling Nell, I hope you don't mind but Wales was cancelled, the cottage wasn't just double booked but quadruple booked, all of us had to leave when the owner decided they were going to stay there and we were not welcome, a little bit of fisticuffs ensued as the buggers wouldn't give any of us our money back, anyway we're going to go back to London – stand up to those bloody neighbours and ride out the storm in relative comfort at least. I didn't think you'd mind us using your amenities again, as you were so generous last time. Just a cuppa will do, and we'll be on our way again. Is that okay? You wouldn't begrudge your little brother and his friends a pee, would you?'

'No, Nigel. Of course not. But please go easy on the toilet roll and only flush if it's brown.'

Dada follows the crowd into the kitchen, staring at the back of Nigel's head. I refuse to use up my thinking time on their difficult relationship and different generational male expectations.

'Nice to see you, son. It must be nearly four years since I last saw you.'

'Has it really been that long? Sorry, Dada, but time flies when you're as busy as I am, running a big company.'

There is no eye contact between Nigel and Dada; there's no point when there's so much emotional baggage blocking their view of each other.

'Oh, you're running it now? I thought you were only a manager.'

'Well, managers run the show – you know how it is. Although I know earning money wasn't your thing, was it, Dada? Running around a dirty field on your belly holding a gun was your idea of breadwinning, but it doesn't matter, does it? We're all individuals, aren't we, got to make our own mark on the world? We can't just replicate the past, can we?'

Nigel rarely pauses for breath, but now takes a moment to outstare Dada. They haven't kept pleasant company since Nigel walked out of the officer barracks Dada had pulled strings to get him into. They are not the same person. It's a good job Nigel is my twin, otherwise Dada would have sworn Nigel wasn't his child and would have taken a paternity test. He knew I was his; I have his eyes, but Nigel appears to have nothing of Dada's that he recognises or admires about himself.

I try to break the icy atmosphere. 'I'd love to make you all a cup of tea, but we've just used the last teabag. All I can muster is a shot of fruit squash and four hula hoops each.'

I squirt some fruit squash into my Kahlo mug. It looks wrong against the hardened tannin stains, but I add some bottled water. Nigel watches me, horrified.

'It's alright, sis; we won't stay; we'll get off soon; don't want to be in anyone's way. We'll be off back to London as soon as you can say—'

WHOOOOOOP!

Fuck! The entire room was lit up by something in the sky. There was a distant but loud crack outside, and the ground shuddered. Everyone stands still; do we need to see what that was? It was bigger than thunder, and it wasn't a fucking supervolcano.

'For fuck's sake, what now?' I sigh.

Dada seemed the least surprised by the noise as he quickly heads for the front door. He opens the door and stares at the eerie sky across the fields in front of him.

'What the fuck was that, Dada?'

'Don't swear in front of the kids, Nigel.'

'Sorry, sis. But what the fuck was that?'

Dada straightens his neck. 'That…that was a nuclear bomb… and that…I think was London.'

Dada would know; he had been trained for this decades ago. Nigel and I stand behind him in the doorway. The last time we stood like this was when they carted Mama off to the hospital. I can't really take in what he just said. It doesn't seem real. I feel as though I'm in a movie.

The strangers gather behind us in the hallway to stare blankly too. Gigi sits on the stairs, swiping through the banisters at anyone who goes past. Scraps buries his head under my cardigan.

Everyone stares in silence as the peculiar sky swirls about as if someone had just popped an enormous balloon amongst the muddy clouds.

Nigel makes the noise he makes when he's trying not to cry.

'Who would…why would…What have they done?…London… beautiful London—'

Nigel can't hold it in; he cries like he did when they took Mama's Morris Minor to the scrapheap. Dada closed the door as if an unwelcome guest had been standing there.

We follow the strangers as they slowly make their way back to the kitchen. Dada turns the radio on, but it isn't working. He looks for some batteries in the drawer, but can't find any. He grabs the radio and looks for the battery compartment, but he can't find that either.

'Give it here; it's clockwork. Sam got it.'

I wound the radio up. Dada finds a channel that is working and places it on the kitchen table; everyone gathers round. It looks nostalgic, like we're in the war, but it actually feels overwhelmingly sad.

The radio confirms Dada's suspicion, but it's not only London – many major cities have been wiped out all over the world. All the images of major cities being destroyed in movies flood my brain. I've seen the Eiffel Tower fall so many times it feels like a repeat.

They don't know who fired the first nuke. Most media outlets have been destroyed. As soon as one went up, many others followed. If there is a God looking down on us, that must have looked like a firework display. Was this part of his big plan? Maybe he and Mother Earth got together and decided to eat all their babies. The death toll has gone up even more significantly now. There will be no one left to explain this soon. Collectively, we knew everything; who knows which working parts have been left?

It looks like those world leaders finally found someone vulnerable to fuck and destroy with their Viagra-laden missiles. Nuclear weapons should only be used by people who can do the maths. There shouldn't have been a big red button, but a complicated equation that only geniuses could control. Nuclear weapons were the stupidest thing man made. Those four horses are at full gallop now.

'See, the media knew this was going to happen, Dada, they were prepared!'

'Peter, this is not a conspiracy; this is World War Three. Or it was. It ended in one afternoon. The biggest pissing contest in the world finally took place; nobody has been left alive to claim a trophy.'

'I bet the government survived in a secret bunker. I bet they're having a party!' Peter claims.

'No-one's having a party. They're all dust now. This won't be pretty.'

With London gone, it feels like a parent has died. The kitchen is full of people, but I can't even hear them breathe. This is the worst wake I've ever been to. In the distance, I can hear faint crying.

The Great Flood

The saddened silence broke as Sam burst through the door, out of breath. 'Did you see it? I mean, did you see that? What the fu—'

'We saw it; we heard it. What happens now?' I ask.

I'm so relieved he's back. Which confirms that I do still need him; I do still want him. Would I take a crowbar to his mistress? I think I would right now.

Dada stands tall and adjusts his beautifully ironed collar. 'Empires fall all the time; the world adapts. We can either fall or adapt.'

Skye comes out of the toilet looking bemused by the stony faces. She sits quietly at the end of the kitchen table, smiling at Nigel, who hasn't noticed her as he stares at the radio with tears streaming down his face. Is he crying for the billions dead or the fact that his beloved vinyl collection was evaporated?

Imelda scuttles frantically through the front door. I knew she could move faster than she lets on. 'What was that explosion? Was it a train crash?'

'No, Imelda, it was London; they've nuked it, they've nuked everybody,' Dada explained.

'Who's "they", Bill? Who nuked London? Why? Why London? Oh, the King, oh, the palaces!'

'Palaces! What about the millions of people? Bloody palaces!'

'But that's our cultural heritage gone up in smoke.'

'Millions of people were just vaporised and you're worried about some bloody Chippendale furniture!'

'I was just saying!'

'Well, don't bloody just say stuff for the sake of it; try thinking before you open your big mouth!'

That's the angriest Dada has looked in a long time. He storms off, slamming the front door behind him. That's not enough to penetrate Imelda's self-generating force field.

'Well, at least Majorie Halls won't be going to the royal garden party now,' she mumbled.

The British stiff upper lip can sometimes be mistaken for a trivial, catty sideswipe. Silent tears streamed down everybody's faces except Sam, who kept them in his eyes long enough to make them go red. He still has a sensitive side; he still has emotions to bleed.

Zoe rushes into the kitchen, opening every cupboard door and slamming them behind her. 'Where's Tom? Has anyone seen Tom? He's cheating; I know he is. He always hides where I can't find him.'

I'm sad, I'm worried, I'm frightened. But I'm alive, and I can't dwell on the loss of so many. All I can think about is that I will never need to be beach-body-ready again, which is the only positive I can cling onto with my last white knuckle. In a couple of weeks, the civilised world has been burned, suffocated, drowned, ignored, starved, shot at, mugged, frozen and now vaporised. I can't think about tomorrow; I can't think about who's in charge anymore. I can't think about rebuilding society; I can't think about hoodlums in leather jackets and heavy eyeliner burning rubber down the street with their motorbikes. I'm not even worried about running out of toilet paper anymore, there's not many people left to be shamed by.

I want to know where Amber is; I can't track her phone anymore. 'Where's Amber? I want her here. This isn't right. She needs us; we're her family; she should be with us.'

'She'll turn up sooner or later, Nell. All phones are definitely dead now; she'll get very bored, very quickly.'

Sam clutches the clockwork radio to his ear; the news reports are just repetitive statements.

'What are we supposed to do now, Sam? Who's in charge?'

'There's little to be in charge of.'

'Are we supposed to go and help bury the dead? Help the survivors? We're a bit far, but shouldn't we do something?'

'They won't need burying. There are millions burned, not enough doctors and hospitals to help them. Even if we did rally round to keep them alive, there will be no food for them when they recover. All the big cities were attacked, even New York, and it was empty. It seems everyone had a grudge against someone else.'

'What is left?'

'Confusion, anger, disbelief. It's going to take a while for people to reorganise themselves; we're all starting from scratch now.'

'So nowhere is safe then, Sam?'

'Not really.'

'We haven't been caught yet.'

'That's one advantage of living in the middle of nowhere; we're far from anything interesting, so not much of a target.'

'Does it mean we could go anywhere? We don't have to stay here? We could find an empty stately home; in the movies, there's always an empty stately home you can take over.'

'If it's in the movies, then that's where everyone else will be heading, especially the criminal masterminds. Anyway, stately homes might sound nice, but they need even more fuel to keep them warm.'

'Couldn't we find a paradise island, live off coconuts?' Why am I asking that? I don't want to be beach-body ready ever again. 'I heard once that all the people in the world could fit on the Isle of Wight. We should have designated it the world's post-apocalyptic meeting point. Although there's probably only enough people left to occupy Osborne House.'

'Have we got a yacht!? Anyway, we wouldn't be able to get to Portsmouth on the petrol I've got left in the car.'

'At least it has nice beaches.'

'Can you stop fantasising? I'm not driving to the Isle of Wight for a coconut picnic.'

'What are we goi—'

'PICNIC!!!'

What the fuck?! Tom just burst out from under the stairs. Every single morose adult jumped out of their seat.

Sam is clutching his heart. 'For fuck's sake, Tom, you nearly gave me a heart attack. What were you doing in there?'

'Sorry, Dad.'

'Found you! I've been looking for you for ages,' screeches Zoe.

'Are we going on a day out, Dad? Are we going out for a picnic? Pleeeease Dad, I love picnics, pleeeease pleeeeeeease!'

'We're not going on a bloody picnic, Tom!'

'Oh, that's not fair. We haven't been out of this house in ages; I want to see grass and mud. I want to go somewhere nice. I want coconuts, and sandy beaches, and ice cream, and a ghost train, and donkey rides, and soggy chips, and laser quest and—'

'Okay, we get it. Maybe one day.'

'You always say that, Dad, but we never do those things.'

'Can we play a game of Nonopoly then?'

'Not now, Tom, all those places don't exist anymore.'

'Why not? What has been catastrophicized now?'

What will it take to get these kids scared? Not sure I can ever play Monopoly again. We'll have to play the *Star* Wars version. That world can't be destroyed by petulant avarice, although some tried.

Sam looks around the kitchen at the strangers he doesn't recognise. He unplugs the kettle, puts it under his arm and leaves the house again without saying a word. Imelda follows him.

At least without a kettle, I don't have to worry about using up my last teabag. That's one less tantrum to have. I look at Nigel and the group of strangers and then back at Nigel. Our telepathic powers don't appear to be working, like everything else.

'So, have you decided what to do, Nige?'

'Um…we don't know what to do; we haven't got anywhere to go now. I'm not sure what I'm supposed to do.'

'Me neither.'

For once, Nigel is speechless. What would I do if I were him? I wouldn't burden my sister with his friends, that's for sure. I feel bad about thinking that. They've just been made homeless. Why don't I want to take them in? Sometimes instincts take over rational thought processes. He gets up and starts walking towards the front door.

'I do think it's time we went our separate ways, though. I need to get this lot out of your hair.'

Good, there is a trace left. The random strangers, who still haven't been introduced yet, take the hint. Nigel opens the front door, and they shuffle out of the house.

I whisper to Nigel, 'Thank God for that! Sorry, Nige, but I've got enough mouths to feed without you bringing more home.'

'Sorry, Sis, I wasn't planning on staying here, anyway. Look, we'll head off now.'

'But where are you two going to go? Your house has been vaporised. I don't mind you two. It was only that lot – I didn't know them.'

'I know, and that's very sweet of you; it was only a house. I think you will be better off if we are somewhere else; our needs are different from you lot. Don't worry, we'll find something. The land underneath the house still stands; it's not going anywhere. At least the hole our neighbours dug has been levelled as well. We will figure something out. Look, it's been lovely seeing you, but we really must get going. Come on, Skye.'

Now I'm pissed he doesn't want to see the end of the world out with the person he started life with. He'd rather hold hands with someone he's only known four years.

Nigel and Skye saunter out of the house, get into their sports car and drive away slowly. I looked round the kitchen. I'm the only adult left in the house, sitting in an empty kitchen with no kettle. There's no electricity to boil the kettle anyway. Maybe I'll have to eat the last teabag.

The Ice Age

I didn't realise there were this many levels of cold. I've never been as freezing as I am this morning. I didn't realise there were different levels of quiet, either. Billions of people made a lot of noise. This is a new level of existing. It's even worse than a bank holiday weekend in a static caravan. At least that was only for a few days, and a warm bed awaited me at home.

I've wrapped three fleece throws around me several times and tied them in the middle with my dressing gown cord. I look like pipe lagging.

Zoe is curled up in my bed instead of Sam. 'Morning, Mummy! You look beautiful.'

She squeezes my waist so tight I'm not sure whether to burp or fart. She's mighty strong for a small child. 'You're like a giant, squishy marshmallow, Mummy.'

Zoe jumps off the bed and runs downstairs. I don't want to look out of the window, but I must check if outside is still there. Everything is a muddier brown or dirtier yellow. The skies look and smell poorly. I miss those big, beautiful John Constable skies.

How would he add sentiment to this scene? I long to see a horse and cart. I think we're stuck in an Atkinson Grimshaw painting now; sombre, nocturnal silhouettes on the edge of pervasive darkness.

I shuffle along the corridor and down the stairs. Sam sits at the kitchen table, holding his empty pint mug. The clockwork radio plays haunting music; it feels like we're in a doctor's waiting room, waiting to hear bad news. I don't like it when he looks like this; then I've got to step up and do even more.

Zoe skips into the kitchen. 'Daddy, can I go to the playground today? I haven't been for aaaaaages, can I, Dad? Can I?'

'It's a bit dangerous, sweetie. Why don't you play in the garden for a bit instead?'

'Okay.'

Sam looks at my pipe lagging outfit and briefly smiles like he used to. Instead of buying sexy lingerie, I should've dressed up as a spirit level; that would have got his attention. I'd let him rip this duvet off me with his teeth if it wasn't so cold.

I wash my Kahlo mug out with a little bit of bottled water. I have no desire to fill it with anything anymore. The tannin has been compromised.

It didn't take long for Zoe to come back into the kitchen. She walks extra dramatically slow with her chin touching her chest.

'Why is the grass yellow? The rain looks like God has been grating cheese…my tractor is all furry…and the jumpoline is broken, nothing's shiny anymore…and my ball is all flat, and my mini golf clubs stung me when I picked them up and—'

'You'll have to play inside then, sweetie,' says Sam.

He gets up, locks the back door, and sits back down, holding the radio to his ear. Zoe finds Amber's eyeliner pencil on the floor and climbs up Sam's legs to sit on his lap.

'What's that box of noise saying now, Daddy?'

'Just the same repeated message. Telling us to go to the local leisure centre.'

'I liked it before everyone got all bombsy.'

Zoe draws on Sam's face with the eyeliner pencil. She draws large eyelashes on his forehead, big circles on his cheeks, and lines coming out of the corners of his mouth to make a big smiley face.

'That's better.'

He does look happier, although the long eyelashes do not suit him. Tom and his hungry stomach are thundering down the stairs towards the kitchen. The fridge has no food in it, so it doesn't matter that it isn't working.

'What's for breakfast, Mum?'

'I don't know, one tin of tomato soup and…some Jif lemon… and three dried mini marshmallows for pudding.'

Sam turns the radio off while we sit round the table in complete silence eating the scraps of food. Sam looks hungry; it is his default setting, but this is a different level of hungry. He looks as if he would kill for a bar of chocolate. I haven't seen him like this since our attempt at a Boxing Day walk last year. He starts hunting through the empty cupboards.

'I thought you said you would get us more food if we ran out, Sam?'

'I'll get some later.'

'What are you looking for now? There's nothing left.'

'I need something to barter with, something someone thinks they need. I can't get food without giving something, unless you want me to steal it?'

'No, I don't want you to steal. Is that where all our things are going? You're swapping them for food?'

'Sort of. I told you I would provide, and I will. I've got all those tins of beans stashed away where no one will find them. We won't starve, but we might have to cut back a bit and make it last. If I fill the cupboards, you'll all just eat it, and then there will be nothing left.'

'So we're on rations? Are we actually at war?'

'Probably. Not sure who with though.'

Zoe runs off to the front room and quickly comes back with Willow, who still has lipstick chicken spots but with dust and debris stuck to them.

'There you go, Daddy. You can swap Willow for more food. But make sure she goes to a good home, someone who will kiss her goodnight and wrap her up warm. Can you swap her for some hot dogs, please?'

Sam smiles at Zoe and stands up quickly. He puts Willow down in his chair. He winces. He looks stiff. Obviously, having end of the world sex with his mistress is finally taking its toll. The bastard, I would love to have the opportunity to make him wince.

'Where are you going now, Sam?'

'Is Amber still out?'

'Yes, I can't track her or text her or phone her.'

'She needs to be here; we need to know where she is. I'll go out and find her.'

'Where will you look, Sam?'

'I don't know – anywhere she shouldn't be.'

'You stay here. I know where her friends live.'

'It's too dangerous, Nell. I'll go.'

'I'm a big girl, Sam.'

'No, you're not; you're average.'

'Girls aren't measured in height or width. Stop worrying about me; you find us some food for lunch. I'll get Amber.'

My confidence is growing. This task requires a certain sixth sense: a knowledge of teenage hangouts and the ability to eavesdrop on teenage conversations without getting noticed. I need to be inconspicuous. I'm an expert at being ignored. Sam isn't; he sticks out like a giant's sore thumb. He doesn't look convinced.

'I'm trained for this, Sam. Sex, pregnancy, childbirth, and child care teach a woman to have patience and gritted teeth during the worst of horrors and to develop the negotiating skills of an international diplomat in a genocidal war zone. The same things only teach men to shout from the sidelines and complain about something not being done right.'

'Actually those things teach a man to give a woman whatever she wants whenever she wants without questioning her, be humbled and sometimes injured watching something out of your control and realise you are way out of your depth when everyone smaller than you won't accept your authority.'

I remove my pipe lagging outfit. Sam walks away. I don't know who won or lost that battle.

I'm eager to leave for a road trip. I haven't been outside for days. Scraps has been quite happy using the old washing-up basin outside for a toilet than venture out into this bleakness. Gigi rarely leaves the house, anyway. I know there's a secret stash of desiccated cat poo somewhere in the house.

There's a fierce wind outside; it's cutting right through me. The air smells of death and nothing else. I know what death smells like because I frequently find half-eaten mouse corpses in the corners of my kitchen. This smell is more intense; bigger mice, and billions of them just lying around the world, slowly rotting away.

The car engine struggles to warm up as I scrape the sickly yellow ice off the inside of the windscreen. The petrol gauge is low. I won't be able to drive around forever. What would I be doing if I was sixteen? An actual shudder went down my back. I know I'm a hypocrite, but I don't want her doing the things I did back then. We knew less; they know more. I was also lucky; going out for a drink can be a life or death situation for a girl.

The car slowly gets warmer as I huddle up inside. I've forgotten what it's like to be warm and cosy. I want to enjoy this feeling while I can; it may be the last time I feel it. I rev the engine and play the CD that has been stuck in the car stereo since before smartphones were invented. It's a Christmas compilation album, but I don't care; I'm playing it loud. I haven't played loud music in a while. I need music like a hot poultice, too.

I've got control, albeit brief, albeit to find my missing daughter. I'm sure there is something inside me that can find her. She's a part of me, whether she likes it or not. I read somewhere that some of a mother's cells remain inside her children, and some of theirs remain in her. Mothers are the connective tissue back to our ancestors. Mitochondria are the powerhouse of the cell and are only inherited from the mother; the father's are destroyed on fertilisation. If only the pharaohs had known that.

Mothers are given time to build a relationship with their baby before it's even a baby. It's a desperate idea to cling onto, and DNA won't help me actually find her, but it fills me with purpose. I need a purpose. I've been looking for a purpose; I'm realising what purposes I have.

Maybe my circle doodles are the egg cell with the mitochondria reaching out. It's the original family tree with links to the core, the centre, the original, the start. That all sounds a bit grand. The doodles could just represent a speck of dust that keeps floating about, reaching out for a surface to settle on. It's art; it can be whatever I want it to be.

Imelda bangs on the car window, holding onto her woolly hat. 'Are you okay, Nellie? Are you leaving him?'

'I'm fine, Imelda. No, I'm not leaving him. I'm going to look for Amber.'

Imelda opens the car door, letting in an unwelcome gust of freezing air.

'I can't hear you. What did you say?'

'I'm going to look for Amber. Sam's inside if you want him.'

'Oh, it's quite cosy in here. I might stay with you. I could do with seeing beyond the end of the street.'

Imelda gets in the car. All the warmth just evaporated, just like my brief moment of freedom. I turn the music off and drive painfully slowly away. A single magpie pecks furiously away at some roadkill on the verge. It flies straight in front of me. They're taking the piss now.

'Where are we going to look first? Have you got any sucky sweets? You'd better get a move on; it might get even darker soon.'

'I suppose I will have to try every village between here and Burton. I doubt Amber ventured further than a brisk walk home. She's too lazy to go far from her comfort zone. The roads look slippery, so I need to drive slowly. I bet there's no roadside assistance available right now.'

'What will you do if you break down, Nellie? You've never known what it's like not to have someone out there ready to help.'

What Imelda said is true, which is why it pisses me off even more.

The car is reluctant to make this trip; every gear change is a struggle. It doesn't want to find out what's at the end of the street. It could be a cliff edge hanging over a lake of molten lava.

It isn't. The roads are intact for the moment. Familiar landmarks like the pubs and parks don't seem so familiar anymore. There is nobody about. The pavements are empty of debris, let alone life. Every house looks empty except for the odd tussle at the curtains. A yellowy smog fills the air.

'This is pointless. You're not going to find a bright neon sign saying "delinquent children hanging out here", are you?'

'No, Imelda. I'm not. I'm using my instinct.'

'Pah! Just roll the window down and listen for signs of debauchery. But don't wind it down too far; it's nice and warm in here.'

I drive slowly into the next village. Luckily, ex-mining villages are only about half a mile apart because the miners had to walk to work. I stopped the car in the middle of the main street. I've always wanted to do that, knowing no one is going to tell me off for a Highway Code violation now. There are no other cars; I can't hear anything in the distance. It doesn't feel like there is a distance anymore. There are no signs of debauchery, although what does debauchery sound like? It's usually hidden by loud music. Where is everyone? Have they all killed themselves? There's the occasional dog bark and baby wailing inside the dark houses. What brings down a nation will also bring down a woman: violence, confusion, and a lack of control.

I'll have to repeat the same procedure in every village before the petrol runs out. For once there's no one to beep the horn at. There's no one in my way. I like this noiseless world. There are no expectations. Everything has changed. I should fear the unknown, but the creative inside of me sees it as another blank canvas.

I could leave everyone behind. I could kick Imelda out and venture out into this grisly abyss with no worries, no dependency, no stress. This car isn't full of people needing me.

I would be scared if the world really is empty, if there's nothing but more bleakness. There might be nothing to respond to, nothing to react to; even the trees are dying. It could be… boring.

Artists are never bored; we can create anything out of nothing. But I don't want to have to. I quite like the things already created.

Imelda clutches her crochet bag tightly. 'Why have we stopped? What are you doing? Where is your head right now? That bloody maternal instinct kicking in yet? How's your perfect motherly radar doing? If you don't hurry up, your daughter will be sold as a sex slave. Get a move on, Nellie.'

I genuinely forgot she was here for a second. The free world is tempting, but I can't do it alone. I'm not very good on my own; I can remember. It sounds better having complete control, but if there's no one around being an arsehole, who will stop me from becoming an arsehole? Arseholes exist to keep the rest of us in check. I'm usually too scared to fight my own battles because I've always thought of everyone being bigger than me, in size and intelligence. But I know I'm good at surviving. I've battled death at my own hands repeatedly; I always won.

There's marauding gangs out here ready to rape and kill me for the half-eaten bag of pappy crisps stuffed under my seat three weeks ago. If they were going to challenge me to who could last the longest with crippling contractions, then I would win that. Although, if I'm completely honest, I only managed a few hours before screaming for an epidural. Someone at work beat me by being in one single labour for five whole days. They won't challenge me to a battle of wills or a quick-draw with the wet wipes packet either. The strongest and meanest always get their way.

Imelda turns to look at me. 'Why don't you stop effing about, Nellie, and try up there, anywhere? We're sitting effing ducks here!'

I hate it when she's right, because then it looks like I'm obeying her. Let's pick a random road and see where it takes us. On my own, I would probably float around aimlessly.

The Bronze Age

We drive through a small wood before the next village. It's clearly not healthy to be isolated in body or mind. A varied, random, cluttered life is better than a single-track road to a dead end. I need my family to feel secure. I need them to make me laugh. Being part of a unit is always safer physically and mentally.

Imelda raises her chin. She might as well have a beam of light circling her head to warn me I'm in dangerous waters. 'Maternal instinct, my arse. You're going to drive around aimlessly like you've done your whole life, hoping something will magically happen.'

I can't react to her; I have trained myself not to.

I stop the car and get out. I must have some peace. Imelda looks bemused as I step out into the freezing cold.

The pungent wind rattles through the trees. I take my shoes and socks off to let my feet touch the ground. It's freezing. I can't feel how cold it actually is. I have no idea what I'm doing. Am I trying to meet my maker? The goddess? Speak to Mother Earth directly? I don't want to return to the car just now. Frostbite seems a more preferable option.

I need to draw. The mud of this land is my paper; my fingers are my pencil. This land always provides. The mud is hard, though; I can't make a line, only cracked marks. I crouch down and grab fistfuls of icy mud with my hands. Normally my back and knees would be screaming at me, but they're too numb to notice. I force the clumps together while they melt ever so slightly from my warmish touch. The frozen ground has deadened the soles of my feet already. This is why Mother Earth created hot flushes, for when women are left out in the cold.

'What the eff are you doing, Nellie?'

Imelda is shouting from inside the car without winding the window down, but I can still hear her. I don't know what I'm doing, but I'm enjoying it. I'm enjoying it because it's pissing her off.

'Is that a ritual? If it's witches' stuff, it doesn't work. I've tried it.'

Mud is our dust that becomes her new skin. It doesn't talk to the magpies or make your dreams come true. It's arrogant of humans to think their words are enough to bend the laws of physics to their will. I have to touch Mother Earth with my hands and get stuck in if I want to feel it and make it work for me. I suppose this is a type of meditation, a way to focus. Although from Imelda's point of view it does look like I've lost my fucking mind. I'm only explaining this inside my head; she can't hear the reasoning behind making a frozen mud ball.

The world is too quiet, as if it's sleeping. This road used to flow like an artery, cars pumping through like blood cells, the forests breathing air like lungs. Streams and rivers cleaned the land. But now it's dying; the arteries and veins have stopped pumping. I'm a single blood cell; I'm no use on my own. This is what happens when you get up close and personal with Mother Earth. It's like staring at a Georgia O'Keefe painting: you must stare it right in the face, intimately, instead of walking past and disregarding it.

I need mental core strength. The Earth has core strength. I need to tap into it. Focus on the mother, the source. Trees are mere hairs on her back.

I can see Imelda roll her eyes in my peripheral vision. She rummages around in the glove compartment, looking for something.

The world is made up of 70% water, just like our bodies. Did Mother Earth create us in her own image? We're all linked; we all came from the same atoms. The Earth is a living thing, but where is its brain? Where is its soul? Do I need to know where it is before I believe it exists?

Yeah, I might actually be losing it. A lack of sensory stimuli can do this to people. Humans don't do very well without colour, fragrance, warmth, the distant hum and the taste of fresh air on the wind.

I'm not losing it; I'm embracing it. The best things we've ever created have been inspired by nature: burdock burrs inspired Velcro, kingfishers inspired fast-moving trains, birds inspired planes, and geckos inspired gloves to scale the Burj Khalifa. What else can we learn from epochs of experimentation?

Gaudi knew it; that's why he wanted his cathedral, the *Sagrada Família*, to honour nature as much as it honoured any man or woman. We can only attempt to understand the mysteries of the universe through the metaphors that fly, flow and scurry all around us. And we can only surpass our own limitations when we harness what already works with the same elements we have to deal with. When no one else is around, she makes a good teacher, priest, influencer, mentor, guide, and mother. This is my church.

The wind picks up; it makes the cold air penetrate deeper. We created machines as extensions of ourselves to smother the earth, to connect the earth, to cover it like a cyborg cloak. The machine is broken, smothered with ash, flooded by seawater and sprinkled with fallen masonry. The mechanics are dead, their knowledge with them. An army of plants and weeds will break through all the concrete and reclaim what was once theirs. We're back to square one; she's bringing us back into line. We've literally been grounded. We tried to hold her back, contain her, monitor her, assess her, grade her, categorise her and play with her like a toy. Well, hear her roar! She's mad as hell. I'll go where the wind takes me; I've heard branches scream like a woman when they break.

The cold is starting to get to me, even though I can't feel it anymore. I can't help this overwhelming need to go a bit Andy Goldsworthy. He would arrange debris from Mother Earth in an aesthetically pleasing arrangement for an ephemeral connection back to Mother Earth. I need to touch the earth. I need to feel the elements and interact with them. I must understand. I won't have time to take photographs for an expensive coffee-table book, though.

This soil of my ancestors has been thoroughly kneaded by the tatty boots of miners, weavers, and potters. Although I think most of my direct ancestors came from Norfolk. It doesn't matter; the British sculpted our wilderness to suit our needs, from dragging enormous stones across rivers and mountains to make pretty circles, to mowing every verge as if it's going to be used to play cricket on. We sculpted this place. I'm playing my part in what are probably its final hours.

Obviously, I sculpt the mud into a sphere; I won't let this motif go. I crave the sense of a perfect sphere; it reminds me of rubbing my pregnant belly. Hands naturally shape things into a curved shape – I'd need tools to make any other shape.

There's a loose bit of barbed wire from a nearby fence. If I wrap the barbed wire around the mud sphere, I could make it look like my doodle. It looks like the rage of the earth is battling with the man-made wire. I don't hate man-made stuff; I love Wi-

Fi and non-stick saucepans. I don't want this to be a metaphor for destroying everything we've built. I think that what we battle eventually becomes our protector. The wire will protect. Nothing can harm the sphere while it's surrounded by the rusty barbed wire.

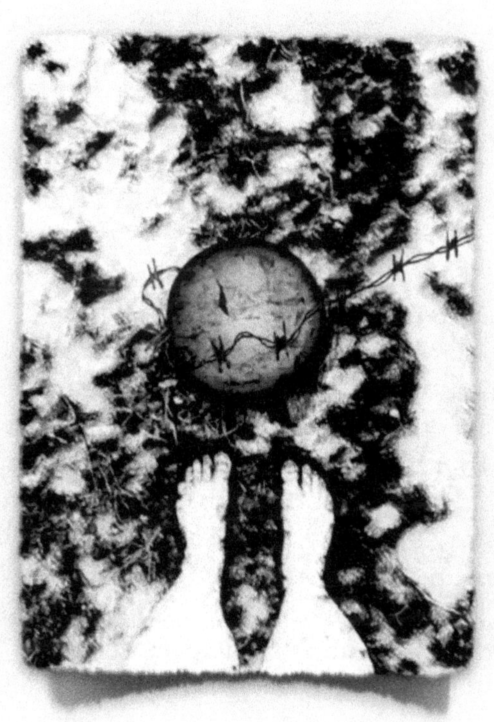

I have to understand Mother Earth. She started this destruction. She's about to consume us all. There's got to be a clue somewhere out here on how to survive all this? She doesn't require us to get on our knees and beg or pray; she doesn't want offerings or sacrifices of things she already provided. What would I want? I'm a she.

'For fuck's sake, Nellie! Let's get a move on!'

Mother Earth doesn't answer me; she's never been anthropomorphised. She's not allowed a voice. How ironic. I'm not looking for a manifesto. I don't need to tell others what I know. Mother Earth learns through creativity and mimicry; everything it makes is art. Mother Earth lets the strong survive, but it also allows the weak to create their own path to find their time in the sun. It might be a lengthier, more fiddly path, but it's possible. My life was never going to be on display at a horticultural show. Mine was not about the pruning or lack of bugs. A well-chewed leaf means a beautiful butterfly will live. We have to accept destruction as a force for life. The bug-free roses might win a rosette, but they don't feed the butterflies. Mother Earth never had a clipboard or gift vouchers; she moves through patterns, fractals and chaos. Like my doodle, these barbed tentacles are like roots from a seed or neurons connecting everything seen to be comprehended as a whole.

The brain of Mother Earth is underneath the soil, connected by fungi and roots; the "wood-wide web" is her nervous system. I'm sure that theory has been debunked, but I don't care; it works for me now. Everything works better with connections. Neurons look like roots looking for water, except they're looking for information, for knowledge, for experience, for happiness, for purpose. A solitary sphere is vulnerable; it has to reach out for stability. I've been drawing Mother Earth all this time. Did she want us to protect her with affordable fencing?

'If I had thought we were going to go at a snail's pace, I would've stayed at home and watched the nuclear fallout make my wallpaper bubble up.'

I can only concentrate on one holy mother at a time. This never-ending length of barbed wire is taking on a shape of its own. It's too unstable just flapping about. I need to wrap the wire around itself. I'm giving it legs.

Is the circle the mother, the earth, the core? Do I want to be the centre? Do I want complete control? Or do I just want to keep everyone together? Or do I want someone to come and stop me from rolling around randomly? The atom is the mother; it splits to create chaos or combines to create something ordered. We are all made from a combination of minuscule, connected circles. The tentacles are the choices we make; sometimes curved, sometimes they come back on themselves, sometimes they wrap themselves around another too tightly, sometimes there's barely a touch, sometimes they connect with others, sometimes they are repelled. All the time they are connected to their core, the centre, their beginning, their origin.

'I'm going to play some music or something. Something that will stop this effing nonsense.'

I'm now making the most significant creation of my life while listening to *Last Christmas* by Wham! Some mothers really don't get it. We can't be experts in psychoanalysis, behaviour control, algebra or war poetry. But we are experts in connections, protecting, nurturing, tolerating pain, deflecting trauma, creating trauma, confiscating, forgiving, loving unconditionally, and putting up with all levels of shit thrown at us. We're natural problem solvers; our physicality forces us to overcome adversity every month. Circles are hard to crack under pressure, which is why it's catastrophic when a mother gets it wrong.

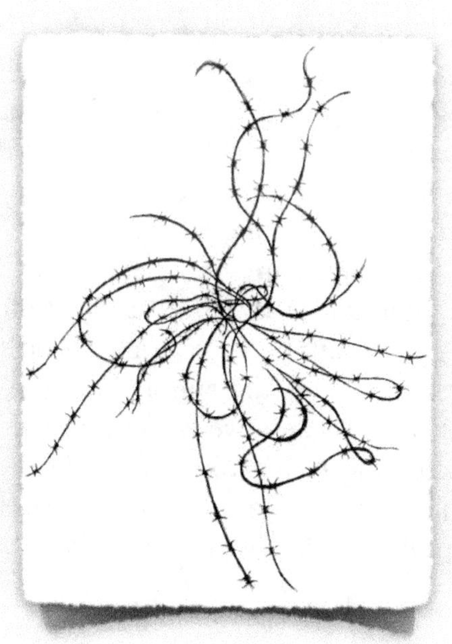

Like the earth, we are not perfect and prone to spontaneous cataclysmic eruptions, but we heal and recover and grow anew. Maybe magpies can talk to Mother Earth; they can probably feel her energy coming up from below, emanating fear, love, protection. It would make sense that Mother Earth is gravity: reclaiming chins, eyelids, boobs and bums, everything she created returns to the soil, eventually.

'I'd be quicker on my mobility scooter.'

I wish I was as good a mother as mine was. She was perfect. My kids don't look up to me like I did to her. I did my best. I hugged them enough to stop them from becoming sociopaths. I read to them enough to open their minds to awe and wonder. I fed them enough, so they didn't know genuine hunger. I sheltered them enough so they wouldn't die of hypothermia. I listened to their incoherent rants long enough to give them a sense of validation. I explained enough so that the world didn't seem too scary. I told them enough to make them curious about the rest. I wiped enough so they knew what clean was. I protected them enough so that they weren't hurt too much. It was the rest of society that ignored them, laughed at them, rejected them, and turned their heads away. Abused children must find it less of a shock when they enter adulthood and discover it can be a cruel and cold place.

Mother Earth doesn't judge; she isn't spiteful or vengeful. Cruelty and cold strengthen us. She's chaotically random but provides everything needed to survive. She doesn't speak a language; she's a visual teacher. Artists are the angels of Mother Earth; we should get our own hierarchy.

Delusions of grandeur are never far away from a creative solution to an existential crisis. I need a delusion of grandeur to force me to create. Oh shit, now I've got a goddess complex.

There's an abundance of metaphors out here, already created and displayed for all to see, but we walk past them, cut them down or spray them with poison. It's ironic that we focussed on building towers and shrines to reach God when really we should have been playing in the mud. We shouldn't go higher than the trees, or where the air gets too thin. She really did lay it all out for us to see; she just needed an audio guide.

'Someone from the council needs to do something about this road; it's dreadful.'

The car is man-made, made in man's image: a body with eyes that can see in the dark and a daft grin on its face. We can't escape what we know; we are limited to our imagination, inspired only by what we can see. Form follows an already evolved function. The car metaphor only works for man-made problems. I must have watched *Herbie Goes Bananas* too many times when I was young.

'If I were you, I'd hurry up. The crows will be picking her eyeballs out by the time we get there.'

My sculpture is finished. I stand up and look back at it. My arms are bleeding from the barbed wire's unyielding design. She has no arms, so can not help herself. She has no head, so can not think for herself. But she has legs, so she can hold the mud sphere securely in place instead of rolling around aimlessly. I've finally made a final piece. This is how beautiful my pain looks. I shall call it Barbie; she has been reborn.

I'm panting hard. I'm freezing on the outside and hot on the inside. I'm scary. Finally, I've achieved a life goal. This is the first sculpture I have finished in over twenty years. That's two life goals in a short space of time. Obviously, I needed more desperation in my life.

I can't solve a random catastrophe with an orderly queue; it will take a random idea in order to survive this. The Earth won't be destroyed by this natural disaster; new things will grow from the ashes.

'Why don't you—'

'For fuck's sake, Imelda, shut the fuck up, will you! I can't fucking concentrate!'

Shit. Did I just open the gates of hell?

Atlantis

I can't leave this here. I made it; it's mine now. I created it; I can't leave it behind. It's heavy, but my strength is returning; I forgot that strength is powered by determination, not wishful thinking. The boot is filled with too much crap. It won't fit in a bag for life.

I put it on the back seat of the car. It looks pretty menacing sitting behind Imelda.

I'm back in the car, still with bare feet. I'm not looking at Imelda; I'm not ready for a critique just yet.

I need to get my breath back, and the feeling in my toes. It hurts to put my socks and shoes back on. Imelda can't stop tapping her foot and shaking her head. I drive off as if all I'd done is just step out of the car to post a letter.

There's an eerier silence in the car than there was outside.

'What have you got to be so angry about, Nellie?'

'I can't control it anymore, Imelda. It comes from a place I don't recognise.'

'The menopause didn't make me that angry.'

'Maybe it's because you were always angry, so there was no discernible difference!'

'I remember it being quite cathartic. No more periods was a positive thing.'

'It's periods that made me feel alive, useful, productive. There is nothing positive about the menopause, like I'm unbearably itchy right now. I mean, what the fuck? Why now?'

'Itching is a sign of healing. Bet your generation doesn't know that; it was never trending on YouTube. Your body is healing all over, all the time.'

'It doesn't feel like healing; it feels like torture.'

'Everything happens for a reason.'

'Really? Why give us thinning hair then?'

'It makes legs easier to shave.'

'Memory loss?'

'So we can watch our favourite programmes again and again.'

'Sore joints?'

'So you have a genuine excuse not to jog round the block and die young trying to look slim.'

'Low libido?'

'So men leave you the eff alone.'

'Irritability?'

'I'm not sure that's a symptom of menopause alone, but we have it every month so everyone can leave us the eff alone.'

'Weight gain?'

'So we're cushioned when we fall.'

'Night sweats?'

'Make us believe we've retired to the Mediterranean.'

'Vaginal dryness?'

'To stop us turning into cougars or what is it, MILFs? And therefore embarrassing our children.'

'Permanently erect nipples?'

'In case you do want to be a cougar or MILF and want to embarrass your children. Or so we can still get the attention of any man when our faces start to look like a Basset Hound. Let's be honest, we need all the help we can to get noticed after fifty.'

'Itchy nipples?'

'Well, at least someone's touching them.'

'Discomfort during sex?'

'That's not a menopause symptom; that's a problem that was always there that no one likes to admit.'

'Difficulty sleeping?'

'Because we're reassessing everything we have ever done.'

'Low mood?'

'Because chocolate cake doesn't contain enough healthy vitamins.'

'Anxiety?'

'Because, like any new part of your life, you don't know what the eff is going to happen to you, it's really just anticipation; it's okay.'

'Brain fog?'

'You only want to think about new things, not the same shit you've been thinking for thirty years. Let it be blocked out.'

'Infertility?'

'New job opportunity.'

'New body odour?'

'An excuse to buy new perfumes, body sprays, body lotions, bath crèmes and indulgent shower crèmes. It forces you to start looking after yourself.'

'Incontinence?'

'So you can adopt a ballerina pose every time you sneeze.'

'Hairs on your chin?'

'To make sure you're still looking after yourself.'

'Unbridled rage?'

'Men have it; women finally get to level up.'

'Zits?'

'To remind you that your youth wasn't as perfect as you remember through your rose-tinted specs. Our minds need new space for new experiences and ideas so you can forget what you've evolved into. Nellie, periods were shit and debilitating, so why should the menopause be any different? Women are subdued by hormones to make them take care of the babies. The menopause lifts the veil. You think it's an illness until you realise it's a strength. It's actually liberating; the realisation of who you were meant to be or always were. Since when did we take everything that was sacred or special and make it a burden?'

Hmm, this day is getting weirder. Did Imelda just spurt out wisdom?

'Nellie, I've been post-menopausal longer than fertile; my baby brain was taken from me a long time ago. I'm like a Dickensian Miss Haversham, but instead of being stuck in her wedding dress, I've been stuck in my giant maternity knickers and incontinence pads. Dickens liked to capitalise on victimhood, with the ghosts of the past clinging to their ankles. But the past won't help us deal with the effing present. The present is not waiting on the side of the road to be offered a lift. It jumps onto the bonnet like a vengeful lover every minute of every day. We can't get anywhere until we drive really fast and the present falls away behind us.'

'But you still believe this is the work of a big old man in the sky.'

'I believe what is necessary to keep my head above water in the crochet club. They are the only people outside of my family who will put up with me. I do what I can to fit in. When you get older, you either get wise or scared. Don't assume you know what I think. I can still learn new things.'

This is why we should still learn from the masters. I had no idea what she was capable of until I studied her up close. I've always walked past thinking it was too much hard work to understand her. Many try to copy and paste from masters without taking it all in. That's why we have art that people don't recognise as art, and why some people don't recognise life as life. Life and art prepare us for what is coming: tough decisions, cliff-edge drama, adulthood, a decaying body, and the greatest mysteries still to be discovered.

'What are you thinking, Nellie? Think out loud, for God's sake! I can't work out whether you agree with me or not.'

'I keep my thoughts to myself because I can't be sure I agree with them all the time.'

'Well, without knowing your thoughts, I can only assume the worst.'

'What do you assume?'

'Every woman wants to kill her husband at some point; I know the signs.'

'I don't want to kill Sam!'

'You hoped he would die, though.'

My head is now frozen more than my feet. What do I say? Is she trying to get me to confess?

That bloody chin of hers has risen again. I hate it when she has the upper hand.

'Wanting to kill your husband is another symptom of menopause. We change, but men don't, and they don't notice the change in us because it's not obvious. Killing everyone who doesn't change with you is a latent instinct that humans struggle to shake off. I should know.'

I'm not sure how to interpret that. Am I trapped in a car with a serial killer?

'It's easier to be yourself than get rid of everyone who doesn't understand you, trust me on that one, Nell.'

This is one time I should keep my thoughts all neatly wrapped up inside this head. Although she's right, she's admitting to having been unhinged for some time. God knows what she's capable of.

'Women like me would have been burned at the stake for talking such truths. Nobody likes wisdom, especially when it contradicts their own beliefs. All women fear becoming the anti-hero, the old crone, the witch, but it can be a lot of fun. You fear your future self too much; embrace it. Wise women stop mad men from going to war; that's why we were really tied to the stake.'

'What happened between you and Wilfred?'

'Fuck off, Nellie. I'm not that vulnerable.'

Worth a try.

'I do hate Sam sometimes. But I also hate myself. I've lost the capacity to love.'

'Don't be stupid, love isn't a capacity, it's a reaction. Sometimes he can be a real dick. You're entitled to hate him for a moment. If you were exactly what he wanted, then there would be nothing for him to look forward to.'

'He has a different set of expectations to what I actually am now; I've turned into a constant source of disappointment.'

'You can't be in love with someone else if you're not in love with yourself. But as self-loathing destroys, so does self-adoration. It's why I've been keeping you humble with all my little jabs. I could see what was happening. Love can't be ignored, destroyed or avoided. It needs nurturing.'

My head is spinning, but at least it has forced blood back to my extremities. I can wiggle my toes again.

'I've used half of the petrol just figuring out what I am doing.'

'Then you better get an effing move on; if you don't find Amber soon, we won't be able to get home.'

Fertile Crescent

Every village is too quiet for a hedonistic teenage party. Maybe they're having a silent orgy like those silent discos. It feels as if all the young people have just disappeared. There are no nightclubs open, nor bars or any other building designed to host the horny and defiant. They must be at someone's house; someone must be letting them use their house. But she's been gone a couple of days; who would allow such a party? Somebody without small children and very low hygiene standards. An empty house; a house with no boundaries, no rules, no owner. What about a new house, one that hasn't been bought? There are so many new estates round here though, which one do I choose? The biggest, they would definitely go for a show house with the shiniest new furnishings in it. Well, I would have anyway.

'We'll try that new executive estate in Appleby. The houses are huge, the light fittings pretentious, and there are deep-pile rugs everywhere.'

'Why there? They're all snobs up there.'

'I don't think the kids of today really care about social class; they'll just want a big empty house.'

'Oh, well, what do I know.'

'I'm sorry I snapped at you, Imelda, but I'm rather stressed at the moment.'

'It's okay, dear, I understand. You lash out at whoever's nearest; I can take it. A woman's physical prime might be when she's young, but her mental prime is now.'

'I've never known so much. I've never had so much knowledge with which to experiment with. My skill set is bigger than I realised, and my hormones aren't making me think about fucking and making babies — well, not all the time. It doesn't look like I've got long before I settle into bitterness, so I'd better make the most of it.'

'Bitter isn't the only option after trauma, unless you enjoy the taste of it.'

'I don't like the taste. No-one is complete until they have made peace and friendship with someone from the opposition by any means possible. I think that's why there are two opposite parents to practise on before we try reality. I need to make peace with my opposite piece.'

I drive at breakneck speed to get to the new estate. Imelda clings to the door handle as if we were in a rally. I was here just a few weeks ago. Gaba's hobby of viewing houses she can't afford might just pay off; she enjoys walking around a pristine kitchen that has never been used. The proportions of the front doors and windows make the houses look like they were designed by any five-year-old. I'm surprised they didn't add fake smoke coming out of a fake chimney.

The estate looks like a drug dealer's hovel now. There are sofas outside on the grass, and the front gardens are strewn with abandoned clothes and empty beer bottles. Every front door is off its hinges. I parked up next to the graffitied cars.

'Are you coming in, Imelda?'

'Good God, no. I'll stay here, thank you very much. Leave the engine on though; I'm warm now.'

'I need to save the petrol; you'll have to blow on your hands.'

I switch the engine off. I can hear the inevitable groans coming from inside the house. I tiptoe around vomit and smashed glass on the newly laid path, and tentatively move the damaged front door to one side.

The large sitting room looks like an updated version of Bosch's *Garden of Earthly Delights*. There are contorted bodies in various positions that I doubt even appeared in the *Kama Sutra*.

Bosch was warning us this would happen five hundred years ago; did we listen? Fuck no. We treated it like an instruction manual. You only know not to touch a burning flame once you've touched it, repeatedly for some. The threat of eternal damnation has never been enough to stop people from doing weird shit.

It's not easy manoeuvring around these entwined body parts. Do I pick up a random arm or leg to see if my child is underneath? Everything and everyone reeks of various bodily fluids that were never meant to mingle. There are definitely Amber's type of people here – this is exactly the hedonism she was looking for. They're intentionally collecting experiences for a future game of "Never Have I Ever." I'm glad I grew out of competitive depravity.

I don't think any of these body parts belong to Amber; I'll have to brave the upstairs.

The floors are so sticky you could probably make candy floss out of them. I gingerly walk upstairs and across the large landing strewn with beer cans and tubes of lube. I can hear the groaning of someone familiar; I'm scared to open the bedroom door.

'Stop. Stop it, please.'

Gaba lies naked on top of another naked woman on the floor. There's a large dog trying to hump her back. She tries pathetically to shove him off.

The enormous dog is very heavy and very keen. I try to help Gaba stand up, but she can't. She sits on the edge of the bed while I try to find some random clothes that are lying scattered on the floor. Can't see my lovely sequined dress anywhere; don't think I'm going to need it until society rebuilds itself and throws a nostalgic party to celebrate.

I try to prop Gaba up as I help her down the stairs. Either she's getting heavier or I'm getting weaker. This reminds me of my eighteenth birthday and hers. If she falls down the stairs, I will have to let her tumble down.

Somehow I get Gaba to the car. She sits next to Barbie.

'I'm going back for Amber.'

'Okay, but if she throws up, Nellie, I'm not helping her.'

Amber is definitely not in the house; I've looked in every room. I checked the not-so-manicured back garden. There is a garden shed, but I can see from here that's being used as an extra toilet. Lovely. The last place to check is the sales office, which would have become the garage. The glass door has been smashed in; the photocopier has been turned over. That's impressive; those things are heavy. And there she is, huddled up under a desk with a boy. She looks awful. She's been sick; it's all down her top, and there are remnants around her mouth. At least she's fully clothed still, although that's not protecting much. I peel the boy's arm away from her and help her stand up. Her legs are walking as if they're made of pipe cleaners.

'Mum… Mum…why… are your hands… covered… in mud and… blood?'

Somehow I get Amber to stagger down the path and through the garden gate. Her legs finally give way, and she collapses in a heap on the pavement. At least the freezing tarmac will numb some of her aching body parts. The boy whose arm I peeled off her has staggered up behind us.

'At least she's got someone to take her home, at least she has a home,' he whimpered.

'Haven't you got a home?' I stupidly ask.

'Nah, my parents fucked off in opposite directions when the food ran out.'

Don't do it! Don't feel sorry for him! It doesn't matter that he's helping to carry Amber into the back of the car. Concentrate on Imelda's tutting.

'Thank you for helping.'

'It's okay, I'd do anything for her.'

'Are you okay?'

Don't give in to the sweeping the pavement with one foot routine; this is peak Dickensian now.

'Why don't you come with us? We haven't got much, but we can look after you.'

What is wrong with me?

'Thanks.'

'You'll have to get into the boot. Just sit on the rubbish.'

'Thank you so much!'

'What's your name?'

'Russell.'

Shit! I don't need this. I feel I have to help; some scrap of maternal instinct still clings on in here somewhere. Russell climbs into the boot and sits on a year's worth of detritus.

Amber gets into the backseat next to Gaba, who is pushed up against Barbie. The barbed wire presses into her skin; she doesn't even notice. Imelda scowls at me as I get into the front seat. She turns around to look at the mess behind her.

'Who's that? Why are we rescuing him? What are you thinking of? Are you mad?'

'I probably am, but I can't leave him there. It's disgusting.'

'How are you going to explain the extra mouths to feed to Sam? You could just dump them at the roadside and race off.'

I do race off, but only to get away from this place.

The White Goddess

Amber groans, 'Everybody else was going, I didn't want to be left out…I thought it would be amazing, I thought it would be fun…it's just a blur…the drinks tasted funny…some girls were crying, some boys were too.'

'It's okay, sweetheart, you're safe now. I've got you. I'll get you home, and then you can rest. No need to talk about it now.'

I try to appear calm, but if I grit my teeth any harder, they're going to crack.

'Why are you being nice to me? Shouldn't you hate me?'

'Why would I hate you for going to a party?'

'You hate everything I do.'

'No, I don't!'

'When did you stop liking me?'

'When you started watching The Real Housewives of Beverly Hills.'

'I had to rebel against something — you and Dad like drugs and alcohol.'

'I don't hate you, Amber. I just get mad when you tell me to fuck off.'

'That's because you're always telling me what to do.'

'I'm not telling you; I'm advising. It's different.'

'I don't want to be like you.'

'I don't want to be like me either, sometimes.'

'Being a teenager is hard. Everyone hates us.'

'I don't hate you; why do you keep saying that?'

'You don't talk to me anymore; I'm not cute anymore.'

'Being critical or defensive does not mean I hate you. Nobody is above criticism. I don't talk to you sometimes because your resting bitch face puts me off.'

'I'm only copying your face.'

'Amber, I don't have a resting bitch face!'

'Yes, you do. It's not there when you look in the mirror, but trust me, it's always there when you look at me.'

'But I'm not a bitch.'

'Well, whatever you're thinking, I modelled my "don't fuck with me" face on yours. It stopped me from being bullied. I hate it, but I have to keep up the act. I'm a method teenager.'

'Amber, you are my firstborn. I know I've made a lot of mistakes, you've made some too, but it hasn't even dented my love for you.'

'I wish you'd told me that before.'

'It's difficult knowing what to say and what to keep back for emergencies. Don't blame me for not knowing what's going on in your head. I've been learning to be a parent from your first breath till now. Every step with you is new to me.'

'So I'm an experiment.'

'You're the biggest badass I've created. I'm proud of you. Not in the way you're currently looking, but because you can stand up for yourself. I still can't do that today. You're a better woman than I am, and you've only been at it a short while.'

'You're not a great advert for womanhood.'

'Ok. Thanks. What did I get wrong this time?'

'You don't seem to enjoy it. You make it look like a lot of hard work and no fun.'

'That's life, not womanhood on its own.'

'I don't want to be a woman.'

'What?'

'It's scary.'

'Really?'

'When I was a child, I thought womanhood was lipstick, heels, flowery patterned dresses, a cute baby on your hip, and hoovering while dancing. Now I know it's napping, drinking pints of tea and saying "Ow!" or "Fuck this shit" every time you get up from the sofa.'

'Sorry I didn't have the skinny waist to be a billboard mother. I've been working on my personality and humour because I didn't have the perfect body. They last longer than your thigh gap and your taut cheekbones.'

'Billboard? You're a con artist. You didn't tell me the reality about never-ending pain, constant fear of humiliation, toxic shock syndrome, being too feminine, being too masculine, running like a girl, all the shaving, anal bleaching, and the gag reflex.'

I'm sure Imelda stopped breathing for a minute there. That's quite a lot to visualise.

'It's normal to hate your body, Amber, even when it's perfectly functional. Blame the adverts for telling everyone you can only be happy when you're skinny and fragile, not me.'

'I hope the anal bleach bottle has Braille on it.' Imelda picks up her crochet bag and unravels a ball of wool. No wonder Sam is an only child.

'Mum, my body can have everything from camel toe to phantom pregnancies. It's crazy what can go wrong with it.'

Gaba heard the word anal, so has awakened. 'The worst thing about being a woman is finding out you can earn better money being a stripper, but they never gave that a stall at the careers fair.'

'Thanks, Gab, but I think I've got—'

'And then there's the blood dribbling down your leg, sperm dribbling down your leg, slut shaming, not enjoying sex, walking round on tip toes, crying rape, rape claims dismissed, actual rape, fear of getting pregnant, unwanted pregnancy, carrying your rapist's baby, freezing your eggs, public proposals and deepfakes.'

I held Gaba's hand through all of those.

'I think what Gaba is trying to say, Amber, is that the career possibilities are limited for women. We can't swing our legs off a mile-high girder while eating our lunch; we're too unpredictable. We can't grease the drill on an unstable oil rig either. The only risk-taking bonus we can earn is sticking our naked arse in someone's face.'

'Women do take more risks than that, Mum. There's breast ironing, contraceptives that make you suicidal, bottom patting, seatbelts that will kill you, incapacitating ovulation pain, stirrups, speculums—'

'I know! And some of us have flushed tiny embryos down the toilet because no-one told us what a miscarriage looks like. Some of us had to carry a dead foetus inside of us for days, and give birth to a foetus that we knew was already dead. Some of us had to let doctors with head torches force a tube into our urethra at 3 am because our labia were so swollen after childbirth we couldn't pee normally.'

'I remember that. You had to pour a jug of water over your bits every time you went for a pee for a week. You were sore!' says Gaba, the expert in soreness.

'The truth is painful, but still the truth, Amber. We surrender our dignity, our privacy, our time, our health, our weight, our bodies, and our sanity. All so we can place ourselves in a position where we are reliant on a man's income in order to survive, while being called "thunder thighs" or "angels". Hairy nipples, stone babies and prolapsed vaginas are the least of our worries.'

'See! Why would I put myself through that, Mum? I don't want all that to happen to my body. Men have it so easy.'

'Men have worries too,' says Russell. He's sitting precariously behind two hungover, angry women who are now staring daggers at him. That was not a well-judged moment to weigh-in.

I stare at him through the rear-view mirror. 'You're right, Russell. All you have to worry about is going bald, a kick in the balls, and your voice breaking.'

Amber leans forward. 'What about glory holes, flicking willies, cottaging and unexpected hard-ons?'

Russell lifts his head and rests his head on the dog guard. 'And fighting, alpha males, beta males, doing dangerous stuff, lifting heavy stuff, being expendable and heroic gestures, proposals, saviour syndrome, showing emotions, being scary, date rape, having your kids taken off you, working long hours, chivalry, lower life expectancy, porn addiction, penile dysfunction, being too tall, little man syndrome, being macho, being a pussy, being treated like an ATM and the size of your penis?'

'And don't forget a finger up the arse after fifty,' adds Imelda.

I smile sympathetically. 'I don't think men need to worry about that anymore; there aren't a lot of rubber-gloved doctors left in the world.'

'I don't want to be a man either, Mum. I preferred my life when Santa would leave me snowy footprints across the floor and the tooth fairy left me a two-pound coin under my pillow to soothe the pain. It was so much easier then. Finding out it was all fake destroyed me.'

'Amber, awe and wonder help expand your horizons. It helps you think beyond the obvious and adds a higher level of enjoyment to an otherwise functional existence. Zebras don't jump off bridges or take pills when a lion approaches. They also don't dream of the circus or a glittery bridle. They carry on. Their needs are simple: eat, fuck, sleep and survive. Wild animals are prepared for stress; they exist in a constant state of stress. Stress doesn't kill you; it keeps you alive. It's desiring no stress that makes you eternally disappointed, and fat. Have you ever seen a fat or diabetic wild animal? The modern world insists you aspire to have a glittery bridle, and if you don't get a glittery bridle, then throw in the towel or litigate. We've created more to lose. Our suffering is human-made. We demand the circus; we insist it's our human right to have a glittery bridle and perform for applause.

Aspiring to live like the aristocracy of the past will be our undoing. All we need to do is not be the last to get out of the way when a lion actually gets here. Instead, we all hide behind the same tree.'

'Why do you have to make everything so complicated, Mum?'

'It's really not that complicated if you live in a metaphorical world, like I do. Why do you think the ancients came up with stories about racing rabbits and tortoises and old men in red flannel suits falling down chimneys? Reality is too boring for our intellect to bother with. We must challenge ourselves; otherwise, we're not living; we're just existing. Life is like a sport. Not everyone wins a trophy; some enjoy taking part, some relish the physical benefits, and some only push themselves as far as they can. It's all about personal bests. Everything hard is training us for losing, not winning, because we will all lose our lives in the end. When times are good, everyone's expectations are a flash car or a boob job; unnecessary things. Now that times are hard, your expectations will be eating and surviving.'

'I'm confused. Do you want me to take up a sport, Mum?'

'I didn't realise I was putting you off being a woman. I suppose dumping all women's knowledge on your daughters is like asking them to be a master craftsman aged 11.'

'Now do you understand why I have anxiety?'

I stop the car on the roundabout so I can turn round and look Amber straight in the eye.

'Being a woman makes us less selfish and less self-indulgent. Because of all the shit we go through, we have a higher pain threshold, stronger immunity, a stronger sense of smell, live longer, better memories, can multitask, can park near the entrance of a supermarket and have multiple orgasms.'

'I don't care about any of that shit; none of that makes you popular or happy. Except for the last one, maybe.'

'It's all worth it. I've realised that now. Every cramp, scream, tear, and urine sample, I'd do it all over again in a heartbeat. We're special. We get to make other humans inside our bodies. It's magic; it truly is. I have never felt so important. You have to accept the bad stuff; otherwise, you'd never know how good the good stuff is. See that lump of barbed wire next to you?'

'I was too afraid to ask what that was. I thought you'd started hoarding scrap metal again.'

'I made that. Just now. I made a woman out of barbed wire, protecting her core self. That's what a woman can be.'

Amber looks at Barbie.

'You're fucking weird, Mum.'

I'll let Amber process all this new information quietly for a moment. It might take another thirty years for her to understand Barbie. It's taken me this long to process. Why are all the answers I can create not instantly ready when I need them? Probably because I didn't put them on a canvas or plinth. Brains are not galleries; they are fluid and fucking hard to control. I continue driving, wondering if I should smash the flashing refuel button.

'Why do men get a finger up the bum?' Russell asks.

'To check their prostate,' I explain.

'What's a prostate?'

'For fuck's sake, don't they teach you anything in school?'

'Only how to put a condom on a banana.'

'Don't worry about it, Russell. You don't have to worry about what's going on inside of you unless you do manage to reach old age or end up in prison. Men endlessly poking things with a stick doesn't prepare them for splinters. If only women could manhandle their ovaries as frequently as men rearrange their bollocks, we could care so much less.'

Let them mull that over. Russell's eyes are very wide open now. He should think twice before getting into a car with strange women. Amber, Gaba and Imelda are looking at me like they're trying to remember the name of the emergency psychiatrist. Amber turns to stare at Russell.

'Who the fuck is this dude, Mum?'

'I was hoping you would tell me, Amber.'

'I've never seen him before in my life.'

'He had his arm around you under the table where I found you.'

'Really?'

Shit. I'm dreading explaining this to Sam. He hates Gaba with a long-held, deeply felt passion. He also said he would maim the first boy who touched his daughter. I'm bringing them both home to be fed and watered when we don't have enough for ourselves. What is it in me that can't leave them by the roadside? Maybe it's the knowledge that one of them knows where we live and would turn up later anyway. Or maybe the knowledge that this will infuriate Sam is what is driving me to do it. I need to stop pushing Sam away; I need him more than ever.

I park right outside our house at a strange angle; there are no phones to preserve this example of bad parking. Most of our neighbours have driven away. Where to? What do they know? I should have shared more sugar with them.

I usher the bedraggled revellers into the hallway. Sam isn't in the house as fucking usual. Peter is in charge, which is probably why Zoe and Tom are running around the house throwing plastic axes at each other. Scraps chases them while wearing the dog skeleton Halloween costume the kids bribed me to buy for him last year. Peter looks really pleased to see me come home. Zoe and Tom stop when they see a strange boy in their hallway. They stand in everyone's way, holding their axes like medieval henchmen guarding a castle. Zoe has drawn a moustache on her own face; it's a bit smudged.

'Who's that, Mummy?'

'This is Russell, Zoe. He was helping Amber, I think.'

'I think I'll get a boyfriend when I'm older, to keep myself occupied.' Zoe and Tom run off, throwing plastic axes at each other again.

Maybe I can hide Russell under the stairs until we need him. Gaba staggers upstairs, probably to sprawl over my bed. I will have to change the sheets afterwards, despite having no working washing machine. Amber goes straight to her bed, leaving a terrified Russell on his own in the front room with Peter and Imelda. Zoe keeps stopping to look Russell up and down. I'm exhausted. I'm not offering my last teabag to this stranger. I'm not sure what to do.

'Well, I've had enough for one day. I suppose I'd better go home.'

That was the most theatrical yawn from Imelda yet.

'The last thing you need, Nell, is another bed blocker.'

It's not like her to be so thoughtful. I'm looking at Imelda differently now; there's a lot more going on in her head than I realised. Old people are messengers from the future.

The Iron Age

Another night I've survived. No ash-filled breath or bored child has brought me down yet. The clean white ceiling is still intact. I haven't even tried to kill myself again. I'm actually doing okay, relatively speaking. My bed is empty of Gaba or any other hangers-on.

Tom and Zoe's beds are empty. Every bedroom door is open; every bed is empty. Where is everyone? Have they all run away, been kidnapped, been dragged out onto the garden and beaten to death with broom handles? My heart is racing. Something has happened!

I nearly went arse over tit down the stairs to find everyone. There was no need to panic; they were all sitting neatly round the kitchen table: Imelda, Gaba, Amber, Peter, Russell, Tom and Zoe, waiting patiently to be fed while playing *Star Wars* Monopoly. It looks like Zoe owns the whole Death Star.

If the ash falls here and cements their bodies in their dying throes like Pompeii, I wonder what they will make of this scene in hundreds of years' time. Especially when they discover a soft carrot stick dipped in what I hope is ketchup in every hand.

Zoe isn't enjoying the new food combinations. 'Your sauces need to leave me, Mummy.'

I would love to have a hissy fit and demand equality, but I'm too tired and I don't want anyone snooping through the cupboards and discovering I don't clean the shelves very often. There's a barbecue sauce spillage that's been there for years. Stop internalising these hissy fits; they're not very effective in my head.

'Can we eat sweets for breakfast instead, Mummy?'

'How do cake decorations and pesto sound, Zoe?'

'Yummy!'

I really need to abandon this poker face. I'm not gambling; there's nothing left to win. Nobody understands what I'm feeling. Everybody looks pale, hungry and tired. I spread the remaining supplies that Sam had left out on the table. There is now officially nothing left.

They devoured the leftovers in seconds, leaving nothing left for me or Sam. I don't know where Sam is, or the baked beans he promised. My stomach is rumbling. I've only got two pieces of dried fusilli pasta to satisfy it; it's not enough anymore. If he doesn't hunt and gather some baked beans, then that is it; I'm off. Although my hunting and gathering got me groped last time.

I wind up the clockwork radio, the only connection to the outside world. A repeat announcement states that an angry mob discovered the Prime Minister and his family hiding in a secret bunker in Fife. He didn't go down with the ship like the King did at Windsor Castle. Apparently, most world leaders had prepared for this event because the scientists had warned them it was imminent. There had been a news blackout to stop worldwide panic. They're playing a sound recording of the moment the prime minister was discovered. You can just about hear him wailing like a small child above the noise of the mob banging saucepans with wooden spoons.

'Well, at least we don't have to worry about the patriarchy anymore,' says Imelda casually, 'maybe this disaster will allow for a matriarchy instead.'

'A matriarchy would make the FTSE graph look like an Alton Towers ride,' I joke, with all seriousness.

'I thought you were a feminist, Nell?'

'I'm a realist. A matriarchy wouldn't create a FTSE in the first place; instead, every company would get a prize for taking part.'

'Women aren't that weak, Nell!'

'I didn't say they were weak; they're just not that greedy, belligerent or as keen to snort cocaine off a male prostitute's anus either.'

Imelda actually laughed at something I said.

'The captain might go down with his ship, Imelda, but the ship doesn't reciprocate; it wouldn't sink if the captain fell overboard, it would carry on regardless.'

'I'm glad to see the government collapse, Nell. They were pretty shit,' says Gaba.

'True, but it's like being in an abusive relationship; easier than being on your own. They made a lot of decisions, so I didn't need to. On top of making sure everyone's teeth and bottoms are clean, I'm now going to have to work out a new fiscal policy and stop the Spanish invading.'

'I don't think the Spanish will be invading, Mum. They were nearer the Italian volcano,' Peter explains, as if I were remotely serious.

Imelda tries to suck on a glacé cherry. 'Help yourself, isn't that the mantra every flight attendant tells us? Put your own oxygen mask on first so you can then help others put on theirs.'

I put my elbows on the empty table and my head in my hands. 'There's no one flying the plane, though. An oxygen mask won't stop us hurtling into the side of a mountain.'

'There's no one to tell us what to do. It should be exciting and liberating, Nell.'

'It should be, Melda, but I'm terrified. I liked having an army at my disposal. I liked the nanny state. I didn't have to make so many decisions, and I got my nap time. I haven't got a church, a knitting group or a squad to fall back on. I should've joined that Pilates class; at least they would have had the core strength I'm so desperately in need of right now.'

As long as I've got sweets in my pocket, the younger ones will follow me, as will Scraps. Will that be enough for Sam to follow me? It might actually; he loves sweets. I should've used sweets for his obedience training rather than sideswipes.

The mother is the centre; she pulls everything towards her, which is why she's a sphere. That sphere is me, reaching out, connecting, keeping things close. I've got to bring everyone–

'What's that noise outside? It sounds like dogs fighting or shagging.' Amber interrupts my thoughts as usual.

'I'm not sure. It sounds like a gunshot in the distance; it's probably just the farmers hunting rabbits,' Imelda replies, while still struggling with the glacé cherry.

Never mind my internal soliloquies; I scurry into the front room to look out of the window. Everyone scurries behind me. I rub a patch of ice off the inside of the window and look outside.

'Shit!'

There are four average-sized young men with bloodied faces fast approaching the house.

'Fuck off, you bastards!' Imelda screams.

'Don't antagonise them. Shit, they're coming this way.'

What do I do? Sam's crowbar is still leaning near the door. Have I got the strength to lift it? Can I weaponise this inner turmoil?

This thing is significantly heavier than it looks, but I haven't got time to think this through; they're coming this way! Fuck, this is actually too heavy. I can't wield it above my head. I dropped it on the floor; it makes a hell of a noise.

'Is it too late to train Scraps to hunt down bad guys?' shouts Tom as he gets in my way.

I open the under-the-stairs door. Sitting in a bag, waiting for me, is Dada's bag of guns. I get my pistol and check it's loaded. I head back to the front door while everyone gets out of my way and hides in the front room. I'm looking through the small glass panel in the door. Everything looks distorted.

Just pretend I'm in a movie. They're not running; they're staggering and swaying.

'Where's Sam when I need him? This is exactly why I had his children – so he would fight the bad guys.'

'Should I throw my Mooncup at them?' shouts Gaba.

'Er…no thanks.'

I drag the crowbar across the floor so it's behind me and hold on to it. I hold the pistol with my other hand, taking a defensive stance like an old soldier. Are these moments hard-wired into our DNA after thousands of years of battles? I'm going to have to put my brain on hold so I can run towards the trouble rather than run away from it. Got to put this heavy-duty body on the line for others, not just myself.

The only way I got out of a fight with Nigel when I was young was by biting him on the leg; I haven't fought a man since. I pray my pelvic floor doesn't let me down against these thugs. I wish Davina had done a video on how to batter pillagers; she did one for every other one of my life-changing events.

One of the young men is looking through the small glass square on the front door. They take a few steps back, ready to run at the door. I take a deep breath. I don't actually need to open the door, but oh well, I'm going to.

One man runs at the door just as I open it. He's holding a golf club above his head. His eyes are wide open and dilated. I shoot. I just made a noise I've never heard before, so does the man as he falls to the floor. I step outside to face the other bloodied faces. One throws a stone at me. I move my head out of the way. I'm trained at the toddler level of angst. Now I need to up my game. I point the gun and start shooting. I can't stop myself; the momentum is building. I don't think I can stop. I have finally found an outlet for my rage.

I think I missed them all. I'm out of bullets. I've seen enough movies to know I should have put some more bullets in my pocket. I lower the pistol, but some latent force runs through my other arm, and I swing the crowbar above my head, hitting someone else. The vibrations reverberate straight up my arm and make my teeth wobble. I shut my eyes tightly. If I look, I'll get scared. Blind people must feel invincible. I swing the crowbar round and round for what seems like forever. I haven't hit anything. Have they gone?

I open my eyes. The men have distanced themselves from my flailing arms and staggered back down the road; the one from the hallway has caught up with them while clutching his bleeding shoulder. So I did get one!

I spin around slowly, winding down. If I stop, I think I will fall over, which won't be a good look. I'm breathing heavily. My arms and wrists are screaming in pain, but I don't care; I know it will pass. I know I should be excited about my bravery, but my instinct is still to run inside. There are throaty cheers from the other side of the bay window, led by Imelda. She does like a bloodbath.

Peter rushes outside holding a handful of bullets and the super-soaker water pistol in the other. He hands the bullets to me. Zoe and Tom stand in the doorway armed with Nerf guns and trying their best to look badass. Those sugar daisies and glitter sprinkles must have given everyone a brief spurt of energy, too. Well, Peter has his zombie apocalypse; he should be the best trained.

'They've gone, Pete; you're too late. But they'll be back unless they were running from someone else. We need to secure the front door,' I wheezed.

Peter isn't interested in the fleeing mob; he's already running up the road towards Freddy's house like a newborn giraffe. I drop the crowbar and reluctantly follow him while simultaneously refilling the pistol and shouting at Gaba to lock the door. I fall over. Multitasking is propaganda. I hope I look stunning and brave as I get back up. I put the gun in my back pocket.

Every door before ours has been broken into, including Imelda's. There's splintered wood where Freddy's front door used to be. The house emanates silent danger as we step over the wooden shards. Peter holds his breath as he tentatively opens the front room door.

Freddy lies on the sofa, still in his filthy rabbit onesie; his mum lies on the other sofa. With their eyes closed, they look like they are sleeping, but there's not enough sound to convince either of us of that. Peter tiptoes over the rubbish on the floor and leans over Freddy. He pokes his friend's body, but there is no movement; it looks solid and cold. The only colour on Freddy's body is the congealed blood from a large wound on his head. I've never seen a dead body before; I have no idea what to do. Peter has seen a million dead bodies before, but none of them were close friends or three-dimensional. Peter pokes Freddy's body again, just to make sure it isn't moving. It isn't. He pokes it again and again. It does not move. Peter puts down the super-soaker, grabs Freddy's shoulders and shakes his body.

'COME ON!!! WAKE UP!!!'

'Let go, Pete, he's gone, you can't get him back.'

I checked Freddy's mum for a pulse. This is why they say "stone cold". She's also been hit in the head; it doesn't seem like they put up a fight. Peter finally lets go of Freddy's shoulders. He picks up the Super Soaker and goes into the hallway. I cover the bodies with a couple of faux-fur throws. Without questioning myself, I ripped a button off his mother's cardigan. Freddy's onesie doesn't have any buttons, so I rip the plastic bunny nose off. I put them in my pocket. There's nothing else that can be done.

Peter stares at a bloodstain streak on the wall. He kicks the wall again and again. The bloodstain is stubbornly refusing to go. Peter takes the end of a nearby broom handle and stabs the plaster repeatedly. The bloodstain is gone now.

'We've got to get out of here. Come on, Pete, come with me.'

'I have to get the pain out of me. I hate the pain in my head. I have to put the pain somewhere else!'

'What do you mean? I don't understand.'

'How could you understand? You're perfect.'

'I'm not perfect!'

'You had perfect parents, a perfect childhood; you didn't suffer. You could never understand how I feel.'

'My life has never been perfect; nothing ever is. I've tried to take the pain out as well, Pete, many times.'

He looks at me quizzically. Why should he understand what's going on in this secretive mind of mine? He looks me straight in the eye as he used to do when he was a child trying to work me out. He has a lot of pain inside. Hate can't be overcome if we make excuses for the hatred. Like dirt, it has to be beaten out.

'We had a pact.'

'What kind of pact, Pete?'

'If one of us goes, the other has to go too.'

'I beg your fucking pardon?'

'We were going to go together; we didn't want to leave each other behind. We don't have any other friends.'

'You can find new friends; you can always find new friends.'

'We couldn't. We wanted to go together. How am I going to survive without him? We were stronger together.'

'Great. Shall I hit you over the head with a golf club then? Would that make you feel better, you dumbass?'

'I wish I were Voldemort right now.'

'Fucking hell! Do you remember when you were younger, when you were fearless? You would ride your bike everywhere, climb trees with Amber, fight Amber, hide in forbidden places, hide in the dark. What stopped that?'

'I grew tall but not strong. I don't know where I fit in. I don't identify with Dad or Dada; I don't know who I am.'

'You don't have to identify with them; I wasn't making clones. It's a shame the one ancestor who you do look like fucked off before you were born. Your fucking generation is obsessed with identity. The whole point of society is not looking for a place to fit in, but creating a space that you fit into. Identity can't be bought in a shop; it has to be found, nurtured, abandoned, rediscovered, carved, and tinkered with until the day you die. Form does follow function. Just don't make the function minimal. If you want to be strong, you need to carry, lift, push, pull, run, and jump. If you want to be clever, you need to read, observe, research, experiment, and create. No one has ever got strong or clever watching a video of someone else being strong and clever.'

'Easier said than done. Lots of people don't want you near their space.'

'Well, a lot of space just opened up. You can't run away from problems anymore; the problems are smothering us from every angle.'

'I don't know what I'm supposed to do. '

'You don't have to know what to do. All you need to survive is to know what your strengths are, but not to compare your strengths to others. You might not have big biceps, but you do have other qualities.'

'Name one.'

'To be honest, Pete, I don't know. You didn't arrive in this world with a destiny stone or a cheat sheet. You don't know what your talents are because they weren't on the National Curriculum. The world might appear to offer you narrow choices and limit your ability to contribute, but that was only to make other people's box-ticking job easier. Those people are counting sandwiches in the leisure centre right now; they don't control your destiny anymore. Your strengths might not be apparent yet, but that doesn't mean you haven't got them. Decide what strengths you want and then train hard to get them. You're only fourteen; it's a bit early to give up.'

'But what is the point? Why put all that effort in for an inevitable death?'

I shouldn't be angry or surprised; I've reached this point so many times myself. Are feelings genetic? Did I make him like this? It's the easy way out. It seems easier anyway. Maybe he has an internal monologue like me. His pain is like mine. There really are so many ways to self-harm. All he needed to do was talk about it.

I remember my first existential crisis when I was a teenager. Staring into the void of inevitable hard work and life-altering decisions is as daunting as looking at the void of inevitable death and life-altering illnesses. I started a doodle to help me out of that one. He's never had to create something on a blank page. All his creativity has been pre-planned, available at the touch of a pre-placed button. He's never been prepared for an existential crisis.

'Pete, the meaning of life is to search for a meaning, not to find one. If you find the answer, then your life doesn't need a reason to carry on. Freddy and his mum died because they weren't looking for anything; they lay still. If you still want answers, then keep living.'

'I don't really want to die, not yet.'

'I'm glad you don't want to die; I don't want to either.'

'Let's go home, Mum. If we're going to live, then we can't stay here like sitting ducks. One thing I'm good at is preparing for an apocalyptic invasion.'

'Yeah, but do you realise you can't respawn?'

'I might know some tactics. You don't know what I know.'

'No, I don't. Let's test your abilities then, shall we?'

I don't fancy our chances, but I'm not telling him that yet. It's lovely just to see him enraged by something. At least he's filling up that terabyte now.

Mary K Hollywood

Exodus

Every front door looks even more sinister knowing that there could be a dead body behind it. We can never be free, not while the dangerous are free too. We replaced marauding mammoths with golf clubs and cocaine. The more we confined ourselves to safety, the more dangerous the outside became.

I feel like we're in Hokusai's Great Wave: most people don't notice the small boats rowing helplessly in the face of a far greater, uncontrollable power, especially if they've only seen it on a pencil case or notebook. Mother Earth is the apex predator; she consumes her own without warning, without reason, and without judgement. We need to paddle home fast. We don't go to hell when we die; hell comes to us when we're not looking.

Peter and I hurry back to the house. It's funny how humans live in neat rows, borrowing cups of sugar and looking after each other's parcels, knowing that if an apocalypse happens, we could turn on each other in a heartbeat.

Imelda is tying her crocheted rabbit Reservoir Dogs diorama on the top of the postbox. If only those crocheted machine guns were real.

The demoralised gang from earlier is at the bottom of the street. Annie and Terry from No. 42 are taking them on in their full re-enactment costumes, attacking them with blunted spears and decommissioned matchlock muskets. They got dressed up before attacking. The thugs aren't equipped with the necessary armour to defend themselves; they're on the ground, whimpering, being kicked by metal spurs.

That volcanic eruption looked harmless from a distance. Everything looks inconspicuous on a wide-screen. Now that the shock wave has finally reached our front door, we can fully appreciate its magnitude.

Amber opens the front door. Imelda has secured her diorama in place and positioned herself in the red telephone box so she can safely watch the battle at the end of her road. Peter staggers in; I slam the door shut behind us. It doesn't matter how this started; I need to be in control of how it ends.

Peter sits on the floor in the hallway with his head down, trying to catch his breath and remove evidence of tears. Sam stands in the hallway with both arms outstretched as if he's holding the walls up all by himself. I'm so relieved to see him.

'Where have you been, Sam?'

'Raising merry fuck. Where have you been?'

'Freddy's. They're dead. We have to get out of here; this street isn't safe.'

'I know. We can't fight them off forever; it's time to go. EVERYONE GET YOUR STUFF TOGETHER, WE'RE LEAVING!'

There's a collective sound of tutting, shuffling and whining combined with Zoe blowing raspberries. He looks at me.

'Where are we going, Sam?'

'Trust me, Nell. I'll take us somewhere safe. Grab what you need; we're probably not coming back, not for a while anyway.'

'What do you mean by not coming back? Where are we going to go? What about all our stuff? Tell me where we are going?'

'I'll explain later; just go and get some clothes, sensible shoes and whatever else you need. But not too much. Don't pack more than you can carry; whatever you can fit in a backpack. I've already taken the suitcases.'

'WHERE ARE WE FUCKING GOING?'

'I can't tell you yet. I will, I promise.'

'There had better be some slain mammoths wherever it is!'

'What?'

'Nothing.'

'I need you to trust me, Nell. If I have your trust, the rest will follow. Please trust me.'

'They only follow me because I keep sweets in my pocket.'

'I was never going to leave you behind, you know.'

'Are you sure?'

'I was making sure I didn't lose you.'

Sam grabs my arm and pulls me to one side of the hallway.

'I want to show you something,' he says.

'What is it?'

'Give me your hand.'

'You'd better not propose. I'll punch you square in the jaw if you get down on one knee!'

Sam unbuckles his belt, buttons, and flies. What the fuck! I definitely don't have time for this! Why now? What's he doing with my hand? Sam's facial expression is confusing. He pushes my hand down his boxers. This is not what I want to be doing right now. Every night for the last four years, maybe, but not fucking now!

'Can you feel it?'

'Seriously, this is what you want me to do right now, Sam? There are thugs on this street, and you want a…'

'How many fucking testicles have I got?'

This is getting weird.

'I'm not joking, Nell. Count them.'

Okay. It doesn't feel the same. I think there's only one testicle and next to it what feels like some knotted string.

'Can't you just explain rather than make it feel like a Saturday night game show?'

'I removed the lumpy testicle. I know you know about it. The ladies in the Co-op know about it, so she must have told you as well. I got rid of it myself. Couldn't get a doctor's appointment, so I've dealt with it. It's gone. It can't hurt me. I'm going to be okay. I'm sure you were really worried.'

I'm stunned. I don't know what to think. I'm not sure if this is a brave or stupid thing. What do I say to make this situation more palatable?

'I hope your testicles don't work like the pendulums do in those ridiculously tall skyscrapers to keep them upright in an earthquake.'

'Very funny.'

'I'm glad you think you're okay, and I'm glad you're not going to fall over.'

My hand is still in his boxers. I don't want to let go.

'I had to do something, although I'm half the man I was.'

'Your testicle wasn't that big.'

Sam puts his other arm around my back. He slowly moves it over my bum. The range of emotions is unfathomable. He touches the pistol in my back pocket, pulls it out, and sighs. He smiles and puts it back in my pocket.

'We don't have to take my mum if you don't want to. I love her, but she'll slow us down, mentally and physically. I'm prepared to sacrifice her for you.'

'Are you fucking kidding! Of course, we'll take her. She's been through a lot. She needs a big man, too.'

'I'm glad you said that.'

'I'm glad you said that; now I have something to emotionally manipulate you with.'

We stare at each other while I hold his healthy testicle. I have no idea what I'm supposed to do next. Should I tell him there was nothing wrong with it in the first place? That's going to sound weird. All I can think about is asking him if he put some antiseptic cream on it, because I know he hasn't. Did the mistress help him tie the string? Has she kept his testicle in a jar? She's welcome to it if she has.

'Mummy! Daddy! What are you doing?' Zoe asks.

Holy shit.

'Nothing Zoe. I was just checking something.'

I need him. I want him. Is that love, fear, or desperation? The same question I asked myself before we moved in together. With nervous smiles quickly abandoned, Sam heads – albeit limply – upstairs. I dutifully follow him.

Sam retrieves his large rucksack from under the bed. I only have one last empty bag for life to fill. He unpacks his bedside drawer into the rucksack: his grandfather's compass, a vape, another vape, a lighter, and four large cigars that he bought for the birth of each of his children. I don't own such things. All I've got is an extensive collection of rubber bands and Post-it notes; my needs were only ever for keeping shit together, not exploring new worlds.

I don't know what to pack. I look under the bed. I've been hoarding since I was little. I've kept every badge, sticker, pencil, and pebble from my childhood. And every cinema ticket, letter, bottle top, and napkin from my relationship with Sam. The space underneath this bed is stuffed with boxes that are stuffed with souvenirs of my life. I can't choose a favourite. I'd rather they stayed together. If I take one, I'll miss the others; if I take them all, I won't have room for anything else. I've got my secret button box I keep within reach – it contains my most special ones. Sam didn't take that. I put Freddy and his mum's buttons inside. I'll just take this; it represents everything else.

I emptied my bra drawer onto the bed. Which bra shall I take? There's the most comfortable one, which makes me look like a matron from the Carry On films. There's the corset one from the specialist shop that forces me to walk like Jessica Rabbit, or the sports one that flattens them into a mono-boob and cuts off the circulation to my head. I can't afford to be dizzy at a time like this. Then there's five that never fitted me and two that still have the price tag attached because I buy clothes that will fit the fantasy version of me rather than reality. The front-opening zip one pops open when I take a deep breath, all the underwired ones are too painful, the lacy ones itch, the nursing one smells, and the night bras don't really do anything unless I'm lying horizontally. Then there's the really comfortable one with no seams or wires, which is great until I reach for a top shelf, and then one of my boobs falls out of the bottom. Why wasn't I panic buying in the lingerie department instead of hunting down teabags?

"Do you really need a bra, Nell?"

"Not unless I had little men down there holding them aloft like Atlas."

"At least they could feed off the crumbs you frequently drop down there."

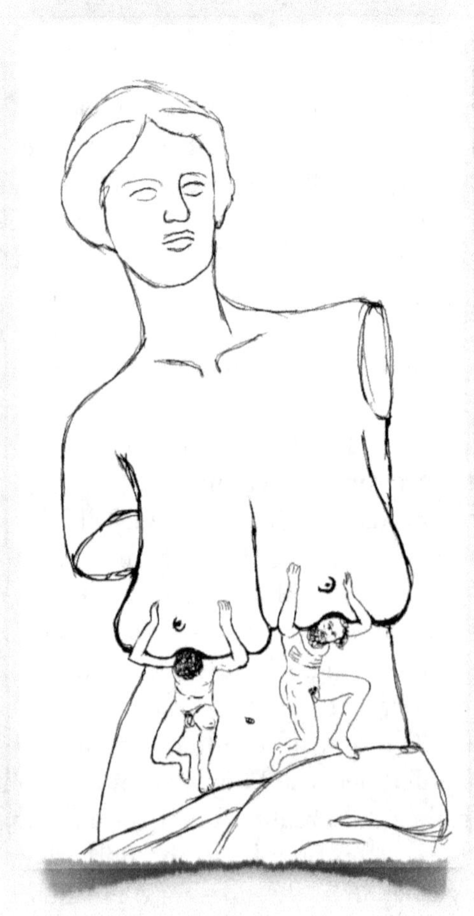

I throw my heaviest bra at him. He laughs a little. I can't believe I'm spending so much time thinking about a bra while the street is being invaded. I don't know what I'm dressing for. Is it comfort, trying to impress, running, or fighting? I threw out my camouflage combat trousers because they were a pain in the arse to iron. I shouldn't appear too attractive; I don't want to be raped or pillaged. Although I should look attractive enough so Sam doesn't dump my arse on the side of the road. I need to look a bit shiny so he can believe I have few miles in me yet. Should I take my favourite jeans? I haven't been able to fit into them for four years. Maybe with food shortages, I might just be able to. I should take the sports bra, I'm going to have to run aren't I? I don't know if I'm packing for a Mad Max or a Sound of Music kind of exit, do I wear all my faux leather belts or my pinny.

I'll take no bras. For once I will let the bastards run free. No one can put them on the internet for the world to see now. Only my immediate family and a few hangers-on will have to witness them swinging from side to side while I run away from whatever it is I'm running away from. I don't have to give a fuck anymore. This is the body I have. I have no choice but to use it to get out of here. Now I can truly look like the Venus of Willendorf, just with jeans and an oversized jumper; it is nippy outside.

I'm overthinking and over-packing, which has never been a good idea: I once took weighing scales to Barcelona. There's one of my many photos of Keanu in my bedside drawer. I'm going to leave him behind. I only need him when I have nothing to panic about.

I pack what few HRT patches I have left and the last of my antidepressants. I can't really think about how I'm going to feel when they finally run out. All I can remember about my feelings before I took these was that I hated everybody all the time. I'm not taking my pocket mirror; I can face the world with a few chin hairs. Chin hair is the least of my problems now. At last. I don't need more self-reflection anymore; my knowledge of art will see me through. Having knowledge is one thing; knowing what to do with it is something else.

My bag is too full; I'm struggling to hold it. It would be a lot lighter if I took the desire to look thinner out of it.

I go downstairs to wait by the front door for everyone else. Amber carries her school bag with her hair straighteners poking out. She doesn't want to hear me explaining that platforms are not essential items, nor that she needs a bigger bag. She wants to be stylish when she runs. Which is why she is wearing the figure hugging nude coloured unitard. She looks like a plastic doll waiting to be clothed.

Peter has all his worldly belongings in his pockets, not even spare underwear. Luckily for him, I packed his clothes a few days ago; he hadn't even noticed.

Russell tries to help by picking things up in the hallway. He holds up one of my bras and asks many people rushing past him what it is. He drops it like a hot potato when I tell him. The excitement and fear are ramping up; it's highly contagious. It helps raise the temperature in the house; I don't feel as cold. Gaba carries my hair products, my jewellery and my toothbrush in my toiletry bag. Tom carries a ball of string and his goldfish bowl. I haven't got time to argue.

Zoe drags a black bin bag filled with, from what I can see, her tap shoes, all of her key rings, her favourite books, her dolly, her magic set, her pencil case, her sketch pad, pretend food, pretend money, a racing car, some building blocks and her bike helmet. I try to stop her from taking the doll's pram and Willow outside.

'That's enough now, Zoe; there won't be room.'

'I'm taking Willow. Try and stop me, Mummy.'

'Why don't you measure Willow to see if she fits?'

'I have measured her; she's two hours long.'

Do I put the bins out? They might resume service once Annie and Terry win the battle. Imelda is still standing in the telephone box, cheering on the battle. Sam returns quickly from Imelda's house with a few of her belongings. He got her bag full of pills, her crochet bag, and a rattling box of that disgusting homemade jam.

Sam tries to pack the car. He sees my sculpture in the back seat. He looks at me pensively. He doesn't ask where it came from. He carefully removes it and puts it on the pavement.

'You can't leave that there.'

'I'm not stupid, Nell. I'm sure we can find a place for it.'

So he does still know me.

He puts everyone's bags in the boot, but there's little room for Willow. Sam takes Willow out to put Imelda's bag in. His sighing increases with every additional bag that keeps being brought out of the house. He comes back into the house and shouts at everyone to hurry and get in the car. I try to reorganise the bags in the boot. Sam watches the encroaching battle that has shuffled up the road near the car. Sam takes a moment out to push over some thugs. Annie tries to stab one man, but the blunted spear bounces off the thug's jacket.

Tom watches from the pavement with his mouth wide open. 'Is this a stiffen the blood and summon up the sinews moment, Mum?'

I smile at Tom and turn to look at Amber standing in the front doorway, staring blankly at her dead phone.

'I'm not going, Mum. I can't do this. This isn't what I want. I want to make my own decisions. I don't need you lot anymore.'

'Who the fuck is this, Amber?'

Sam has only just noticed Russell for the first time.

'That's Ralph, Dad.'

'I'm Russell, actually.'

'He goes where I go.'

'I thought your mum and I put you off relationships?'

'You did. This is different.'

Sam looks at me for clarification, but I don't really want to explain this. 'I doubt he eats much more than Peter; it will be fine.'

He looks mad.

'I'm mad at me as well, if it helps.'

Amber's hands are shaking. She won't look me in the eye.

'I can't do it, Mum, I can't leave. I have friends, I have a life here, I don't know what else I can do. I'm scared, really scared. I don't know what I'll become. I don't know who I will talk to.'

I walk up to Amber and get as close as I can.

'We haven't got time to wait for the energy companies to force their workers back into the power stations just so you can find some distant influencer to tell you what to do. I can't drag you out forcefully. If you want your independence right now, then on you go, but I'm not sure as the world collapses is the best time for that.'

Amber has never looked this scared before. All the people who had her back are nowhere to be seen; they vanished with the power grid. Smartphones replaced more than calculators, clocks, cameras, torches, and folding maps. They also replaced stealing sweets, hanging around, play-fights, fistfights, hanging upside down, skipping, mixtapes, untangling the telephone wire, making a reverse-charge call, and boredom. She's never had to face a consequence in her whole life.

Staring into my daughter's eyes should be like looking in a mirror. But each generation is too wildly different from the last. We don't have the same experiences, knowledge, or skills. She's not ready. I haven't finished preparing her to be on her own. I got distracted by my own problems.

'It's not all cool tattoos and eye makeup out there, Amber; it's real anarchy. The kind that requires submission or your face smashed in. You have to come with us; we're stronger together.'

Sam manhandles the guns and knives that Dada had hidden under the stairs. Is he going to kill Russell? No, he's still trying to work out how to get everybody and everybody's stuff, the dog, cat, the goldfish and the windbreak in the car. He looks at my sculpture and sighs.

'I'll be back in a minute,' he shouts as he runs up the road.

Scraps is getting increasingly excited, either because of the noisy medieval battle or because he thinks he's going to the beach. Amber has her "I'm not changing my fucking mind" face on. I can't use brute force on her; she's bigger and stronger. I've got nothing to bribe her with either. She always has her own stash of sweets. That bottle of gin would also have been useful now. I hug her and hold her close.

'I don't blame you, Amber; I don't want to go either. This is scary; this is genuine fear. I don't know where we're going to end up, but our choices are limited. If we stay in this house, we will get killed. If we venture out on our own, we will get killed. The ones you are stronger than are not looking to take your life; they're hiding or running too. The only thing we can do with our strength is save ourselves.'

'I've got Russell.'

We both stare at the scrawny boy she barely knows, leaning up against the wall. Amber lifts her chin, knowing that was not a great retort.

'I'm going with your family, Amber, at least they are attempting to go somewhere together. I don't want to stay here.'

'Thanks, Russell.'

'It's okay, Mrs… Nell, Amber's mum.'

'You can call me Nellie.'

So he is of some use. But no one who needed to witness it saw it.

'Amber, your life is like a book; each chapter moves your story forward. Do you really want the ending right now? If you want full responsibility for yourself, then okay, stay, but you're starting from scratch. You'll only have Russell to look after you, and that's only if he decides to stay with you.'

Amber watches Terry batter a thug on the ground with a garden spade. She shuffles towards the car and throws her bag in the boot. Everyone is defiant until threatened. Thank God, because if I'd had to take Russell without Amber, I would have dumped his arse at the first available bus stop.

The rest of the battle moves further up the street. I can see Sam driving Freddy's mum's yellow MPV down the road, swerving round it. This car has a roof box and seven seats. He's stolen their car! We shouldn't be stealing from the dead, or anyone, but I can't help but think about the large storage. I hate the colour though; he should have stolen Jackie and Tim's Range Rover from the other end. It looks way cooler. I know I'm a terrible person. But if I think about the seriousness of this situation, I will cry, and that's no use to anyone.

Sam brakes hard in front of us while we wait on the pavement. I'm so aroused and, as usual, my timing is way off. He gets out and folds down the back row of seats.

'We need the seven seats, Sam.'

'But we'll lose luggage space, Nell.'

'This lot is our luggage.'

Sam puts the seats back up and puts Zoe and Tom's child seats in. Tom gets in first. 'Wow, this car has a back back!'

As we fill the boot of the new car with the backpacks and the roof box with all the guns and knives, Imelda saunters back towards us. Sam ties Willow to the roof box. Amber helps Imelda into the back seat. Russell and Peter squeeze themselves into the back seat as well. Zoe and Tom are in their child seats in the back back seats. Sam looks at Gaba and Scraps idling on the pavement. He orders everyone out of the car. He rips the child seats out, puts Gaba in the back back with Tom holding his fishbowl and Scraps.

'I heard that you like dogs now, Gaba,' says Sam, under his breath.

Gaba didn't raise an eyebrow. Either she's not bothered, still exhausted, forgotten, or maybe thinking about it. Everyone else gets back in their seats. Sam tells Zoe to sit on anyone she chooses. She choses Amber to everyone's surprise. Amber holds her tight. Sam looks at my barbed wire sculpture and then looks at me. He hoists it up on top of the roof box and secures it with some bungee cords. Barbie looks like a supreme being riding on top next to Willow. I poke my head inside the car to check everyone is comfortable.

'Zoe, did you bring your elf sword?' asks Tom.

'No, because I know I will poke my eye out.'

I go back to the front door to check. Gigi, who is sitting on the doorstep, stares at me. I open the cat basket and stare back at her. Like a dowager queen, she stretches her whole body, holds her head up high and walks into the basket as if she had been waiting for me to open the door. I put the basket on the passenger seat, but I instinctively get into the driver's seat.

'What are you doing, Nell? You know all the bumps on our car were made by you,' says Sam as he tries to sit in the passenger seat with the cat basket on his lap.

'Who cares? Right now we need a bit of chaos to fight chaos. These people will kill us, not negotiate for our no-claims bonus! I don't have a lot of skills for surviving an apocalypse, but I can drive really fast and really badly. Anyway, your haymaking arms need to be kept available at short notice.'

'While holding a cat basket?'

'Gigi scratches deeper than you.'

I open the storage compartment on the centre console and place the pistol carefully inside. This car has fold-out extra cupholders. Why?

Not sure I can put up with this new car smell. How do you turn this car on? There's no "on" button. Do I whistle? Will it only work with Freddy's mum's voice? Is it activated by a breathalyser? That might explain why Freddy's mum hardly drove it. Sam leans over, touches my knee and shoves it down hard so my foot presses the brake pedal. The car engine starts. Thank God we're leaving the geniuses who came up with that behind.

This car has more petrol than ours too, result. I feel so guilty about that thought, but also relieved. Maybe we will make it to the Isle of Wight. I'm scared. Should we be doing this? Are we more vulnerable in a car? I'm leaving my home undefended. I'm getting in a car with a man who I thought hated me. He doesn't hate me; he put my hand down his boxers. That's middle-aged love.

Have I got everything? I must go through my usual checklist for a long road trip while Sam keeps an eye on the battle in the rearview mirror.

'Wait! I am not facing an apocalypse without wet wipes!'

I race back into the house. I'm not facing any crisis with snot-encrusted faces. I rush back into the house and grab the nearest pack of wet wipes from the kitchen. There's my unfinished painting on the floor. I doubt I'll ever get time to paint again, but I'm not leaving this to be destroyed either. I fold it and put it in my pocket. My Kahlo mug sits alone on the draining board. Do I want to take the old stains with me? I feel it's time for a fresh start. I'll leave it here for now.

The small, sticky fingerprints and muddy paw prints on the walls are our mark. It might not have been immaculate, but it was a lot of fun. I don't want to leave, but I don't want to stay. The house seems weird without people in it. It's too quiet, and already doesn't feel like home. Home is stuffed into that car. I wonder if I will ever see this house again. There are so many memories; from now on, it will all be new.

I stop in the hallway and look back at my home. It reminds me of Rachel Whiteread's *House* installation. She filled an old house with concrete and then ripped away the walls and roof to reveal the space inside: a solid block of concrete that was once space to live, once full of laughter and pain, but now unable to function… I haven't got time for a deep dive into my artistic consciousness. Just get the keyring souvenir on my way out.

I'm fumbling around for my last teabag under the cupboard. It's not there. Where's my emergency teabag? A wave of heat floods my cold body. If there's no teabag, then there's definitely nothing left for me here. I'm back to cold and sweaty.

I step back outside my front door, perhaps for the last time. The street is quiet. The thugs have actually been defeated by the medieval army; they've staggered off. Annie and Terry are exhausted, sitting on the road catching their breath. I wave at them. They waved back exhaustedly.

I look at my new family car. Everybody is squashed up inside despite the extra legroom. Sam looks at me through the passenger car window, smiling. He's dangling the emergency teabag with the tape still attached. He knew he might have to bribe me to get me into the car. The kids would have been enough, although I am keener to get in the car now.

I get in the car and drive quietly away, leaving the exhausted thugs lying on the road. The only noise is Scraps getting very excited and jumping all over Gaba, Tom, and the goldfish bowl.

'Can we play Tig?'

Everyone smiles at Zoe's suggestion. I wish we could play Tig. I've never felt so tense and adrenalised at the same time. At least we're out of the house and going somewhere.

'We'll go to Dada's first.'

'Okay, Nell.'

I have no idea where we're going after Dada's; I have no idea what to do about Mama. I know we can't go back, but we have nowhere else to go. Is there a place without trouble? Sam could suggest we live together in some dystopian ménage à trois with his mistress, or he might take us to a leisure centre or other municipal building and abandon us there with other disoriented families while he goes back to his mistress. Does every possible outcome have to include a mistress? I have no proof of one. She's not here; he's not rescuing her. He could take us to a ditch where he's going to shoot us all in the head, but I don't think so. A nicer man wouldn't necessarily be able to protect me in these times. I'm glad I've got him.

Not knowing what the future holds should make it more exciting than working to a plan. It takes courage to go into the unknown with a man who is twice my size and uncommunicative, but if there are only one hundred men left in the world, I would still need to choose one to protect me from the other ninety-nine. I'd rather have one I know. He's still my favourite pain in the arse. Love emanated from him once, and that's all I need to go on. Can I learn to love him again? Did I stop loving him? Do I need love right now? Will love save me? Love is saving me. We're not in situ anymore.

I can't change him, and I can't change myself. I can change the way I deal with shit though. Turns out I can handle an apocalypse after all. All I needed was a leap of faith.

The bombs destroyed what's left of the bomb makers. What's left are the middle-income, middle-aged, middle-of-the-road middlemen. And middlewomen. As Nigel said, the land is still here. Mother Earth continues to provide. She's shedding the past and embracing the new. This could be her wisest epoch yet.

Sam plays the CD that has been left in this car radio. It's country music. Amber and Peter desperately search for a charger to plug their earbuds into. Ha, they won't work, anyway.

'Where are we going after Dada's?'

'Just drive, Nell.'

'Wanker.'

Sam leans over and kisses my shoulder. I smile. He smiles back. That was always enough for me. The butterflies have returned to my stomach. They're either excited, full of fear, or desperately trying to escape the acid reflux. We've been slowly approaching oblivion, but now we're picking up speed.

Coming next

The Mother of All Apocalypses
Book Two

Last Mum Standing

Mary K Hollywood

Published by TiHi Art

Acknowledgments

There are many people to thank, as many people offered their help, some intentionally. My two daughters, Hannah and Lauren, contributed nearly all the children's dialogue in this book because they were, and still are, significantly funnier than me. My husband, David, provided some of the inspiration for the character Sam (against his will). My father, Ivan, a writer himself, who sadly died in 2016 but read my first attempt at writing this and convinced me I was a writer. My mother, Heather, put up with my every crisis of confidence and tried in vain to explain where commas go. This book has been an existential journey for us. Sadly, my mother passed away recently after a long battle with cancer. I dedicate this book to her unwavering support.

There are other one-off contributors of dialogue I was granted permission to borrow: my mother-in-law Theresa, my brother David, my sister-in-law Jen, and my nieces, Matilda and Phoebe. Also, Donna, a friend.

Thank you to friends and acquaintances: especially Jo who approved at least a hundred different book cover designs and Amanda, Zoe, Celeste, Cat, Sue, Alan and Gill who read various versions of this book over the last fourteen years and provided valuable feedback.

A huge thank you to Kylie for all the professional editing and moral support.

About the Author

Mary K Hollywood (is not her real name so she can continue teaching anonymously!) was born in North Wales in 1974. She was an art teacher for over twenty years and has practised art for over thirty. The Last Teabag is her debut novel (although started in 2012) and is the first book in a trilogy: The Mother of All Apocalypses. She used to live in the East Midlands, where this book is based, but now lives in the West Midlands with her family.

This book started as one thing and ended up as something completely different. Mary K started writing it as a young mother, balancing small children and teaching art. She finished it while being a full-time carer for her elderly mother, just as her eldest child entered adulthood and she entered menopause. This book evolved with her.

www.tihi.co.uk

List of Illustrations

All illustrations/photographs/sculptures have been created by the author Mary K Hollywood. This list denotes whether the illustration is an original artwork by the author or a parody/copy of an original artwork by a named artist (if known) for ease of reference. Please take some time to look at the original artwork referenced in this book and immerse yourself in the amazing creativity and skill of the human mind.

www.ingramcontent.com/pod-product-compliance
Lightning Source LLC
LaVergne TN
LVHW020655110826
845149LV00012B/2011

* 9 7 8 1 0 3 6 9 9 1 7 5 3 *